A Total Guide to
the State of Being Single

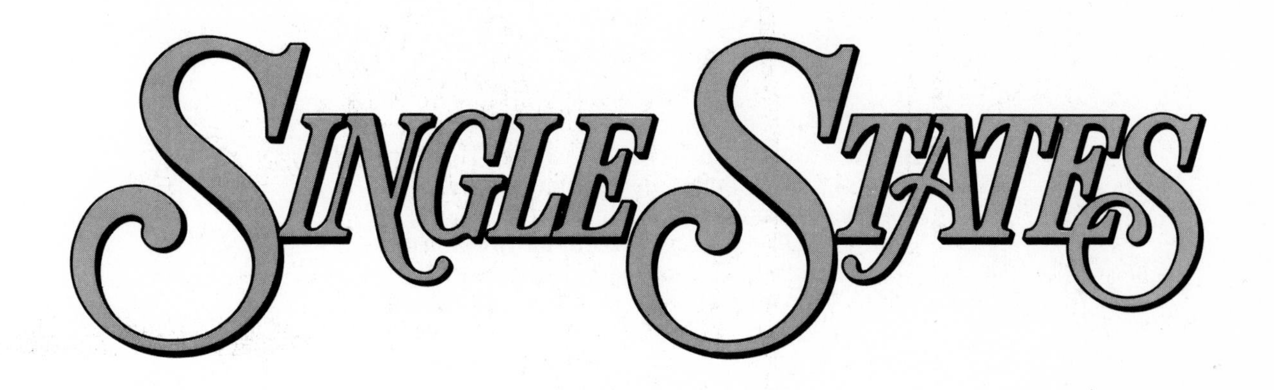

By Singles
About Singles
For Singles

Edited by Peter W. Kaplan

Ballantine Books · New York

Art Director · **David Kaestle**
Associate Art Director · **Leslie Engel**
Cover photographs · **Don Banks**
Cat · **Mr. Tibbles**, Cover design · **James R. Harris**
Monophobia illustrations · **James Sherman**
Perfect Singlicity illustrations · **Paul Meisel**
Technodating photographs · **John Grossman**
Mono á Mono scrapbook · **Leslie Engel**
Single Parenting photograph · **Suzanne Becker**
Single Diseases illustration · **Cathy Canzani**
Hollywood Singlehood photographs · **Jim McCrary** and
Jim Marchese (Paige Matthews) and **Harry Langdon** (Jenilee Harrison)
Nowsweek cover photograph · **Jim Marchese**
House Gorgeous, New Yawk, and
Cozmopolitan magazine photographs · **Jim Marchese**
Playbuy short story illustration · **Michael Gross**
Single Cities photographs · **David Kaestle**
Many thanks to ·
Rob Biggers, Glenis Gross, Steve Bogardus,
Lucinda Jenney, Franie Ruch, Mark O'Donnell

Published in the United States by Ballantine Books,
a division of Random House, Inc., New York,
and simultaneously in Canada by Random House of
Canada Limited Toronto.

Grateful acknowledgment is made to the
following for permission to reprint previously
published material:
Canopy Music, Inc.: Specified lines from "Witchita
Lineman" by Jimmy Webb. © 1968 Canopy Music, Inc.
Used by permission. Helen Gurley Brown:
Material from *Helen Gurley Brown's*
Single Girl's Cookbook.

Library of Congress Catalog Card Number: 82-90844
ISBN: 0-345-30603-1

Manufactured in the United States of America

First Edition: August 1983
10 9 8 7 6 5 4 3 2 1

A Letter to the Single Reader

We get letters up here all the time. One we got recently said:

"Dear Friend,

I had Singlexia. Everywhere I went I'd see people looking at me thinking that person is Single. *I would get on an airplane, and the steward would say, single-seating only, and I'd think,* geez! they know I'm here. *Or I'd read a book about a soldier and see the words* assigned leave *and certain letters would jump out and reassemble, and all I could see was S I N G L E. And I'd think,* they knew I was going to read that book. *That's Singlexia.*

But I was cured. How? I started remembering that I wasn't alone. That I had a lot of Singles around me. That I was part of a Single nation. That reassured me, and my Singlexia disappeared."

This set us to thinking: why is the Single self-image so bad in this country? And if our correspondent is right—and he is part of a Single nation—what are Single *States*?

That's how this book was begun. We wanted to repair the Single self-image. Singles have this tendency to think they are all alone in the world, that they are the first ones ever to undergo the pioneer work that is going it without a mate. Singles forget sometimes that they are part of a great tradition. They forget about President James Buchanan, who was not only President of the United States, but a Single President of the United States. And Elizabeth the First of England, who was Queen of England and also Single. And Walt Whitman, who was not only a genius of the most authentic kind, and Single himself, but wrote *Leaves of Grass* to boot! He didn't skulk around acting pathetic and incomplete. He sang the song of himself. Single! They forget hundreds, thousands of great Singles on a great rhumbaline through the ages. They forget Greta Garbo: *"I want to be alone."* Not, I *don't* want to be alone, but I *want* to be alone.

We put together *Single States* when the abuse had already gone on for too long. Single women and men have spent centuries hiding behind newspapers, sitting alone in restaurants and coffeehouses, dreading recognition and castigation, imprisoned only in their minds. In 1977, the wise adwriters for a Steven Spielberg space epic came up with the slogan, "We are not alone"; that goes for Singles. There are 45 million of us, which means we could probably overrun New York, maybe Texas, surely California, and take control if we wanted to. We could elect governors. We could stop them from making any more TV-movies about Singles starring Bonnie Franklin or Sally Struthers. We could declare each other tax dependents. We are not alone.

In the morning, we are together, as we sit and eat our single eggs around the nation. In the afternoon, we are together as we get ready to leave work for some exciting thing that will probably happen that night. In the evening, we are together as we wait for "The Tonight Show" to come on. Late at night, we romp together in our dreams. Why can't we just federalize and flex with our tremendous strength, instead of cowering?

We can, if we'll just overcome our conditioning. For years, we the Singles didn't think of ourselves as a group. No unity, nothing. We opened the *World Book* or the *Encyclopaedia Britannica*, both of which had so much to say about the *human cell* and the continent of *Asia* and found not a word on Singles. Sadly, we were being hidden by information dispensers—probably single—who weren't even aware that our very numbers had grown 78 percent from 1970, 385 percent from 1950.

Yet, some understood. Many sharp-eyed schlockmeisters saw us as a cotton field to be reaped. They gave us Singles bars and soups for one, rental condos and video dating systems, free-drink vacation clubs and designer clothes. They packaged Bad Advice. They found people to tell us how lonely we were; how to Live Alone and Love It; how to pick up women; how to pick up men; how to have meatloaf, martinis, sex for one. It was crazy medicine, like feeding a sick person iodine. They told us that not only could we be happy on our own if we listened to them, but happier than we could stand. They had the efficiency, but not quite the sincerity, of W.C. Fields' Great McGonigal, and many people fell for it. One wrote in:

"Who are all these profiteers of bathos, anyhow? They keep getting me. I go into a disco, and I feel like day-old meringue. I read advice on how to avoid loneliness and I feel like the Count of Monte Cristo. I send away for pamphlets on how to pick up dates and I feel like I've taken dramamine. Why do I feel like I'm orbiting in a one-man space station? Why can't we unify? Is there no march, or anthem, Fight Song for us?"

We sent along one verse of one we had around:

(Rah! Rah! Rah!)
We're not alone, we're Single!
We often dine on Chinese food in bed
We're not alone, we're Single!
On Us is where we'll tell you please Don't Tread!
A union are we
We'll rise up from the mist
Our 40 million soldiers will be marching in a Tryst
We're not alone, we're Single
We tingle, for Single are We!

We knew this would be just the thing to perk almost anybody up. Hundreds of thousands of us experienced depression when faced with the culture's approach to Singlehood. In quest of affirmation we Singles have gone in search of a kind of Dr. Spock to burp our anxiety out of us, only to keep running into psychoshysters with easy answers and all the trustworthiness of the bad foxes in Walt Disney pictures. Yet it was not only these that misdirected.

Magazines, very often city magazines, revelled in giving bad advice for the Single millions. They would tell us where we had to eat, where we had to dance, what kind of clothes we had to have slapped onto us. They'd tell us why we were down-the-drain if we didn't find love-partners whose general aspect was reminiscent—male or female—of a blonder Bjorn Borg. To them, and the advertisers who caught the scent, Singlehood became a kind of designer jean to be put over the head, to make us all look alike no matter how distinctive the sculpture underneath. When they tired of it (and, while still growing as a demographic, Singlehood began winding down as a vogue in the late seventies) these stock manipulators began playing up the seamy side, trying hard to cheapen the statement of independence and self-reliance enlightened Americans knew Singlehood to be.

Singles needed a friendly voice. What could we do?

Years ago, before they went into the trend-analysis business, magazines used to see things like this as a chance to put writers on the case. In the days when they were commercial and literary storehouses—from the twenties through the mid-seventies, some were amazingly vital and fun—and before they got so scared and pummelled by the economy and television that they forgot the writers came first, magazines used to reach out to their audiences with issues that would devote all their stories to a single cluster of a topic with big, fat heavy issues that had the bass and the treble both on high. It didn't matter what they were running issues on. They'd throw in all the silverware, on Communism or Suburbia or Hollywood or the Negro and the New Society.

We kind of wanted to put together a big, nice magazine on Singles and give it the old multiple pop. Nothing high pressure, nothing hyped—just a focused bunch of pieces by the best writers we knew about. So we began to call around America. We made hundreds of calls. We called lots of magazines and small papers. "Who's good that we don't know about?" we asked. We got an oceanic overflow of responses, and then we went back and chose 22 writers, most of whom we already knew, but chances are you don't. We wanted writers who are working on the kind of short fiction, journalism and humor that seems to find fewer and fewer slots in an ever more scientifically-managed market. We wanted eccentric dancers.

The 22 writers we found had already tnought about being Single, and each found something salient they had to say on the subject. None of them wanted to give advice that had the smell of practicality, none of them wanted to get analytical. Not that they couldn't have, but we wanted comrades, not lecturers.

Singles have a tendency not to take too much talking at these days. We're like people with chronically big pupils who can't stand getting night headlights turned on us; we flinch. We forget what a big bunch we are, that we're not just loose molecules dribbling here and there, into bars and out of offices—that we're part of a single multitude that transcends its numbers. We forget these important things. Our self-image needs work.

For instance, when we commissioned the New York pollsters of Glemp and Bone to perform statistical work for us at Single States, we never dreamed of the results. They called a scientifically adequate sampling of the unmarried, and here's what they got:

Americans who are single and claim to be married	12%
Americans who are single and admit to it	6%
Americans who are single and cough when asked	28%
Americans who prefer not to discuss it	52%
Americans who remember voting for John Anderson	2%

Up here at *Single States*, we'd like to get that second number up to 65 percent by the end of 1984. That's why we're here. We thought we would do our little bit by preparing this kindly companion. We wanted to cover things around the country, drop a little info, speak to all the sexes, and keep it shorter than Norman Mailer's *Ancient Evenings*. We wanted to say to Singles: "You never asked for the rank of Single, but you got it. So long as it's yours, take a walk with it on your own as though it was a Decoration Day medal. And if you're not the man or woman to wear it, why, go on, get married. We'll still have you to dinner once in a while!"

That's what we wanted to do, and we hope to some extent we have done it. We are mostly Singles, and we like our kind, who have the strength and the courage to get through the wilderness on foot. It is to all of them we dedicate this book, to the independent and the self-confirmed; to them, and if they marry, to the new Singles they will bring onto the earth.

Peter W. Kaplan
New York, New York
June, 1983

CONTENTS

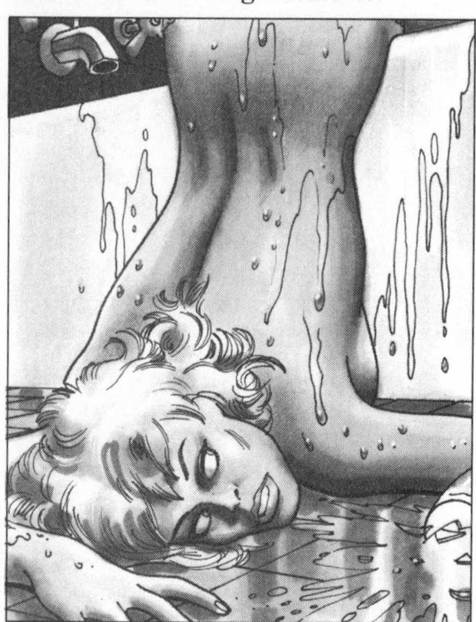

1

As Alfred Hitchcock used to say,
Good Evening.
Among the unattached, no late-night activity is more avidly pursued than the anxiety attack. For the convenience of those who wake in the middle of the night and are stuck as the opiate "Mary Tyler Moore Show" is replaced by a test pattern, for those of you who can't decide which of a myriad of anxieties to indulge, here are the eight major fears of the single life, a syndrome we call Monophobia.

MONOPHOBIA

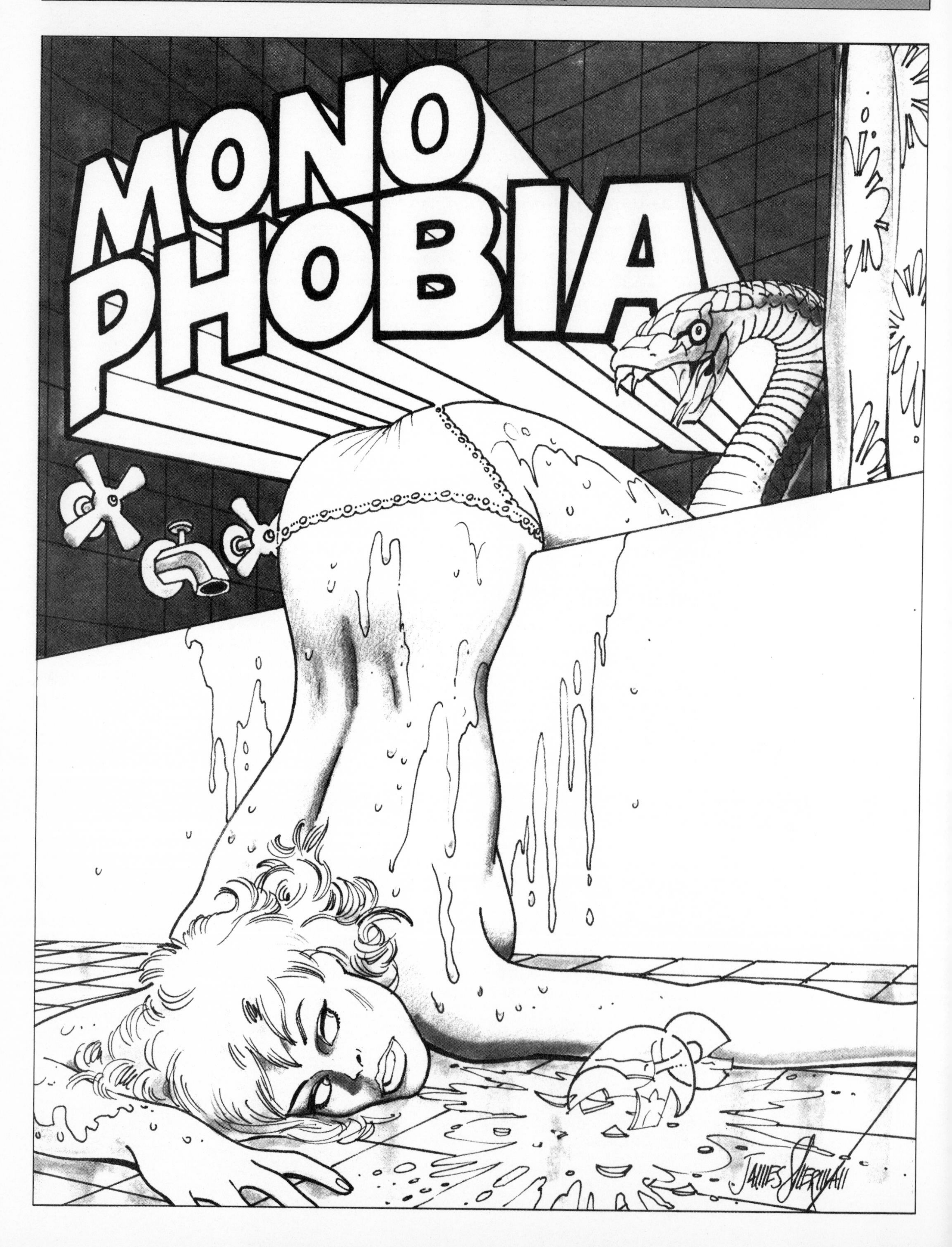
MONO
PHOBIA

A Catalogue of Single Terror

1 YOU WILL TAKE THE SHOWER OF DEATH. You slip on the soap, fall down, hit your head against the hot water tap, and bleed to death because you have no spouse to hear your fading cries for help. The cops won't discover your body for weeks, and even then it won't be because anyone really misses you, but because the neighbors report a "strange smell" emanating from your apartment. Remember how important it was always to wear clean underwear in case you got hit by a car, so your family wouldn't be embarrassed when they took you to the hospital? Well, this is much worse. When the police finally break into your apartment, you won't be wearing any underwear at all. (Unless you shower in your underwear, and then the police will *know* that you're weird.) They'll see your stolen towels (not even from good hotels), and they'll gossip around the precinct house about how messy your apartment was.

Of course, it might not be that bad. Perhaps you'll collapse on top of the drain so that the water quickly fills the tub, overflows, and soaks through the floor to the apartment below. This way, they'll discover your body promptly, and the words "peculiar odor" won't appear in your obituary. So you see, you've blown this thing way out of proportion; you got all upset over nothing. Unless you own your own home, in which case there *are* no neighbors downstairs, just your rec room. They might not find your body for months. Years.

Even if you elude the Shower of Death, you still have reason to fear the Bath of Doom. It's evening, and you're having a leisurely soak. As you relax in the tub, a radio plays, a glass of brandy sits in easy reach, there's a magazine in your hands. You feel the tensions of the day dissolve in the hot water, and filled with a sense of security and well being, you begin to drowse, slip beneath the water, and drown.

Of course, you might manage to escape both the Shower of Death and the Bath of Doom, but then you must face the horror of Incredible Filth.

These are the most common bathroom fears; there are others. It is admittedly unlikely, but not impossible, that a deadly viper—perhaps a water moccasin—could swim up the pipes, slip out into the tub, and bite you on the behind. You'd just die! Or, you could get your big toe stuck in the tap and be trapped there, slowly starving to death, unless you had the guts to gnaw off the captured digit. The longer you're single, the greater the risk.

How can you escape? Get married. Make bath time a civilized occasion. Picture it: she is soaking in the tub reading the Paris edition of *Vogue*. The tub is filled with bubbles, the air is perfumed, her makeup is perfect. He stands at the sink, a towel wrapped around his waist, shaving. His pecs are perfect. They carry on an astonishingly witty and romantic conversation. Nobody gets killed in a ludicrous accident. Which would you prefer: this interlude of ease and affection, or being bit on the behind by a venomous snake?

Many bathroom-related accidents can be avoided by observing a few basic safety rules. While taking a bath, never change the radio station (even if Sammy Davis, Jr., comes on singing "The Candy Man") and never try to change the light bulb above the tub until all the water has drained out. Never shave in the shower, particularly if you use an electric razor.

The very design of the bathroom offers a few built-in safeguards. If you were smoking in bed, you might doze off and let the cigarette slip from your hand; it would ignite the bedclothes and burn down the building, killing you and most of your neighbors. This can't occur in the tub. If you fall asleep there (assuming you don't drown), you'll awake unharmed a few hours later in a disgusting pool of water with soggy butts floating around you, and then twenty-five years later you'll develop severe respiratory ailments and die. So you needn't let fear of the bathroom dominate your life, although you may want to continue to dread being in a reenact-

ment of *Psycho*; if only you were married, you'd never be attacked in the shower by an ax-murderer played by Tony Perkins.

2 YOU'LL BE AT HOME ALONE EATING DINNER, AND A BIT OF FOOD GOES DOWN THE WRONG WAY. There is no one with you to perform the Heimlich Maneuver, so you choke. And die. The end.

Terminal, and, even worse, humiliating. Remember Mama Cass and the fatal ham sandwich? Remember Liz Taylor's near miss? I can still see the headlines in that sleazy tabloid (which I didn't buy, but merely glanced at in the checkout line at the A & P): "Liz Chokes on Chicken Bone... Star Rushed to Hospital." Nobody wants a cartoon death, and that's the risk you run each time you dine alone.

Eating is a social act that, when practiced alone, is transformed into a solitary vice. It's apt to be joked about nearly as much as that other, more celebrated solitary vice—that's why you are reluctant to perform either of these acts solo in a restaurant. You might not die, but people would give you funny looks. It was in response to this fear of embarrassment that Chinese restaurants began offering takeout food, and cable TV began offering at-home late-night adult entertainment.

Beyond the terror of becoming a food fatality, there's another dread. What will you do if it's dinnertime and there's nothing good on? Many lone diners find it less important to consult the *New York Times Cookbook* than to check *TV Guide*. Eating in front of the television is a challenging situation. If you sup during the local news, there is the loathsome possibility that the health-and-science reporter will do a piece on new techniques in stomach surgery right in the middle of your Stouffer's Spinach Soufflé. If you dine during the network news, you face the even more sickening prospect of eating while Caspar Weinberger announces his latest step on the road to World War III. You might delay dinner until the "MacNeil-Lehrer Report," but even so, there's no telling how appetizing their topic will be. And once you enter prime time, the possibilities for nausea increase geometrically. Another TV trepidation: the set could explode during dinner, and you'll be killed in a hail of shattered glass. When the cops find your body, you'll be face down in a Salisbury Steak TV Dinner. Talk about total humiliation...

Even if you survive the meal, you're not out of danger. Fear stalks the fridge. As you clean up and put things away, you place yourself in peril of infection from that green furry mass on the top shelf. Is it the ghost of pork chops past? You risk severe frostbite if you venture across the great glacier in your freezer compartment. In fact, considering the multitude of terrors surrounding an ordinary meal, your only hope is that NASA really will come up with those little pills you eat instead of food.

3 YOU'LL NEVER RECEIVE ANOTHER PHONE CALL. This is it: total isolation. You can tell, because the phone hasn't rung in quite a while. You might as well call the phone company and have it disconnected. Why keep it around if all you ever use it for is to order pizza?

Of course, you may be getting many exciting phone calls when you're out. The phone could be ringing off the hook when you're at the supermarket or the cleaner or any of the other provocative liaisons that make up your social life. Many modern singles deal with this by hiring an answering service, allowing themselves the chance to develop an entirely new scare-scenario: the people at the answering service are laughing at you because they know you're such a loser that no one ever calls you. You hate phoning for your messages because there won't be any, and you're sure you'll hear the people at the service giggling in the background as your hopes are crushed once again. For this misery you pay them $17.50 a month—the little rats.

As the situation deteriorates, you begin phoning the service from work, disguising your voice and leaving suggestive messages for yourself. Let's be realistic here. Will your service believe that Al Pacino called to say he'll meet you at the usual place? Is it a good idea for you to care what the service thinks? Why not just cancel those punks and get an answering machine? Get the kind with a beeper that lets you get your messages from any phone in the world. Then, even if you're thousands of miles away, you can call home and get the awful truth. It will keep you from over-extending your fantasy life. If, however, you begin phoning your machine from work, disguising your voice and leaving suggestive messages, then you've indeed attained a major obsession, and you should phone the clinic for professional assistance. If the doctor isn't in, leave a message with his service; it will make him feel needed.

There is another telephobia, a vestige of the era referred to by local newscasters as "that tumultuous period of upheaval that threatened to rend the very fabric of our nation," by which they mean 1969. You are convinced that the FBI has been tapping your telephone, but they find your life so incredibly dull that

their agents keep falling asleep on the job, so they decide to drop your case. Using the Freedom of Information Act, you get hold of your FBI file and find official government documents certifying that your social life is boring, and your lovelife nonexistent.

Some phone fears grow out of the odd sense of intimacy created by a telephone conversation. Many singles have the irrational sensation that the caller can "see" that their apartment is a mess. Similarly, some people are embarrassed to talk on the phone if they are naked. Sophisticated singles exploit this sensation, arranging teledates. She's in bed watching a movie on TV, and he calls. He switches to her channel, and they watch together—a tele-movie-date. This sort of thing often leads to telesex, but you can keep your self-respect by insisting on first having teledinner.

Most telephone mannerisms are harmless if kept under control. For example, some singles refuse to pick up on the first ring lest they seem too available. Others, when phoned for a date, refuse simply to accept the invitation but instead say, "Let me check my calendar." These are common subterfuges. If, however, you've made a cassette of party sounds that you play in the background whenever you receive a call in the evening, then you've gone too far. Likewise, it is impolite to say, "Let me put you on hold; I've got a call on line three," if you've only got a single line. And it is pathetic to attempt a ruse like "Let me put you on hold; the red phone to the White House is lit up." Once you've gone this far out of control, the only remedy is overcompensation. Disconnect the phone and carry on all communications through the mail. Or buy a brace of carrier pigeons and go cold turkey.

4 YOU'LL SPEND SO MANY YEARS ON YOUR OWN INDULGING YOUR OWN ECCENTRICITIES THAT YOU'LL BECOME UNABLE EVER TO LIVE WITH ANOTHER PERSON. You'll cultivate little obsessions about cooking, cleaning, sitting around. You will insist on a particular place to store the canned goods, a particular way to fold your jeans when they come out of the drier, a particular order to stack your records on the shelf. You'll know that these are arbitrary tics, but you won't be able to help yourself. You'll have had it your own way for too many years. It will be too late to change even for Mr. Right, let alone for Mr. Barely Acceptable.

In English movies that take place in the twenties, such male eccentrics are called "confirmed bachelors." They often dine at their clubs. Today in America, such fellows are often called "lone assassins." They end up dining in jail.

Oh, it's not so bad yet. You can put up a pretty good front for a day or two. "The wine? Put it anyplace," you tell your weekend visitor with a totally false suggestion of nonchalance. But you'll never pull it off for long because the wine doesn't go just anyplace. It belongs on the second shelf next to the anchovies. And all weekend long, you'll hear that bottle of Bordeaux whispering, "Help me, help me. I'm out of place." Soon, even the pose will be beyond you. You'll end up keeping four cats, and you'll let them sleep in your bed. (Or even worse: tropical fish. Wet sheets.)

As time goes by, your bachelorhood itself will become an obsession. You will be preoccupied with the term "premarital"; it's so exclusionary, so accusing. It will infect your thinking until you find yourself driving a premarital car, taking a premarital vacation, shopping for premarital shoes. Other, more innocent phrases will remind you of that despised usage, and you'll grow sullen and withdrawn if you watch a pregame show or eat a slice of precooked Virginia Ham. Eventually, whenever you spot that discriminatory term in a newspaper article, you'll dash off a hysterical letter to the editor demanding that it be altered to the more democratic "predeath."

It's a modern anxiety. Several generations ago, you'd have been married by seventeen, and you wouldn't have had the time to let your obsessions reach full bloom. But now there's the very real threat that you'll end up a crotchety eccentric, and be portrayed in your movie bio by Ruth Gordon.

5 YOU'LL BE CRUSHED BENEATH AN AVALANCHE OF DIRTY LAUNDRY. It must surely be that singles, and single men in particular, become alarmed in the face of soiled clothing. How else to account for the efforts these fellows make to avoid a confrontation with yesterday's socks? They kick them under the bed, hide them beneath the sofa, heap them on a chair—in short, they'll do anything except take them out to be washed. Psychiatrists speculate that such men are driven by an awful unconscious memory of being brutally bathed as infants, perhaps connected to fears of bath-toy separation.

If the pile of dirty clothes in your apartment is high enough to be charted on local topographic maps, it's time to get a grip on yourself. If, on one of your rare excursions to the launderette, you notice a pair of jeans that you haven't worn since the big demonstration against the bombing of Cambodia in 1972, it's time to seek professional help, if not from a therapist, then surely from a laundress. A trip to the coin-op is not meant to be a sentimental journey. One solution: link up with a victim of the unrestrained quirkiness mentioned in the previous section. You and the fellow obsessed with properly folded jeans can establish a symbiotic relationship. In any case, you really will have to stop thinking of underwear as a disposable item to be worn once and thrown away. Or at least stop regarding the floor of the bedroom as "away."

6 YOU WILL ALWAYS HAVE A ROOMMATE. Rents will keep climbing higher and higher, and studio apartments will become quaint anachronisms like drawing rooms. The only way you'll be able to afford housing is to spend the rest of your life with one roomie after another.

Despite your cautious screening, you'll be sharing with a succession of screwballs among whom Freud's patient the Wolfman would not feel out of place. One will be a lapsed monk with a collection of Gregorian chant albums that he plays after midnight on his massive stereo. Loud. One will constantly borrow your clothes without asking your permission or sharing your gender. One will converse in a language he claims is Dutch, but you suspect is of his own devising. One will steal your TV, and another will steal several of your dates.

They'll have better lovelives than you do, as you will hear through the bedroom wall, late at night, when you are lonely and depressed. Each will get married and leave you in the lurch the day before the rent is due, and you'll have to scramble frantically for a replacement.

Sooner or later, the replacement will be a member of an obscure political cell who will fill your living room with inflammatory tracts and your closets with Soviet AK-47 assault rifles. While you may never live to read your own wedding announcement in the society pages of the paper, you'll get to see your photograph on page one beneath the headline: "Didn't Know of Bomb Plot, Sez Terror-Gal's Roomie."

7 YOU WILL HAVE TO PERFORM THE ULTIMATE ACT OF MORTIFICATION, ADMITTING TO YOUR FAMILY THAT THEY WERE RIGHT, YOU WERE WRONG. They loom before you, the dreaded relatives—your fatuous cousin Phil, your smug brother-in-law Howie, your busybody Aunt Constance—ready to accept your confession.

Hers. OK, OK, I should have gone out to dinner with that nice Arthur the dentist; it wouldn't have killed me. I see it now. I'm going to end up a lonely old woman in Miami Beach with an annual cat-food bill running into the low six figures, to be covered by a Social Security check that doesn't even scrape the high fours. There will be a ratio of 5,000 single women to one single man, and he won't even be a good dancer. His name will be Lance, and he'll be a total no-goodnik, but everyone will be nice to him anyway. If only I'd listened to you . . .

His. It's true: if a man's not been married by the time he's thirty-five, there's a fundamental flaw in his character. I guess what my last eleven girlfriends said was right; I *am* an emotional cripple, and there's not a thing I can do about it. I suppose I'll go out and buy a twenty-five-inch remote control television set; that's about the only sort of commitment I'm capable of. Things would have worked out a lot better if only I'd listened to you and just called up that nice Elaine the lawyer and taken her out for a drink. It wouldn't have killed me.

8 YOU'LL BE SINGLE FOREVER. It is estimated that one endangered species becomes extinct each day, and for singles, no species is more endangered than the potential mate. Your other fears pale beside this one: all the good ones are taken. You've really blown it; you've waited so long to hook up with someone that there is no one left. Everyone decent you meet is, if not actually married, part of an established couple. The unattached are all badly damaged, and it is entirely your own fault for squandering your wonder years on a series of wildly inappropriate types just for the fun of it. It's like the grasshopper and the ant, and now you'll be stuck with some little insect.

Your lamentable circumstances will inspire your friends to help you, engaging you in an endless round of fix-ups. It's futile trying to stop them; they're only doing it for your own good, as they will remind you again and again. As you spurn each of their ludicrous suitors, they will begin regarding you as someone lacking all of his faculties, someone incapable of running his own life. They'll invite you over for home-cooked meals of insurmountable boredom, and view your refusals as a sign of false pride disguising pathetic loneliness. They will assail you with magazine articles discussing the health problems of the unwed—the high rate of heart attacks, depression, and suicide; the latest, most virulent strains of venereal disease—and they will be amazed that you are not delighted to receive dispatches. They will discount your opinions on every subject, because as a single you can't understand what it is to be a mature adult, participating in the real business of life. As the years roll by, their condescension will grow until they ignore your views not merely on domestic affairs, but on books, movies, politics, and which restaurant serves a good veal piccata. And—the most dreadful prospect of all—you will come to share their opinion. You'll think of yourself as a doddering coot, inept, lonely, miserable. You'll find yourself tearfully thanking them for giving you new insight into your own life. After all, what are friends for?

* * *

Of course, there is hope for the unwed. Sustain yourself by drawing up a list of famous singles who led lives of interest and accomplishment. Neither Chopin nor Ralph Nader nor Jane Austen ever married, and neither did Hitler until his bunker period, and what did it get him? Joan of Arc, Governor Jerry Brown, Virgil, and Pope John Paul II all stayed single, as did Queen Elizabeth I; she was known as the Virgin Queen, but there's no reason to go overboard.

Your greatest source of inspiration is to be found in the skyrocketing divorce rate. Divorce makes potential mates a renewable resource. As the rate climbs from one-third to one-half to nine-tenths, you should be suffused with optimism. Each CBS special or *Newsweek* cover story on the decay of the American family will cast a ray of sunshine upon your life.

Think of these things when the single life has got you down. Would Queen Elizabeth have been scared to eat dinner alone? Would Ralph Nader be afraid of his shower? Would Joan of Arc have been intimidated by her telephone? And when you are terrified of your roommate or your dirty shirts, cling to the thought that somewhere out there is a special someone just for you, in a marriage that is about to go bust. It's all a matter of recycling.

We are going to teach you to achieve Perfect Singlicity. Oh yes. Perfect Singlicity lifts you above the miasma of a nondescript existence.
Ah yes. Perfect Singlicity brings your life into focus.
It teaches you the value of oneness.
It is this Singlicity that eastern philosophers (particularly the ones in Boston and Brooklyn) have sought for eons, and that we pass on to you immediately:
We teach you to drink alone, and to know yourself as you do. Ah yes.
We teach you to cook for yourself, and to reach a knowledge of your food, as a woman.
We teach you to provide for yourself, with the speed of a fleet sprite, if you are a man.
We teach you to dress yourself, as most suits one of your single place in the great haberdashery of things.
We teach you to decorate your home and place of life, oh happy one are you.
We teach you the beauty and breadth of the single universe as you say your mantra over and over: "Saturday Night . . . Saturday Night . . . Saturday Night."
With these things, and with a true understanding of that, you shall have achieved Perfect Singlicity.
Do not deny it.

PERFECT SINGLICITY

How to Achieve It

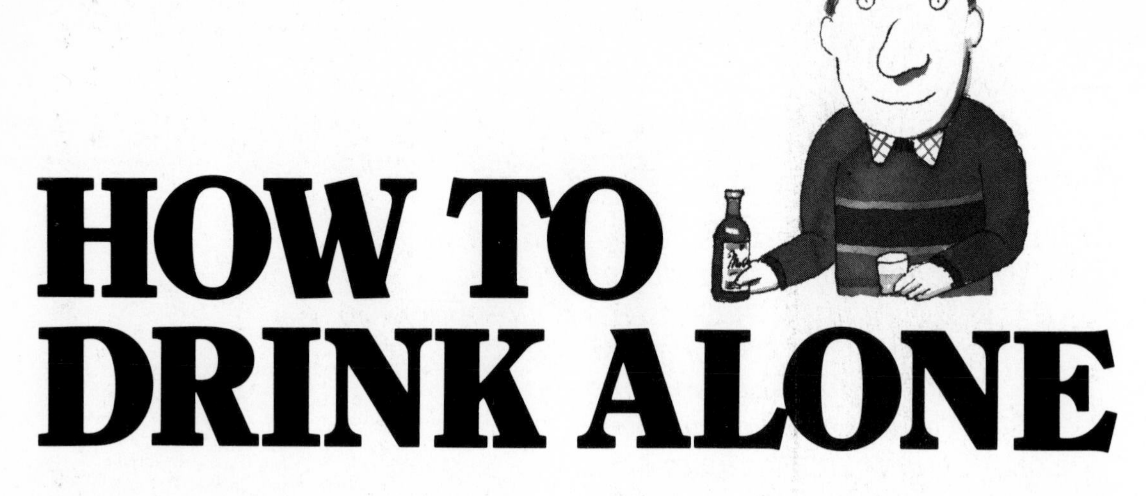

HOW TO DRINK ALONE

They will tell you that you should not drink alone. They will point out that having a social drink or two is no more than courtesy and cordiality demand; that a Napa varietal jug over a game of Dictionary with friends is part and parcel of the fun; that a couple of jolts in thick fist-cased glasses while waiting for the entrées of a business lunch is good business indeed; that a shared nightcap is the most reasonable pretext for inviting a date back to any apartment not containing a 16mm movie projector and a clean print of Mickey One. *All of these, they will say, are occasions on which drinking is all right, because it is a means to an end or a responsibility to be borne.*

But on drinking alone they will take a baleful pass. They will suggest that drinking alone is drinking for its own sake, and reflects an unfathomable desire to withdraw from the chummy company of one's problems, or to apply to those problems a kind of liberal welfare-state quick fix, resulting inevitably in a troublesome emotional deficit while failing to forestall the decay of one's psychic inner cities. The implication seems to be that there is something *dark*, something self-despising, even, about drinking alone.

You must be ready to answer them trenchantly, cogently, point for point. You must tell them: their mama.

Drinking alone is one of the great private pleasures, and makes enormous good sense besides. Many people believe that drinking puts them at their conversational best. Nearly all of them are wrong. If you are like most people, drinking actually puts you at your brilliant best for talking *to yourself*. With whom, then, should you drink? In point of fact, there are few things that can be done alone in such engaging company.

There is a sympathy of spirit between the institution of the saloon and that of the solitary person that should not go unremarked. A bar is a place where you can be alone and be a first-class citizen. Even in this enlightened epoch, a person eating alone in most restaurants is made to feel like a subject for the famous still-life *Leper with Mixed Seafood Platter*. This problem does not obtain in bars. Therefore, if you are going through a particularly sensitive or self-conscious phase of being single, you may wish to leave restaurants be and use bars to address your meal needs. If this seems nutritionally sketchy, remember that the signal injunction for good eating, back there in grade school, was to interact with the four basic "food groups" every day. This is still true now that you can no longer make a yo-yo "sleep," except that your nutritional needs have changed along with your body. Nutritionists tell us, if we pay them enough, that for a mature but still quite arresting person such as yourself, the four basic food groups are boilermakers (see "What to Drink," below), smoke-flavored almonds, complimentary hors d'oeuvres, and some more of those almonds. (See the monograph "Vastly Higher Quantities of Niacin and Riboflavin in Free Swedish Meatballs Than in the Special K Breakfast," by Dr. Maurice Minor of William and Mary and Ted and Alice University, 1977.) Some bars have pickled pigs' feet or "Scotch" eggs available as well, but I am not writing this essay for health nuts.

The Physiology of Drinking

Drinking alone will be a much more richly rewarding experience if you understand the biochemical wherefore of alcohol's effect on the brain. Scientists tell us that there are two brain hemispheres: the Northern Hemisphere, in which ideas go down the drain clockwise; and the southern, in which they go counterclockwise.

Tests show that alcohol molecules actually act as tiny "transporters," carrying neural impulses across the "International Date Line" that separates the two hemispheres. Just as seasoned world travelers "gain" or "lose" a day as they traverse the "real" International Date Line, the timing with which thoughts "pass through customs" into our conscious minds may be similarly sped or delayed by the action of alcohol.

Thus, certain perceptions seem to arrive "early" as boilermakers are applied. These perceptions may include the laughable but quite possibly legally actionable attempts by jealous business colleagues to sabotage the drinker's talent in the face of the clear hopelessness of ever competing with same; or the deep, initially hidden thematic content of the dots bouncing up and down along the arcs in the electric beer sign behind the bar; or of the koanish humor eloquently conveyed by that guy over there's blue shirt. Other sorts of perceptions arrive "late," notably those concerning the dynamic referred to by scientists as "accretion of the tab."*

When alcohol molecules are acting most efficiently as "transporters," "steaming" on the "clear seas" of bar hospitality under the "Norwegian registry" of intoxication, a condition exists that scientists call the "jake" (or "copacetic") state. In this state, small particles called "okie-dokules" are produced. Scientists have made numerous attempts to catch these particles on slides or in specimen vials. However, shortly after the particles are observed in action, scientists' heads sort of fall down.

What to Drink

"When you are drinking, a great difference as to the degree of your enjoyment and other salutary effects is made by your choice of beverage, and so an essay on 'How to Drink Alone' should, of natural necessity, include a section on what *to drink alone."*

—*Voltaire*

Voltaire was right. Some drinks are the key to man- or woman-sized beverage enjoyment at its best, while others are depressing. The most depressing drinks are the ones in the Smirnoff Vodka advertisements and the Southern Comfort brochures that are found next to the cash registers in liquor stores. These drinks have cute names, such as the Francis Ford Coppola Fizz ("Take two shots and you've blown the whole week!") or the Two Pernod Aces ("Try staying poker-faced after *this* one!"). If it were legal to suggest mixing Southern Comfort with Seconal, this favorite recipe of modern high-schoolers would be in those brochures too, advertised as The Down Comforter. As it is, these brochure drinks are even more depressing than the other leading cute from-a-recipe drinks, the ones in articles subtitled "Potables" in *Playboy* magazine. (Is there a recorded instance of a human being saying "potable" in conversation? This is hardly the only *Playboy* coinage that prickles the skin. Have you ever referred to a woman you knew as a "miss," much less "our peripatetic modeling miss"? Where were we?)

The Comfort and Smirnoff drinks are more depressing than the *Playboy* drinks partly because the ads and brochures always feature couples (*exercising* while drinking! *Remodeling the spare room* while drinking! If you please!) or covens of recently embalmed suburban twosomes of whom the women will be calling the sitter a lot and the men will be saying, "Let's party!" like to make you cringe.

It is not only the depiction of their use by zombies, however, that makes these drinks so depressing. It is also the notion that you would, in a million years, be so suggestible at the hands of the Eastern Media that you would actually pour all that melon liqueur and peppermint schnapps and other unpotables into three-quarter-teaspoon measuring spoons in order to mix these things. A friendly warning: If you do this, you will be only one precarious step from going out and buying all the dopey clothes in the *Playboy* Fall Fashion Forecast. And the people in the extensive Buffoon-Gulling Division of the Southern Comfort organization will be *laughing* at you as you try for the seventh time to float the Chartreuse properly.

Elaborate mixed drinks can be fun, of course, if they are served flaming in hollowed-out fruit halves at a place with big-band music, little spareribs, and a mirrored ball on the ceiling. (Astute readers will recognize this as a plug for Kelbo's on Pico Boulevard in Los Angeles, and *really* astute readers will recognize this writer, over by the tiki.)

The ideal drink, when you're drinking alone, is half a beer. Wait a minute, hear me out on this. When you're drinking alone, no external party is monitoring your level of intoxication. This is good as far as it goes, but there is always the danger that you will feel called upon to monitor your *own* level of intoxication which is ℞ for no fun. This is where the half-beer comes into play. The effect of alcohol in half a beer (4% or so of six ounces, or roughly none) is very slight, an ineffable little mayfly of a buzz that won't even show up on a Kirlian snapshot. It serves, however, to *remind* you of being drunk, to *conjure* intoxication—in short, to get you just drunk enough so that you will realize you aren't drunk enough.

Now you will order a little something to season the half-beer still outstanding in alternate sips. This little something may be tequila, may be scotch, may be one of the important Caribbean rums (Cockspur, Mount Gay, J. Wray and Nephew Overproof, Avery's, St. James, and Appleton's, whose slogan on its native Jamaica is "Appleton's—The together feel that's right in there!"). In any event, a neat shot, and you're now drinking a boilermaker (a shot and a beer, side by side), which is what I like to see. The interplay of straight liquor and beer is one of nature's marvelous syntheses. It is light and shadow, *lingam* and *yoni*, Apollo and Brooklyn Fox.

So: Isn't that half a beer something? Before you consumed it, you probably conceived of "boilermaker" as just another word for "troublemaker." *After* it, you recognize a boilermaker as necessary equipment for any happy home, just under "knotty pine rumpus room" on the docket. And after the boilermaker *lui-même*, you will be in the "jake" state mentioned above, and will want to hear "Giant Steps" by John Coltrane, "Telegram Sam" by T. Rex, or something else that will almost certainly not be on the jukebox where you are drinking. However, the strength of the "jake" state will probably be sufficient to make whatever *is* on the jukebox—even if it is only "Suspicious Minds" by the late Elvis Presley—seem just as good as what you had in mind. It is, as Sammy Cahn and Jules Styne might have put it, magic.

If you have any lingering doubts that boilermakers are the drink for you, go watch how washed-up hoodlum Robert Mitchum orders them from Mob-controlled bartender Peter Boyle in the seriously underrated movie version of *The Friends of Eddie Coyle*. Watch how, without speaking a word, Mitchum holds his thumb and index finger a shot glass's height apart, kind of squinching his facial features up, and then, as he expands the finger gap toward the height of a highball glass full of beer, widens his eyes and raises his brows to complete the equation. If ever there was a guy

**Attempts have been made to test the effects of alcohol on both hemispheres simultaneously, chiefly by mixing tequila with akvavit. The freedom to essay such experimentation without terrifying one's trusted associates is only one of the benefits of drinking alone.*

who needed to sit and work things out over a swallow or two, it is Mitchum in that picture, and what does he drink? Also, notice that he looks about a million years old in this one, proof that boilermakers are key in achieving that aspect of road-tested wisdom that will be so desirable as the baby bulge continues to mature and our nation's embarrassing Humbert Humbert youth cult closes up shop. If you pay attention to no other celebrity endorsement, take Bob's unspoken word about boilermakers to heart.

Dealing with Certain Insecurities

"For a depressed person, bar talk is much better than Bartok."
—*Racine*

"Yes, but are gay bars better than Zabar's?"
—*Verlaine*

"Both of you stop it." —*Rimbaud*

The solo drinker is subject to certain insecurities. One superstition to which you may be prey is an unrealistic conviction that the people who work in bars are actually some kind of Women's Christian Temperance Union missionaries who frown on your drinking, and, particularly, your drinking alone, and, more particularly, your drinking so much. The idea may take hold, while you are enjoying your first sultry, heritage-rich double gold tequila with its sparkling, life-embracing beer back, that when you ask the lady behind the bar for another of each, she will engage you in a conversation in which she probes for the *root causes* of your behavior and makes some Straight Talk for Teens kind of points about how you can run and run but you can never hide from *yourself.*

Don't give it another thought. This is not going to happen.

Every Drinker His Own Pinter

You may also be plagued by the unfortunate notion that sitting around drinking constitutes "a waste of time." The simplest way to disabuse yourself of this is to make drinking a "worthwhile" activity, by keeping a *Log of Overhears* and updating it frequently. Drinking in our nation's taverns, you will overhear some really prize stuff, and be in an optimal condition to appreciate it.

A notebook, however, undercuts the spirit of the thing. On hearing something especially oracular and poignant, root through your wallet for something on which to jot it down. In the cold sober light of the few hours between wakening and the first frosty, bracing beer of the next day, these stray bits of dialogue—preserved on the back of a Kim Lee Finished Laundry ticket or the fringe area of an emergency-reserve traveler's check—will have a refreshing aspect of total unfamiliarity, of having drifted into our galaxy on free-floating interstellar radio waves in exchange for an old Bickersons program.* Tell yourself that, since there is no WPA Writers' Program here in the present-day downturn, it is up to you to record the voices of the plain people, the roiling and striving common folk, as they enact the eternal pageant of reaching for the stars, climbing toward Eldorado, asking of God only that tonight they might make moofky-poofky with a junior partner in a view co-op. Say to yourself: In no way did I come away from last night's experience empty-handed. For one thing, I have a laundry ticket on which is inscribed:

"So we're having a good time and then all of a sudden she says, 'Well, how much *is* your father worth?' That was it. As soon as she asked me that (Gets really mad here) I said, 'You're history, pal. Take a *hike.* You are history.'" (*Repeats story several times, exactly. Guy with him keeps saying, "You did the right thing."*)

If nothing else, Mrs. Kim will look at you through new eyes.

The Cocktail-Frank Problem

Drinking alone is sometimes a reasoned response to the termination with extreme prejudice of an *affaire de coeur.* This in itself is fine, so long as one doesn't make the mistake of expecting an unrealistic degree of pleasure from being alone in a bar at such a juncture. As you may have gathered, we are about to address the question of Frank Sinatra, and the very difficult problem he poses to the newly single drinker.

It is true that Frank Sinatra is one of the finest singers in the history of the world and sets an inspiring personal example as well. This, however, contributes to the problem under discussion. Some of us are—understandably—a little too susceptible to the image of saloon loneliness evoked by the middle-young Sinatra, particularly in his definitive version of "One for My Baby (and One More for the Road)" and on the jacket of *In*

**Some overhears, of course, are phantasms. That one a few moments ago, where the tourist lady seemed to say to her husband, "It's up to you, now that that Haas boy is drunk," is a classic example. Disregard these just as a rational person would.*

the Wee Small Hours (the one with the cigarette under the streetlight). Some of us have even been compelled to *yearn* for the opportunity to savor the bittersweet moments therein portrayed, because it is Frank Sinatra's genius to romanticize loneliness—palpable, existential, terminal, French-Foreign-Legion loneliness—into a desirable hep stance. Is it too much to think that a few people out there have broken off perfectly good affairs *for the express purpose* of crushing an empty Pall Mall package while closing a bar at two in the morning, expecting the armed might of Nelson Riddle to well up behind them as they announce, "We're drinking, my friend, to the untimely end of a brief episode"?

The problem is that, for you and me, savoring is not really in the cards. Bear in mind that Frank's very best turns are on these dejected songs, that they are what show him to be a better interpreter than any of several pale young women in headsets behind the scenes at the U.N., and that if not for this whole saloon-closing thing we might be walking around today referring to him as, "Oh, yes, Joey Bishop's friend." The pitfall for the single drinker is the way The Chairman seems to *welcome* loneliness, curling up into it as if it were international fame and untold millions of dollars. After considerable experimentation, I have concluded that the international fame and untold millions are what Frank actually *is* enjoying, rather than the loneliness. So go ahead and drink it off, but remember that it is not really in your nature to feel like anything but human junk at these times, unless you know that every time your nouveau ex picks up a magazine he or she will have to look at you in there, posing with your personal friend Lee Iacocca for a Chrysler ad in which he explains the Imperial's onboard computer to you.

Singles Bars

The advice in this essay, by the way, has been tested for your safety in the friendly boites of San Francisco. San Francisco is, of course, on the Pacific waterfront, and the air is chock-full of negative icons.* One such negative icon, which abounds here, is the singles bar, a place where people go to "meet" other people on the pretext of enjoying beverages, ignoring the obvious fact that the mental rehearsal of classy repartee and the attempt to assess an individual's social and financial suitability by dividing the number of pushbuttons on his Casio calculator watch by the apparent age of his Wallabee shoes are both activities incompatible with enjoying anything.

In any event, the world is full of better ways to "meet" people than in singles bars. For instance, I have been told about a supermarket in Fashionable Marina Del Rey, California,* where it works like this: around the knock-off hour, each man goes into the supermarket, takes a shopping basket, and places in it two steaks and a bottle of red wine. Then he wanders the aisles.The women walk around checking out the contents of the men's baskets** and deciding who to go home with. I'm not clear on whether the women have baskets of their own, for romaine and Ore-Ida purposes, or what. Anyway, if you think this is cold-blooded and mechanical, I put it to you that it is no better or worse than a singles bar.

It is not just the Chicago Mercantile Board aspect of singles bars ("Get me Lauries! I need Lauries and Seths!"), but the way most of them are named and appointed. The formula, especially in the Sunbelt cities, seems to be to name the place for some nonexistent codger out of the quaint past, i.e., Orville/Homer/Cyrus/Phineas T./J./P./K. Pettifogger's/Pennypacker's/Whippersnapper's, and to decorate it with rusty old headlamps and make the staff wear collar stays.

None of this means that you will not meet people in bars and wish to start liaisons with them. This can happen in financial district bars, waterfront bars, collegiate beer-pitcher bars with bluegrass bands still gritting their teeth through "Charley on the M.T.A.," and airport Ramada Inn bars (you *dog*).

However, because drinking engenders a certain elasticity of judgment, it is possible that you will meet a person and invite that person back to your home, only to discover en route that this person, as evidenced by his or her use of "plus" as a conjunction, or a professed admiration for the cinema of Frank Perry, is not someone you will want to have in your life on any continuing basis, and perhaps not even long enough for what NASA engineers call "docking." But what to do? One cannot exactly dump this person on the street.

Fortunately, there is a way out, through the investment of a little forethought. Have on hand in your residence a recording of Glen Campbell singing "Wichita Lineman." (This is the one that starts, "I am a lineman for the county, and I drive the main road," and has the woodwinds making those odd little power-outage sounds.) As the undesirable person starts describing his or her favorite scene in *David and Lisa* or *Mommie Dearest*, get "Wichita Lineman" going, hold up an instructive, silencing finger, and say, "Excuse me, but this is *Glen's* time of the evening. *Glen's* time is a very *special* time of the evening." You will have fought fire with fire, and this person will soon pass out of your happy single life.

Drinking Alone at Home

Many people like to drink at home. I can see few advantages to this, other than the short distance to approved sleeping surfaces and the opportunity to build up a more comprehensive library of the important Caribbean rums than most stateside bars have managed at this writing. Some people—most of them Associate Producers or Creative Group Heads—have their own pinball machines or jukeboxes as well. As long as you stop short of cocktail napkins featuring the cartoons of Virgil Partch, I think you're okay.

The Use of Cooking Wine When Every Place Is Closed

Just don't tell me about it.

Going Home

Finally, it should be noted that no episode of drinking alone should go on forever. Here is my handy rule of thumb for judging when enough has become enough: Every now and then, take a look at the matchbook display beside the cash register of the bar in which you are drinking. At a certain point in the evening, the legend "For Our Matchless Friends" on this display will seem to you to be (a) new, and (b) the very soul of wit. You will go up to the proprietor of the establishment and say, "Wow, did Noël Coward come in here and do that match thing for you guys?"

Go home.

**New Age joke.*

**The City Council there has recently voted to add the word "Fashionable" to the city's legal name.*

***Sorry, this just happened.*

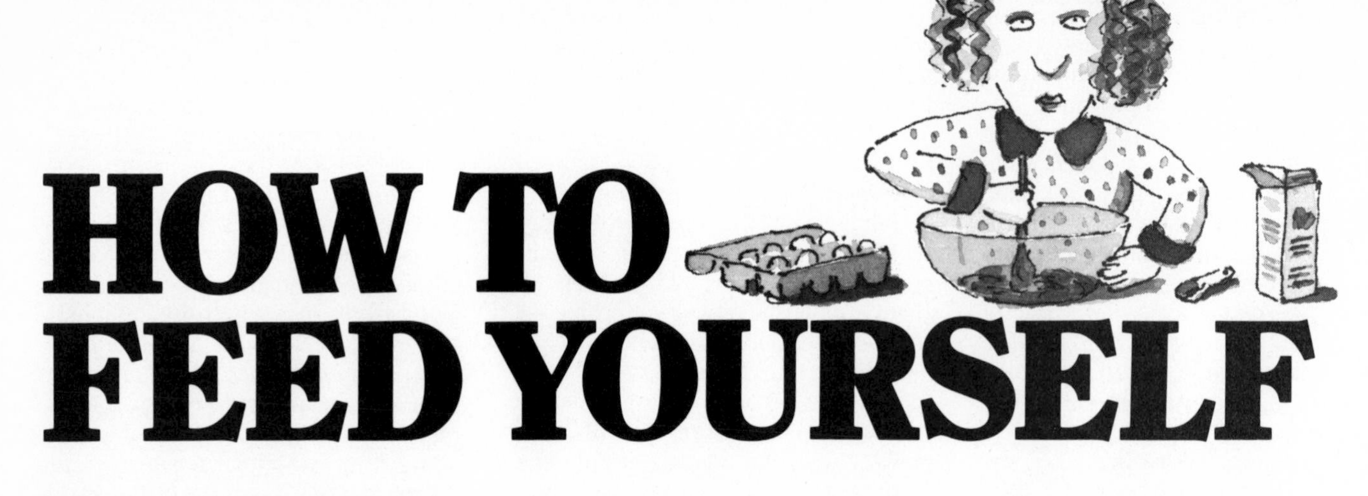

HOW TO FEED YOURSELF

(If You're a Single Woman), Or, Are You Finished with That Plate?

In 1969, Helen Gurley Brown published *Helen Gurley Brown's Single Girl's Cookbook*, which included the following recipe:

Rhett Butler Casserole
You Can Feed *Any* Man

2 pork chops per person
1 large can (1 pound, 13 ounces) sweet potatoes
2 oranges, peeled and sliced thin
Brown sugar
Butter

Grease skillet by rubbing the fat edge of 1 chop across it.

Brown chops for about 10 minutes on each side. Butter a large casserole. Slice sweet potatoes 3/4 inch thick and put a layer in the casserole. Add a layer of orange slices (you can leave the peel on if you're a health nut like Margo and me)...

It was 1969. Serving a lover, a boss, or a landlord orange food with pork in it was not automatically alienating. It was OK for an unmarried woman, in miniskirt and white boots, to heat up the kitchen with her panic (*"Should I leave the peels on, or will he think I'm a health nut?"*). The object of excitement was a guy with shaggy hair, bell-bottoms, and a wide tie, who sat in her living room, also panicking (*"What if I don't know what it is?"*). Mutual torture was the rule for single people, and they practiced ardently. If they ever got good enough, they'd go pro together.

If *she* got good enough. In the kitchen, she swigged cooking sherry for courage and memorized Helen Gurley Brown's reassuring instructions for Red Caviar in Sour Cream: "When ready to serve with cocktails, place this dish on a flat platter, surrounded by potato chips. Carry to the living room." Maybe if she followed the instructions carefully enough, she could escape her single life, just like Helen did.

Some things have changed. Now, we play the theme song from "The Outer Limits" when we flip through *Helen Gurley Brown's Single Girl's Cookbook*. We are looking not just at the past, but at life on another planet. There, food was a girl's only defense against a life of desperation. She could be a poor bum, eating cold baked beans out of a can; or she could be genteel and take what Helen called "bowser bags" home from her restaurant dates, to whip that leftover beef into civilized meals. She could let a cad get away, or she could remember (Helen would remind her) that single females outnumbered Steak Balls. And if that didn't work, and life veered out of control, Helen knew what to do. Go to bed. Take some Milk Toast Like Mama Used to Make with you, or some Soothing, Nourishing, Calming French Toast. Helen herself preferred ice-cold milk, and a handful of stale gumdrops.

Have we come that far since 1969? We've come farther.

Your Food Heritage
A Quiz

Please check any of the following foodstuffs that you might have eaten frequently during your Wonder years:

☐ *Wonder bread*
☐ *Wonder bread rolled up in balls*
☐ *Pizza (frozen or from the bowling alley)*
☐ *Cinnamon Toast*
☐ *Hawaiian Punch*
☐ *Lucky Charms*
☐ *Velveeta*
☐ *Homemade corny dogs or homemade candy apples*
☐ *Canned peas*
☐ *Sandwiches made of toasted marshmallow, a plain Hershey's bar, and two graham crackers*
☐ *Popcorn, non-gourmet*
☐ *SPAM*
☐ *Nestle's Quik artificial strawberry flavor stuff*

Scoring: 4 or less: milk-drinker
4 to 8: lived on Jujubes
8 to 15: my people

No matter where our mothers came from, we are all part white sugar. That's a key ingredient in our American heritage, a heritage, by the way, that includes these contributions to the English language:

beeline	girlfriend
boyfriend	hamburger
cafeteria	iron lung
chop suey	moron
fraternity	refrigerator

My favorite Donna Reed show of this period was about a teenage girl who was trying to ace a tough home-ec course. Her final exam was running a family household for a whole week, at the end of which she had to play hostess to her home-ec teacher. This girl planned a fabulous meal for her final grade, with baked Alaska for dessert, but something horrible happened—someone got mixed up about the nights and so on—and she panicked and had to order out. She had to pass off *take-out* food as her own home cooking! Of course the home-ec teacher knew the real story, but as she pointed out to all of us at the end, sometimes a real housewife gets surprised by company, too, and she must never be ashamed to be resourceful. Then, to emphasize her point, she gave that girl an A.

That was prophetic television. By the time I waved good-bye to my mother's avocado kitchen, the freeze-dried craze had just peaked, the two main places to cash checks were the liquor store and the supermarket, and everyone was buying crock pots. You didn't have to cook anymore as long as you were resourceful—as long, that is to say, as you could thaw. Was I warped by the fact that three of the staples of my childhood—frozen Popsicle sticks, frozen fish sticks, and canned fried shoestring potato sticks—were called *sticks*? And how many residual maraschino cherries do I have in my body? Who knows? By the time I peeled the last slice of Wonder bread from the roof of my mouth, home was no place to get a home-cooked meal.

Grandma's Creamed Tuna 'n' Toast

1. Combine one can of tunafish and one can of Campbell's Cream of Mushroom soup in saucepan.
2. Make toast.
3. Spoon tunafish in mushroom sauce over toast and eat.

Everybody is so obsessive about food these days, we forget what a single person needs to survive. The truth is, not much; but not much of what? The granolaheads threw us off track with their groats and brewer's yeast, and now even Wonder bread is on the defensive. What's wrong, plead their commercials, with stripping all the nutrients, making what's left all soft and fluffy and white, then washing it in a bath of twelve essential vitamins? So what if sprouted rye and wheatberry has more bulk; do you really want to feed your sensitive tummy *bulk*? It's not an aggressively stated question, just a puzzled inquiry. If Wonder bread isn't basic, what is?

Good question. Sometime during our childhood, when Mom was boiling all the remaining nutrients out of the canned spinach and packing Casper the Friendly Ghost lunch boxes with Twinkies and pimiento cheese sandwiches, whoever decides these things decided to reduce the number of basic food groups. Yes, in America. There were seven, then suddenly there were only four. Butter and margarine were their own essential food group; then suddenly, they were merely part of the milk team. Now how could we build strong bodies and jump higher if someone was going to be banishing major food groups, even while we were eating them?

Better Homes and Gardens understood the new streamlined nutritional categories, but they didn't take the hint; what the hell, they told the American cook, "let your imagination run." And so did theirs. The meal menus in their red-and-white-checkered cookbook were marvels of nature, even in 1969, when the first packets of trail mix began sneaking into the drugstores. *Better Homes and Gardens* called it a meal only if it included a main meat dish, a "starchy complement," a vegetable, a salad (if you can call Pineapple Rings With Stewed Prune Centers a salad), and dessert—pies, parfaits, or our old friend, cupcakes. Then *Better Homes and Gardens* took their own advice and invented an additional food group without which a meal was incomplete. They called it "accents." What was an "accent"? Oh, sometimes it was nothing more than a wedge of cheddar cheese on your apple pie, or a pickle next to your Outdoor Burger. Sometimes, though, it was a dollop of melted marshmallow "atop" your squash. Americans don't do that anymore, not even to their vegetables.

The concept is useful. For example, I live alone, which means I live on "accents." My kitchen, like the kitchens of most single people, is ideal for the munching of this unofficial and neglected food group. In the drain are a few spoons from United Airlines and some oyster forks the previous tenant left; my knives are dull, perfect for hacking off chunks of cheese. I have one big pot (popcorn), one frying pan (eggs), and one saucepan (Progresso Lentil Soup, to which I add—call them "accents"—vinegar and quantities of black pepper). In the refrigerator are garnishes, condiments, and cosmetic food trifles: chili sauce, hot mustard, cherry tomatoes, and hard-boiled eggs. I root around these with my dull knives for nourishment, or I eat things raw straight from their brown bag (how basic can you get?); once in a while, I even try to scratch up a meal. My definition of a meal: hot or cold, liquid or solid, gooey or crunchy, it's got to fit in one dish, and it's got to have the same consistency across the dish. No surprises. No bones, gristle, fat, garlic chips, or dirty pieces of sponge in any bite. The same bite, every bite: that's my standard. I don't want to have to watch my food when I eat. I want to watch "Family Feud."

Maybe you have more pots and pans than I do and a more sophisticated idea of what a meal is, but if you eat alone, you know what I'm talking about. I'm talking about grown men and women eating bowls of hot cereal for supper. I'm talking about pawing through little white cardboard boxes of cold leftover Chinese afterthoughts—bamboo shoots, hard yellow pellets of rice, congealed pepper sauce—looking for one morsel of beef, one nugget of shrimp: a metaphor for eating alone. I'm talking about a state of mind so bent it can't manage a square meal.

Consider: Any idiot can cook, right? You just have to pay attention and follow the recipe. I could do it perfectly well when I lived at home; I was a regular little flour-sifter. And when I lived with friends, I wokked demonically. But what will I had to cook mysteriously evaporated when I moved into my own apartment, and now I suffer from a bona fide condition. I'll take a friend out to dinner rather than open my refrigerator. There's something furtive about my meals, something embarrassingly private about my eating habits. If I were surprised in the act of scavenging—say, someone turned the kitchen light on—I'd hit the floor. All accumulating evidence, I began to realize, of the psychological effects of discrimination.

It's a new sort of discrimination, one that attacks people where they eat. It flips the food right off your fork, and kicks you out of restaurant booths during the lunch hour rush. The message is: Eating alone? Why bother? Think of all the racial and ethnic and cultural groups suffering from discrimination; every single one of them has a native cuisine. To have your own cuisine is to have a history (not to mention a future). I think of my people's, a blend of poor Catholic pancake eaters and suburban convenience consumers. But people who eat alone have no tradition, no spontaneous culinary response to a unique situation that could grow into a tradition; we have no cuisine of our own —not yet, anyway. Instead, we've had foisted on us a really disgusting, really patronizing, really chiseling fake cuisine.

I'm talking about Campbell's Soup for One.

How could they? How could *Campbell's*? True, I've shifted to the post-hippie Progresso brand, but Campbell's is my heritage. I mean, there they are in my Grandma's Creamed Tuna 'n' Toast. When I was a little girl, they made it all right to be a kid with freckles; I'm indebted for that. They were there for my first off-campus dinner party—chicken breasts baked in Campbell's Cream of Mushroom soup, undiluted, on a bed of flat noodles—and there when I walked through dangerous neighborhoods with cans of it in plastic bags to swing for weapons. Always, there were Campbell's soup cans in my cabinet, like rows of red and white soldiers with their gold medallions, the prize of the 1900 International Exposition, the definition of stalwart.

Now, in the eighties, betrayal.

I knew something was fishy because, first of all, who needed Soup for One? A regular can makes a little over twenty-one ounces, enough for a full bowl and a dab more for seconds. I've always been able to handle it, and so what if I haven't? It's nobody else's business.

But they didn't ask me, and I bet they didn't ask you, either. They just went ahead and produced a new squat little can, designed to make single people feel flattered and cozy. Not a can, a con! Suddenly, the familiar Campbell's script shrinks in the shadow of the bold Soup for One. Suddenly, we get a color picture of a bowl of soup, in case we're so far gone we can't visualize. No fleur-de-lis, no gold stripes, no two-toned letters spelling S-O-U-P. Suddenly, Cream of Mushroom soup is Savory Cream of Mushroom soup; Vegetable is Old World Vegetable; Chicken & Noodle, Golden Chicken & Noodle; and plain, sturdy, rainy-afternoon Tomato is Tomato Royale. What's different? It's semi-condensed, not condensed; you add half a can of water, not a full can; you make eleven ounces, not twenty-one. Otherwise, it's the same old thing, only different.

Now, pretend this is "Let's Make a Deal," and guess how much more the regular-sized can of Cream of Mushroom soup costs, for almost exactly twice as much mushroom soup. Did you guess four cents? At my supermarket, the savory small can costs 39¢ and the regular no-comment can costs 43¢. Four cents is nothing, a margin of error, a trickle from your pocket. You can't buy a thing in a supermarket for four cents, except adjectives. If you're friendly with the manager and you don't have four pennies, he'll wave you off. Four cents? Forget it. Catch me later. No, Campbell's should have just finished their insult to us and made those two different sizes the exact same price.

Let's nuke them.

O.K., Campbell's isn't the worst. The worst is going to the supermarket and trying to find the worst. I've always thought of the supermarket as a toy store for adults, full of gratifications, and bright and noisy in the way that a person living alone thinks of as comforting. It's a spontaneous place; I don't use shopping lists because it's so much fun to run back to the Red Apple for a box of Little Friskies, a tomato, a light bulb. Dominic, the manager, and the checkers, Sheila and Francine, know me as one of the sneakered ones who stand in the express line once or maybe twice a day, flipping through *People*. They don't bother giving me a hard time if it takes an hour to find just the right TV snack —this is a neighborhood of derelicts and oddballs, and the aisles are full of people dreamily comparing ingredients and prices and pictures on the labels, and couples having sincere conversations about how to dress their pork chop. In the Red Apple, we are all suspended in the hours before dinner in a zone of security, trusting Dominic, Sheila, Francine, and Campbell's.

It is, of course, a false security. I went there immediately after the Soup for One fraud was revealed to me, and the place was suddenly alien. "Hey There, Georgy Girl" was the Muzak selection, and Vienna sausage was the sale of the day. The stockboys stood back by the bacon, muttering as female shoppers strolled by. It was Tuesday, dusk, and busy. I wandered for a minute, just to get the sense of it, and found myself on an aisle flanked by lovely Lido cookies on one side, and on the other, revolting Ken-L Ration burgers—giant boxes with obscene red curlicues pressed against the see-through windows (4 ways better than hamburger! the boxes swore). A few yards away, chicken bologna and olive loaf hung against a pegboard, above which towered big blue stacks of feminine hygiene products. There was no sense in these juxtapositions, just hostility. If you paid attention, you could lose your appetite.

The Kellogg's cornflakes were stacked in a corner by the aspirin and laxative. Every size package had an inviting, appealing American face on its cover. Bill Cosby, Miss America, a woman in a military uniform, a little Boy Scout. Kellogg's with fresh strawberries, Kellogg's with pure white sugar, Kellogg's cornflakes straight from the box while watching cartoons . . . I stood there in a reverie. The clanging of the cash registers and the checkers' cries of "Dominic! Dominic!" faded in the background as the Kellogg's faces beckoned me closer.

What a sucker. If Soup for One was a lesson, why didn't I learn? Once you get close enough to see the leer in the little Boy Scout's eye, you see what sort of punishment Kellogg's has in store for sentimentalists. Oh, if you're sentimental and have a family of six, you buy the giant military woman—a pound and a half of cornflakes—for a little over a dollar a pound, and that's not too big a bite. But if you're sentimental, shop only for yourself, and like to keep your provisions fresh, you buy the cornflakes in the Handi-Paks, for a little over three dollars a pound. Now, a person can pay that difference ignorantly and still be a happy person, but a person can't understand that difference and be anything but transformed. I was transformed into Charles Bronson of *Death Wish* and *Death Wish II*. There by the gigantic boxes, my attitude grew gigantically. Certain parties had taken my trust and messed with it. I felt as cold as cold cereal, as cold as cold tablets.

I lurked down the aisles of infamy, waiting to strike. Down the aisle of sodas, pulsing in the giant, two-liter plastic containers. How large would they grow? Down the long aisle of fruit juices—more juice, juice combinations, reconstituted juice, juice substitutes, and cocktails than one mind could absorb; the deep purple of prune, the flaming orange of cranicot, the flagrant red of clamato, the unnatural green of lime. Even in all these varieties, the principle held: everything small is expensive, everything large is cheap.

At last I arrived at the aisle against the wall where the conglomerate food group "dairy products" was kept. It was hard to separate the unfair from the disgusting in the dairy case. Here one could buy frozen toaster pancakes and two pound tubs of something called SPREAD, solidified vegetable oil with 25% less fat than margarine. Here one could also be slapped in the face by more of the fake cuisine: an abomination called Kraft's Singles, individually wrapped slices of pasteurized process cheese food in three varieties, American, muenster, and "sharp," don't ask sharp what. (Resist them. They live forever in your refrigerator. The only way you can make them die is by ingestion. Not even mold can stand them.)

But also here in the dairy case lie the only food items that don't cost more if you buy less: eggs and butter, friends to all. Tear a carton of eggs in half, and Sheila and Francine will charge you half price; liberate a stick of butter from a package of two or four, and they'll charge you a half or a fourth. It seems so fair; everyone has the right to fresh eggs and butter. But the scene is one of decimation; a war has been fought here and lost. Half cartons of eggs lay strewn around, butter wrappers clutter the floor. Why aren't the eggs packed in half cartons? Why aren't there at least perforations through the middle? Why are the butter sticks wrapped uselessly and redundantly in extra waxed paper, so two and four come together, go on sale together, march out of the supermarket together, and together tyrannize the kitchens of America—that is, unless some lone shopper rips them apart? What is going on here?

I kicked over a milk carton and stepped right up. Over the strains of an orchestrated "Baby Love," I shouted my dismay to the stockboys and the winos and the girls in flat shoes choosing yogurt flavors.

When I was a little girl (I shouted), I ate like a little girl. I got a piece of whatever my family was eating, and if I ate it fast enough, I got two pieces. Pretty soon I grew up, and now that family of six is scattered all over the country, and we eat in smaller units. Some of these units are as small as one. But we are not fragmented people; we are whole people. And we are not miniature people; we are regular-sized people. We just can't eat together anymore. It's the way it is, and we've suited ourselves to it.

Now, there's a plague in the land. It's not a plague on the crops and fields—look around you, there's plenty to go around. No, this is a plague of greed. This is a greed that has decided that you and I and others who eat alone don't eat enough to line some particular pockets as fast as they'd like to be lined. Two things happen as a consequence of this greed. Number one, there are rewards for those who consume large quantities of food in short amounts of time. Number two, there are penalties for those who buy small quantities of food and use them all up before they buy more. A lot of help is going to the people who eat in crowds, and a lot of hurt going to the people who eat alone. An injustice is what I call it, and an indignity is what I suffer. No more, no more.

Whenever I can buy economy, I'm going to buy it. Whenever I can avoid a big name brand that spends its money on ads and labels, I'm going to walk around the block. Whenever I find an item that costs the same per unit in the little sizes as it does in the big, I'm going to go on a diet and eat only that item. I resolve not to just look at the middle shelves, but at the top shelves and the bottom shelves, too. I *will* compare. I *will* pay attention. I *will* try using a coupon, just to see if it works.

Someday soon, the single eater will achieve recognition. It will take us time. It always does. Here's how we'll know when that day comes: When we leave our parents' homes, no matter which road we take, that's when people will throw us a big party and send us toasters, blenders, flatware, Tupperware, and monogrammed dish towels to wipe up our mess.

I stepped down from the carton and wandered toward the red meat. For the first time in years, I recognized the gnawing in my stomach as *appetite*.

The Speed Chef Method of Power Cooking and Power Shopping for Single *Guys*

Most of you know me as The Speed Chef. You've undoubtedly heard of my revolutionary approach to transforming the grim business of cooking for yourself into a tolerable, if not actually pleasurable, experience. Thousands of single guys and gals have already thanked me for teaching them how to prepare savory gourmet treats in seconds, and now I'd like to share my secrets with you.

First, however, let's bury once and for all those two conventional wisdoms about the annoying task of cooking for yourself. I'm sure you know what they are.

Number one, virtually every singles guide advises you not only to shop sparingly, but to relish the art of loading your grocery cart with the perfect lone lamb loin chop, transparently thin wedges of gruyere, and the smallest amount of commercially prepared potato salad allowed to be sold by law.

Number two, the conventional wisdom is that the unattached should prepare their meals slowly, basking in their proud independence and the freedom of catering to only one palate. This blithe advice is based on the notion that epicurean pleasures, if prolonged, will somehow mitigate the despair of solitary cooking. "Don't be afraid to experience your own loneliness," instructs one bestselling singles guide, with the implication that there's something to be gained by taking an hour and a half to broil a chicken leg.

If these suggestions seem like sound ones to you, it is only because your loneliness and frustration have robbed you of the common sense necessary to see that they are exactly the opposite of what you need to do to lead your life as a single *guy* with dignity.

Power Shopping

Take the first instance, food shopping. If you fill your shopping cart with those depressingly petite portions of food, you succeed only in revealing your status as an undesirably lonely person and in causing other people in the checkout line to either move politely away or else offer the name and phone number of an equally lonely relative of the opposite sex who has recently moved to town. (Under no circumstances are you to write the number down; studies show that a large percentage of relationships begun in this manner end up in custody court or homicide.)

No, the trick is to follow The Speed Chef Method of Power Shopping: buy as much food as your budget will permit. No one can mistake you for a lonely single in the checkout line when you begin to heave, say, several self-basting turkeys and a steamship roast beef onto the conveyor belt. To the contrary, people will jealously assume that you have either countless admirers, a large family, or a severe glandular disorder.

But the advantages of Power Shopping are even more pronounced when it comes to your refrigerator. I hardly need to tell you that the most tragic thing in the life of a single person is Singles Icebox Syndrome (SIS), whereby your refrigerator is discovered to contain two tiny cartons of Yoplait yogurt, a half-pint deli container of macaroni salad, a 5 oz. can of V-8, and an object which, were one to extrapolate from its present condition, might very well have been a slice of Genoa salami at some point during the previous month. Anyone greeted by such a collection will automatically infer that its owner is not someone for whom human contact is a frequent occurrence, and is therefore someone to avoid.

Now, on the other hand, if someone opens your refrigerator and finds two or three rump roasts, a twenty-five-pound wheel of Jarlsberg cheese, and a large amount of fresh okra, he or she will quickly deduce that you are an important person to know, and—even more dramatically—one of the few people around who actually knows how to prepare okra in bulk. A general rule of Power Shopping is that your romantic prospects will bloom in direct proportion to the number of assorted pork chop Family Paks in your freezer compartment.

Another advantage in having a well-stocked refrigerator is that the smaller the amount of food, the more it is apt to go bad. How many times have you purchased a small portion of ground beef in May, eaten some of it in the form of a miniscule hamburger, only to find the rest sometime in August in the back of your refrigerator, wearing a beard? You know the feeling: Is that a piece of blue felt in that bowl, or merely the remains of the cioppino you lovingly made for yourself in your last year of graduate school?

Large items of food can go bad, too, naturally, but they are noticed more quickly and discarded. A neglected whole salmon that has taken on the odor of the inside of a running shoe is rarely overlooked for long. But chances are that you will already have cooked the salmon for one of the dinner parties at which you entertain the many close friends and lovers you've attracted simply as a result of having an impressive amount of food on hand.

Power Cooking

Now you're ready to learn The Speed Chef Method of Power Cooking. Why the Speed Chef Method? Because cooking for yourself is a profoundly depressing activity, yet one in which you must indulge often. The only solution is to know how to cook and eat a stylish meal at home in a matter of minutes, minimizing the trauma and leaving you plenty of time for more pressing matters, such as fighting off crippling anxiety, scouring the personals in the *New York Review of Books*, and preparing suicidal gestures.

According to The Speed Chef Method of Power Cooking, breakfast never takes longer than one minute to prepare, lunch no longer than three, and dinner a maximum of five.

I can already hear some of you saying to yourselves, "Is this *guy* nuts? Every time I try to make an omelette, I have to clear my calendar for the next three days." Yet, although a few single people lack the imagination and manual dexterity to master the sample recipes below without either maiming themselves or undergoing psychotic episodes, it is easier than most of you might think to grasp the essentials of Power Cooking:

1) At no time must either the right or the left hand be idle.

2) Clear your mind to concentrate on the task at hand. This is called Food Focussing. Mental lapses—for instance, wondering what's on public television that evening or why God has deprived you of the joys of a devoted companion—can ruin the meal or at least result in improper spatula technique.

3) At no time measure any of the ingredients, except in a general sort of way.

4) Never be afraid to improvise. But remember: not every ingredient enhances a dish (the addition of Karo syrup takes the edge off a sauce piccante), nor are all ingredients interchangeable (the substitution of cottage cheese for rice in Instant Risotto—see below—changes the character of the dish for the worse).

5) Never plunge any part of your body into a pot of rapidly boiling water, no matter how often you may be tempted.

6) Never underestimate the pivotal importance of the following condiments:

Spanish olives, capers, pickled jalapeño peppers, garlic, lemon, and Frank's Louisiana Red Hot Sauce. These can be used quickly in various combinations to enliven any dish that does not contain sliced peaches.

Now let's go slowly through the steps of preparing a day's worth of Speed Chef meals, beginning with a breakfast of cinnamon toast, half a grapefruit, fresh ground drip café au lait, and shirred eggs. You'll need to buy, according to The Speed Chef Method of Power Shopping:

3 loaves white bread
2 lbs. butter (unsalted)
a 1½ oz. jar of ground cinnamon
18 grapefruits
56 maraschino cherries
2 lbs. honey
8 heads garlic
4 dozen eggs
6 lbs. coffee beans
2 gallons whole milk
salt
pepper
Frank's Louisiana Red Hot Sauce

Can a breakfast as good as this one be prepared in just a minute? Am I The Speed Chef?

0:00–0:19 sec.

With left hand, boil one cup water and separate one half grapefruit with serrated knife while using right hand to peel and score one clove garlic, pre-heat oven to 500 degrees F, and butter two slices white bread.

0:20–0:47

Crossing over with left hand, sprinkle cinnamon on buttered bread and place in Toast-R-Oven while rubbing garlic clove on bottom of shirred-egg dish and heating one tsp. butter in it on top of stove with right hand. Use left to grind coffee beans and pour them into filter, while with right pour boiling water over coffee, break two eggs into shirred-egg dish, place dish on cookie sheet in upper third of pre-heated oven, and baste each yolk with a tsp. melted butter.

0:48–1:00

Remove cinnamon toast with right hand and, while slicing toast diagonally with left, deposit maraschino cherry in center of grapefruit, heat 2 oz. milk in saucepan without bringing to boil, and pour into coffee cup while left hand is dribbling a spoonful of honey onto grapefruit and removing shirred eggs from oven, seasoning with salt, a grinding of black pepper, and a healthy splash of Frank's Louisiana Red Hot Sauce.

Although this looks easy on paper, a few of these split-second operations are tricky; it is not uncommon for novice Speed Chefs to make the mistakes of shirring the maraschino cherry or buttering the sports section of the morning paper. But with a little practice and diligent observance of the principle of Food Focussing, in no time you'll be ready to tackle Lunch à la Speed Chef.

A light, contemporary meal consisting of eggplant parmagiana, Romaine lettuce salad with Speed Chef soy dressing, and black raspberry–flavored gelatin with navel orange slices is a great way to spice up the middle of the day. The one item you'll need to prepare a few days in advance—or a few months in advance if you're extremely maladroit around the kitchen—is the tomato sauce, for which you'll want to sauté four diced garlic cloves, one diced medium onion, and a Tb. of finely diced carrot in olive oil over medium heat; add bay leaf, oregano, thyme, canned peeled Italian plum tomatoes, salt, pepper, a small diced pickled jalapeño pepper, some chopped pimiento-stuffed Spanish olives with a few Tbs. of the olive juice, a slug or two of dry red wine. Simmer uncovered over low heat until the flavors fuse or you get bored, whichever comes first.

For the rest of the lunch, you'll need:

19 medium female eggplants
3 dozen eggs
2 loaves stale Italian bread
6 lbs. parmesan cheese
8 heads Romaine lettuce
12 bottles Kikkoman soy sauce
18 cloves garlic
8 gallons vegetable or safflower oil
4 gallons olive oil
8 lemons
red wine vinegar
16 packages black raspberry–flavored gelatin
1 crate navel oranges
kosher salt
pepper
oregano
basil

Ready? Now watch closely:

0:00–0:41 sec.

With your right hand, cut five or six ¼-inch slices of eggplant, place them in colander, and sprinkle liberally with kosher salt to absorb the eggplant's excess water, then quickly wash several leaves of romaine lettuce, break into pieces, and dry, while putting one cup of cold water into pan, transferring pan to right hand, setting to boil, and, with same hand, heating up tomato sauce, and breaking and scrambling a single egg into a shallow bowl.

0:42–1:25

Open black raspberry–flavored gelatin and place in mixing bowl with left hand while peeling and sectioning one navel orange with right, then crossing under with left to pour into salad dressing cruet the following ingredients: vegetable oil and soy sauce in roughly 4:1 ratio, a Tb. each of red wine vinegar and fresh-squeezed lemon juice, and finally the two cloves of garlic you have peeled with right hand as soon as you have completed sectioning orange. With your free hand—your left—stir tomato sauce, check water for boil, and heat 2 Tbs. olive oil in pan while now idle right hand cuts quarter-loaf of stale Italian bread into small cubes and throws them into smoking olive oil with pinches of salt, pepper, dried oregano, and basil.

1:26–1:58
Keep turning bread with spatula to brown on all sides with right hand while pouring boiling cup of water into mixing bowl with gelatin. Mix thoroughly while using left hand to wash kosher salt off eggplant, then pour sufficient olive oil into large iron skillet to cover bottom over high heat, and place two cups ice cubes into bowl of gelatin, while coarsely grating, with right, a handful of parmesan cheese.

1:59–2:34
Use left hand to stir ice cubes around in gelatin mixture with rhythmic circular motion while placing now evenly browned cubes of bread into clean paper sack and gently stomping on it with right foot until a consistent crumblike texture is achieved. While placing bread crumbs in shallow bowl next to shallow bowl with beaten egg in it with right hand, continue stirring ice cubes with left while watching olive oil to begin smoking slightly, at which time use right hand to dip each slice of eggplant first into egg, then coat on both sides with bread crumbs, then repeat with egg, and place in skillet while stirring tomato sauce again with right, remembering to continue stirring ice cubes until gelatin mixture reaches the consistency of mucous, at which point remove unmelted ice cubes and arrange navel orange sections in it.

2:35–2:55
With left hand dry romaine lettuce leaves once more and place in salad bowl with 1 to 2 oz. of well-shaken Speed Chef soy dressing, toss thoroughly, while with right turn over eggplant slices, making sure they are golden brown. Spread grated parmesan cheese evenly over top of eggplant with right, covering skillet now to melt cheese.

2:56–3:00
Set table with right hand while heating plate in warm oven with left, removing plate with right and spooning tomato sauce in thin layer onto plate, with right hand arranging eggplant slices on top of sauce, then adding a healthy dollop of sauce on top of the melted cheese on top of each slice. Garnish.

Sounds incredible, doesn't it? Well, now you're cooking the Speed Chef way—a hearty meal in no time, including a colorful dessert of barely solidified Jell-O, in the *nouvelle cuisine* manner.

One word of warning: don't be disappointed if the first time you try this lunch it takes you as long as three and a half hours. Practice does make perfect, and you are undoubtedly going to slip up now and then, such as grating your left hand instead of the parmesan or, in your frustration, ordering out for a sausage pizza.

However, when you get the hang of it and graduate to making five-minute dinners, you'll discover how easy it is to reach the pinnacle of The Speed Chef Method: a frenzied euphoria I call the Automatic Cooking State (ACS). Those who meditate have their nirvana and satori; joggers hit "the wall" and pass beyond. Speed Chefs have the Automatic Cooking State, when you are operating purely on instinct, liberated from the normal constraints of time and space, living entirely inside of the culinary experience, at one with your ingredients as you dissolve the mind/food dichotomy.

Singles who achieve the ACS not only experience a pleasurable loss of ego and heightened fusion with all of Western cooking, but find that the phenomenon is a more than adequate substitute for sex. When I am preparing dinner the Speed Chef way, as in the following recipes, I often become so excited that I seem to lose consciousness, only to wake up later slumped over my empty plate in a state of contented exhaustion.

For the following dinner of smoked mozzarella and sweet red pepper appetizer, shrimp coriander, and instant risotto, you'll need to have purchased the following items:

8 lbs. smoked mozzarella
1 peck of sweet red peppers
6 heads of red leaf lettuce
3 gallons olive oil
50 lbs. medium shrimp
24 heads garlic
10 jars of pimiento-stuffed Spanish olives
36 shallots
12 lemons
10 jars capers
40 lbs. rice
11 lbs. parmesan cheese
7 lbs. unsalted butter
1 case Chablis white wine
salt
pepper
fresh coriander leaves or ground coriander seed

0:00–0:50
While shelling, deveining, and washing 12 shrimp under cold tap water with your left hand, boil with your right 1 cup water in a pot, peel 2 cloves garlic and 2 of shallot, and melt 2 Tbs. butter in a sauté pan, using left hand to dry shrimp in paper towels and leave in colander (or on a calendar, if it's handier and is particularly absorbent), using right hand to slice 3 oz. smoked mozzarella into 1/4-inch slices, put 1/2 cup rice into boiling water, stir, cover, and simmer, seed and slice one small sweet red pepper into rings, chop garlic and shallot and brown lightly in melted bubbling butter, and finely chop 3 Spanish olives.

0:51–1:45
With left hand, wash and thoroughly dry one leaf red leaf lettuce, and arrange it on a salad plate under alternating slices of smoked mozzarella and red pepper, place shrimp in pan and add a handful of fresh chopped coriander leaves or 1/2 tsp. ground coriander, using the right hand to check the rice, sprinkle olive oil over the mozzarella and pepper rings, turning the shrimp over when pink and opaque on one side.

1:46–2:30
With your left hand, grate 1/2 cup parmesan cheese and quickly place it in rice along with 2 Tbs. butter, salt and black pepper, and stir, while, quickly, with your right, pouring 2 oz. of dry white wine over shrimp, with your left squeezing half a lemon, yes, then the capers, with your right, okay, with your left the olives, the salt, with your right, the pepper, your left, quick, reducing over high heat, your right hand, for 10 seconds, your left, your right, yes, yes, oh my God, the garnish, LEFT hand, the GARNISH, your RIGHT, YOUR LEFT, YOUR RIGHT
Add frozen Stouffers, and stir gently.

HOW TO DRESS YOURSELF

You, as a single, suddenly have the responsibility to dress yourself. You also have the responsibility to do the opposite, but that is another chapter's territory.

I have discovered, in twenty years of scouring *Vogue, Harper's* and the spring Sears order book as though each were the complete outlay in my life of the Realm of Possibility, that you can do better for yourself, and you can do worse, than you ever knew when it comes to presenting yourself as an entity in the world. In those years between the last time your mother dictates and your spouse inhibits, you've got one shot at establishing yourself as the draped representation of humanity on which you would most like visiting spacemen and Mr. Blackwell to pass judgment.

My purpose here is not to tell you what to wear, but just how to achieve a fast and reasonable point of decision-making. This is, after all, yourself you are sending out onto the street to be seen—but the point is to get you there, and away from the paralytic agony of trying on different disguises as though you were a millionaire child attempting to try on every Halloween costume at Woolworth's. Your dress is not a costume; leave that to the Children of Many Lands who dance at the U.N. As an American, you are not required to wear anything that doesn't appeal to you, unless of course you are a friend of Nancy Reagan's, which is your business.

Let me add that, in short, I am not exactly what you would call exquisitely in control when it comes to clothes. My first memory is of a dress. This is an age-three memory: I was at a summer party in a backyard and it was 1956. A woman walked by in a white dress, princess silhouette, bare neckline, close-fitting bodice, and flared, three-quarter-length skirt. There were polka dots—off-colored, slightly less than quarter size polka dots. The woman in her dress was the most beautiful thing I had ever seen. Now, appreciation may come early, but power comes later. When it came time to pick out kindergarten clothes, my Peck & Peck mother with her lovely conservative taste and sure sensibility for prettiness picked out a dress for me on a Saturday afternoon in a suburban mall children's clothing store, and let me tell you: I THOUGHT SHE HAD LOST HER MIND. The problem was the color; at five, it was hard to think of mustard gold as a decent color for a dress.

If love for clothes came late, you may have missed out on the early frustration of powerlessness. If you were a normal five-year-old you were probably happy enough to get your damned snowsuit on. Not without fierce pride comes the quote of the small child: "I can dress myself." Which of us can say it this week?

I'll give you this: it does mean more to say "I can dress myself" at 18 than it does at five. It means you can communicate an individual with aesthetic authority. Nevertheless: if you liked a red T-shirt at five, you knew from whence you came, and the point seems somewhat the same—to tell the bastards, not be told, what you like.

OK; let's go.

I. Shopping

As lone explorers, some of us have to make a point of *appearing* as customers in a wonderful store. We go in disguised as customers, and we masquerade so professionally that even the most alert of the selling squad can't smell the absent credit card. Researchers don't need credit cards to collect their information, they need a good breakfast. It takes stamina to make the rounds. Shopping is a joke compared to visiting.

A limited clothing budget calls for judicious purchases. Make a point of coolly checking out what the clothing industry came up with for the summer or winter season. Fashion is no big deal: it's about two ideas and many variations. It can't victimize anyone who doesn't let it. Know what you look like and what you need: put fashion in its place. Squish it like a bug. You have time for style and that's it.

Research: it's important. Find out if that idea of yourself exists; if some designer was sympathetic to your coloring and your body. Look at clothes you can't afford—you'll recognize the lower-priced approximation when you see it, or get ready for the sale. Memorize the salient details of that suit you will not, on principle, pay $400 for and have fun. Go to a tailor. Tailors and dressmakers are not storybook characters like tinkers and cobblers. They're real.

Spending money when confused or pressured (the party is at 9 and the sales clerk wants to close his register) may cause feelings of panic. Who needs to waste that kind of emotional strain on clothes? That's why you do your homework. A serious purchase deserves thought ("If I need this garment for several different kinds of situations, will it make it? Is it too conservative—even for something I'll be wearing all the time? Does this jacket or dress have too much fashion for me—more personality than I do? DOES IT FIT?") and a night's sleep.

The luxury of having to plan a wardrobe with a definite budget in mind is that you get to fall out of love. Sure, you may feel intense lust upon discovering something you really want RIGHT NOW; and intense chagrin as you make yourself leave the store for some fresh air ("OK, right foot move forward. Left foot, look at right. Get . . . me . . . out of here!"). But in the cool air, or a few hours later, you're the lucky one. You don't have to open a drawer to see some mean-spirited, wrongheaded purchase stare up at you ("Hey, sucker!") taunting you with the memory that sometimes you lose your self-control in stores.

Preliminary research turns the action of buying into something precise, swift, and fleet. There are times when, engaged in research, you will come across exactly what you have been looking for a very long time. At that moment, stop being a researcher. Be a customer.

II. Basics and Essentials

Basics are the pieces of clothing that cover the most area of your body, and in some cases will protect you from weather. These are raincoats, sportsjackets, pants, blouses, skirts, sweaters, and suits. (You've had basics in your wardrobe before—this time around make sure they fit). Essentials are the accessories that give charm to basics. (They cover the least part of you and yet they make you feel dressed.) You can't kid around with basics because they have to do a lot of work for you. Buy a good basic, and you won't feel like prancing around the room, you will feel broke, mature, and relieved. Collect the appropriate stock of basics and have a wardrobe. That's all a wardrobe is: basics.

Belts, scarves, watches, and luggage punctuate your basics. Do not depend on Christmas to surprise you with the accessories you need. Accessories are gifts to buy for yourself. If you are lucky, a friend with spectacular taste just may give you an accessory. I know. I received a scarf once that transcended all my ideas of what a scarf could be, handwoven with silk and metallic threads. My humble but warm-as-hell down jacket almost burst into tears when it found it was to be accessorized by the splendid scarf.

III. Color

When you were little, you may have noticed a flesh-colored crayon in your box, on the floor, or squished on the back of your shoe, at some point. I'm sure you saw it. It was pinky beige and it was used for making skin. Doubtless, you've noticed since that you have never even met one soul who has possessed a skin tone equal to the Crayola company's vision of life. The Impressionists were right. You may have trouble changing jobs, apartments, or partners, but your skin, at least, will always be colorful.

Green, yellow, gray and red give skin its predominant tone. Any woman who has the equivalent of a Ph.D in makeup knows exactly what colors will betray her. It never matters what color your pants are, it's the color you choose to wear close to your face that matters.

Take the time to find out which colors will always feud with your skin and which are in permanent sympathy with each other. The first is easy, the second requires a little more effort because, in effect, I'm suggesting you go to an art school. Do go to a department store and try on as many different colored Lacoste shirts as possible. At least two of your tries will make you think that you've spent the night before drinking.

The business of mastering color relationships is best begun by finding the neutral color that suits you and from this base, adding accent colors. First of all, of course, find your neutral color. Calvin Klein has spent a good part of his career investigating beige—there are neutral colors and then there are the many shades of the neutral color. Sorry. Discipline yourself to keeping your wardrobe within the bounds of a limited palette. In this way, mating separates will not be tasking.

It's upsetting to find that a very beautiful color can look absolutely disgusting on your body. Don't be upset. That color can be in your life; just put it somewhere else. Buy an address book or a wallet in that color.

IV. Fabrics

Once you've limited yourself to a few colors, your sensibility for textures will become more alert. It's time to spoil yourself with good fabric, even though you may associate the patronage of unalloyed wool, cotton, or silk with just plain snobbery. Snobs may wear pure fiber fabrics, but it's the fabric that has the real attitude problem—it's smug. Good fabric looks great, and knows it.

The burn test establishes the identity of pure fabrics. If you set fire to your closet and notice your clothes shrinking from the flame, then melting, then burning slowly (the whole time giving off black smoke and smelling sweet), then finally settling on the floor in piles of tiny black beads, it's clear that you have invested too much of your income in manmade fibers. Try some of the fibers God came up with.

V. Discard Wisdom

The difference between great old clothing and clothing that is simply old is that despite all the glory your Jr.–Sr. Prom was, if you can't wear that dress tomorrow it doesn't belong in your closet. Closets are containers for the way you want to look now. Get rid of everything that you haven't worn in the last year. This includes newly purchased mistakes. It's hard enough to be awakened by an unfeeling clock radio without adding a visit to a time-machine closet to the ordeal of morning.

VI. Breaking In Your Clothes

No one wants to look like they've dressed for the first day of school. Get to know your new clothes. Practice wearing whatever it is while you have all this privacy on your hands. Nonchalance is not one of the big virtues, but it's a good one to keep in mind. The only thing worse than appearing self-conscious in your finery is affecting cool-guy mannerisms. Don't turn up the collar of your jacket unless your neck is in danger of breaking off from the assaults of cold blasts of wind. Be careful with hats, too, unless again, it's freezing, or you are directing a ridiculously expensive motion picture.

VII. Juxtaposition and Balance

Please, one focal point per person. Other people's wedding bands do not count as a focal point, as attention-getting as they may be; a neckline is an example of a focal point. An interesting neckline should not be upstaged by a not-to-be-forgotten waistline or intriguing footwear. If you are a woman and wear glasses, say, watch out for hanging earrings and the Indian necklace and the focal point neckline. Just as you shouldn't want to distract from a good detail, you should veer away from clogging that focal point with an overload of extraneous statements.

That's just part of composition strategy: balance. When you're pulling things together, remember to keep changing time zones. Wear the new shirt with the riding jacket you've had since high school. Wear the thrift shop tuxedo jacket with the perfect black pants you bought last week. Your clothes should convey the fact that you have a past —that all through the years you have

made careful decisions about style and necessity.

The first fashion rule I made for myself was to try to look like old money, because at the time it seemed appealing to look like my clothes had never, for a second, been new. (I also wanted to look like someone who hated being away from her horse for any great length of time.) It wasn't much of a trick to pull this look off: I wore the same turtleneck sweater, jeans, and gold bracelet every day. I'm still making payments on my college loans, and yet friends tell me I had fooled quite a few of them into thinking that I could have bought the school a video-game amusement center.

It is not a trust-fund look that I am promoting, it's the grace of wearing expensive new clothing as comfortably as the cheaper, newer stuff—and wearing them together. If the idea of casual elegance grabs you, you should understand that personal dignity can be expressed through carefully considered outfits.

To go on in this vein, remember how we subsidized the garment industry of India in the sixties? What about the army surplus look? Do you recall when the tennis craze was followed by a mania for jogging, and running shoes left the track for the street? Remember the outdoor life you pursued and the great clothes you discovered for staying warm and dry in your backpacking days? Ethnic clothing, surplus clothing, active sportswear, outdoor sports clothes, boy's department clothes, and thrift shop clothes still stand as excellent resources. For the record, these resources individualize any look. Erase the sharp edges of too much fashion/not enough you with these.

VIII. Shoes

Some people have the same affection for footwear that others have for small pets. This fact wasn't apparent to me until recently when I noticed the tone a friend used when she spoke of Stanley, her new kitten. It was familiar. It was the same tone she used to describe her Susan Bennis/Warren Edwards leather confections.

The pound-cake theory of dressing is this: start with a simple foundation; add topping. Shoes are the accessory that count the most—more revealing than the bag, the scarf, or the belt. Doormen at The Plaza, the story goes, look at feet to distinguish the VIPs from the crowd.

Shoes and boots have become the hats of our generation. It may not be fun to buy a pair of classic gray flannel pants, but notice the mood swing when you buy shoes. Shoes have all the personality, and like any good source of pleasure, they can be extra fragile.

Women often make the mistake of forgetting that their feet are connected to their legs. They wear shoes with ankle straps. Unless you have extremely narrow feet and need to be bolted into your shoe, think twice before you break that line of leg. For some reason, it is hard to find a summer slingback sandal. Watch out for the shoe designers' conspiracy to make summer feet look bad.

Men and sandals? I don't care if you like them. They are ugly, ugly, ugly. Wear old sneakers. Wear espadrilles. Wear "old man" canvas shoes. Rethink your summer foot. Sandals on men are like boots with zippers. Please don't wear them.

Another thing for women to watch is the heel variation factor. For my money, I'll stay close to the ground, thank you, but if you like experimenting with height, remember that you change the proportions of everything you put on with each change. Disaster lurks. Don't forget to be really careful about the shade of stocking you wear with your boots, by the way. Just as our mothers knew to wear nude underwear with white blouses, we are responsible for never wearing skin-colored stockings with our boots.

IX. Fashion Magazines

Fashion magazines were invented for reading on beaches and while using public transportation. They can also be used as a source of minor entertainment for those draggy moments of the day: at the tail end of a lunch hour; upon entering your apartment after work before you find the strength to prepare spaghetti for one; after dinner before you find the strength to eliminate the traces of spaghetti for one, etc. They can also be used to validate the time you spend in front of the sitcom that only you and your dog will ever have to know you watched.

As you know from the days when you improved your study habits, all books are not alike — biographies of obscure movie stars can be read with greater speed and less attention than essays about sweetness and light. Your *Vogues* and your *GQs* require the attention and rate of reading speed that can only be compared to the concentration and dispatch you display when making your bed.

In other words, fashion magzines are meant to be inhaled, stored for a year, and then enjoyed. It takes about a year for a fashion magazine to age properly —for shrill fashion to make its way onto the backs of the trendy few. It's fun to look at pictures of clothing that people are actually wearing.

When spending time with a fashion magazine, remember not to confuse the editorial message with the ad pages. Sometimes advertisers can come up with pretty good fantasy situations, but it's the editors who are the real pros at making you feel like you've been living your whole life on another planet. I used to try to train my dates to imitate couple situations I had memorized from various fashion magazines. This was at a time when I thought having a good time meant having a photogenic time. Wrong.

X. Sexiness

My single, romantically ambitious friends, it is our duty to appear sexy, especially at parties. It's so easy to blow it. We face party nights alone in our apartments with warm-up drinks at hand, getting-dressed background music playing, and, for reassurance, a hostile mirror. I can imagine a caring husband preventing disaster ("Oh my God, you've got to be kidding"), fastening my pearls, and zipping up my dress. Singles have guardian angels for companions, and those guys are no help when it comes to offering opinions on the special effects we try to create.

It seems unfair, but trying to look sexy somehow always looks like an imitation of looking sexy. "See that person over there trying to look sexy?" they'll say. The truth is that you just have to leave Hollywood behind if you want to avoid caricatured sexiness. Button up the desire to bludgeon folks with your version of Marilyn or Rita or Clark or Burt on a good night.

Looking sexy does not mean wearing tight clothes. It means having self-confidence about the way you look. The ability to look sexy is related to spirit. It's a function of exploiting your sense of fun and your sense of style. Everybody can do it. As Norma Kamali has said, "Bianca has great self-confidence. But there are girls from Flatbush who come in here and they pull themselves together just as well as she or Diana Ross can. They've got it in Queens, too, you know." The same applies for men. A tight suit with boots does not Travolta make.

XI. Vision and Taste

Norma Kamali, the consistently inventive designer who really understands sexiness, is known to have showed up for class in the sixth grade wearing nine starched petticoats and white bucks, which she powdered to keep white. She had trouble fitting between desks when she walked, and wherever little Norma went a trail of white powder followed close behind. That's not the early dressing behavior of a girl with vision. No wonder she grew up to design jumpsuits made of parachute material that can be seen on display in the costume exhibition rooms of the Metropolitan Museum of Art. Normal people get through their days on taste. The good news is that taste can be acquired; the bad news is that it takes a lot of practice. Dressing well has to be a habit.

How do you feel about habits? Listen to this horror story and you'll feel better: after I'd spent a year of wearing a waitress uniform, my habit of dressing had atrophied to the point where I let my mother talk me into buying a *maroon polyester pants suit*. Holy smokes. Don't let this happen to you. Don't make the mistake that has scarred me for life. Remember: the other side of habit is a maroon polyester pants suit.

HOW TO SET UP HOUSE

OK, you're setting up shop on your own. Let's talk about your present furniture layout. If it strikes you as jumbled or uninteresting, chances are it is. Start by picturing your room as an empty shell. See the space as if for the first time. Note any distinctive architectural features (moldings, fireplace, paneling) worth highlighting, as well as less attractive features (radiators) that can be downplayed.

To help evaluate your layout options, draw up a floor plan to scale. It's not hard to do. Using the squares on a sheet of graph paper, establish whatever scale you want (e.g., one square equals six inches). Now draw a plan of the room on one sheet and your furniture in the same scale on another. Cut out the furniture drawings and move them around on the floor plan, experimenting with various configurations. Record the layouts you like best on sheets of tracing paper; by comparing these you'll discover which are physically awkward, which are graceful, and which you want to try.

Whether or not you make a floor plan, push your furniture around to see what looks good where. Once furniture is in place, people rarely rearrange it. But until you do, you won't know what you might be missing. Besides, a fresh arrangement can give a room a sense of renewal. So experiment. Put the table where the arm chair now is, slide the sofa to a new location.

In my apartment, the paintings just sit against the walls. Their transience pleases me. I move things around all the time, and I hate to have pictures stay in one place because then you stop seeing them. I remember once going to Philip Johnson's house in Connecticut and noticing that the places for the ashtrays were marked on the tables with red dots so they could always be put back in exactly the same spot. That's very spooky. I love disorder.

—*Ward Bennett*

If you have enough space, try "floating" the main seating out from the walls. Placing a sofa away from a wall by even as little as eight or ten inches can make both the sofa and the space around it look airier and more graceful. Always lay out your room in terms of both positive and negative space—that which is filled and that which is empty— as any good painter does in designing a canvas. Don't obsess about symmetry. Everything doesn't need an exact counterpart directly opposite it. The goal is not Noah's ark.

If your room is large enough, try positioning the sofa on a diagonal in a corner. Given the right corner in the right room, this can be very elegant.

Rooms in which most of the seating faces the same direction are socially awkward. Excessively long sofas and banquettes make it almost impossible to discuss the season in Palm Beach with anyone who is not seated directly beside you. Unless you plan to screen double features on the opposite wall, arrange chairs and sofas so that people can chat easily without getting stiff necks.

How much furniture is enough? How much is too much? Mies van der Rohe continuously proclaimed "Less is more." Robert Venturi, with his passion for the chaotic juxtapositions of American "strip" architecture, countered with "Less is bore." In other words, my dear, it's all subjective. But when in doubt, don't overfurnish. Leave yourself some breathing space, both literally and visually. Remember, what you leave out is as important as what you put in.

Finally, don't worry about rules. Keep experimenting until you find what looks and feels right to you.

When I look at things, I always see the space they occupy. I always want the space to reappear, to make a comeback, because it's lost space when there's something in it. If I see a chair in a beautiful space, no matter how beautiful the chair is, it can never be as beautiful to me as the plain space.

—*Andy Warhol*

Painting

Preparation of the walls is two-thirds of the work in a quality paint job; without it, you are settling for mediocrity. No matter what color or brand of paint you select, walls covered with cracks and orange peel will never look topdrawer. So sand, steel-wool, plaster, and sand some more.

God is in the details.

—*John Saladino*

Woodwork that is caked with generations of chipped paint must be stripped. It's a hideous chore, but you get what you work for. Use paint remover and steel wool (be sure to keep the room well ventilated—you don't want to inhale those ghastly fumes). If you can handle a blow torch, it's a much faster method. In either case, finish by smoothing with sand paper.

Flat paint doesn't wash well, so paint the more vulnerable areas—woodwork, doors, and kitchen walls—with semigloss. Glossy finishes on walls and ceilings magnify imperfections (although

Benjamin Moore makes an eggshell finish that leaves a very subtle sheen and can look wonderful provided your walls are in good enough condition).

Never paint ceilings anything but flat. There, even more than on walls, gloss paint throws cracks and bumps into startling relief. Don't even consider a glossy ceiling unless you've retained a decorator who's decided to glaze the ceiling (in preparation for which a team of specialists will spend weeks replastering and canvassing the surface until it's as smooth as glass).

Color

Color is elusive, mercurial. It grows darker, lighter, warmer, cooler, gains and sheds subtle hues, all depending on the light, which itself changes dramatically according to regional differences, weather, and the time of day. A color on the walls of a friend's room may appear very different on your walls.

Color also changes with the amount of space it covers. A color covering four walls, reflecting off itself, may look nothing at all like what you had imagined when you chose it from a small paint chip. So buy a pint and try it on the wall before proceeding.

Your color options are theoretically unlimited, but some options are more equal than others. White, a classic of the International Style, reflects the maximum amount of light and lends a room a sense of spaciousness that darker colors do not. But if white feels too safe and dull, and you still want airiness, choose a shade like gray-beige, sea-foam green, or a pale gray-blue—the color of an overcast day. These soft, moody colors are understated but can make a space feel more finished than plain white walls.

Natural colors—those actually found in nature—are the easiest to live with. Dyed-looking, garish colors don't wear well. If you have a natural object whose colors you are drawn to—a tulip, a seashell, a piece of driftwood—let it suggest a paint color to you. Or take your color inspiration from the palette of terrain you like: forest, desert, ocean.

If you want to surround yourself with rich dark colors, stick with the classics: a deep forest green, a Chinese red, a terra cotta. Avoid strident colors. A color that adds punch to a room in a small amount on a throw pillow can be a disaster on four walls.

A technique frequently used by interior designers is to make the walls, ceilings, and floor the same color. This creates an envelope of color that immediately lends visual order to the space. The remaining colors in the room can then be used to augment or counterpoint the monochromatic shell.

Study the colors in a room apart from the objects that contain them; see the room as pure color. Is there balance and harmony, or chaos?

Lighting

All lighting should be kept low to protect women with double chins.

—*David Hicks*

The mood of almost any room changes dramatically from day to night. Artificial light focuses attention, carving vignettes out of the nighttime shadows. What is not lit at night fades into background, and what is comes to the fore. The lamp on top of the chest of drawers highlights the vase of flowers also sitting there; it draws attention as well to the mirror over the chest and to the piece of furniture itself. (This is assuming that the entire room is not ablaze with bright, even light, which is helpful if someone loses a contact lens, but otherwise creates a flat and boring look.)

When choosing and placing light, decide both what you want to see and what you need to see. Experiment. Move the lamps around the room until you get a feel for where they work most effectively. If you have an indoor tree, consider lighting it from below or above, thus casting leafy shadows on the ceiling, walls, or floor.

Not everyone likes its theatrical look, but track lighting has some distinct advantages. Since the entire track is electrified, you can position fixtures anywhere along it. This saves the messy and expensive task of channeling wires through a plaster ceiling. The flexibility of track lighting allows for a wide variety of fixtures, which can be changed at will. To wash an entire wall with soft, fairly even light, for instance, you can use a flood bulb with its broad spread of light. To light something smaller on the wall—a painting, a print—you'll want a spot with an appropriate beam spread.

As with other types of lighting, experiment once the track is up. One client of mine, an elevator magnate who bought his new last name from a Hollywood screenwriter, had rigged up an elaborate array of track fixtures in his dining room: spots, floods, colored gels, spread lenses, and large, theatrical framing projectors. The effect was smashing, although I had to wear sunglasses at dinner.

I met Matisse and Picasso and Giacometti when I lived in Paris, and I loved the way they lived. Usually there'd be lots of plants and an old rug or something around. There was a certain kind of disorder and spontaneity. Matisse and Picasso lived in a total mess but it had a marvelous beauty to it. Even now, for me to stack a pile of books beside a chair pleases me.

—Ward Bennett

Modernism—and After

Thank God comfort is "officially" sanctioned again. Not that I was ever a slave to minimalism. They say Modernism died somewhere back in the mid seventies and we are now living in the post-Modernist period. (They named it that to buy time to figure out what's happening now.) People apparently got miffed with living in those sensory deprivation chambers. It was probably that endless sea of gray industrial carpet and the perpetual hum of neon wall sculpture that finally did it.

In any case, it is now okay once again to mix contemporary pieces with period pieces, to use more color—to do whatever works for you. Of course, some will still prefer the classics of the International Style, such as the elegant, sculptural leather and steel chaise designed by LeCorbusier in 1928. When you recline on this chaise lounge; you lounge as "Corbu" would have you lounge; you have little choice about it. You are bent at the waist at a 120° degree angle, bent at the knees at another 120°, and your eyes are cast skyward at a similar angle.

Living Rooms

Do visitors seeing your living room for the first time leave with a sense of who you are? This could be why you never hear from some of them again.

Some living rooms feel vacant and chilly, coming to life only when crowded with people, while others work well enough for one or two people but seem ill-suited for much more than that. Ideally, a living room should function well as both private and public space. There's no reason it can't.

The idea is to make the space as graceful and livable as possible so that your bedroom is not your only refuge when you are alone and want to relax. Pick a comfortable piece of furniture and put it in a good location; one with a view would be nice, or perhaps next to a fireplace. Be sure there's something to put your feet up on. Surround yourself with whatever makes you feel cheerful and cozy. You'll probably want a table close by for books and magazines, plus a good reading light and maybe your TV set. Billy Baldwin once wrote, "Something to sit upon—which must have beauty and comfort; something to look upon—which must reflect the personal taste of the owner; and something to put upon—which means tables of comfortable height, conveniently arranged."

If you find that you often have more guests than you can comfortably seat, consider buying some oversized pillows. They should be elegant to look at; those lumpy things that look like they were bought at an ashram tag sale simply won't do. If your bare floor seems cold and off-putting, cover part of it with an area rug, throw down the floor pillows, pull up some extra chairs, and you'll have created a more inviting spot.

Bedrooms

Everything is more glamorous when you do it in bed. Even peeling potatoes.

—Andy Warhol

The bedroom is the most private of all rooms. You don't entertain there, at least you don't entertain groups there, at least, well, forget it. It's a place to pamper yourself, to indulge your wildest and most arcane impulses. If you carpet only one room, make it the bedroom, where so much time is spent barefoot. (If you consider a carpet aesthetically objectionable, politically bourgeois, or financially preposterous, at least put a small area rug next to your bed as a toe-warmer.)

The optimal bedroom includes a dressing mirror, spacious bedside tables with drawers, good bedside-reading lamps (wall-mounted with swivel arms are the most functional), and ample drawer and closet space. If you don't have enough space for clothes, consider building a new or larger closet; whatever space it eats up will be more than compensated for by the diminished sense of chaos. An alternative solution is buying an armoire—one made of old country pine is an affordable possibility.

I lost the biggest job I ever had when the lady told me she needed a closet large enough for 3,000 dresses and I told her no one needed 3,000 dresses.

—John Saladino

Your closet should be a totally separate piece of space so you don't use it as a crutch too much. If you live in New York your closet should be, at the very least, in New Jersey.

—Andy Warhol

A headboard, though not critical, is a grace note. It makes the bed feel less adrift and gives it a more finished look. Luxurious bed linens enhance, just as shabby ones detract.

Dining Rooms

If you are living alone and have a dining room, it's probably your least-used room. Most singles don't have the energy or the resources to give even small dinner parties more than five or six times a year. And eating alone in a dining room can be a gloomy proposition. (I know that when I've been between husbands, I've found myself eating in the kitchen or the living room, or watching TV.)

So put your dining room to work as something more than simply an eating area. Let it double, for instance, as a library. There's something reassuring about eating among books; there's no reason Beatrix Potter and Welsh rarebit can't coexist. A dining table makes a spacious desk—there's all the room in the world to pad your expense account.

The dining room provides the perfect opportunity for a more dramatic design scheme than you might be willing to try in rooms where you spend more time: a rich, dark color on the walls, moody lighting, a sprawling, beautifully lit tree . . .

Now that you've installed the bookcases and painted the walls hunting green, don't forget that you still want the space to work as a dining room.

Nothing will help more than a piece of furniture—a sideboard, a cabinet, an extra table—in which to store glasses, liquor, serving pieces, etc., or whose top can be used to serve a buffet or to hold serving dishes during the meal.

Bathrooms

Being single is no excuse for living with a bathroom designed in the gas station mode. Although it's a room with a clearly defined raison d'être, the equipage can easily become part of a setting of honest elegance. Even if you can't afford to transform your bathroom into a mirrored spa complete with whirlpool, hot tub, and Nautilus, you probably can improve upon what you have now.

Bathroom motifs usually err in one of two directions. The first is the cold, comfortless bathroom. It has all the charm of an operating room. A single bare bulb (150 W.) in the ceiling sheds an even glare on the sea of white tile. An anemic Turkish towel is slung over the towel rack, and the plastic shower curtain, fogged with soap and plankton, hangs limply from a corroded rod.

Equally popular is the claustrophobically comfy, cutesy bathroom with its deep-pile, acrylic wall-to-wall rug and matching toilet seat cover, its multi-tiered chrome rack stuffed with damp magazines, and a shower curtain featuring lingerie ads from old Sears catalogs or hundreds of hideous Queens of Hearts.

Between these extremes is an efficient, gracious, comfortable bathroom. With their abundance of porcelain and tile, bathrooms are by nature fairly clinical spaces, so it helps to balance the hard surfaces with some soft touches: large, luxurious bath towels; a fabric shower curtain (you need a plastic liner); a bath mat that is neither furry nor synthetic-looking (try something with a flat pile or a colorful cotton rag rug like those made in Haiti).

Natural materials can also do much to offset the starkness of a bathroom. Towel racks, shelves, and picture frames can be made of wood, wastebaskets and laundry hampers of straw, bamboo, or rattan. If you have a window, a plant will help bring the bathroom to life; most thrive on the humidity from the shower.

Hang small prints or photographs in the bathroom. They will enjoy greater visibility than in a larger room and, if strategically placed, are guaranteed a captive audience.

To create a unified look, match the wall and shower-curtain color. Choose something flattering to skin tones: peach, beige, cream. I love small-scale wallpaper prints and matching shower curtain fabric—subdued two-color prints, small flower prints, or "soft" geometrics. Beware of too much color, vibrating designs, or large prints in small spaces. And please, no foil papers; they'll make the bathroom look like a kleenex box.

A shower curtain can be custom-made; if you know how to sew, you can make it yourself. Try to avoid using hanging sheets. The best-looking ones hang from ceiling to floor (on hospital-style ceiling-mount rods) and are generously gathered (enough panels to equal three times the length of the rod). Such a curtain creates a wall of fabric that softens, unifies and reaches high chic.

Miscellany

Taste and style is not dependent on the dollar.

—*Albert Hadley*

Assuming your budget is limited, buy essential items first. Even if you suspect that you'll soon be moving on, a good bed, sofa, armchair, and coffee table will serve you well wherever you go. If you see something you need, like, and can afford, buy it now. It may not be available later, and even if it is, it probably will cost more.

Whether you can spend a little or a lot, it pays to buy quality. Well-made furniture usually looks better, works better, and wears better, and almost always is a better long-term investment.

The right antique piece can add depth and a sense of history to a room and is often an excellent investment. Most furniture depreciates with use and has no marketplace if you decide to sell it. An antique in good condition, on the other hand, generally can be sold for a profit. When trying to sell a piece to a dealer, you will be appalled to discover that he's offering you 20 to 40 percent less than what he is asking for a similar item already in his shop. Worse still, he'll probably want you to pay for trucking. He can't pay his rent without a substantial markup, but drive the best bargain you can.

And avoid these:

- *Astro-turf*
- *Round beds, unless you're Walt Frazier*
- *Cement dwarfs*
- *Matador paintings on velvet*
- *Conversation pits*
- *Fake books with Harold Robbins covers*
- *Carpets with more than six inches of pile*
- *Framed autographed photos of game show hosts*
- *Porcelain poodles with ash tray top-hats*
- *Electric fireplace logs*
- *Needlepoint pillows that say "Je suis sleeping"*

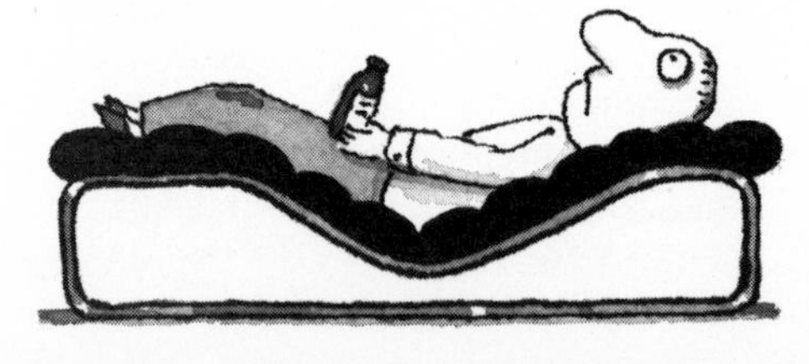

*Here's good news! This important piece
of journalism proves that capitalism has brought us
a better world once more, a world devoted
to a year-round open season on
twenty-first-century foxes. We've gone beyond
personal accidents, and into binary
romance—Technodating.
In singles bars, on television, and on the radio,
software and display systems have
a new meaning. What Duke Ellington once called
the prelude to a kiss—soft music—
is still with us, but the sound is synthesized,
and so is the mystery of the erotic.*

TECHNODATING

The Shape of Things

It must have been back in 1970 or so that my friends and I heard about the Dial Tone Lounge. Someone we knew had actually been there. As he explained it to us, every stool at the circular bar had a large two-digit numeral hanging above it and a telephone in front of it. The idea was that you would sit at the bar, survey the room, spot a woman who struck your fancy, and then *call her on your phone*. You'd dial her number — 47, say—and her phone would ring. She'd answer it, you'd say, "Hi, this is 62!" and she'd scout the horizon . . . 59 . . . 60 . . . 61 . . . and then she'd see *you*, coyly smiling and waving a few fingers from across the room. Maybe you'd ask her to dance, and maybe she'd say yes. Or maybe she'd take one look at you and hang up, in which case you'd muster your courage and ring up 32, who appeared more approachable anyway.

Singles bars, as everyone who frequents them can tell you, are among the dreariest places on earth. Whoever dreamed up the idea for the Dial Tone Lounge clearly knew this, knew that there is no intelligent, humane way for men and women to meet each other in such absurd surroundings. Only by compounding the absurdity, he must have reasoned, can singles experience anything approaching joy in their pursuit of each other.

What supernatural force compels men to singles bars to engage in behavior that only they could possibly find charming? What atavistic trait compels women to be so reflexively *nasty*? It is a self-perpetuating syndrome. Men behave like assholes and women treat them like assholes. Who can say for certain which came first? All I know is that women who under normal circumstances would be delighted to talk to me, will walk into a singles bar and suddenly not have anything to do with me. Did I become an ogre? Or did they?

It's a sad state of affairs, all right, and many a barkeep has tried to do his bit for the cause (and for his nightly receipts) by instituting novelties that will keep discouraged singles coming back for more abuse. Wet T-shirt contests, for example, come to mind.

So, yes, my buddies and I were intrigued by the notion of telephones at a singles bar. What sort of pathetic coward, we wondered, would be unable to walk up to a woman and introduce himself without some artificial, technological intermediary? What kind of desperate fool would resort to such a cheap gimmick?

On the other hand, what sort of woman would be so bold, so upfront about announcing her desire to be approached?

We rushed right over to the Dial Tone Lounge to find out.

I got to thinking about the Dial Tone years later when I was in Houston writing an article about the sudden proliferation of country-and-western theme bars. The perpetrator of many of these bars turned out to be a company called McFaddin Kendrick, which is a leader in what is broadly referred to as "the hospitality field." By studying trends in music and fashion, and by conducting marketing surveys of its intended clientele, McFaddin Kendrick has been able to keep one step ahead of the competition. Its revenues approach $100 million a year, and its concepts are quick to find imitators.

The company's first singles bar was Todd's, a disco located in the heart of Houston's affluent singles community. Unlike most discos that opened in 1975, Todd's is still around today, a testament to McFaddin Kendrick's willingness and ability to keep its finger on the national singles pulse, to anticipate subtle shifts in climate and attitude.

Their first national-scale success was *Élan*, a multitiered members-only nightclub for the aspiring-to-glamour crowd. Since its debut in Houston in 1976, *Élan* has been successfully cloned in Atlanta, Dallas, Denver, Memphis, Philadelphia, St. Louis, and Washington, D.C. A one-year membership card runs as high as $450. In addition to providing self-perceived elite companionship, and over-

To Come

priced food and drinks, *Élan* mails to members a glossy quarterly, *Communique*, that mainly features photos of members *having fun* on the premises and news of upcoming wine tastings and fashion shows. It's all part of an attempt to make you feel like *one of them*... busy, professional, well-heeled, well-traveled, sophisticated, on the go. Somebody who deserves to shop in this supermarket. Somebody worth "meeting."

In 1978, two years before the movie *Urban Cowboy* opened, McFaddin Kendrick discovered that Macy's in New York was doing one heck of a business in Ralph Lauren Western Wear, and that country music was starting to cross over onto Top 40 playlists. Out of its test labs and off its drawing boards came a bar called Cowboy and its cousin Rodeo, country-and-western theme bars in which no self-respecting cowboy would be caught dead. There are now Cowboys and/or Rodeos in Atlanta, Austin, Dallas, Denver, Houston, Montgomery, Memphis, St. Louis, and St. Petersberg.

What I was not aware of before I investigated this new trend was the astonishing amount of forethought that goes into the design of each bar. You might even say that McFaddin Kendrick has it down to a science. An affiliate company, TMHI, supervises the interior design and decor; a subsidiary company, Soundscapes, formats and produces tapes of "foreground music" (as opposed to background Muzak) that are blasted over their clubs' elaborate sound systems. Every element of its bars' design—lighting, color schemes, floor plan, furniture, music—has been calculated and planned not only for optimum comfort and enjoyment, but for—and here's the surprising part—*optimum mingling potential*. This is accomplished without the minglers themselves ever being aware that they are being oh-so-subtly manipulated.

On the surface, for instance, it would seem that Cowboy's decor consists of soft-sculptured (i.e. pillowed) cacti, soft-sculptured cowskulls, real cacti, real cowskulls, beer signs, hanging serapes, wagon wheels, saddles, rope, and all manner of ersatz western paraphernalia. But there is more here than meets the eye! McFaddin Kendrick is understandably reluctant to divulge specifics of its master plan for subliminally jiggling romantic sensibilities—like Coca-Cola's formula, it is proprietary information—but some generalities can be intuited.

The barstools, for instance, are constructed so that the women sitting on them will be exactly eye level with me as I walk past them...

Zucchini is a hip, healthful happy-hour hors d'oeuvre, but if it's fried, then you can bet I will join the flow of customers toward the restrooms... and the

This is Todd's. Here's Merle, living in Houston, searching for the woman who might lead him into the twenty-first century. Merle was a lonely guy with an eye for the future. He went to Todd's. He ordered himself a frosted drink; it was called the "Howling Coyote." He looked around for his designated. He could find neither Debra Winger nor Claire Trevor. He couldn't find the woman.

passageway is wide enough for only two bodies . . . so that I'll be forced to smile, as though to say, "Excuse me" . . . though what I'll really mean is, "Hi, there!" . . .

But if I really want to talk to this young lady, then I'll have to lean over close and intimately scream in her ear . . . because the music is so loud, but somehow not annoyingly so . . .

You get the idea. This is more than just putting a phone at my barstool, and less blatant. To inspire me to mix it up, to get my amorous juices flowing, McFaddin Kendrick has thought of every strategy, it seems, short of slipping a Mickey in my drink. So you can understand why, when I wanted to find out what singles bars planned to do about making it easier for me to meet girls in the 1980s, I thought a McFaddin Kendrick bar might be a good place to start looking. I went to Todd's in Houston.

At another McFaddin Kendrick bar, Confetti, they hang Honda motorcyles from the ceiling. For all I knew, they were there for decoration, but once one learns the secret of McFaddin Kendrick's success, one is instantly suspicious of decoration. Even though I don't ride motorcycles, and even though the sort of woman I'm apt to date would not be inclined to give a moment's thought to motorcycles, these hovering Hondas, I would bet anything, were part of the elaborate formula devised to perform its hypnotic magic on me.

Why Hondas? "They're fun," says Judy Meyer, McFaddin Kendrick's senior vice-president of marketing. "They put a smile on your face. Besides, they're unusual. When was the last time you saw Hondas on the ceiling?"

It had been a while, I'll admit. But then other aspects of the Singles Bar of the 1980s began to seem familiar, and it took me a while to realize why. Though it is touted as a neighborhood bar, it bears zero resemblance to Archie Bunker's Place. It is located not in a blue-collar residential community, but smack in the center of a suburban-styled shopping mall. It is not one big room with booze, raunchy posters, and a dartboard; it is many rooms, each with its own purpose.

In one room, there is a pool table, backgammon tables, and a slew of two-player video games. Another room features low, comfortable chairs and wide-screen television. In another room is a full-service restaurant, and that room is adjacent to the dance floor.

As I roam from room to room, it dawns on me: this is somebody's house. Not just anybody's house, but a millionaire's house, a veritable pleasure palace, a public version of Hugh Hefner's Playboy Mansion, complete with living room, dining room, ballroom, den, and servants.

For all the singles who were disenchanted with the hustling and pressure of singles bars, McFaddin Kendrick has designed the non-singles singles bar. You can amuse yourself for an entire evening here—with pre-dinner cocktails, dinner, after-dinner drinks, dancing, or TV, or billiards—and feel like you're at a very rich friend's house. Like the phantom Hefner, the friend is hiding somewhere, but he's given you full run of the place. Meyer, with her marketeer's penchant for converting nouns and adjectives into verbs, says that even Todd's had been "humanized," so that Todd, like Hef, is the mythic man of La Manse, the keeper of the castle. Appropriately, the ads feature a beautiful woman sighing, "Todd, you've always been so good to me." There is, of course, no Todd.

In the comfortable surroundings of an elegant home, women can feel comfortable chatting it up with their woman friends, adhering to a new mating code; this is a place not to be picked up, but to hang out.

"People are getting into people on a real basis," says Meyer, "not on a plastic basic. If that's what they want to do, we want to make it easy for them."

Accordingly, we will be witnessing relaxed dress codes. "America is casualizing itself," is Meyer's prognosis; why should we have to get decked out if we're just stopping by to visit Todd? Dancing is on the decline, says Meyer, because the two-step got too serious for the "tongue-in-cheek ambience" that today's single prefers in his leisure time. No more Donna Summers disco or Johnny Lee country. The sound of the eighties bar is Olivia Newton-John pop rock—upbeat, lighthearted tunes that will put a smile on your face.

Meyer even has a name for this new bar concept: the Adult Playpen. Now do the Hondas make sense?

The Adult Playpen, where someone has provided all the sights and sounds and colors and music and games and stimulating shapes and forms . . . because I am incapable of functioning on my own. There is no pressure to interact, just *encouragement*. They want to make it easy for me to meet people. To meet girls.

And so at an Atlanta singles bar called Confetti, I don't have to hustle at the bar, or even attempt anything as serious as dancing. Now I can chat *casually* while watching the big-screen TV in those deep, comfy chairs, or while I'm helping her with a three-cushion shot. And those dangling Hondas are like colorful mobiles, to gaze at, to wonder about, to attempt to make conversation

about. No, a playboy's mansion wouldn't have Hondas . . . but a baby's crib might.

The sad joke of singles life is that as the years roll by, you polish and perfect your girl-meeting skills, and right when you have it down to a science, you suddenly can't find any girls worth meeting. Where did they all go? They're not at the singles bars, that's for sure.

Well, if you can't find what you want at the supermarket, at any supermarket, then you'll have to check the newspaper ads, the catalogues, the mail-order houses. If you want to peddle your wares, and you don't want to peddle them at the supermarket, then you'll have to advertise—in newspapers, on radio and television.

And that's precisely what singles began doing, shopping for each other in ever more modern ways. It all started with the "personals" ads in the alternative newspapers of the 1960s; Single White Male desires loving woman to take sailing and share good times. At first the idea of advertising for love seemed outrageous, something only weirdos and losers would resort to. But like so many outrageous concepts before it (i.e. crotchless panties, a.k.a. intimate apparel), it would be only a matter of time before it won mainstream acceptance. Even the *New York Review of Books* runs personals.

Gradually the phenomenon has crept into every medium, and singles now deliberately partake in the ultimate marketing scheme. It's not the beer you drink or the jeans you wear that's for sale, it's ol' lovable *you*, packaged and presented like any other new age commodity targeted for young trendies on the go. Unlike those who have plugged in to computer dating services, this modern set of consumers not only gets to do its own advertising, but its own shopping as well. In keeping with the times, the ingredients and instructions—not to mention creative recipe suggestions—are conveniently listed right there on the label.

The unabashed purveyors of this crazy little thing we'll call technodating have provided efficient means by which all of us busy instant-gratification seekers can improve our lovelives. Thanks to technodating, we are now better equipped to pursue true romance for the simple reason that we can now eliminate much of the clumsy guesswork. Or, as some might say, the mystery.

Let's tune in to WRKO in Boston, 680 on your FM dial.

Our first caller today is a twenty-five-year-old grad student who is telling talk show host Dick Syatt and his Saturday morning audience that he arrived here a year and a half ago from southern Europe. He says he is six one, weighs 150 pounds, and has brown eyes, black hair, and a dark "perplexion." For fun, he says, "I like sports a lot, especially swimming and the movies." Then he describes his ideal woman.

"She must be fairly attractive, warm, and have a good sense of humor. But especially, Dick, I want her to be honest and sincere."

"Are you cute?" asks Syatt.

"Fairly cute," says our grad student, and then, heaping honesty upon sincerity, adds, "but I'm no Burt Reynolds."

Well! Welcome to Hotline, Boston's classified ad of the airwaves, where the cost is free and the product is *you*.

Every Saturday between 10 A.M. and 2 P.M., some 42,000 Boston singles dial 720-4080 ("Seven! Twenty! Forty!

Then . . . yahoo! She sat there like . . . like . . . like . . . Victoria Principal. Like Linda Evans. Like Dale Evans! "Howdy, space cadet," he said to her, "Howdya like to ride with me inter the twenty-first century?" "Lessee whether yer can dance or not," this glorious desert flower responded. He stood up. He knew he could shake it with the great ones. He banged his Teflon spur on the dance floor.

"Not bad," she said, "for a guy who I took for a regular Doogie Saddlebags." "Is that a saying in these here parts?" he asked. "Naw, I jes made it up," she said, "I like yer Horace. Lemme kis yer knuckles there, but I won't know whether yer the man for me until we play some video games together. Out here, we've got to check up on a feller's mettle." "Yahoo!" he said, "yer some wild woman."

Eighty!" in peppy radio parlance) in a mad attempt to be one of the fortunate forty or so who actually get to go on the air with Dick Syatt to be asked, "What do you look like? What do you like to do? Who do you like to do it with?"

The responses to these questions, and the ensuing banter between host and caller (one is reluctant to label them "conversations"), range in tone from lighthearted to poignant to pathetic, depending on how charitably one is willing to view the human race and its quest for fiery romance.

Callers describe themselves in terms of height, weight, coloration, and occupation. Their pastimes and special interests as a rule come under the umbrella of "having fun," and many a caller, perhaps taking care not to turn away any potential suitors, has gotten no more specific than that. Another favorite is "taking walks on the beach," which is uttered with such frequency as to set mathematicians calculating whether there are enough grains of sand in the universe to accommodate so many seaside strollers.

And who are these self-promoting singles looking for? Generally, someone who is honest, sincere, and has a good sense of humor. (Ask yourself: If you had to describe your ideal mate, what adjective would *you* employ?) Judging from the frequency with which these particular attributes are requested, you'd think they are in frighteningly short supply. And yet breathes there a soul who will admit to being dishonest, insincere, or unfunny?

It is the task of twenty-nine-year-old Syatt to ferret out more specific data—information that will make a caller stand out, as he would put it—and he achieves this by congenially kibitzing with his callers. He is not, he emphasizes, a matchmaker; rather, he is a facilitator, a conduit. Each on-the-air guest is assigned a Code Number (no names are ever broadcast), and listeners may phone the station to learn the first names and telephone numbers of prospects whose voices, self-descriptions, and criteria for companionship have appealed to them. Then they're on their own.

By any standard, Hotline provides more of a public service than most radio entertainment, and is more entertaining than your average public service program. In his confessional-sized studio at WRKO, the bearded, bespectacled Syatt resembles a Semitic father confessor, taunting a city of singles, of all ages, from all walks of life, to bare its collective soul.

After Syatt helps the fairly cute grad student make his pitch, he takes a call from an Andover woman, to whom he assigns Code Number 185. She is "half a hundred years old," but tells us that her friends persuaded her to add that she looks much younger. Like many a talk-show guest, she prefaces her personal plug with an appreciative nod to the host.

"First of all, I want to thank you, Dick. The cheerfulness and happiness which you engender can't be accurately measured. I know you think your job is tedious,"—she pronounces this *tee-jus*—but I enjoy your vocabulary. You come up with such interesting words."

"That's the first time anybody's said that," Syatt allows.

Ms. Half-a-Hundred has "escaped" from secretarial work, and is now employed as a florist: "my natural habitat." She is five-six, and weighs 132 pounds: "my ideal weight."

For activities, she prefers "the usual

—dining out, ballroom dancing, candlepin bowling, swimming, wallpapering and painting—"

"Wallpapering and painting?" queries our host, disbelieving.

"I'm very handy to have around the house."

"*Wallpapering* and *painting*!"

"Well, not *all* the time." (Silly boy!) "But I regard my body and my habitat as artistic endeavors, so I enjoy being color-coded and doing my best in that sort of thing."

Syatt proposes pairing her off with "somebody who does floors," but, seemingly oblivious to his remark, she proceeds to describe her preferred mate: "I like strongly practical men, ones who have pulled themselves up by their own bootstraps. I like to hear engineers sit around and tell how they've acquitted themselves well in work. Bragging, I guess that's what it is."

"Boy," says Syatt, "we're in for some really great weekends—hanging wallpaper and listening to engineers talk."

In the next hour, Syatt will yield center stage to ten more callers, among whom it is difficult to detect any one common denominator, except that they are all unattached and looking.

We will hear:

☐ a twenty-six-year-old man who works "in retailing," likes to party, and is looking for a woman with "a nice personality" who enjoys "intellectual discussions."

☐ a twenty-seven-year-old office equipment salesman who sails, boats, and water-skis, and wants a woman who "can carry on an animated conversation" and who "likes to laugh."

☐ a thirty-eight-year-old office manager who says she is turned off by the bar scene ("Everybody wants to stare, and nobody wants to meet anybody"), and who is in the market for a man "who I could hit it off with right away."

☐ a twenty-two-year-old stand-up comic who describes himself as "dashing," and puts in his request for "somebody whose feet don't smell."

☐ a twenty-eight-year-old antique dealer who desires a woman who is "independent, but likes to be treated as a lady... someone whom I can talk to and be a friend to."

☐ a twenty-seven-year-old draftsman who says others have described him as "sweet looking," and is on the prowl for a "nutty" woman who shares his passion for "music, music, and music."

☐ a "nervous as hell" bank teller, age thirty-two, who says she is "an extrovert trapped in an introvert's body," and is attracted to "a man who likes his mother."

☐ a forty-one-year-old carpenter who is "an incurable romantic," and will get involved only with a woman who "doesn't put her career ahead of a personal relationship."

☐ a thirty-five-year-old lawyer who says she is "shaped like a sixteenth-century Renaissance painting," and is "more interested in making acquaintances than in meeting *a man*."

☐ a jovial sixty-five-year-old widow who wants a dance partner "sixty to seventy who's full of fun... who's very conservative but not a stuffed shirt."

Hotline, in short, is for people who want to meet people. (Grotesquely stretching that parameter, a woman new to the area phoned in her request for a "grandmother" for her kids. She got eight calls.) Some callers sound so downright ecstatic about having gotten through ("I persisted and I'm here!" exclaims one woman, as jubilant as a lottery winner. "It's my lucky day!" enthuses another), and so many express such strong dissatisfaction with the bar and disco scene ("Too noisy, too crowded," is a typical complaint) that one can't help but wonder what the world has come to when people have to depend on a radio call-in show to snare themselves a decent date. The host's major talent lies in his ability to make the whole thing seem so respectable, so *damned normal*.

Syatt got the idea for Hotline while he was at a Miami station in the mid 1970s conducting a call-in show called Jobline, which matched jobhunters and employers.

"I had the idea that a spin-off of a dating show would be big," he says. "It was just a smidgen of an idea. It was so unimportant I mentioned it to the general manager in the hallway. He said, 'It's a stupid idea. Don't you dare.'"

Syatt moved to a Dallas station in 1976, just as it had switched to an all-talk format and was searching for an attention-grabbing gimmick. He saw his chance. When he took it on the air, he had no idea how the logistics would work. For the first hour he kicked around the idea with callers. All agreed that anonymity was important, and so it was decided that code numbers would be assigned to each "guest." Gradually, the rules of the game evolved, and the name "Hotline" (from the Sylvers's hit song) was selected.

At 9 P.M., Syatt announced he was open for business: "If you're single and you want to meet somebody, call!"

Five minutes went by, and nothing.

He begged and beseeched his audience. "If you're shy, call! Otherwise, you're missing out on a good idea."

Ten minutes, the lines were still dead.

"Chance of a lifetime!" pleaded Syatt, adopting the pathetically rabid manner of a public TV fundraiser.

Fifteen minutes, no response.

"Okay, this is a great idea, we're doing it for *you*, but if you don't want it . . ."

Then, one by one, the lines started lighting up.

From that moment to this, Syatt says, he's never had an empty line.

Syatt took his act to Providence in 1979, and then to Boston in 1981. Though its audience-share ratings have never been spectacular, the show has always enjoyed a high profile. Commercial spots—for jewelry, clothes, condos—are sold months in advance. Most tellingly, radio programmers who once sneered at his early success have now found their way into Syatt's corner. Hotline imitators, most without the good-natured warmth of the original, have popped up in Orlando, St. Louis, Denver, Buffalo, and other cities.

Syatt now wishes his show bore a more descriptive name, such as Dateline or Loveline, but on the other hand, he is thankful he doesn't have to labor under the title of one station's version: Dateless and Desperate.

"That's so *dreadful*," he says, wincing. "It's ri*dic*ulous! That's the image you're trying to stay *away* from. It's like naming a car a Shitbox. 'Buy this new Chevy Shitbox!'"

In their ad-libbed ads, Hotliners portray themselves as anything but losers; they tend to rely most frequently on images of specific celebrities when attempting to describe either themselves or their ideal mates. One woman claims she has been "likened to Suzanne Pleshette." One man's perfect playmate "should look like Natalie Wood." "It wouldn't hurt if he had some resemblance to Gregory Peck," says another woman of her preferred gentleman. And in one of the more demanding casting calls, a woman requests "someone who's a cross between Woody Allen, Dick Cavett, maybe Omar Sharif, and Al Pacino."

What we don't hear on the air, of course, is what happens after contact is made, whether such lofty aspirations are, in fact, fulfilled. Hotline does not purport to be a panacea for lonelyhearts in search of love. There are many roads to riches, weight loss, and romance, and what works well for some may fail abysmally for others. To its credit, the show has received few complaints from participants, and for a method of bringing strangers together in which even the moderately paranoid can detect potential danger, there have been no reports of untoward incidents.

"No Mr. Goodbar stories," says a relieved Syatt. "Nobody's ever been hurt that I've heard of."

Rather, the complaints Syatt has received are the sort one would expect to hear regarding any social situation.

"Occasionally someone will say they got ten calls and a few of them were rude. Well, what can I say? I'm sorry! Or, 'I made a date with this guy and he never showed up.' I'm sorry! But it happens. My feeling is, if you meet ten people in a bar and only one or two are rude, then thank God!"

The compelling question, of course, is not whether Hotline diminishes the chance of error, but whether it enhances the possibility of rapturous romance. Can true love blossom from a radio speaker? Can hearts be paired in the same starkly logical fashion in which jobhunter finds employer?

As hokey as the whole idea of calling a radio station to find a date may seem, the very least that can be said about Hotline is that, because of the show, thousands of singles met someone they probably would not have otherwise met. (In one enchanting instance, Hotline introduced a man and a woman from the same small town in England. "They were living together, last I heard," says Syatt with a smile.)

Almost as icing on the cake, Hotline has been the first step to the altar for at least 150 couples, several of whom have chosen Dick Syatt, Mr. Hotline himself, to be their best man.

"I was married six years, and now I'm not," says Syatt of his own status. "Both had advantages and drawbacks."

Syatt met his wife, Jane, at a party in 1972. His sister introduced them. He remembers the occasion as "uneventful." After they divorced, Syatt regained his appreciation of the inherent difficulties of singles life. "Meeting people," he says, speaking for himself and for his code-numbered congregation, "is hard work."

Asked how *he* would tout himself on Hotline, Syatt ponders a moment and then remarks that he can appreciate how difficult his callers' task really is. Unaided by the written list that most Hotline participants have prepared for themselves before picking up the phone, Syatt introspectively free-associates:

"I don't think I'm that confusing," he starts. "There aren't that many mysteries about me. I don't have a fetish for anything weird. I consider myself pretty normal . . . I'm very spontaneous. I have a lot of energy . . . I'm not crazy about sports . . . My job brings me into all sorts of different things: new restaurants, plays, movies, meeting interesting people, going on junkets and trips. In my free time, I like to be with good friends. I like bike riding, walking,

sailing, just keeping active. I like to have fun."

And here, realizing that he sounds like any other Hotliner, he breaks into laughter. "'I like to have fun,'" he says, chiding himself. "What the hell is that supposed to mean?"

Fearing perhaps the sort of vengeance a distraught coed might wreak upon a dallying professor, Syatt has avoided becoming romantically entangled with any of his callers. Instead, he has joined a state-of-the-art dating service called Couple Company that is remarkably similar to Hotline in every way but two. One, he has to pay for it. Two, for his money a year, he not only gets to hear a woman before he consents to take her out, he gets to see her as well. Likewise, the woman will get to see and hear him.

Dick Syatt, progenitor of audiodating, has eschewed his own service in favor of *videodating*.

In the summer of 1982, Channel 11 in Los Angeles premiered a weekly show called "Singles Magazine." It featured short segments on such provocative topics as "Why Some Older Women Date Younger Men," and "Why Singles Go to Singles Bars." It featured obsequious interviews with "singlebrities" such as Rick Springfield and TV stars Judy and Audrey Landers. And it featured, for the first time on home television screens, videodating.

Producer Barry Jaffe got the idea for the show when he saw a local TV news feature about dating services.

"Videodating looked like a good idea to me," he says, "but I thought, why pay for it?"

Jaffe placed a newspaper ad calling for volunteers, expecting maybe 100 responses. In one week, he got 1500.

"For the most part," he observes, "the responses were from articulate, intelligent, attractive, middle-class people. These were not losers. Losers are losers because they don't get involved. They're not attempting to do something about their social life. But these people *are* getting involved.

"Plus," he added, "it's an ego trip to sell yourself on TV, there's no doubt about it."

Of the 1500 who were eager to strut their stuff on the air, Jaffe taped 150. Each weekly installment of "Singles Magazine" contains six to eight self-scripted pitches from singles, each pleading with eligible viewers to come forth and love them. As with the Great Expectations tapes, these self-promoters offer only their first names. (You can write to them in care of the station; be sure to include a photograph!) Otherwise, these tapes differ dramatically from those you can see in the privacy of a curtained booth in Westwood.

For one thing, they're shorter; each is no longer than 30 seconds. For another, there is no off-screen interviewer or phony hidden-camera technique; rather, the "Singles Magazine" self-promo spots are shot on location, with the stars looking you square in the eye. So what we now have are not simulated first dates, but real TV commercials.

We watch one middle-aged man make his play from the driver's seat of his Rolls; a young woman performs her bit on roller skates; a plumber, wrench in hand, peddles his companionship from under a sink; a musician croons a singles jingle while strumming away on his guitar.

"You have to have production values," says Jaffe, explaining the varied settings and situations.

"More guacamole?" asked the waitress. "No thanks," said Merle, "I got all the avocado I can handle right here on my left." "You better watcha-yo-mout," she said moving closer. "No, you watch it," said Merle moving in. Singles bars and wild women, video games, and lazer hors d'oeuvres. If this was the future, he could see he liked it! It was late when they left Todd's. Maybe midnight. They were exhausted by their future-hunting. They thought they'd finish the evening with an old fashioned date. They went home to watch her Betamax Red River. *In Merle's heart he could imagine himself to be just like old Monty Clift. He took her arm and smiled. "Yee-ha!" he said, "on to the twenty-first century!"*

Consequently, the finished product is an eerie combination of an ad for a soft drink and an ad for a political candidate. Yes, it is as though the young hipsters in the Pepsi commercials are running for President and they want *your* vote.

As amateurish as these spots are, they make the Great Expectations tapes seem as plodding and antiquated as those live Frigidaire ads of the 1950s. On the other hand, their slickness and superficiality could send any potential videodater packing in search of an out-of-town business convention, where genuine human warmth and enduring relationships are abundant by comparison.

Watch and listen.

To Jill, a magician: "If you haven't caught my act, well, you really should. I'd like to give you an opportunity for a private showing."

And Jeff, perched on a barstool at a singles bar: "I'm an actor, a lawyer, and an all-around good guy."

And Jo, a highway patrol officer. And Guy, who enjoys outdoor sports.

And Margie: "I fly, model, and act... If you're a goodlooking guy who knows how to treat a lady, take me dancing."

And Tamara, on the tennis court: "I'm a twenty-three-year-old aspiring actress, and I thought this was a great chance to get on TV. I love great Italian cooking and hockey."

And Red, in his Rolls: "I've also got a Cadillac Eldorado convertible, and the largest antique penny-scale collection in California."

And Doug. And Bryn. And Florence, and Bill, and Shari, and...

And by the time you read this, "Singles Magazine" may be on your TV. Jaffe plans to nationally syndicate the show—local stations would supply the videodating spots—so that curious singles coast-to-coast can get a taste of videodating.

Yes, you, too, can be a star for thirty seconds, right up there with Rick Springfield and the Landers sisters, inspiring the creation of your very own fan club.

"Singles Magazine" eliminates both the expense of a subscriber videodating service and the necessity of trekking to a central office to screen dates. But, as anyone can see, it has problems: it lacks the limited privacy and the illusion of exclusivity that Great Expectations offers; the video aspect of it is not reciprocal; and the spots are preposterously short. (What meaningful information is conveyed by a woman who tells us only that she likes horseback riding and roller skating? Never mind getting to first base; we don't even feel as though we've had a chance at bat.)

Well, then, how about a selective breeding—a Great Expectations–type service you can plug into inexpensively at home?

Get ready. It's almost here. It's called telecomputer dating.

How does it work? Simple. Let's say I want to find a mate to go sailing with me in Newport Bay next weekend. I can do it by using the same apparatus I would use to shop for food or clothes: the telecomputer, a home computer with a video display and telephone access to every other telecomputer. They'll be as common as pocket calculators before 1990.

STEP ONE: I punch in the information pertaining to the type of partner I desire. Who will it be this weekend? Oh, how about a twenty-five-year-old nonsmoker who's, say, 5′4″, 115 pounds, with dark hair. Religion? We'll punch in "not applicable." Can't be too fussy. I want her to live within twenty-five miles of me, have her own car. And, just for kicks, let's make her a nurse. Haven't ordered one of those in a while.

STEP TWO: On the video display, I see a list of first names and code numbers of women who meet my criteria. I punch in the first one: Veronica, number 046483229. Veronica's self-authored profile flashes onto the screen. She tells me a little about herself: relationship, her favorite activities. Uh-oh. She has a fear of water. I punch in the next number, and the next, sequentially reading about each candidate until I find one who strikes my fancy: Amy, number 177835901.

STEP THREE: Amy looks good on paper, so to speak, so now I'll command the computer to play her self-produced videotape. I like what I see.

STEP FOUR: Through the telecomputer, I relay a message to Amy that I want to take her sailing next weekend. I tell her my first name and code number.

STEP FIVE: Amy sees my tape, reads my capsulized biography. The attraction is mutual. It is as though our eyes have met across the city.

STEP SIX: Amy and I go sailing off into the sunset together.

Now what can be easier or more methodical than that? I found the girl next door right in my own living room; I just let my fingers do the walking.

Cold? Artificial? Mechanical?

Before long, I promise you, the stigma of prescreening dates will vanish completely. Rather, there will be a stigma attached to dating someone I *haven't* prescreened. When someone asks me "What did you see in *her*?" I should at least be able to produce a list: 5′4″, 115 pounds, doesn't smoke...

What kind of person will telecomputer-date?

I imagine one of your more adventuresome friends will try it out, just for the novelty. Then a few magazines will print articles about it, initially skeptical, but ultimately positive in tone. Films and novels will incorporate the phenomenon into their plots. More of your friends will give it a go, just on a lark. Then, sooner or later, intrigued by their experiences, you'll try it. You won't want to appear old-fashioned, will you?

Eventually, an entire generation will be raised in ignorance of what life was like without telecomputers. Shopping for love on a home video screen will seem as natural to them as phoning someone for a date seems to us.

You want to hear my prediction? When the day arrives that telecomputers become the standard means by which boys and girls meet each other, some forward-thinking entrepreneur will open a radical new business. All he'll need is one large room and some comfortable furniture, and he'll charge singles $700 a year to come in and experience the excitement of meeting each other in the flesh... *without having seen each other on TV.*

Maybe he'll serve some booze, just to grease the wheels of interaction, to lower inhibitions, to encourage banal chitchat, to fuel the hunt, to revive the numbed exploratory instinct—to get his customers acting silly and unscientific.

He'll open his doors to the masses, welcoming old ladies, cripples, illiterates, and, yes, even fatties.

He'd call his enterprise something like Chance Encounters or Happy Accidents.

What sort of women would rely on such a haphazard, inefficient way of meeting men? Couldn't tell ya. But, knowing me, I'll be the first in line to find out.

There are a great many reasons to establish an intimate relationship with another person. In the four pieces that follow here, you'll find a documenting of four stages of singlehood, in which you share yourself with another, or two. In the first piece, "First Lines: Translations from the English," you'll find out how to make your approach. Next, "Promiscuity and You," or, as we call it, Poly-singlicity, will tell you how one man found dissatisfaction yearning in all his title bouts. "How to Cohabitate" is a piece on the process we call singlicide. It is a diagramming of the end of singlehood, the hurtle toward commitment. The last piece is on Last Lines: "The Collected Letters to Dear John." It is a short and vivid glossary of circumstances, none of which you'll ever, we're sure, encounter.

Your Single Relationships

SCOTT WEISS
LICENSED REAL ESTATE BROKER
HARPOON REALTY LTD.
516-725-2252
MADISON & MAIN STS.
SAG HARBOR, NEW YORK 11963
Easthampton
ANTIQUE
FAIR
We meet: I put on the irresistibles for her.
Love is like tap water!
THE BEACH HOUSE
BAR & RESTAURANT
Last blast of summer passion!
Don't drive (you know Harry's drinks!), the aspirins on u
Har-Har!
DATE September 5
TIME 7:30 until Sunrise
PLACE Harry's Burning Ember on-the-beach (off Route 8)
GAULOISES
CAPORAL
GAULOISES FILTRE
SEITA FRANCE
20 CLASS A CIGARETTES
"WARNING: THE SURGEON GENERAL HAS DETERMINED THAT CIGARETTE SMOKING IS DANGEROUS TO YOUR HEALTH."
11,0 mg TAR . 0,60 mg NICOTINE
FILTRE
MADE IN CANADA
GAULOISES
FILTRE
She likes the French. The French! Yahoo!
She sees me totally nude for the first time.

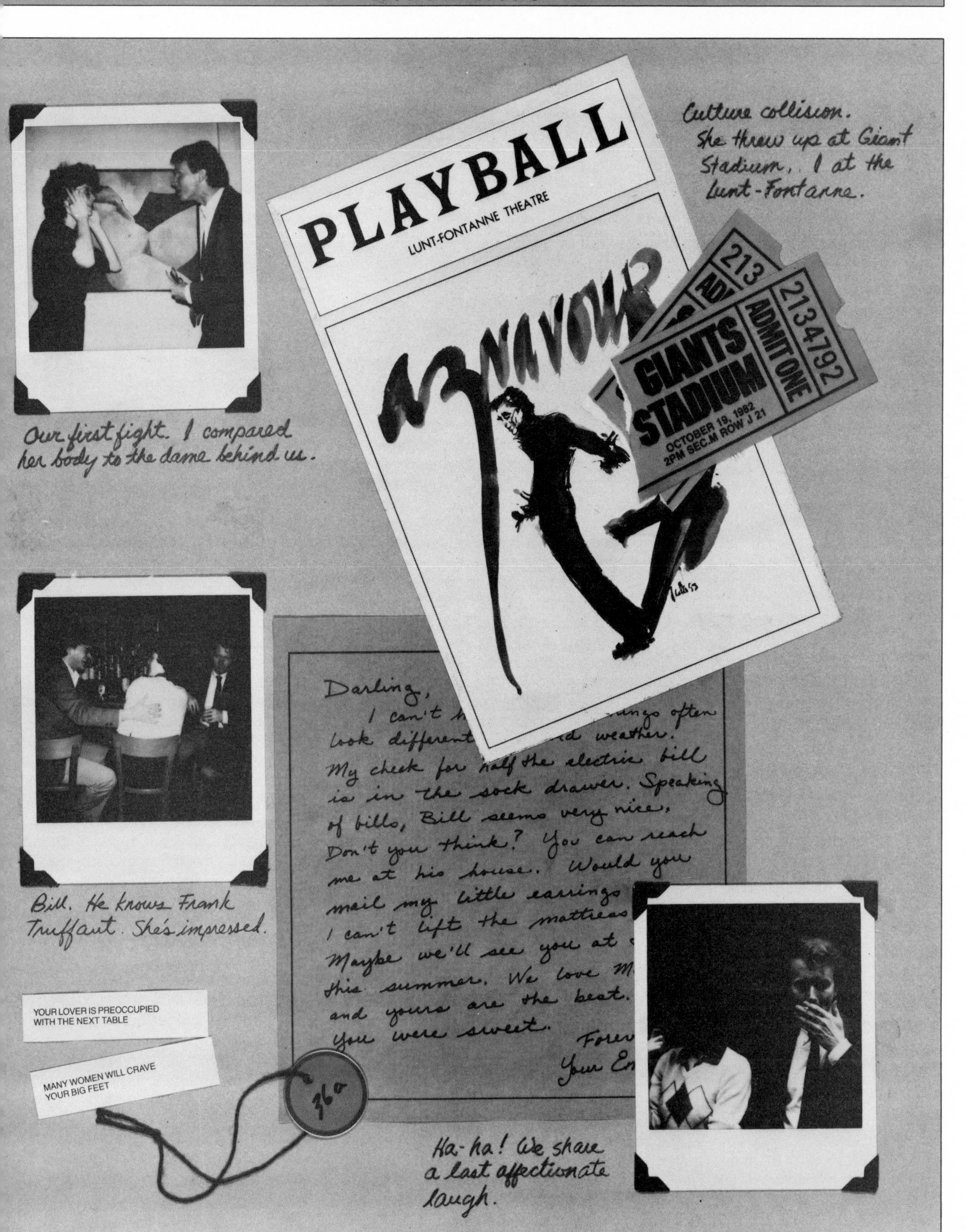
Culture collision.
She threw up at Giant Stadium, I at the Lunt-Fontanne.
PLAYBALL
LUNT-FONTANNE THEATRE
AZNAVOUR
213
ADMIT ONE
2134792
GIANTS STADIUM
OCTOBER 19, 1982
2PM SEC.M ROW J 21
Our first fight. I compared her body to the dame behind us.
Bill. He knows Frank Truffaut. She's impressed.
Darling,
I can't h
ings often
look different
d weather.
My check for half the electric bill
is in the sock drawer. Speaking
of bills, Bill seems very nice,
Don't you think? You can reach
me at his house. Would you
mail my little earrings
I can't lift the mattress
Maybe we'll see you at
this summer. We love M
and yours are the best.
You were sweet.
Forev
Your Em
YOUR LOVER IS PREOCCUPIED WITH THE NEXT TABLE
MANY WOMEN WILL CRAVE YOUR BIG FEET
360
Ha-ha! We share a last affectionate laugh.

First Lines:

Translations from the English

For Men

Sooner or later the chemical chains that add up to *you* are going to start militating for maximum insane expansion, and when they do, you're going to think it's love you're after. Sadly, the much criticized complexity of life makes assurance of true and further available love unlikely without conversation first, so brace yourself for some of the symbolic higher-primate exchanges that have made man sweep the honors in Bartlett's *Familiar Quotations*.

Unless you're a lawyer, though, you can't force anyone to talk to you, and even then, the talk might be strained. Therefore, some Open Sesame or verbal pageboy is needed that will dispose your object to receive you, although the time-proven candidates for First Line are depressingly if purposefully unmagical. Intensely conservative as our chemical chains are, they like to sight solidity before lowering the landing gear, so regardless of the cute ripostes that are meat and drink to underage checkout girls and James Bond, it's the plain, even the wan phrases that excel in actual highway tests.

Here are the five most lusterless and qualified choices for Opening Line, one of which just may be the appropriate salvo for your next targeted dreamboat.

1. "Hello."

The Tiffany of greetings, this elegant little black word commits you fully to your prospect without in any way limiting the scope of what's to come. Studies have shown that your quarry is likely to match your hello, however reluctantly; then, of course, you must start from zero again, but you've "opened Japan," as historians say, and it's now a relationship, even if they turn away coldly. After all, now it's *you* they're avoiding, and only seconds before you were mere strangers.

When inflecting this word, avoid the musical comedy "va-va-voom" subtext, however much you wish to fly your enthusiasm's colors. You may mean "My astral mate at last!" but it'll read as "I see supper!" Also, "Hi" is a tolerable sleeveless variant, but under no circumstances is "Yes!" on its own.

2. "My name's ———."

This sacrifices both mystery and coyness immediately, but it does show a certain forthrightness, even a compulsion to divulge what many associate with intimacy. Its openness (he or she could go right to the police with the information, after all) obliges anyone honorable to offer up their own name, and, by primitive superstition, their very soul, in response.

If your name is Crusher or Peewee, it may be a provocative general introduction to you, and, in any case, your partner can always get the chat, and destiny, rolling by saying, say, "Tony? Oh, are you Italian?"

Again, watch inflection, or your intended may suspect you're seizing a narcissistic opportunity to recite your own name, especially if you include any roman numerals that may follow it. If you choose to bill yourself above the relationship, then offer your name factually, like a placard at the zoo. Curiosity is most likely to explore in safety.

3a. "Are you a model/dancer/Swedish?"

Only the stupid will be fetched by this superficial tribute, though you'd be surprised what a longstanding good time many stupid people can show you. As vulgar come-ons go, this one's pretty subtle; it's even phrased passively, as a question. The lesser, old-school variant, "You look like a great painting," might lead to schoolyard Picasso jokes or, worse, feeble classroom discussion. Comparisons to flowers and deities (film stars excepted) provoke prickly unease in these literal times, and mother/old girlfriend–type analogies unnerve even an eager subject. Even objective observations like "My mother had a pin like that" land somewhere uncomfortably between the Gothic and the homely. Specific praise seems fetishistic, even maniacal, so again, generality is the ticket: let them make their own sundae.

3b. "I just want you to know you're beautiful."

As modestly winning as it may seem, this oil-tinged zephyr doesn't quite sell the way you would think. The saintly mash lacks the promise of Question Form, and though we love to hear ourselves say it, the selfless compliment always engenders suspicion in the recipient. There is, of course, the pathetic implication that, having delivered your gift horse, you will now slip into the gloaming, so if you don't poignantly vanish, your motives will begin to smell up the romantic glen you've evoked. If ever, this socko approach is serviceable for those rare right-before-getting-off-the-subway moments; at least you might run into the beauty concerned another day, premoistened for second-level blandishments. Needless to say, your chemical chains hate high-risk long-term sallies like this.

4. "May I ask the time?"

Though one of the top five, this one is still very bad. It exploits and dismisses the beloved before you've even been introduced, even though you might think it's an ingenious way to have the two of you thrown together by business matters. True, it obliges the Watched to converse with you, but nothing of a very scintillating order. It implies you have interests elsewhere, or are restless where you are, or, if it's late, that both of you should be in bed, a finally rather defeatist argument for togetherness. Still, mechanistic as it is, it beats such other dull data as "Do you live around here?" or even the lewdly solicitous "Are you having a good time?" As for "Do you come here often?"—its inquest into a stranger's figurative virginity lacks even camp potential to excuse it, except perhaps on a Nobel Prize dais, and even then there's a likely language barrier.

5. "Excuse me: Don't I know you?"

This is the closest to magical of all because it attempts to bypass completely the problem of speaking to someone for the first time, by pretending that in fact you've already done so and can now just relax and try to remember each other. It can be followed with a quick rifling of the past, using whatever you perceive as your best credentials: "The Winter Olympics? Northwestern? The Video Fair?" Everyone doubts his own memory, and even if your fascinator demurs, you can coast into Where-Or-When metaphysics with "Well, it feels as if I know you." The Reachable Rose may incline its head into some other warm wind, but you'll have the consolation that anyone who'd spurn an old friend isn't good enough for your chemical chains anyhow.

Well, there they were: admittedly an unprepossessing clutch of phrases, especially when prepossessing is the goal. But if you think flippancies like "Which way to the frozen yak?" will disarm a fellow shopper, you've been reading too many quack guides to sensuality. Also, as a last warning, contentions of inferior drama aside, beware of the spirited wrangle that you plan to turn to passion. If you challenge a prospect with "Do you really eat that junk?" or "What are you so smug about?" don't expect the scuffle that follows to melt into a helpless embrace. No, let your spoken emissaries be drably dressed to imply great wealth. Begin with an aura of effortless health. Dupe them with a competent phenotype. Let their chains think yours are less hysterical than they are. It's high time you fooled nature for once.

For Women Only

Since Mae West has moved on to the place where you'll have to wait until you can come up to see her sometime, women who speak English have been somewhat deprived of good advice on a first line. "Is that a gun in your pocket or are you happy to see me?" has hardly ever been beaten as an entryway to further interaction, but the eighties have offered a few more opportunities for women than even the brilliant Miss West was allowed to see. These include:

1. "Why don't you get out of that heavy Walkman and into something comfortable?"

This subtle invitation to the senses has the strength of avoiding an overt sexuality, while communicating a provocative acceptance of technological contemporaneity. It suggests that although you have spent your waking hours taking pleasure from a cold and portable unit, an alternative source might be as invigorating, particularly a source powered by something with a little bit more kick than two AA batteries. Thus, an incitement to seek a crescendo from another system besides the one bought for $40 from a street-corner electronics salesman might have some impact, even on an input-sated late-century model male.

2. "Say, are all your ties that thin and bunched up?"

Just say it, wait a beat, see what happens in the next ninety seconds. Even if your addressee has never read a Classics Illustrated "Life of Freud," you're sure to get an uncontrollably aggressive response of self-defense. Look away for a moment. When he goes to the knot of his tie to straighten it out, you know you're in business. Don't let him change the subject. This one's a lulu.

3. "I know an exercise that will triple your Pac-Man score."

So it's a little phony and panders to a trend that you probably, if you've got an iota of decency in you, detest. So it's manipulative. So he'll probably make you come up with the quarters, afterward, to prove it. So. The point is, in eight of nine cases, it works; and the score *is* subsequently tripled. He'll be forever grateful, and will return to you as often as he needs to play. This fast opener will do more than just establish a conversation, it will lead to a permanent relationship and leave a devoted sportsman attesting to your clinician's skills wherever video athletes compare hints. Sure, this first line succumbs to Pacmania in the worst possible way, but if you're really interested in a new relationship, and if you own Warner Communications stock, you'll put it on in public.

4. "Didn't I see you sweep five last week on 'Family Feud'?"

This is the kind of first line we don't give out for free. Usually we charge as consultants with this kind of information, because with a formula this surefire, we give it away once and it's giving away the ballgame. They never come back, because it works forever. But for you, we give it. Look, the guy's an American man living in 1980-something, if you tell him you saw him on "Family Feud," he's either going to go through the roof with delight (it's the eighties equivalent of telling him he reminds you of one of the Beatles) or ask you what "Family Feud" is, in which case you've got the opportunity to instruct him with the kind of arrogance usually saved for college hipsters talking to classmates who have never heard of Charlie Parker. At any rate, your target victim ought to be grateful and happy and entirely at your feet, which is what you want at some point—later, and in the dark, if you can swing it—and ready to book you in at 7:30 each night for the rest of his natural viewer's life. Make sure to write and thank us for this one.

5. "Is that a microcomputer in your pocket or are you happy to see me?"

This is just to make the guy feel like a whiz, and to give him the opportunity to say, "Computers? I never touch the stuff." Despite the success of *The Soul of a New Machine*, computer expertise is still considered among heathens to be the kind of knowledge one ought to know but not bring up in public. It's cool, but abstruse, and finding a man who knows computers but is reluctant to talk about them is one of the surest signs that you're onto something triumphant. But even if he doesn't know a bit from a nit, this lovely opener brings forth the true essence of the man you've chosen to confront, a man of complexity and strength, with a readiness to see the new century. If, by the way, he really does have a computer in his pocket, kick the bastard down the stairs and tell him he can plug his instrument where the data's less refined. Find somebody who knows how to put his work to bed at night, and, as Miss West would say, visa versa.

Promiscuity and You

Many people dwell on promiscuity. Daydream, temptation, self-dramatization, forced or acquired habit. Sleeping around a lot is a phase plenty of people go through at one time or another, some by sheer voracious choice, others out of repeated disappointment, impulsiveness, and indecisiveness.

Many people just aren't ready to get married. They're not ready to settle down, not ready to commit themselves, not ready to make up their minds.

The situations one finds oneself in, such as college, are for many draining and hellishly all-consuming. One studies, promises oneself all sorts of improved, stable, future versions of oneself, devotes all one's essential energies to self-definition, labyrinthine charts made up of promises and likely self-deceits. Intuitiveness isn't so trusted. One studies the opposite sex as one studies oneself. Getting laid a lot implies vitality and a questing disposition, and even a sense of self-control. You run the gamut of mates like a Willie Mays fouling off pitch after pitch, trusting that you won't lunge and blow it when the right one comes along.

Promiscuity as an acceptable way to be was first introduced to America by the media disguised, I think, as Sweden, that country where pretty blond fourteen-year-olds all went on the pill. Before that it lived in legends such as Marilyn Monroe and bohemian Greenwich Village—a way for other troubled, gifted sorts to be. To be ungifted and promiscuous was just slutty. Marilyn Monroe, in retrospect, always seemed doomed, but now she would seem no more doomed than anyone else. And now, as is obvious, Sweden is all around us and Warren Beatty is King. He's obsessively working on a movie like the rest of us want to work on our lives. Lots of lovers is an energy source and in step with the times. Everything you do is in step with the times as long as you acknowledge its imperial finiteness.

"I want to go out with lots of people," they say.

"I can't be ready to marry because I still think about going out with other people."

"Maybe she's right for me. I won't know until I've gone out with a lot more people."

"Maybe this is love. Maybe it isn't."

"You better be the one to make me happy. Because if you don't, someone else will."

"There's lots of fish in the sea."

"I see someone, and he's built like an Adonis, and I have to find out whether or not I can lay him."

"Let's go to the lingerie department."

Do I have any idea what I'm talking about? Many people are promiscuous, but many are not. It seems strange to seek advice on how to go about it. But plenty of us are not ashamed to think of ourselves as nerds. Generally, nerds are good at one thing, such as computers or telling jokes, and are not at home doing anything else. Nerds have been vaguely fashionable for about five years now. In a world where fads and fashions seem to carry so much moral weight and come and go so quickly, many of us rarely feel at home, many of us often feel like nerds, and we'll listen to advice regarding just about anything. There are self-help manuals for everything. They're all written by nerds who take something that used to seem quite simple and think that just because they can explain and overcomplicate it the rest of us can profit from it.

Penthouse magazine is really a monthly self-help manual for those who wish to be promiscuous, for those who want to put some sleazy muscle into their daydreams and quests, thus obscuring their deep timidity and, should push come to shove, lack of finesse. Rev those sex engines, boys. Three dollars.

In "Penthouse Forum," where people write in about their unexpected sexual experiences, guys and girls are always going about their daily, mundane businesses when suddenly they have their sudden, unexpected sexual experience. I read an interview where noted author Truman Capote said that sudden, unexpected sexual experiences were what he enjoyed most in life. I pictured Truman walking onto a train, eager to cuddle up on the seat with a book. Suddenly the conductor walks down the aisle, takes one look at him, and flings off his clothes.

I mean, I don't know anyone who lives the life that guys in "Penthouse Forum" live. If I am that out of touch with mainstream America, just raise your hand and if enough of you do I'll shut up. It's hard to tell where most of "Penthouse Forum" takes place, but somehow I always picture condominium complexes in Florida and the Southwest, the stale air-conditioned air, suntan lotion, beery breath, headaches from too much sleep and television.

The girls in *Penthouse* magazine always remind me of the most promiscuous girls in my high school. The most beautiful girls in my high school just happened to be the most notoriously promiscuous, although they confined their extravagances to the same group of tough guys, and carefree, irresponsible sex by older people has always seemed to be an ill-fated search for what, back then, I dreamed those exalted teenagers enjoyed. The closest I ever got to that group was when one of the most famous girls went out with my best friend just to clean up her reputation. He was a good boy. He'd been accepted early decision to Yale.

Coincidentally, he was also the one who introduced me to "Penthouse Forum." I don't think it did him any good, nor did it do me any good. The advice I have to give is based on the following experience. In college I had a girlfriend. (But I didn't have one in high school.) I dropped out of college and the girlfriend and I came to New York City, where we broke up. She suddenly realized just how many fish there were in the sea. Nerdlike, I went and spent a year in Central America living alone in a cottage on a lake in the mountains, reading and writing. When I came back to New York City, I didn't want to fall in love. I wanted to go out with girls for the first time in my life, and I had no idea how to go about it.

When you start out you are just lost in well-traveled territory without a map, pretending you know the way. Shyness blinds you so much you feel like you're sitting on a camel in a desert sandstorm. You're not used to this kind of conversation. Conversation that is supposed to be so much more than what it sounds like, conversation that is supposed to be seductive and somehow a sample of your bed. In a way, promiscuity is nomadic, and you carry your bed in your words, your looks, your initial touch. For the true nomad, the easy exit surrounds him, and so does the front door.

In the little Central American lakeside town where I lived, I used to see this pretty, dark girl riding around on the back of a motorcycle driven by a macho half-Indian who was always dressed like Zorro. She always wore the pale, waistless dresses the local Mormon missionaries gave out, and her dark curls stuck to her neck in the heat. I had a hot crush on her. I thought about her all the time. Then one day I went to the bordello in that lonely town, and to my surprise, she was the only girl on duty. That, I guess, was about the sexiest thing that had ever happened to me. But she was blackly insane, and she begged me to take her to New York, telling me what a wonderful wife she'd be.

You have to be ready. You can only spend so much time wondering why it seems to come so easily to everyone else before you scare yourself into giving up. There are ways to ease yourself into it. You have to be ready, and I was almost ready, and it served me to tell the first few girls I went out with upon my return to New York that I couldn't go home with them because the girl in the Central American bordello had given me v.d. Which was true. I let that drop early on those first awful, spastically selected, pragmatic dates and then we spent the rest of the night acting as if we'd go to bed if only we could. If you are feeling shy about dating a lot and never have and want to get your moves down, this might be a good thing to try.

Expect to be halted and unmasked. The best girls can see through anything and are proud of it. An experience I had I think is typical. I had kissed a girl at a bar. And then she dropped a bomb on me. She pulled back and said, "Oh God. I can't do this to you. I'm so promiscuous. I'll hurt you so much."

And nothing I said could change her mind. What really burns me is that the dashingly confident bartender just heard the word promiscuous and he instantly got horny and started hovering around. He thought *he* was going to have something to write to "Penthouse Forum" about. So she wasn't going to hurt me. She was promiscuous, and it was a game she and all the others out there were playing, and somehow she could tell I wasn't yet up to that game so I wasn't going to be allowed to play anymore. Like I was lacking that telltale insouciance. I felt like Casper the Friendly Ghost sitting on a barstool. Like my lack of insouciance meant I was looking for love and only love in the most deadly serious way, and she could tell.

That telltale insouciance can do everything for you. Some teenagers are born with it. Others must travel far into the nomad's desert to get it burnt into their skin. In the meantime, just concentrate on looking good. On looking at home with yourself. At the video machine in the back of the bar that you have never played before, slap the buttons as if you know what you're doing. The most insignificant gesture might be the one that pulls the stopper and sucks her in. Sitting at the bar, pretend you are moving in slow motion. Sudden gestures, starts and stops, may startle.

"Then wear a gold hat if that will move her;/If you can bounce high, bounce high for her too/Till she cry, 'Lover, gold-hatted, high bouncing lover,/I must have you!" Those words are by Thomas Parke D'Invilliers, and they are printed on the title page of *The Great Gatsby*, and it is the best advice.

My experience was limited because the thing in college was a great love. A really great love. We met in a freshman course called Great Books. As for women, all I really knew about was great love.

So I didn't want to fall in love, but right away I did. I fell in love with the girl who, at the bar, told me how promiscuous she was. She was beautiful and smart and had a disposition I swear is the prettiest thing I've encountered on the planet. But she also had this air of Nothing can hurt me if I don't let it.

I went home and I kept hearing her say: "I'm so promiscuous," and "I'll hurt you so much." I kept trying to recapture her tone of voice as she'd said it, trying to figure out what it meant to her and how she felt. She practically sang it out, and it was a moon tune to me. She seemed to be saying: Nothing is more fun than being promiscuous. I won't give it up for anything.

While you are getting into training at singles bars and rock clubs or wherever, you should probably get your body into training, too. Everybody seems to be making a very big deal nowadays about bodies and being fit. Flabby and poorly shaped consigns you to spectral oblivion. Health clubs are good, if for no other reason than that they keep you out of bars in the afternoons or early evenings. The health club I joined was full of dancers and models working out. On my tour, the guide told me the afternoons were best because you got all the girl dancers and models in while most of the guys were at work.

But there were always just as many guys as girls there, and hardly any flirting went on. The guys all wore their college sweatshirts and lined up to use the blowdryers in the locker room. There was a room to sit in by the pool that made you smell like eucalyptus leaves. Everybody displayed a devotion to their bodies that was a little humiliating to be around. I liked the mirrored wall around the jogging track. I ran track for five years, in junior and senior high school, and never had any idea what I looked like.

Eventually I came to one conclusion. Anyone can sleep around a lot once they decide they really don't care who with. You develop a kind of ease. As if your skin, like a hat in the movies, is being worn at a telling angle. It can pass as, and is often mistaken for, that rare kind of natural attentiveness we call warmth. I like finding it in a bar, spotting sluttishness in a bar. You're walking to the jukebox at the back of the room and there she is sitting on a barstool, legs crossed, talking to the bartender, shiny-eyed, hands propped delicately on the bar as if it were a keyboard, this girl you've never seen before. I can't get over it, and I'm sure I will never change.

There is sleeping around for the fun of it, and for the need of it. There is sleeping around because you need to know your pain is true, and you hold strangers in your arms and call them by your loved one's name. Many people who are not in love sleep around to prove that they are formidably alive, pretty, desirable, what not. You get used to being led around, learn all about the insides of peoples' apartments and how people kill time on Friday nights. You become sensitive to the poetry of finite acquaintances. The clammy hand over the heart, and the long walk back to your apartment on a Saturday morning, her taste on your lips for the last time, her laugh and expressions never to be thought of again. (Until they turn up in that dream on that night of feverish tossings and turnings in a Mexico City hotel room years from now.) There are no expectations, no crushed hopes, no demands or responsibilities.

Summer is best for sudden, unexpected sexual experiences, especially those days that follow those howlingly monotonous heat waves like a kite bouncing lightly on a temperate breeze. It is important to pay attention to weather conditions. It is important to pay attention to everything. You come through the door of the bar with that breeze that has everyone in a grateful pagan rapture. You sit down and order a beer from the waitress. You are convinced that the waitress made eyes at you.

It takes so much energy to believe things like, "Wow. She made eyes at me." That's why teenagers who are inflated with egotistical sexual energy are so good at this kind of thing. The routine that follows always feels familiar and at the same time always seems unprecedented. After a while you lead her back to your table with your eyes and order another. Waitresses, unlike most girls, will always respond to a long, desiring stare with the question, "Can I help you?"

Now, ask her something dumb and ponder the degree of animation in her reply. Not yet certain, you get up and go to the pay phone in the corner and pretend to phone someone by dialing your own number. While the phone rings and rings, watch the cute waitress to see if her eyes register disappointment or surprise when she sees you're no longer at your table, relief when she spots you in the corner pretending to talk heartily into the phone. Stare thoughtfully at the phone after you've hung up, as if everything matters to you. On your way back to your table, stop at the video game and look as if you're racking up a high score while you stare down into the screen and slap the buttons. The waitress stops at the end of the bar to place her drink orders, and then she has to loiter there, waiting for the bartender to pour them. Move to the barstool closest to where she is waiting. It's as overt a gesture as asking her to dance, and yet it doesn't make it look as if you're going too far. Now every time she comes to place a drink order, she's coming to you. The bartender is impressed and gives you a free beer. You learn that the waitress is eight years younger than you. She's a freshman at NYU. Every other word she utters has no consonants. But she seems to like you, and you'll follow her home. But it's ten-thirty and she gets off at two-thirty in the morning. That's okay. You'll wait. Roll up your sleeves, have another beer. (And try to stand yourself.) On your way back to her place, stop at a bar that stays open until four, have another drink or two, and ask her if she wants to go back to her place. At this point she can hardly refuse.

My waitress lived with six other eighteen-year-olds in a third-story East Village walk-up. When I got there they were all awake, some of them dressed in nighties and pajamas. There were posters on the walls, books shelved in orange crates, a stereo set put low on the floor on a trunk, all the records currently on view in the record-store windows. The murky repetition of synthesizer passages was cold and intimidating. The music seemed to be checking me out with the girls. What do you want here? it seemed to ask, placing an insinuating hand on my heart. The girls talked among each other about boyfriends. The night before none of them had come home, not even my waitress. They'd all been with boys, even the fat one, and they giggled over the fact that the cat had not been fed. The waitress suggested we go out to the all-night grocery and get a few bottles of beer. Leaning against a car, we kissed, and she said, "Are you heartbroken or something? You kiss like you're heartbroken."

Everyone hopes to find their truest, best self in love and, lacking that, looks for standing ovations in the shifting glances of strangers. Standing there under the streetlight with the waitress, I did not feel so unnoticed and unknown. The moment blazed like an old Frank Sinatra song, and I felt as at home in tender, vicious New York City as a Mayan sitting on a temple's steps back at old Tikal. To kiss like you're heartbroken, you must find some young girl rare and innocent enough to notice and you must truly be that, because I was doing the best I could. But she said she was heartbroken too. The boy she loved had just gone into the Marines.

Sooner or later you will find that sleeping around isn't such a thrill anymore. The true nomad doesn't ask questions, he wanders diligently, and if he finds himself fenced in or out, he turns around and heads toward some other sweet sunset. Should he ever find himself left with no way out, no-trespassing signs and border patrols all around him, watch out —he'll probably reach for his rifle. The true nomad is immune to heartbreak.

But you probably aren't immune to heartbreak. And the true nomad has long ago stopped listening to my advice. Willed promiscuity brings dangers; crash victims fill our streets.

So what do you do when disillusionment has set in? Go back to your com-

We kissed, and she said, "Are you heartbroken or something? You kiss like you're heartbroken."

puters? Tell jokes? Read "Penthouse Forum" to get yourself interested again? If you have done everything right, you finally fall in love just as you were getting bored with promiscuity, and you just forget about it. Often the convert to promiscuity tries to propel himself frantically towards some perverse mirage. We all remember withered Jack Nicholson at the end of *Carnal Knowledge*, slumped in the prostitutes' corner, peeling off bills in an attempt to buy one last sensation.

You feel that you've lost the art of looking into yourself. You have to feel ready to fall in love. No matter how much you deny it, somewhere inside you there must be a readiness to fall in love, and some cookie cutter of longing must have pressed into you the shape of someone you know is right. But you look into yourself and find your soul is so muddled it resembles a *New York Times* fashion supplement, and you leaf desperately through the same old gory selection of glossy, gorgeous daydreams, none of them resembling any girl walking the streets. You stop at the newsstands and run your eyes over the models posed on the covers of the magazines hanging like wash from a clothesline and wish you could phone them up.

And what if you've been playing the sexual nomad's game and you suddenly run into a real nomad? If you are fortunate enough to fall in love with some open, wonderful charmer, you might be unfortunate enough to find out that she could care less. Or if she is truly wonderful, she might feel flattered or touched and will be as careful with your feelings as she can. But what can she do if she thinks of you as one more nice place she's stopped off at. She'll sigh and say, "Oh no, I'd hurt you too much. I'm so promiscuous."

Having shaped your self-image to project promiscuity, it's no surprise that you'd step through some barely disguised hole in yourself and fall for someone who really is that way.

What can you do, indeed? Move into the apartment across the street from her? Stalk her? Serenade her from the street below her window? Offer to do her laundry? Take a job as the elevator operator in her building? Hey! Forget about it. You can't do anything.

The French author Stendahl was sort of a true nomad. He went after every girl he liked as if planning an invasion. He wrote out—that's right, *wrote out*—whole complicated strategies. He hid among the bags of flour in the pantry of one married lady and waited for her to sneak down to him there at night. He fell in love with opera stars who wouldn't have him. Most of the time he was happy that way, but eventually even he caved in and longed for his opera star and found no great thrill in being covered with flour days on end just to get a little.

You may learn to kiss as if you're heartbroken and see how many girls notice. There's some satisfaction in others noticing that you are heartbroken without your telling them. It tells you that you're not fooling yourself. If you do meet a girl who is sensitive enough to notice, the smart thing to do is to try and force yourself to fall for her. But if she did notice, it's probably because she's in love with someone else herself. Two people going at it halfheartedly don't stand much of a chance.

I don't think that the nomad's life is for me, after all. And so once more I stand at the mirror in the bathroom in my pajamas, brushing my teeth, preparing for bed. I wonder why things aren't different. The girl I love lives just across the street but she might as well be running wild through the jungles of New Guinea. I realize that if I hadn't met her, things might be different. I wouldn't have lost my momentum at all. I might be Marco Polo.

The answer, somehow, is in the mirror and out the window. The exotic lights of New Jersey pillar the river's banks and stripe its currents. I am what I am. I feel I know the river but it does not know me. I will open a beer, pull a chair up to the window, and sit there for hours, thinking about it. On my way to the refrigerator to open another beer, I will stop at the mirror. I play my stereo loud.

LIVING ALONE AND LIKING IT

The bachelor is the envy of the dead—
his mobile frame improves his chance of fun.
He can't be forced to make his unmade bed,
and he can chase all things beneath the sun.

It should be fun. It really should. It should.
It is. At least, for they the dutiful
who don't insult their youth by acting good
or pausing as they eat the beautiful.

As godly as pornography may be,
though, don't they ever lie down and relax,
or dawdle, convalesce beside the sea
and let the breeze refresh their drenching backs?

And love, that famous fountain overseas,
rococo, vaulting, absolute, and far:
its jets may spray, then drop without reprise—
and that's assuming you could get to where they are.

So dodge things as they come. And be prepared
to see a schoolboy falter as he runs
too near your path, and, in the glance that's shared,
that bolt of doubt that fathers fear in sons.

But yours is island, natives, God, and clime—
all the explorers have forsaken it.
You're free to scratch yourself at any time.
You've made your bed, now lie awake in it.

How To Cohabitate

Cohabitation

"In the beginning we were nothing like we are now. For one thing . . . there really was a man-woman in those days, a being which was half male and half female....Each of these beings was globular in shape, with rounded back and sides, four arms and four legs, and two faces, both the same on a cylindrical neck, and one head, with one face on one side and one on the other, and four ears and two lots of privates, and all the other parts to match. They walked erect as we do ourselves, backward or forward, whichever they pleased, but when they broke into a run they simply stuck their legs straight out and went whirling round and round like a clown turning cartwheels. And since they had eight legs, if you count their arms as well, you can imagine that they went bowling along at a pretty good speed."

—*Aristophanes' speech in* The Symposium

Of the various forms of mating, none has been so widely misunderstood as living together, a phenomenon unique to the advanced industrial nations and to France. Mexicans do not live together. Botswanans do not live together. Two unmarried Indians would no more think of shacking up than of running over a cow. Uruguayans do not live together. Israelis would like to live together, but their mothers won't let them. Chinese would also like to live together, but the government won't let them. Russians live together, but it's only to spy on each other. Only in Western Europe and North America is the practice a common and accepted alternative to marriage, on the one hand, and cheap sex, on the other.

Men and women have sought to assuage their loneliness by sharing it since the dawn of history. Java man, for example, was terrified by lightning; during violent storms he'd scamper over to Java woman and offer to share his half-eaten haunch of mastodon. One thing would lead to another, and pretty soon she'd be picking giant insects out of his hair. The bliss would never last. For one thing, she noticed how bad he smelled and that it did not seem to bother him; in fact, he thought the smell was macho. He never cleaned the walls after he had finished doodling on them. He left mastodon bones all over the cave floor. She liked to take long walks around the savannah. He liked to hang out with his pals and argue about whose was longest. After a few days, she gave him the boot.

Well, Java man was not having any of this. If he could be on top during sex —the missionary position had recently been discovered by a woman with a bad back—he could be on top in all other matters. Imposing his more powerful physical presence, he demanded that early woman clean up and raise his kids. In return, he agreed to give her a bite of the daily catch. The woman agreed, but only under duress. To get even, she began refusing him sex. He started seeing a hairy little cutie from a nearby tribe. Marriage was born.

And there matters remained until the onset of late capitalism, which was inaugurated at a party in Greenwich Village on June 7, 1922. The pressures of living in such a society have led to a disastrously high divorce rate, while the one-night stand, though more common than in previous eras, is less fun now that it can be had for free (the principle behind psychiatry as well). Yet men and women, like the cells of which they are constituted, still felt the need to join. Cohabitation was born.

What, then, is this living arrangement, this purgatory of human relations which is neither here nor there? Even in the United States, where men and women are free to lifestyle as they please, even here confusion reigns when an unmarried pair want to keep their underwear in the same bureau. It is commonly assumed, for instance, that all one needs for cohabitation are a man, a woman, and an apartment. Not so. These might be the ingredients for a raffish little French movie, but they hardly add up to a successful experiment in keeping off the streets, particularly streets on the Upper East Side of New York. Two lives uniting until they break up is a matter of more than gender and real estate.

Cohabitation is, first of all, a matter of marital status. Only a single man and a single woman can do it. (The reader will note a reluctance on my part to discuss gay living arrangements. This is simply because I know so little about them. Those interested in the subject are advised to pick up any issue of the *Village Voice*.) A married man with a single woman is said to be not cohabitating, but *screwing around*. A married woman with a single man is said to be having an *affair*, unless the man is her son, in which case they are having a *complex*. Married men and married women have been known to live together, especially when married to one another. Nevertheless, they are not true cohabitators. Yes, they have fallen in love and decided to spend time together like true cohabitators, but they have also decided to get married. True cohabitators discuss marriage a lot. Sometimes they even manage to convince themselves that living together is a dry run for the real thing. But deep, deep in their hearts they know that they are living together not because they want to get married, but because they are afraid to. Marriage is too big a commitment, and married people, they believe, tie the knot only around each other's throats.

The second requirement is incompatibility. Man and woman should have in common as little as possible in order to guarantee an interesting few years together. People are essentially dramatic animals; without a daily dose of conflict, they shrivel and become Moonies. Disagreements also give the cohabiting couple something to talk about during dinner. The most famous couples in the world have been radically mismatched, two socks of a different color:

Frank Sinatra and Mia Farrow
Simone de Beauvoir and Nelson Algren
Errol Flynn and Tyrone Power
Ernest Borgnine and Ethel Merman
Liza Minnelli and Peter Allen

J. D. Salinger and Joyce Maynard
Howard Hughes and Errol Flynn
Elizabeth Taylor and anybody

It is true, of course, that these couples ultimately split apart on the rocks of incompatibility. But at least they stayed afloat on the Flotsam of Excitement before the Waves of Boredom carried them back to the Desolate Beaches of Singledom, as W. H. Auden once said. In other words, they had a good time.

Political arguments add particular spice to living together. Few conservative men will ever know the thrill, as I have, of setting up housekeeping with a member of the Spartacist League, a neo-Trotskyite group whose favorite activity is coming up with new last lines for that famous chant, "Two, four, six, eight..." As in: "Two, four, six, eight, we don't want no fascist state." Or the lyrical "Two, four, six, eight, Reagan's an invertebrate." Poetry aside, such relationships can never grow dull, for the couple always has plenty of good arguments from which to select: Should one vote Republican or Communist? Does Barry Commoner further the cause of the working class? Is it OK to have sex, even though the Chilean junta is still in power? For a variety of nonpolitical reasons, the Spartacist and I eventually broke up. She subsequently married a member of the party; before you could count to eight, they were divorced ("Two, four, six, eight, now we want to separate"). Their continuing abstention from sex in protest against U.S. imperialist policies in Africa probably contributed to their problems as well.

Couples who do not have politics standing between them can try fighting about cleanliness. An unimpeachable tactic is for the man to leave his underwear and socks on the floor, just like in the days when he was single. Rational discussion of the matter will fill up hours that otherwise would have been spent in fatal harmony. Since men associate well-organized women with the overwhelming presence of their mothers, female cohabitors who rearrange a guy's books by size are also doing their bit to keep the relationship lively.

Marital status and incompatibility: these constitute the ontology, if you will, of cohabitation. Yet the cohabiting couple must fulfill a number of other criteria before they can be said to have fully explored the phenomenon to its outer boundaries. From my own experience I have extracted a number of guidelines that should help see you—two people who love each other, are terrified of marriage, and don't get along—through the areas of greatest turbulence.

The Space

Assuming you are both pressed for cash—in other words, poor—you will be strongly tempted to move into the apartment you already share with a number of similarly poor people known as roommates. Don't do it. If you are male, consider that nothing will disgust a woman more than walking into an apartment decorated by three guys—particularly unemployed history professors—swilling Budweiser and watching the Yankee game, unless it is three guys swilling Budweiser and watching a football game. Remember, also, that regardless of how tidy you guys are, the bathroom is doomed to fall below the standards women require. Moreover, the three guys will always be there, if not physically, then in spirit, in your mind. During loud bouts of lovemaking, you will cup your hand reflexively over her mouth: "Shhh. They'll hear it," you will whisper. This tends to inhibit romance.

A woman who installs her boyfriend in her apartment is also asking for trouble. Nothing will please a man more than the prospect of every evening opening the front door on the scene of three women in sexy nighties swilling Tab and dancing with each other to the music of Billy Joel. Moreover, the three women will always be there, if not physically, then in spirit, in his mind. He will urge you to scream louder, because he really gets off on the idea of having breakfast with three women who respect his sexual prowess.

Once you have accumulated enough of each other's clothing, look for a place of your own. A studio will do in a pinch, though there's something depressing about waking up in the kitchen. Studios also interrupt long-standing television habits. At 11:30 most men get the urge to turn on Johnny Carson. Most women get the urge to sleep, and if not to sleep perchance to dance—anything but television. A larger place will eliminate such squabbles. In a serious negative cash flow process, earphones are the answer.

A one-bedroom is a pleasant size: big enough to offer privacy, small enough not to give you tachycardia on your way to the bathroom. Since one-bedrooms do not grow on trees, especially when they're on very expensive pieces of Manhattan real estate watched over by doormen who instinctively feel that you're not the kind of tenant such a swank property deserves, try a realtor. A realtor does not care what kind of person you are, as long as you give him his cut. You could be Adolf Eichmann. He doesn't care. As a result, you, the two of you, needn't pretend that you are married, only that you can afford the rent.

Realtors do have drawbacks. They will, for example, try to sell you on the virtues of southern exposure. Tell them no, you prefer as little light as possible, or at the very least a western exposure. This will prevent you from seeing each other in the morning the way you truly are. Realtors also will try to palm off on you an apartment w/fplc (with a fireplace). Decline firmly but politely. Even if you and your partner should live together 20 years, you will never light the damn thing. It will simply sit there in the middle of your living room, a black, sooty, useless hole, a constant reminder to the lack of romance in your relationship. Besides, fireplaces warm your front but leave your backside cold, a perfect formula for getting sick.

The apartment should be furnished as sparsely as possible: a bed, a couch, a table, a bureau, a few chairs. The *New York Times Sunday Magazine* will do a feature on your space. You will save money. And you will be spared the grief of haggling over the carpet when you decide to break up.

Last but not least, check the water pressure. Is it strong? Good. One of the chief pleasures of cohabiting is taking showers together; that spot on your back that you could never reach can at last get scrubbed. Pleasure will quickly turn to ashes, however, if instead of being pounded by a waterfall, the two of you are standing in the tub naked as bird pee-pee drips on your heads.

Romance

Living with someone, as opposed to not living with someone, is primarily distinguished by the gradual disappearance of romance from your life. By romance I do not mean sex, though the two are often confused inasmuch as sex also tends to disappear (see next section). I mean rather that warm state of illusion in which everything is surprising and mysterious. This has been dubbed the Casablanca Syndrome (Jung and Wienerschnitzel; Baden-Baden; 1947). The most common symptoms are a belief on the part of the man that the woman is Ingrid Bergman; on the part of the woman that the man is Humphrey Bogart; and on the part of both that they are in Paris before the Germans and Victor Laszlo showed up. All is champagne, intimate nightclubs, gauzy evening gowns, faraway looks, hidden pasts longing to be revealed, lyrical sex scenes.

The Syndrome occurs during the time-frame of early courtship. After the lovers move in together, the reality principle sets in (Lacan and Poulet-Poulet; Filthée-dans-les-Bains; 1960). He discovers that she doesn't just happen to look stunning night after night. She has to *work* at it. She spent hours shopping for that midnight blue dress, hours more deciding whether to wear it or some other fleecy dress in light mauve, hours more after that finding a pair of matching shoes. She in turn starts to realize that the reason he combs his hair so strangely is because he's balding and within a few years will look like E. L. Doctorow or some other distinguished Jewish writer. He spends his spare time not running guns to the rebels in Ethiopia but watching television. His toenails need clipping. Champagne gives him gas. He's really Peter Lorre.

Living with someone is distinguished by the gradual disappearance of romance from your life. This can be slowed if attention is paid to following rules: 1. Perform no bodily function in front of the other. 2. Refuse to meet your mate's parents 3. Eat only certain foods together . . .

Can nothing halt the decline of romance? Nothing, but it can be slowed if attention is paid to the following rules:

1. Perform no bodily function in front of each other. Nos. 1 and 2 are inherently unromantic. In fact, it is best to avoid going to the bathroom when you are living with someone. Did Humphrey Bogart excuse himself to go to the john in *Casablanca*? Did Ingrid Bergman say, "Sam, I have to go to the potty, but when I come back I want you to play it again"? The great poets understood that love and elimination do not mix. Romeo and Juliet never went to the bathroom. Neither did Tristan and Iseult. Nor Heloise and Abelard. If they could hold it in for the sake of romance, so can you.

2. Refuse to meet your mates' parents. No man is Humphrey Bogart to his mother, no woman Ingrid Bergman to her father. The shock of discovering this has scuttled many a cohabitation. A thirty-year-old man arguing with his mother about why he did not finish the broccoli humiliates all parties involved except the mother. Equally embarrassing is a father who pulls a thirty-year-old daughter on his lap to ask, "And how's my little girl?" A boyfriend witness to such a scene may also decide that Oedipal ties run rather too deep for his taste.

3. Eat only certain foods together. Some foods fire mystery, others extinguish it. Among the passion-killers are chili, herring, anything boiled, particularly chicken, anything that can be found in a chef's salad, particularly lettuce, onions, fried brains, mashed potatoes, cauliflower, tuna fish, and all Eastern European foods, which are fine for marriage but not romance. Foods that inspire passion include: hot dogs, grilled steak, White Castle burgers, Veal Zurichoise, fried chicken, lobster, whipped butter, fresh Italian bread, sole almondine, artichokes, asparagus, garlic, zucchini stir-fried with a splash of sesame oil, endives, caviar, cheesecake, all fruit except the obscene kiwi, fresh coffee, chocolate, and, of course, Häagen-Dazs ice cream. You can lose the extra pounds when you break up. While you're together, eat.

Making It

Sex will be a constant source of friction between you. Many are the days you'll wish the Malaysian Basket Trick and the Crouching Tiger Position were still ahead of you, instead of fading memories. Let's face it. Nothing poses a bigger threat to the stability of cohabitation than sexual monotony—a monotony which settles in around the end of the first year and against which constant vigilance must be exerted, lest it lead to marriage.

The problem can be explained arithmetically. Say you are the average New Yorker, male or female. Before you met your true love you had sex with between 0 and 10 people a year. (The statistics exclude Gay Talese, who brings up the average dramatically.) Statistics show that you had sex with each an average of five times before deciding that the human emptiness next to you was polluting your bed. That adds up to between 0 and 50 sexual contacts yearly. At this stage, sex is news. Even when you reach 50, you can call up a friend to tell him, "Hey. I just made it with Heather." "All right, man. Way to go." (Try this only if you are male.)

But now you have moved in with somebody, and the fact of your having sex is no longer news to you or your friends. Here's why: During the first few months you and your mate remain passionately crazy about each other. You make love two, three, sometimes four times a day. In three months that already adds up to 360 contacts. For the next six months it drops to once a day, for another 180 contacts. Three times a week for the next three months, and we arrive at the grand total of 576 contacts a year—and all with the same person. This figure explains both the charm of cohabitation and why the Crouching Tiger Position becomes history.

It would, however, be a grave mistake to call the whole thing off on account of a little boredom. Now is the time to unleash the dormant imagination, to learn new tricks, to boldly go where no man has gone before.

1. *Home Video Equipment*. Take advantage of the wonders of modern technology to enhance your sex life. A Betamax and a camera will run you about $1000, but will offer years of novel experiences. Simply set up the camera on the far side of the bed, turn on the machine, and go to it. Pretend you're Ricky and Lucy, Larry Hagman and Morgan Fairchild, Barbara Walters and Harry Reasoner. Your great moments no longer need fade away on postcoital wisps of cigarette smoke. At your leisure, rerun the tape and critique your performance: a little more of this here, a little more of that there. In addition, should you two get married, you will have a permanent record of your sexual activities to delight and instruct your children. "See, Johnny. You were born right . . . wait . . . right . . . *here*!"

I've also found that intercutting your sex tapes with TV programming results in more interesting viewing. Hardcore shots edited into "Washington Week in Review" serve not only as a metaphor for the governing process, but transform dreary fare into sensuous entertainment. Foreplay shots interspersed with any program on public television will improve it, even if the broadcast is an action-packed thriller like Mahler's Symphony No. 5.

The trick in using the equipment is to be natural. Do not become obsessed with performing for the camera, or you will wind up like a pair of old vaudevillians fighting for the limelight.

"Hey, you're blocking me."

"Well, of all the nerve. Who's the star here anyway?"

2. *Different Places, Different Times*. Sex, regardless how varied in position, will lose its luster if performed regularly in the same place and at the same time. Try 10:37 instead of 10:30. Try it in the spring as well as in the summer. Stop using the bed; try it under a desk, in a closet, or under the bed (but watch out for the dust balls). Do it in the back row during a punk opera, where your noise will blend in. Do it in a car—not a Datsun, or only the Roto-Rooter man will be able to get you out. Japanese alone can have sex in a Datsun, but they don't. They like to spend their spare time at the factory, discussing the most efficient way to humiliate Americans.

3. *Different Folks*. Every once in a while, sex between cohabitors becomes so stale that they refuse to have any. This stage is usually characterized by any of the following lines:

"Are you finished yet?"

"Oh, God. Oh, God. I forgot to wrap the turkey."

"I need some personal space tonight."

At this point, cohabitors may want to decide that the solution is to start having sex with other people. If you choose this course, however, remember that the goal is to improve your sex life together, not to have fun.

You should first try cheating in secret, preferably with someone who is a dull contrast to your steady mate. NYU professors and stockbrokers are apt choices. Start arriving home an hour later. Within days your mate will be consumed by jealousy and will set out to prove that they are just as exciting as on the day you met. When that happens discontinue the dalliance; it has served its purpose. Women squeamish about taking on a new lover can accomplish the same end by hiding their diaphragm case. Men regularly check to see if it is in its usual spot. A bit of bathroom tile instead will send a sure signal to any man that his mate is seeing another. Men can get away with staying faithful, too. They are naturally suspect.

A second possibility is cheating in the open, or swinging. In the time of your parents, this was an activity reserved for married couples. In a movie theater during showings of *Ben-Hur*, one couple—not your parents—would pass a note to another couple asking them over for cocktails and group sex. Today swinging can be initiated without shame everywhere and is a perfectly acceptable alternative for cohabitors. You should, though, avoid places like Plato's Retreat, unless you enjoy watching your mate making it with a politician. Try rather to have group sex with your friends, who appreciate you for what you are and who have always been curious about what you're really like in bed.

4. *Hit Me, You Fool*. There is nothing wrong with tieing up the one you love, as long as you don't slip out for a pack of cigarettes and forget your address. More violent forms of excitement should be avoided, however. Too often, couples decide to try S&M only to discover that they are both M and must call in the doorman for help. Also, whipping tends to be more amusing than being whipped. Sadists seldom wind up in hospitals (except as doctors); masochists often do. Finally, it is well to keep in mind that two people facing each other in leather underwear will crack up hysterically with laughter, rendering sex an improbability.*

That about covers the major problems confronting would-be cohabitors. As long as they are attended to, minor matters like money, his friends/her friends, who gets to go out and buy the Sunday paper will all resolve themselves.

In the war between the sexes, to sum up, cohabitation is a truce. One is free but not lonely; together but not married. Cohabitation is also a force for honesty. Within the walls of their apartment, two people will attempt the great experiment: to exorcise the ghosts that haunt them—the ghosts of their parents, of Hollywood, of women's magazines—and to become, simply, themselves. The experiment fails as often as it succeeds; even then the ghosts have learned their lesson. It is an experiment to be recommended. Singles of the world, unite!

**Sometimes S&M is not funny, as a friend of mind, Pinky Axelrod, discovered. Pinky, excruciatingly shy, never had much luck with women. The moment he'd pick them up, they'd demand to be put right back down. No one quite knew why, until he decided to move in with Jane. On a warm June day, Pinky carried two cardboard boxes filled with his belongings from Soho, where he lived, to the Upper East Side, where Jane lived. She helped him unpack. Lovingly she took out his shirts, his one pair of Levis, his four pairs of Fruit of the Loom, seven pairs of socks, and—hold on here! What's this at the bottom of Pinky's box from Gristede's? It's a ... it's a ... it's a set of HANDCUFFS! And more: a pair of leather underwear, a bottle of Chocolate Mint Lubricant, two feet of chain, a vibrator as big as a club, and oh my God, a whip—a whip long enough to scare the shit out of Jack Palance. Jane looked up at Pinky. He smiled shyly. "Right," Jane said. Before Pinky knew what was happening, his socks, his pants, his shirts, his doo-dads, everything—went flying out the window onto the pavement four stories below. By the time he got there, only his clothes were left. The good stuff, he told me, had disappeared.*

Last Lines:

The Collected Letters To Dear John

Dear John,

While you have been overseas defending freedom, I have fallen in love with someone new and wonderful. He has a bum ankle (that's why he's not in the service) but can he chacha! His name is Ramundo, and your father used to work for his father. He told me how you were probably living it up with all the beautiful girls there in Antarctica, and I just couldn't take being hurt by you anymore.

We are to be married during your next suicide mission (July, didn't you write?), and I will keep all the furniture you bought me as a memento of what once was. If you would like a last chance to give me something to remember what once was by, Ramundo says you should send us a popcorn popper—the kind with the clear top so you can watch the kernels pop.

I saw your mother in town last week and she seemed upset because your younger brother may be shipped overseas (Hawaii, I think she said). She said if I ever write to you, I should send along her regards. I think she meant you but she said Jim and I know there's no Jim in your family.

Forgive me, though I don't know why I'm apologizing when this is all just a natural process. Stay well.

Yours, at one time,
Sally

Dear John,

I look forward to our wedding, I do. It may take longer than we had first calculated, though, since I now think it would be best to wait until you are the last man on earth.

Sincerely,
Janice

Dear John,

Writing this is so painful, very painful, and difficult. I don't like writing this letter at all. It grieves and saddens me. If you only knew how difficult this is. Heartbreaking, for both of us. Oops! Just looked at the clock. Have to run—but I'll write more soon.

Till then,
Nancy

Dear John,

It's been ages, just ages, hasn't it? Things are *super* here. I'm *très* busy, what with the receptions after every one of my friend Carl's concerts. Listen, sweet one, you must tell me something. Did I say I would marry you. I *know* you asked me, I do remember that, I'm not that hopeless! But what did I say? Yes? No? Well, *anyway*, I'm supposed to marry my friend Carl, but I do not, repeat, *do not* want to just rush ahead until I've double-checked with you to make sure I had in fact said no. Did I? Do write. I hope your dog is fine.

XXX,
Marla

P.S. You are the one with the dog, aren't you?

Dear JohN,

How are you? I aM fine. My brother swallowed a bottle cap last night. I can't merry you, I have to go to camp. Plus you have cooties.

CINDY

P.S. I shoud tell you I lied about being fifteen by a couple years.

Dear John,

I have eyes. I see what's going on between you and Lurleen Krieger. I didn't just fall off the turnip truck. What did you think you were doing, calling her up *in my presence* and asking her if she knew your cousin's address in Boston? As if I don't know code when I hear it. I have ears.

I remember that week we were camping in Vermont, just the two of us, and you let slip how you had borrowed one of the quilts from Lurleen. I was ill, I really was. I sneaked off into the woods and was ill.

I've never mentioned her to you in all these months because I was hoping it would blow over. But no. You had to stop by her place with me *waiting in the car* while you did God knows what in the five minutes you were in there. I'm not stupid. It doesn't take five minutes just to return a quilt.

This is good-bye,
Henrietta

Dear John,

It's more your fault than mine but no one is to blame really. You should stop beating around the bush by asking me to marry you and live with you forever and have children with you. I know you want to end it so I will do the noble thing by giving in without your having to ask. I am marrying Hoagie Farnsworth this Saturday. It would be fine with me if you came, but Hoagie says no.

I hope we can still be friends via the mail.

With a kind of love,
Marcia

P.S. Don't answer this letter too fast. I hate owing people letters.

Mrs. Walter King
2022 Cresthill Drive
Colvin, Illinois

Dear John,

~~The funniest thing abou~~
~~Life is so odd when you come t~~
~~Just think, you introduced me to Wal~~
Call my mother and ask her how I am.

Love,
~~Mrs. Walte~~
Joan

Dear John,

I think we were both awfully drunk last night. See you at the club.

Best,
Doug

Dear John,

I knew by your shortness that you weren't a basketball star in school even though you said you were. But now I realize you aren't rich like you said either. My mother saw you going through the trash baskets outside Piggly Wiggly's.

Good-bye,
Sharon

P.S. No, you can't have ten dollars till next week.

Dear John,

There are many beautiful ways to say good-bye forever. This is just one of them.

Love,
Natalie

5

Most of us are not *single parents, but most of us also think that, at one point or another, it might not be such a bad way to go. No pandering to a spouse's ego; no conflicts in "it's-bedtime-lights-out" philosophies; no arguments over how to break it to the kid about birds, bees. Sometimes single can mean simpler, sometimes not. In no area is this line less clearly defined than in the realm of the single parent. Well, you're about to meet one: Eileen O'Malley Walsh.*

SINGLE PARENTING

An Interview

Eileen Walsh is thirty-one, and has worked for seven years as a registered nurse at the Presbyterian University of Pennsylvania Medical Center in Philadelphia. She is a single parent with two children: Nora Walsh, nine, and Peter O'Malley, four. After graduating from nursing school, Eileen married at age twenty, but was widowed while pregnant with her first child. Five years later she had Peter and decided not to stay with Peter's father. She owns her own home in West Philadelphia. Currently she has returned to her mother's home in Long Island, while contemplating a career change.

EILEEN:

I went over to Nora and Peter's school, and the school nurse said, "Oh, you're the little girl who lost her husband." So I said, "Yes, I'm the little girl who lost her husband." She said, "Well, who's this?" I said, "This is my daughter, Nora. She'll be ten in May." She said, "Ten, it couldn't be ten years ago. I remember that wedding as clear as it could be." And she started talking all about my wedding. The only thing she remembered about my existence is that I married some man and he died. And that's it.

She said, "And who's this?" I said, "This is my son." And she said, "Oh! You're remarried!" I said no. She said, "Oh! Oh, I didn't mean to ask such an embarrassing question." I said, "I'm not embarrassed. This is my son Peter." She said, "Oh! Well. Well, their health records have to be in and I hope you'll see to it

I went over to Nora and Peter's school, and the school nurse said, "And who is this?" I said, "This is my son." And she said, "Oh! You're remarried?" I said no.

that they get done." And that was the end of the conversation.

I've never really considered myself a single parent because I've never been alone. I have an incredible network of people; my friend Mary Pat lived with me for a year, and Mary Pat was wonderful because she really helped me a lot. A typical day would be we'd all get up at

6:30 in the morning and take an hour to get dressed. And what I used to do is that I would dress both kids when they were still asleep, because then they couldn't fight me, and it was less aggravation; when they'd wake up completely dressed, it was always a source of amazement for them.

I would get dressed and go downstairs and make Nora's lunch and Pete's. We'd all have a quick breakfast, and then we'd run out the door, jump in the car, and I'd drop both kids at the babysitter's. That was about a quarter to eight, and then I would zoom to the hospital and clock in.

I was nineteen. I got married just because of this one man. He was too hot to let get away. We were married a short time but were together two years altogether.

At noon Tuesdays and Thursdays, I would leave work because I would drive Peter's car pool to nursery school. If I had an emergency, the nursery school would be on the phone: "Eileen, can you come for the car pool? It's 12:20; the kids are supposed to be picked up at noon." I'd say, "I know, but I'm sewing someone's finger back on, so could you wait a minute?" "Oh, sure." And then I'd zoom over and pick up these little cherubs, take Peter back to the babysitter's where Nora would be having lunch, and we'd all kiss and hug—good-bye, Ma—and I'd go back to work.

For a long time I didn't have any time for myself. I'd run to pick up the kids, and I decided this is absurd, I need to have my own hour. So, I managed. Sometimes I'd leave work at four, and I would go swimming, or I'd work out at Nautilus for a while. That was really fun. Or I'd meet a girlfriend for a drink. I really enjoy being single more so than when I was involved with somebody. The only reason I got married was because I knew this man Larry Walsh who I could not live without. If he wasn't around, I didn't want to be attached to anybody. I did not want to have children; I was nineteen years old. I got married just because of this one man. He was too hot to let get away. With my husband, we were married for such a short time, but we were together two years altogether. But somehow, to think that one or the other has to be the boss (which isn't true now, but it was then), or to think that one person has to take some sort of responsibility in keeping the home because the other is the breadwinner —even though you're both working —that was really a weird concept.

Yet it continued when I lived with Peter's father. I ran the home, and his only job was to bring home money. And that's how he saw it. I was working, too. But he took no interest in my home; he couldn't care less about the home, whereas my home was my castle, my palace and my paradise, and I wanted a home in a particular fashion to raise my children. They weren't—well, one of them was his child, come to think of it. But it didn't work out that way. They were my children and my home, and I prepared the food, and I did the washing, because I liked doing it. I liked how I did it. He didn't do anything.

That's what happened to the relationship; he just didn't feel like he belonged there at all. He didn't make his wants known, and I didn't involve him. So when he left, I was really glad. Because I had my own structure and my own world and I ran my life the way I wanted to run it. I don't know if I could frankly get along with any one man, some man who wanted to come in and share my home and my children; I don't know.

I like having my children and not sharing them with anybody. If they turn out good or bad, they're mine. People say the joy is so much greater and the sorrow is lessened when you share it. Well, I don't want to share it. They're mine. I am *it* as far as they're concerned. Even though my nails are broken, and I've got a pimple, and my hair is turning gray, and I look awful, and I'm feeling lousy—my children think I'm beautiful. They think I can sing, because I sing to them at night to put them to sleep. They like my jokes. And when I'm away from them, they miss me. Nobody can replace me in their eyes. And I like that; that's really really important to me; that's really neat.

This summer, my kids and I traveled. We just got in the car and we went, and I didn't have to tell anybody where I was going, or explain why, or how much money I was going to spend, or who I was going to spend my time with. Nobody's business but mine. I really like that. I like owning my own home. And if I want to put up a wall or take down a wall, it's my prerogative to do so. I like that feeling of strength. And when the pipes are broken, I have pliers. I know how to fix that stuff. My car breaks down, I know how to fix it. Anything like that—I do my own income tax return. I just don't mind at all being as independent and as free as I am. The part that I miss is that I don't like sleeping alone at night.

Unless I find that perfection again, I'm not getting married. There's no reason for me to. I suffer from loneliness, but I don't think that it's anything that any other human being doesn't suffer from. That's why humans are so motivated to create and to use up their time, to entertain themselves. And then every once in a while, the loneliness crops up anyway, and it does become overwhelming. So, what do you do? You go to a therapist or something, and you cry a little, and then it gets pushed back down again. And you continue. So I don't think I'm so unusual.

I have a friend right now in Connecticut, and every once in a while I just take off, and I go to Connecticut for the weekend. And it's very pleasant. He treats me very well: he cooks dinner for me and takes me to a show, and we just have a very good time, and then I say thanks a lot and I leave. And I don't ever have to talk to him again if I don't feel like it.

Lots of times I feel—I'm a mother. Even people in the neighborhood call me Mom. But when I do something like that, I feel very much the vamp. I feel very womanly . . . a woman with a past . . . it just gives me a little kick somehow, a little thrill to feel like, well, you're not just a nursing mother with your wet blouses from all your milk all the time,

It gives me a little thrill to feel like, well, you're not just a nursing mother . . . but that I've got legs . . . and I could be a Playboy centerfold

but that I've got legs, and I look great in high heels, and I could be a *Playboy* centerfold if I felt like it. I don't have to because I know that I am good-looking and attractive and I can turn somebody on just with a wink. That somehow still makes me feel vital to myself, not just "Mommy I need you" kind of thing, or "Sister, I need you," or "Daughter, I need you," but "Hey, Honey, I *need* you." And that makes me feel good.

6

Good health is important among singles, who do not, no matter what you've seen in the press lately, carry virulent diseases brought on ourselves by uncleanliness. We're as clean as anybody. We wash our hands. And sanitized? Nobody beats us for sanitized. The recent terror concerning certain herpetic strains was clearly a wily plot conceived by the KGB to undermine the single morale of our most vital and productive social group.

Nevertheless, let's be careful! The first piece in this section on single diseases, "Tissues and Answers" is to reassure even the least virulent among us.

Next up: "I Have Herpes Simplex," by Mr. X—a sobriquet—is a confessional with a thrust. It is not pretty, nor fun: just a telling of the real by a man waiting for a cure.

SINGLE DISEASES

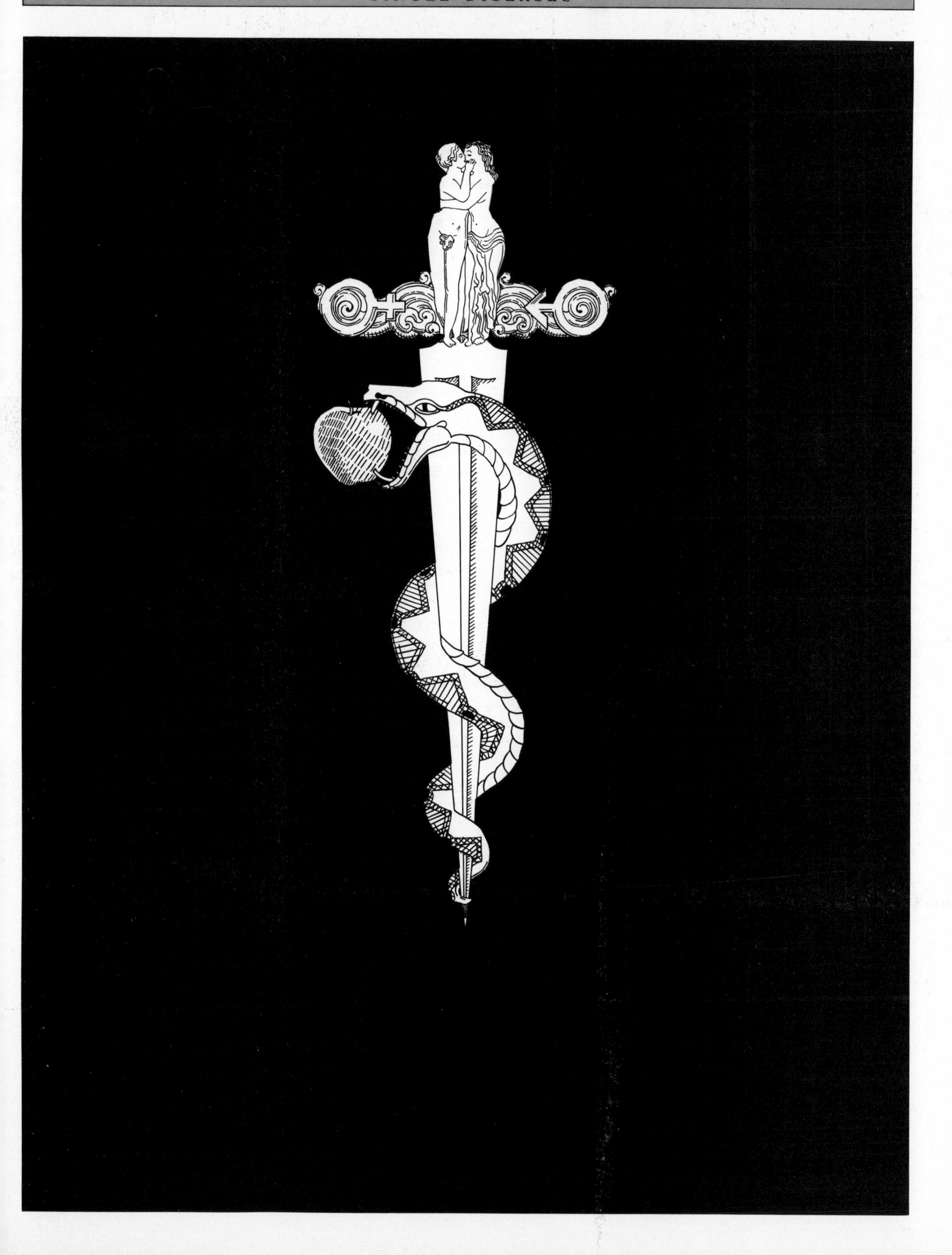

Tissues

The data has quietly accumulated, for years, and now some conclusions seem inescapable. Ever since Ike left office, the number of Americans living alone has been steadily climbing. Throughout that period, the U.S. cancer rate has risen at more or less the same pace.

Coincidence? Perhaps. But perhaps not.

Doctors are puzzled by these trends, and troubled by their implications. Does the single state cause cancer? At medical conventions and hotel bars—the distinction is often a fine one—this question has sparked fierce debates lasting several minutes before yielding to discussions of heart disease and whether Jack Nicklaus is really washed up. At last, a consensus has emerged:

Researchers can find no evidence that being single causes any special diseases. The converse, though, is not necessarily true. A great many diseases are virtually guaranteed to keep you single. Leprosy, herpes, and whatever it was that the Elephant Man had leap immediately to mind. But: another matter, another book.

Nevertheless, statistics have shown that singles have a higher than expected death rate. What can this mean? One explanation is that single patients experience an illness more acutely than others. They just don't do as well without someone to bring them ginger ale and coo, "Goodness, your pajamas are soaked! Let me get you another set." In contrast, enduring an illness alone is a grim affair that can erode the will to live. Sometimes, a bad case of hay fever is enough to make a single patient want to throw in the towel.

Physicians do not completely understand this phenomenon. Their work has been slowed by penny-pinchers in the Reagan Administration, and the discomfort of doctors induced by any work involving perspiration.

In the meantime, though, single people around the country have become understandably anxious. They want to know whether smoking low-tar cigarettes is safe. (No.) They want to know whether cocaine is dangerous. (Yes.) They want to know what we think of that little mole below the left shoulder blade. (Hmm...)

To relieve this fear of the unknown, and replace it with a well-informed terror, we studied just what single people want to know about their bodies and those of others. We devised a questionnaire encouraging them to voice their anxieties, to raise the issues they refuse to bring up with their doctors in person.

The response was gratifying, to say the least. At noon on May 15, 1982, we mailed out 2,500 forms. Within 45 minutes, we had 8,579 completed questionnaires. By the next day, we had been forced to move our offices, unlist our phone number, and adopt disguises to avoid harrassment in the street.

We carefully analyzed those forms that had been filled out by people we know, and quickly thumbed through the rest. Almost immediately, the study revealed a shocking void in knowledge: we could hardly answer any of their questions.

So we did our homework. We went to the library. We consulted several specialists and some of the most attractive social workers in the Harvard hospital system. And here we present the most common questions that we received, along with our answers—the very same answers that we would give you in our offices after looking at you naked.

All of the medical information is true, and the studies described are real. It is with a sense of grave responsibility and imminent unemployment that we release this data to the single public.

and Answers

Q. I am a single woman who lives alone. Ever since I hung a poster of Burt Reynolds in my bedroom, I have experienced a great deal of difficulty in getting to sleep. Every time I *do* get to sleep, I have a dream in which I am the only person on a train leaving a destroyed city. The countryside is empty, save for the ruins of burned farmhouses. I enter a white hotel, and my doctor is Burt Reynolds. He sets my hair on fire. What is going on here?

—S. G., Cleveland, Ohio

A. Many of our patients ask us for help in their quest for sleep, and appropriately so. Sleep is one of the most wonderful things that can happen to you. It is your body's time to rest, your mind's chance to dream, and your throat's opportunity to make small snorting noises.

Scientists believe that humans developed sleep eons ago, before Johnny Carson was even born. It was one of the few inventions that Marco Polo brought from Europe to China instead of the other way around. Due to overcrowding, the Chinese refined sleep into "sleeping together," which may have made matters worse. An ocean away were the Americans, who adapted sleep to their mobile culture, and developed the concept of "sleeping around." But those are other stories for other books.

Despite this long history, physicians only recently began to study the mechanisms of sleep. With the use of EEGs (not to be confused with EKGs or EGGs), they learned that we all go through five stages of sleep several times a night. The most crucial phase is the fifth, Rapid Eye Movement or REM sleep, during which the eyes shift from side to side in their sockets. If a patient is awakened during REM sleep, he will usually say that he is in the middle of a dream, while if he is awakened during other phases, he will merely be very angry.

Researchers have conducted experiments in which they repeatedly woke "volunteers" just as they reached REM sleep. These subjects were allowed to get eight hours of non-REM sleep per night, but the REM deficit took its toll, as they became irritable, fatigued, and even hallucinatory. Through such work, scientists came to believe that REM sleep is essential to the integration of information into our memories—in other words, learning itself.

There's obviously much more to the learning process than sleeping—otherwise President Reagan would be a genius by now. Still, this data has frightening implications for medical education when one considers how physicians live during the most important year of their training: internship.

The problem you present is different. You can't even get to Phase I, let alone REM sleep. You are one of those unfortunate folks who are forced to embrace alcohol, drugs, or, even worse, "Don Kirshner's Rock Concert." Too bad. Research in this field is still primitive, but you may have a defect in your sleep mechanism, the complex interaction between brain tissues and chemical messengers in the spinal fluid that bathes the brain to get out that ground-in dirt.

To put it in simple layman's terms, the brain cells responsible for stages one through four of sleep are located in the medial tegmentum of the medulla, pons, and lower midbrain, with projections to the hypothalamus and thalamus. In contrast, the cells that drive REM sleep lie in the lateral tegmentum of the pons, the locus ceruleus, the substantia nigra, and the hypothalamus. Stimulation of these critical sleep centers causes release of a hormone called Factor S, which seems to induce sleep. In everyone but you, that is.

Scientists hope that one day Factor S can be synthesized and lead to a safe, reliable sleep-inducer. Others say that it already has been mass-produced, and that it is the secret ingredient in Gardol. We don't know, and can only advise renewing your subscription to the *Journal of the American Medical Association*. It is the most potent sleep inducer we know—far more effective than alcohol, and a lot less fattening.

Q. I live by myself. I have been alone since the age of sixteen, when my parents went out to do the laundry and never came back. I remember that when I asked my mother why she was washing the suitcases, she began laughing, and stuck her chewing gum in my hair as she walked out the door. In the eighteen years since my gerbil escaped, I have been the only living thing in my dingy apartment. I didn't particularly mind being single until I recently read that people who live in isolation have poorer health. Is this true, and what can I do about it? Emotional scruples prevent me from considering any plan that violates Hegel's postulate that reason is the conscious certainty of all reality.

—D. B., Eugene, Ore.

A. Yes, it is true that people who live without strong social bonds tend to die sooner. Paradoxically, compared to those who are the center of large and happy families, it usually takes longer to get them buried. These conclusions are derived from years of research, including a recent study of 2,754 adults in Tecumseh, Michigan. This data showed that socially isolated people have *double* the normal death rate. Our guess is that the risk on the East Side of New York is several orders of magnitude higher.

Why is this? Some theorize that anxiety contributes to a much higher incidence of cancer and heart disease among singles—yet another reason for singles to feel a little jumpy. Others speculate that poor health is why those living alone tend to stay alone, a theory that gets no arguments from anyone who has ever been to a movie with a date with a runny nose. Since singles may be more ill to begin with, their higher death rate cannot be considered a surprise, or, for that matter, much of a disappointment.

Interestingly, the data has shown that almost any social contact reduces the risk of death—"social contact" being defined as marriage, friendships, religious affiliations, or informal clubs like the American Automobile Association. The important point is that people benefit from *any* kind of social intercourse.

Thus we advise our patients to throw themselves into life as the surest way of dragging out their own. We tell them to go ahead and answer chain letters, join cults, or, better yet, start their own. They can find fellowship in organizations like church choirs, political clubs, and paramilitary groups, and we encourage them to take it. If all these measures fail to improve their sense of well-being, they should consider giving up drinking and smoking.

Q. I don't get it. I recently turned thirty. I just got my PhD in Interpersonal Communication. My thesis is being published as a book, *You Can't Hurry Love*. I'm finally getting a little hair on my chest, and am able to grow a modest beard. My apartment has a jacuzzi and a Cuisinart. My life should suddenly be coming together, but now I find that I'm going bald. What's the story?

—R. T., Santa Cruz, Calif.

A. No mystery here. One of the paradoxes of nature is that the same hormonal changes that make hair fall from your head also cause a sudden sprouting all over the rest of the skin. This irony represents one of your body's insider jokes, and we encourage you to laugh along as if you get it, too.

Actually, if you look closely with the aid of a microscope, your entire body is covered with a thin fine growth called vellus hair, except on your palms and soles. This growth makes you a mammal, and serves as your evolutionary link with primates and professional athletes. We ignore these hairs, because we cannot see them, and because the very notion of their existence makes most Americans mildly ill, unless they are Italian, in which case they are aroused.

The hair on your scalp is qualitatively different, however. Dermatologists call these fibers "terminal hair," and not just because they are at one end of the body. The fact is, once one falls out, it doesn't grow back. You are issued about 100,000 of them by the time of puberty, and what happens after that is your own fault.

Endocrinologists have found that your chances of losing your hair are determined by several factors, among them, your age, your genetic background, the way your body metabolizes testosterone, and how often you think impure thoughts. Subtle changes in the ratio of the breakdown products of testosterone are what make your chest suddenly fertile ground for hair growth, while your scalp comes to resemble the dark side of the moon.

Most men lose half the hair in a region before they even realize that their hair is thinning, and then begin to search desperately for a cure. Magazines are full of ads for plans that involve implanting synthetic fibers into the scalp. Most doctors feel this approach should be discouraged. One reason is the considerable risk of infection from a foreign body in the skin. Even more compelling is our distaste for anything resembling double-knit.

Some patients resort to transplants of their hair from other parts of their scalp to their bald spots, an expensive and painful procedure that nevertheless has the distinction of working. Others have tried smearing various hormonal creams on their scalps—a tactic that has never been proven effective, and can attract packs of dogs in the street.

Few are desperate enough to resort to the simplest surgical procedure that stops baldness: castration. Cutting off testosterone at its source leaves you with a head of hair as full and lush as, well, a young boy. And all the opportunities of one as well.

Q. I'm a thirty-two-year-old dealer in computer software, whatever that means. I spend a lot of time in my bathtub. The other night I was soaking there, thinking about that movie where Marilyn Monroe got her big toe stuck in the faucet and had to call for help even though she was naked and all. After about an hour, I noticed that my fingertips were getting wrinkled. Why does this happen? Will other parts of me wrinkle, perhaps permanently, if I stay in too long?

—M.B., Lexington, Mass.

A. We have been studying this same phenomenon since the age of eight. Until recently, our conclusion was that it was just one of those things. After all, God didn't want us to understand all the ways in which He works. Wasn't it enough that He made us permanent press?

But in the tradition of Galileo and other heretics, some researchers have pressed on. Two schools of thought emerged on this subject. One was that the skin was expanding. The other—which still has its proponents—was that the body was shrinking. Resolution of the question was delayed because most investigators lost interest in the issue five minutes after leaving their baths.

Now, however, it seems clear that the skin is indeed expanding. The fingertips have a special layer of skin called the *stratum corneum*—ordinarily among the driest tissues in the body. This sandpaperlike skin evolved to enable us to perform fine tasks like picking locks and putting in contact lenses. When soaked, the stratum corneum expands, forcing the skin into folds. The net effect is an appearance resembling that disgusting little patch of skin on the back of your elbow seen when you straighten your arm. The process can be prevented by the simple precaution of wearing rubber gloves at all times.

As for the rest of the body, there is probably little need to worry. Dermatologists say that there are no tissues that will expand when wet like the stratum corneum outside the fingertips. Nevertheless, they admit that they too get a little nervous when their fingers crease up, and immediately jump out of the tub. As they see it, there's no sense in taking any chances.

Q. I am a thirty-one-year-old divorced mother, living with my little three-year-old, Orelia. After my marriage broke up, I went back to school, and since then, I've been drinking more and more of my favorite diet cola. One reason is that it helps me stay awake. Another is that if I don't drink it all in the same day, the cola tends to eat its way through the sides of those plastic two-liter bottles.

I'm not concerned about the dangers of the soft drink for myself. Since I started drinking it on a diet, I don't notice that funny taste anymore, and I've

lost 80 pounds—down from a plump 140. And there haven't really been any side effects other than the prolonged nose bleeds and occasional blackout spells familiar to all diet cola addicts.

But the reason I'm writing is that now my little girl wants to drink it "just like Mommy." Is it safe? Should I be worried?

—R.L., Seattle, Wash.

A. We believe that the entire medical community is behind us in urging you to let the child drink all the diet cola she wants. There is really no good evidence at this point that diet sodas can cause any serious illnesses, except maybe cancer. Besides, you and Orelia may help resolve one of the most hotly debated controversies in medicine today —whether a child will continue to grow if allowed to touch the stuff. We are betting that she will, and are willing to give odds.*

We feel that the dangers of synthetic foods have been vastly overplayed. We lived off such foods throughout medical school, because they were the only nutrition available in the hospital vending machines. We almost starved during the 1974 oil shortage, when many of our favorite items became mysteriously scarce.

Actually, food additives and other synthetic edibles have been much more rigorously tested by the Food and Drug Administration than any of the so-called "natural" foods. Do you really think an apple a day can keep us away? And when you drink a glass of water, do you have any idea where it has been?

So let Orelia have all the diet cola she wants. And with it, we advise serving "cream"-filled cupcakes. But first break them apart and throw the cake part away. It may have flour in it.

Q. My boyfriend is very, very fat. He is wider than the Four Tops, and when he eats, he looks like Siamese twins joined at the lips. Recently, he fell down the stairs, and didn't realize it until I told him. I've tried to help him lose weight by counting calories, fad diets, exercise, and dangerous drugs, but nothing has worked. What can I do?

—K.L., Media, Pa.

A. Unfortunately, there are no magical ways to lose weight. Exercise can help, as can dangerous drugs, but there is simply no substitute for the mental commitment to limit daily food intake. We know how difficult such commitments can be, for food has pleasant associations for all of us. It not only tastes great, it summons sensations of being loved, of maternal warmth, of happy family events like the time the dog grabbed the chicken right off Grandpa's plate, giving him his first heart attack.

You must reverse such associations for your boyfriend. Once you have got him by his mind, his fat is sure to follow. There are many ways of dwelling on his fatness, but remember, you must be incessant and consistent.

A few tips: Reassure him that as long as he is fat, he has no other good qualities. If he comes to you concerned about personal problems unrelated to his weight, laugh at him. Use dinner dates to instill a sense of purpose. Bring along a scale, and make a little game out of weighing him before and after the meal. Announce the results to others in the restaurant. Ask the waiter to put two plates at his setting, and order him his own turkey at Thanksgiving. Act surprised and roll your eyes when he says he doesn't want dessert. Wink at the waiter, and say that he should leave a piece of pie for your boyfriend on the side. Make a bet on how long it lasts there. Pretend you don't notice when he walks out. He'll thank you later.

Q. I am a thirty-six-year-old martial arts instructor, and I am really steamed! Today, I was at the doctor's office getting some cuts on my knuckles sewn up plus my tetanus shot. The bastard told me that he knew why I didn't have any friends. He said that I had Gilles de la Tourette syndrome, and that was why I kept getting in fights! I told the son of a bitch that no one calls me a fairy, and stomped out of his goddamned office! Just what the hell was that jerk talking about?

—A.B., Buffalo, N.Y.

A. Thank you for your letter. Our response was delayed by some difficulty in pasting it together. You seemed to have torn the paper in several places while dotting i's and making exclamation points, sir.

It seems that you *do* have Gilles de la Tourette disease, a rare neurological disorder characterized by sudden uncontrolled outbursts of profanity called coprolalia—literally, stool in the mouth. Its victims are also prone to facial twitching and obsessional ideas, some magnificent, some not.

This disease may explain why you yelled those things at Mother Theresa on her world tour last year, just as it explains much of Teddy Roosevelt's foreign policy. Today, it can be effectively treated with a drug called haloperidol, but if you begin taking medicine for your condition, we advise you to keep it a secret. Why not enjoy the luxury of being able to say whatever you want as long as you can?

Q. I am starting to get a little anxious about being single. My mother used to warn me about strange waitresses; now she introduces me to them. My computer-dating agency has retired my number. I have begun sweating heavily during "Ozzie and Harriet" reruns. I am so nervous about going home alone that I have started to eat slowly at my favorite fast-food restaurant. Can you offer me some medical advice on how to relax? Do you think meditation will help? Also, send any pills you have lying around.

—D.C., Tucson, Ariz.

A. First, we'd like to say unequivocally that pills are not the answer. Granted, they're a pretty good way of stalling for time, but they don't solve any problems. They can be both psychologically and physically addicting, and are responsible for destroying many fine American families. Besides, the government has warned us that it doesn't want us sending them through the mail anymore.

Nevertheless, we are sympathetic to your plight, as many of our single patients have come to us with similar complaints. They cannot relax. They are obsessed by the possibility that if they should fall in the tub, no one would know until the bank foreclosed the mortgage. Eventually, some resort to tactics like calling home before leaving work so there is at least one message on the answering machine that evening. Others waste their money on the records for loners, advertised on UHF TV, with rewritten classics like "I've Got Me Under My Skin," "I Do Something to Me," "Embraceable Me," and "I Can't Hurry Love."

For them and for you, meditation may be helpful. Researchers are only now beginning to understand how this calming technique works. Apparently, it

**5 to 4.*

affects the patterns of electrical activity in the cortex of the brain. For example, meditation decreases the amount of beta waves—the rapid electrical activity that predominates during waking intellectual activity. On the other hand, it increases alpha waves—the slower frequency activity that normally occurs during sleep or while watching golf on television.

This increased alpha activity is associated with the physical characteristics of light sleep: lower blood pressure, muscle relaxation, and a sense of drifting tranquillity. It's not as good as taking drugs, but it may be the next best thing. Not surprisingly, meditation has been shown to help chronic hypertension, normalize irregular heart rhythms, and dramatically improve your tax bracket if you can grow a beard and talk with an Indian accent.

How can you learn to meditate? There are several courses available at varying expense, some with religious overtones, many of which require active duty at airports. The core of their teaching is that you must concentrate all your attention on a word or concept, sometimes called a mantra. Ordinarily these mantras are closely guarded secrets, but our suspicion is that this policy is merely designed to increase enrollment in meditation courses. Thus we don't mind if you use one of these secondhand mantras bequeathed to us by former patients. The next time you feel anxious, just try murmuring one of these over and over:

1. Toy Boat.
2. Unique, New York.
3. Red Leather, Yellow Leather.
4. There is someone in the basement.
5. This mole is probably benign.
6. Floss your teeth.

If these fail, we recommend biting your nails.

Q. I'm a thirty-year-old journalist. I've had a lot of medical problems in the past, but my doctors have been so incompetent that they've been unable to come up with a diagnosis. They're so bad, I've never bothered to go back to the same one twice. It's a miracle that I'm still here.

The reason I'm writing now is that for the last three days, I've had a fever, muscle aches, a runny nose, and a cough. My girlfriend has the same thing. Could this be cancer?

—S.K., Los Angeles, Calif.

A. It could be, but there's also a chance that what you have is a cold, a common illness due to one of the many viruses placed on earth by God for fun. If your disease *is* a cold, it will clear on its own over several days, during which your closest friends will understandably avoid you. There's not much medicine can do to speed your recovery. (We can slow it down, but that costs extra.) The trick is getting through that mandatory period of misery without doing anything foolish like making out a will leaving everything to your housekeeper, just because she brought you aspirin.

A few words of advice are nevertheless in order. There's not much point in staying home alone and feeling sorry for yourself, as gratifying as that can often be. You might as well go to work, even if only for a few hours, and make other people feel sorry for you. When you're sick, and everyone knows it, you can get away with the most incredible things. You can lash out at friend and foe alike, and then hold your forehead, mumbling, "I'm sorry. I'm just not feeling very well." And they will forgive you. It's great.

The main danger lies in forgetting your tissues, forcing you to resort to those paper towels in the lavatories—the ones with wood chips added for extra absorptive power. Several of our patients have required skin grafts to their upper lips after such errors. We recommend that if you are caught short in this fashion, make a lot of disgusting noises while pretending to breathe. Your co-workers will almost surely go out to find some tissues for you. Some may even return.

Q. I'm a magazine editor in his fifties who has everything except a casino. Still, I find that I feel vulnerable and lonely. To me, the worst thing that could happen, the fate I fear most, is dying in my sleep and being found several days after the fact. I've gone to extraordinary lengths to avoid such an event since the breakup of my marriage. At the Mansion, we have parties around the clock. I sleep with beautiful women every night, sometimes two or three at once. I publish a well-known magazine to celebrate my lifestyle, and to help me meet girls. Few know that the women I choose are selected not for their beauty, but for their expertise in cardiopulmonary resuscitation and willingness to stay up all night watching me breathe. It's not pretty.

I guess I'm kind of afraid of sudden death, or maybe just of being alone. Is something wrong with me?

—name and address withheld by request
Los Angeles, Calif.

A. Not at all, Mr. Hefner. The fear of dying unexpectedly and alone is normal in a man on his own, as is the desire to sleep with twins that you have raised in previous letters. The prospect of sudden death reminds all of us of how many of our worldly affairs are unsettled, how many personal debts are unmet, and how many close friends will never know how much they were appreciated.

It also reminds us that we had better throw away those dirty magazines and clean out the medicine cabinet. Such thoughts can dominate your life. Many of our patients have described a recurring nightmare in which, after their deaths, their mothers sift through their belongings for mementos. She weeps softly as she combs every square inch of the apartment, including behind the bookcases. She seems somehow smaller and older. Her nightmare has come true, and she is outliving her child. Almost inaudibly, she murmurs her child's name over and over. Suddenly, she inhales sharply, straightens, and snaps, "What's *this*?"

At this point, the dreamer usually gives up any desire to come back from the dead.

What to do? Well, here are the facts: About 400,000 Americans are victims of sudden cardiac death every year. Most either have symptoms of heart disease, such as episodes of chest pain, or the so-called "risk factors" for coronary artery disease, such as high blood pressure, smoking, diabetes, and a family history of heart trouble. Thus, few deaths are truly unexpected. There's not much you can do about a family tendency toward heart disease, but you *can* control some of the other risk factors, and you could start by rubbing out that cigarette. Now.

Beyond that, we tell our patients to make lots of dinner engagements with responsible friends. That way the newspapers will quote them saying things like "We got worried about him when he was a half-hour overdue at the restaurant. He's never late."

Instead of some neighbor you hardly knew saying, "We've been smelling something terrible in the hall for days."

Finally, invest in some pets; we suggest fish and birds. If you have to go, you may as well take someone with you.

I Have Herpes Simplex

By Mr. "X"

As a six-year-old I waited with the other first-graders in a line on the sagging wooden floors of the classroom for the polio vaccine. It was an oddly delicious moment: a crimped white wax paper cup and a bright red sugar cube, taken in the company of other children—and so all my tangled fears of needles and knives and sharp implements of health dissolved in a sweet grateful crunch.

Back then, my mother tells me now, in that way she has of giving me the straight poop now that I'm old enough to understand, polio generated hysteria. My mom was pregnant then, and feared to walk outside. And when she saw suspicious characters coming from the other way, she had crossed the street.

The baby my mother had that time is now a grown woman, my sister, and herself steps to the other side of the street on account of disease. In her case the phobia is herpes—should I say *HERPES!!*? —and the stepping across the street is the questioning she undertakes with would-be lovers. My sister is a robust, full-blooded girl—she's got va-va-va-voom—and so I can't help chuckling to imagine her with all her clothes on and her legs tucked under her, sitting on her bed and mistrustfully eyeing the palpitating youth who is thwarted. He has got red apple cheeks and clear eyes, but in the vision, he cannot convince my sharp-eyed sister.

That scene has an emotional impact for me because I failed to conduct bedside interludes. How can you reconcile such application procedures with hot-blooded Passion? *I tore at my clothes as the mattress sank with the weight of her naked body, etc.* And so, you see, I've sipped for a second time at my generation's crimped white cup and vermilion cube. Many others have tilted it to their lips, too. No, it doesn't inoculate you *against* something. But with it: I've got herpes.

That is one thing right off about herpes: you become part of a vast silent community and in ways are made to feel special about it. Really. I am not talking about the sad long faces visible in photos of the herpes self-help groups. No, no. More like this: a heavy steel door has swung closed behind you, *clank* like in prison movies, and you are in. You can listen to the mournful sound of the door echoing, or you can take a look at the others who have come alongside to take your coat and welcome you. They will tell you of all the good people you have known and would never have imagined in a million years, etc., but who also have herpes. It is a collegiality—like the masons, like academic hoods, like Mensa (!).

I was taken by this treatment, especially finding out about certain friends of mine. I came to think that we were an elect, that other qualities must unite us besides just the disease: an elect of risktakers, and more than that, risktakers who had been let in on a deep emotional secret.

It was a happy way to think of it. Again, I picture my Mom's street, populated with its fears of infectious disease. On the one side were all of us sufferers. And on the other side were people like my sister, her sensuality withering on the vine. Or my lughead friend. He talked to me on the phone about a woman he had gone out with for four weeks and just a kiss on the cheek in all that time, so that he *knew* she had herpes. He spent the night with her but had not even touched her, he bragged. "I was wearing armor," he laughed. Ha ha. I felt closer to the girl than to him, though I had never met her. I half expected him to launch into a tirade about promiscuity. That girl and I have been on both sides of the street, I wanted to tell him. If we had pain, well, we had a widened vision, too.

Oh, I am not saying that any of us with herpes would not get rid of it at once, happily. What I'm talking about is how an epidemic enters society. It is something secret, a touch in the night, and touching millions. Everyone is made different for it, some widened. In Edgar Allan Poe's story "The Masque of the Red Death," those who don't have it bolt the doors of a castle and party endlessly, till the end comes for them, too. Just so, I imagine my sister and my lughead friend peering fearfully over the edges of their beds at night. No way to live. (I love my sister and all, but sometimes you've got to take off the kid gloves, especially when you're writing *anonymously*.)

The hysteria goes deepest on the other side of the street. My friend and my sister have become advocates of celibacy, and a little paranoid—moving among them are preachers, haters of sex, and *Time* magazine with its talk of the dan-

We were on her parents' bathroom floor, while a couple of sheetrock widths away, her parents were having cocktails and sourly discussing the new boy.

Weeks later I got the word in a telephone booth. The way she blurted it out—it was staggering. It was as if three gentlemen in black tie had come in my door in the middle of the night and dragged me by my legs out of bed, the way some secret societies at Ivy League schools inform their new members of the honor. There was nothing really funny about it, though when I think of the scene on the bathroom floor, I can't help but think of an exploding cigar.

gers of oral sex. Or, as Groucho Marx once said, "Booga! Booga! Booga!" No doubt others will soon seize the moment to declaim against certain institutions, races, hangouts: against abortion and cohabitation, against "dandies, clerks and students," and "vari-colored demoiselles," as a syphilis pamphleteer put it nearly 135 years ago. Someone back in school says that in the dining halls herpes is all anyone talks about (and in the bedrooms?). "The Pope's best friend," he says.

When the secret touch comes in the night, everybody gets the heebie jeebies. Vision narrows to a squint.

So, I tell myself, it is we, the herpes sufferers, who have the advantage, we who have felt that sweet and grateful crunch, inoculated against worse things. My girlfriend—I'll get to the mechanics and romantics of the transmission of the disease in a minute—likes to say that it is a personal secret binding us together. And though herpes has a notoriety, bandied about on the other side of the street, for destroying couples, it also confers on the bearer a badge of courage worn away from embattled times. It's the response of the sensitive, in this view, and one of life's painful deepeners.

Like all sufferers, I have a home in the past. Seeking the roots of my disease, I churn up rows of memory and fork apart caked clods of old episodes. If herpes can be a gift of vision, well, I still don't know *who* made it to me.

At the time I got it I was engaged in what the hysterics might call a fit of promiscuity—which sounds about as stimulating as St. Vitus's Dance. When I look back on those lovers it's with a fresh eye; the disease's eye. Just what, after all, was their *depth* of motivation?

The sodden old lover of mine in the midwest, who had grown even more heavylidded; years before she had waited days before telling me she had no birth control—maybe her nostalgia for me last summer was tinged with contempt. The actress my sister fixed me up with had me going in a number of ways—I thought I was being cruel to her, but now I hear she is gay. What else didn't she tell me? And then an old steady tells me that a sore has been showing up for years on her lower back, a site for genital herpes. Did it and I show up at the same time, I wonder? And did she want me to do anything unorthodox with the base of her spine?

The past can be very rich.

I would be more acid about this, and more vengeful, if I didn't know that women can shed the virus without even knowing it. Besides, these are not women on whom I ever had the right to make demands—the new morality, remember! "Live by the sword, die by the sword," as the old moralists are chuckling happily. Even so, it is more fun to dig up the past with the archaeologist's eye, and speculate on the liaisons and lies by which the little red blossom was passed around. There may be a collegiality to the family of herpes victims, but it's obvious that there would not be so much of it if people were more honest. Like the Moonies, a little deception is always there at the inception.

So I wonder again about the sodden one, a pretty blonde, her face getting too fleshy: Was that why she looked so sullen after? And why she did not want to see me two days later? Worst of all, I doubt the girlfriend I had been *living* with for so long. There's enough emotional wreckage to pick through as it is, but how can I help but think that she was cavorting even while we were keeping house? Did she gambol in the lilies while I sat home reading, and bring a black flower back for me?

On it goes, kissing, lying. The evidence is never very good.

I spent a weekend about that time with a medical student. She was thin and dark, with a trilling laugh. We'll call her Dr. H. She regaled me all weekend with stories of people coming into the hospital with genital injuries. TV antennas, poisonous snakes, you get the picture.

There was one episode that, if it *was* Dr. H.—and of course Dr. H. says it wasn't, though even she might not know, Hippocratic oath notwithstanding—seems pretty splendidly ironic. It makes you wonder about how cynical medical education is these days.

A man comes into the emergency room with his cock flayed open like a slinky—I'd like to wind that down, but those were Dr. H.'s words. At first he lies, makes up something about the butter knife slipping. The doctor smiles and repeats the question, and it all comes out. He was lying in bed that morning, a hot summer day, fan on, and his lover beside him stroking him seductively. You're so hard, she cooed, I'll bet you could stop that fan with it.

The poor schmuck, I cried, howling with laughter. How little empathy I had then!

So now I wonder: When Dr. H. told me that story, weren't we lying around in bed, and wasn't it hot? And shouldn't I have been looking around a little more to see what sort of fan she had prepared for me?

That story sounds suspiciously like the age-old male phobia of a vagina with teeth, but it *was* about then that I discovered the red glowworms on my cock. Perhaps they had been there before, years ago—something I hadn't even thought of before I began typing. Which goes to show you how much more digging I must do.

These glowworms, anyway, I didn't know what they were, and, with all due respect to Dr. H., attributed them to friction. For sex is not always a long, smooth slide into bliss. Days went by. The glowworms stuck around. And they were there, the friends, when I hooked up with a woman—let me be mysterious—who is special to me.

"Oh those things," I told her. "They're just some old glowworms." It really was something like that. We were on her parents' bathroom floor, it was in a time not chronologically that long ago but psychologically a different era, when I was glibly charming—and besides, who was in the mood to go to the hospital? A couple of sheetrock widths away, her parents were having cocktails and sourly discussing the new boy.

Weeks later (I was traveling) I got the word in a telephone booth. The way she blurted it out—all the anger and superiority of long suffering in her voice—it was staggering. It was as if three gentlemen in black tie had come in my door in the middle of the night and dragged me by my legs out of bed, the way some secret societies at Ivy League schools inform their new members of the honor. Of course there was nothing really funny about it, though when I think of the scene on the bathroom floor, I can't help but think of an exploding cigar. In some lights even that can be funny.

I didn't laugh at all then, hearing those clanking steel doors. She felt dirty and used: a pariah. She could not imagine making love again, because her sexuality seemed to have been annihilated. There was the direct pain; she waited till the bathroom was empty to pee at work lest anyone hear her cry out. And she felt fury for me, too, and had not been able to express it.

Here I ought to tell some of the grotesque refinements of my situation when I heard the news. For there is a grim, human-condition ring to them.

I had been waiting for her call in a waiting room, and been sitting with a Spanish-speaking gentleman. He was a gray and ugly Spanish-speaking gentleman, sensual in a reptilian, voracious way. You must know the type. He wished for me to fix him up with loose girls. "They like to sleep, OK? They do not want to get marry?" Could I send them his way? "Of course!" I was contemplating all the vicious practical-joke potential in this, and taking out my book to get his address (Was there some woman I couldn't stand who would be heading this way?), and then the phone rang.

I was on the phone a long time. My dear friend stuck around, twiddling his thumbs; he had yet to give me his address. When the door at last opened, he met me with an enormous smile, but it had as much effect on me as on a mummy. I was stunned. I had done nothing so terrible as this in all my life. A few words of hers reverberated, clanged. I wondered what I was doing here at all. How could life keep going on in its muddy course—the man, the room, that town—without sloshing over the banks, as my mind was sloshing.

Something then happened that I don't understand. I guess I was just lonely. The gentleman, that reptile, was smiling his iguana's smile at me; he could tell I had taken a blow and he wished to know everything. *Every*thing. He was prurient, seeking detail too sordid to consider now, but—and this is what was so strange—it was painless to render them to him in broken Spanish. He nodded happily at all I told him.

Who could feel any tenderness for that Spanish-speaking gentleman? I did. It meant so much to hear, as he assured me shallowly, that all would be all right. We walked down the street, him in his rumpled suit, talking lasciviously about girls, and me in my jeans and emotional tatters.

"I feel like a shit," I said mournfully to him, suggesting in my diction that it was what I had done to that special woman that mattered most of all. But he was practicing his English again, and got it slightly wrong. "Me siento como un mierde," he repeated. Then, "I feel like shit."

I had a classic reaction. There are moments when you realize that life in its honest, naked grimness has thrown aside all the festive illusion it's often clothed in, and this was one of those moments. I felt cut off from the mass of people, and in some inner effort to confirm that terrible impression, I went at night often to an area of town where celebrants gathered to sing and put their wineglasses on the tops of their cars—people happy over a new job or a wedding. I moved through these scenes like a ghost in a museum. The way their lives spilled and sparkled had nothing to do with mine, and they would surely discover what illusions had sustained them one of these days. My acts, I knew, were fastened with plumblines leading straight to the black muck that underlay all this—which I had seen.

They talk of a crucial Picasso painting in which two thick women tear open a background as being the opening to a new space, ultimately a cubist space. Well, the disease had torn open some

At first sex seemed like something I would have to learn all over again, like batting for a baseball player who is beaned, and then things were all right. Despite all the hysterics, nothing has been ruined. Oh, there may be some people who won't want to sleep with me because of it, but they don't know what they're missing, of course. Sex is still everything it can be: the colored lights, the big top, the roaring animals, the claws, even the trapeze...

I went to the library and read some of the things syphilis used to do to people and was horrified. Next to that, why, herpes could be like *sun*burn.

new space in my mind. As a kid I had escaped the knowledge that hurts you caused would last and last. A happy ignorance. I had been careless, free from empathy. I remember that once for days I discussed epilepsy with an epileptic, a man whose life was wrecked by the disorder. In all that talk I don't think I once really entered his consciousness of it. It was a self-centeredness; I saw no connection between me and his problem. In fact, his hysteria seemed a little curious.

Now I had injured myself and someone else in a forever sort of way. Of course I had not *known* I was giving it to her—that was something in my favor, yes. And yet for long intervals each day I could be trapped in those moments on the bathroom floor with her, and all the moments before that, and the ways in which I had dismissed the significance of the sores, scoffed at them.

I was changing. About that time, I went to see Leonardo Da Vinci's anatomical drawings. They were exhibited in a dark hall with soft illumination on the sketches, and people filed through hushed as a church. You must know of these: there is that famed picture of the fetus that embraces itself in a cutaway womb. They are pictures that had never engaged me before—what was all the fuss about? I wondered. Well, it is the spirit of these pictures, their devotion to the human form, the ennobling sense of calm in them. There was a drawing of people making love, done with such nonpornographic and unexcited care as to seem passionate in admiration. Praise for the human being sounded like a song everywhere.

And I felt chastened. The temple of my body had been defiled, and I hadn't even known it was a temple.

When I speak of the disease as an inoculation—my sugar cube in the paper cup—it's the same lesson Leonardo was scratching at: feeling myself to be part of that humanity, bound to my girlfriend and hordes of others. The youthful feeling of being outside it all had vanished.

In time the glowworms formed brownish crusts. Then they dropped off, leaving red patches. For a month or two these spots got inflamed during sex. When I went blinking into the light of the bathroom minutes afterwards, my features would be flush and full, but there were angry red cracks in the flesh down there, sometimes with a drop of blood.

At first sex seemed like something I would have to learn all over again, like batting for a baseball player who is beaned, and then things were all right. Despite all the hysterics, nothing has been ruined. Oh, there may be some people who won't want to sleep with me because of it, but they don't know what they're missing, of course. Sex is still everything it can be: the colored lights, the big top, the roaring animals, the claws, even the trapeze.

Deep in my pelvis, of course, the virus is hanging out. Just where I don't know; maybe it has its own bloody brier patch down there from which it picks red corpuscles to stay fat. In fact, the virus is invisible, its presence almost metaphysical. It doesn't obey laws of physics or chemistry, I imagine, but laws of the spirit, the same bloody laws it came in on, buried in a sweet tangle of lies. So it seems appropriate that it could descend at times of mental tension. As if the whole business were an invention of young people who crave understanding.

After all, I had written letters about my herpes to friends, and suggested that maybe it had come at the right time. Sure, it bothered me that medicine and technology hadn't yet collaborated to purge my body of herpes. But I knew that the disease wasn't such a terror; it just wasn't one of the real tragedies of our time.

"What are people worrying about?" a friend said, leaning over lunch to me. "In the fifteenth century they went to bed with one another when their bodies were rotting apart. *Rotting*!"

She was right in her way. I went to the library and read some of the things syphilis used to do to people and was horrified. Next to that, why, herpes could be like *sun*burn. So, you wear a rubber, I thought.

But that wasn't the point. No, every age would have its own medicine, and good old metaphysical herpes was ours. What lovers we had considered ourselves! And each of us so caught up in the unique trajectory of his or her life. I'm not against the new morality, I like it fine. But I can't help but think here of friends of mine who thought they had achieved some higher consciousness among themselves by abolishing jealousy. They were free of desperate human nature, free of Leonardo's images—which is why late at night one of them would sit in the kitchen, convincing himself he didn't care about what his erstwhile lover was doing in the bedroom.

What innocence! Not the sort of innocence I regret losing: the belief that you might touch someone else as much as you pleased and never really touch them at all. You *were* touching them, that was for sure, there was a great interconnectedness beneath it all. A bunch of us had been in on the secret.

Hollywood is good to singles because,
in many ways, Hollywood is *singles. Single dwellings,*
single cars, single—you know.
Almost everybody knows about Hollywood and
single people: it's the lamp from which
the single image is projected
to America.
So, what have we got: five Californians, ready to
tell you the truth about the Coast.
One of them's a movie star. One lived life on the
casting couch. One is what we
used to call a swinger. One's a millionaire
business woman. One's on "Three's Company."
We think, after reading these pieces,
you'll understand the essence of that strain of
singlehood that is becoming,
much faster even than Napa Valley wines,
exportable.

HOLLYWOOD SINGLEHOOD

The Truth in Five Voices

*Even with the best of breaks, the struggle to survive in Hollywood is rarely an easy one. Few actors ever get a bigger break than the one **Martin Hewitt** pulled off two years ago when the darkly handsome unknown was selected by director Franco Zeffirelli from a field of 5,000 hopefuls to play the male lead, co-starring with Brooke Shields, in his movie* Endless Love.

For the first few months after the release of the film, Hewitt confidently awaited the calls to come rolling in from the studios. He received a constant stream of fan mail, much of it prepubescent, much of it pleadingly obscene. Then he sat in his new apartment in high-rent West Hollywood and, to his surprise, nothing much happened. Today Hewitt, 24 and affable, lives with his cat in a small, faded apartment in Glendale, not far from where he grew up. But he's still not ready to settle down, he wants to return to the glare of Hollywood success—by himself.

The life I led while shooting *Endless Love* was something that I had never experienced before. I had cars, I had suites, I had everything. I was pampered and treated like royalty, and that's very attractive. That keeps me going.

Because I was a nobody at the time of the movie, I didn't really get that much attention to start with. When I was in Italy, when the film opened in Italy—it was in Florence—they had a special screening. I walked out at the end of this screening, and there seemed like hundreds of girls waiting. This is where it really blew me away: I had girls coming up and grabbing me, and the looks in their eyes; I mean they were just adoring, these adoring eyes, these eyes seemed to say, I'll do anything for you. You know, and they were grabbing me and screaming at me, and it was wonderful. I had never experienced anything like that before.

I thought when I moved to West Hollywood, things would happen: I'd be partying, I'd be meeting people, and I'd get caught up right in the whole scene, you know, the whole shot. But nothing happened. I spent many, many nights just sitting there wondering where the action was. Now what was I supposed to do? Nothing happened.

It's a tough town. There's a lot of competition as far as acting goes. There's a lot of jealousy, envy. There's a strange aura about Hollywood. It's got a bad aura.

Hollywood is sort of like a make-believe town. People expect Hollywood to be a lot more than it is. I think that when they think of Hollywood, they think of constant Rolls Royces rolling down the street, movie stars running around saying hi, drinking martinis, champagne, golden streets. I'm sure they feel that I'm always partying with movie stars and meeting different people, up every night til 3:00 in the morning, dancing around town, nice clothes, probably doing drugs, doing coke every half hour, have a few, la de da, you know, generally having a good time. When actually, it's a lot more serious than that, for me. That's not the way it is.

I felt alienated the moment I moved in. I didn't know the area at all, I didn't know anybody out there. I went to one party, at Barbara Carerra's house. There was this nice-looking girl and she came up to me—and it was pretty much like the Hollywood party I expected, not really, but close. Peter Straus walked in la de da de da and I go oh, there's Peter Straus, this is a real Hollywood party—and I could care less. And this girl comes up to me and she tries to hit on me and everything. A couple of days later I found out it wasn't a girl, but a guy who had had an operation. Oh God! So I don't know. I thought it would be all partying, all glamour, all flashbulbs flashing wherever I went, getting the front table in the restaurant, whatever. It just never happened. That's not to say that it could never happen. I mean if I go on to do ten more movies that get twice as much attention as *Endless Love*, that may happen one day.

I know there are a lot of phonies out there and I've been warned by my agent time and time again that I've got to be careful who I make friends with. There are a lot of people out there who pretend to be your friend and they're not your friend. They're just using you on and on and on. OK, I'm a pretty good judge of character. I can figure out who's there to use me. What I've figured out is that if what I've done is going to affect people enough to where they all want to be my friends, that's fine. I'll just have a good many more friends. It's sort of like a tool. It's like a tool to use to cultivate friendships. And I'll just use this tool to my own advantage.

I have no illusions. I used to have illusions, but no more. After living there, I realize that it's just another city and it's a special city because of its name and its history, but it is a sad city, really. It's tinsel town without the tinsel.

What you have in Hollywood is a lot of "actors" that have come from everywhere imaginable, expecting to be caught sitting in a malt shop drinking a malt, and swept off their feet, put in a limousine, taken down, have their hair changed, given another job, put on a set, and made into a star. There are thousands of people down there. Santa Monica Boulevard is just crawling with male hookers; they'll fuck anything to get ahead in this town.

And all of the hookers you see on Sunset Boulevard are actresses—or would have been actresses. It was just that illusion that drove them here in droves.

I'm sure that a large percentage of the people working the street down there have had the opinion that they could screw their way into a nice little part or a nice little soap opera.

I was sold as beefcake, whatever they call it, in *Endless Love*. They showed my little fanny and they had me work out every day for an hour and a half at the gym. That's the sort of product I was pushed as. And I think that's what people expect to see me in next. If they found out I was married and had three kids, it would take away from that. I think if John Travolta was married and had three kids, he'd lose a lot of his attraction. You do have to be ready to just pack up and leave and be gone for months at a time.

My life right now is dedicated to that place where I can have that cake and eat it too. I'm trying to find that perfect line in between. I've lived with my girlfriend. I've gone out on her and been with other girls. And she'll leave. She'll move out and I'll go, "Shit, damn, why did I do that? I'm such a fool? We have a good relationship. We get along really good. We have fun. Why do I go chasing other girls?" I get on the phone and I call her and say, "Come back," and she'll come back and I'll go out and do it again.

Because emotionally I'm tied up with a girl. We think on the same level; we're on the same level all the time. We can anticipate the other person's response. I need her... she's like me; she's like a second me; she's my companionship. She is actually more like a buddy than a sexual partner or a girlfriend. I want that sort of mother image that my girlfriend has and I want a tall, leggy blonde at the same time. If I could have both, then my problems would be solved.

I like the one-night trips. They're easy and fun. But I don't have a lot of them because I feel guilty when I wake. It's a trap, you know. But I keep doing it. A lot of people think I'm a bigger stud than I really am, I'm not. I'm pretty decent.

People think I'm a bigger stud because I co-starred with Brooke Shields. A lot of guys promote this image. "Aren't you the guy with Brooke Shields in that movie?" I say "Yeah." And they say, "Hey, man, I just want to know one thing, did you fuck her?" And they think, they actually... there is that space in their mind...

Sweet little Brookie is nothing like people imagine her to be—this hot trampy little sixteen-year-old that loves to get it on with guys. Let's see, in *Pretty Baby* she was fourteen, I think, and she played a teenage prostitute. People believe what they see. And they believe now that she's maybe just a little more grown-up prostitute. She still has the same role. She has body doubles that she always uses. In *Endless Love* she used a body double, but a lot of people don't know that—a lot of people. They think that is fifteen-year-old Brooke Shields up there...

A lot of people think there is the distinct possibility that I got down her pants. Brooke Shields is a hot number these days. She's on every magazine cover. And I think a lot of people have created the illusion about me, but not as much as I would like it to. I'd like it to become really easy for me. Come on, now, it's the devil talking. Guys always fantasize about how they'd love to have girls swarm all around them all the time. How they could go out and just pick up anyone out of the crowd and say "OK, it's you tonight." I don't think that happens to too many people. It happened to Elvis Presley, I'm sure it happens to a few people now. I'd like to see myself in that position.

Don't let my mother hear me say this.

I'd like to be in a position that I could do what I want. I like having the freedom to be with one girl as long as I want and I like the freedom to feel I can sleep with anyone I want who will let me. I like the space. I don't like it when people say no. Nobody does. Nobody likes being stuck where you can't move.

***Paige Matthews** had the makings of a star. As the protégée of the late Vivian Vance (best remembered as Ethel on "I Love Lucy"), she entered Hollywood with considerable industry contacts as well as an impressive list of theatrical credits. Tall, voluptuous, dark-haired, looking a bit like a younger Barbra Streisand on a good day, Matthews has been widely displayed on billboards and television commercials promoting everything from Coca-Cola to Ultra-Brite toothpaste.*

But for all her credentials, her beauty and talent, Matthews has faced rough times in a Hollywood where sexual favors are frequently the most effective currency. While many actors and actresses readily accept the persistence of the casting couch as a Hollywood institution, the 28-year-old Matthews, the daughter of an upper-crust Marin County family, has spurned the opportunity to engage in Tinsel Town's sexual economy. As a result of her adamant refusal to "play ball," Matthews fears she may well have ruined her chance to climb to the top of the Hollywood hill.

The actress spoke of her frustrations with the film industry, the loneliness and disillusionment that afflicts many of Hollywood's gifted and aspiring singles.

I have very few friends. I keep to myself a lot because the value system here is unbelievable. It's very bad.

People's loyalties—to each other as friends and people—are not there. Everyone's doing a lot of climbing the ladder and stepping on a lot of heads to get to the top.... As a matter of fact, I've rarely been in a situation where it hasn't been using. And most of the time women are as vicious as men, as using as the men are.

I think younger women are much more aggressive and they're not as—feminine. I think they're all becoming ballbusters. They're tough. And the thing is that they have these little façades of being sweet little innocent things and then they'll stab you in the back. They're scary.

I think it chastises men, so they are always threatened; they're always frightened; they don't want women to win. Not really. They look at them and they say, oh honey, I'm not going to let you win. As if I'm competition. I'm a threat. I'm smarter than they are, which they aren't used to. I'm not saying that I'm brilliant, but I do have a tendency to speak my mind in a thoughtful way. So I have a lot of problems with men in the industry.

Number one, I don't put out energy that's kind of, "Hey, baby, you might get it," because they're not going to and I've never dealt with life that way. I've had a couple of people in the industry who—agents, or managers, or whatever—have literally called me into their offices, and said, 'Listen, you're not putting any energy out that would give anybody a hint that you might have a relationship with them or something might happen, and you're not going to get anywhere unless

you let them think that they might."

The casting couch is alive and well. If you want a job in this town, you're going to have problems. You're going to have to play a really good game. I'm sure there are lots of people that never have this problem, that don't put out and do make it in the industry, and that's terrific. I haven't necessarily made it in this business, but then again, I'm standing here with my head up and I have a lot of self-respect. I also know that if I had slept with certain people, or had relationships with certain people, I would be a star right now. I am positive. That's obnoxious, but that's true.

There are a lot of managers out there—there's one in particular, he's a little man, he's sort of big and obnoxious, he's what you would call that sort of comical manager of the worst kind. He called me all the time and he said, "I want to represent you, but listen, for you to get something, I have to get something." And I always laughed at him. I thought it was just hysterical. And one day he called up and he was very funny and I had lunch with him and he said, "Just think of it as if you're making a guy happy. Just sleep with me and I promise I'll have a job for you within a week. You'll be a star in a year, but I'm not going to do it for nothing." He also wanted 10% of my money. I couldn't get up in the morning with that one. You want to slap them in the face, but you can't do that. You have to react very nicely and say no thank you and leave.

There are hundreds of good-looking, talented women in this town. I was Vivian Vance's protégée. Vivian told me—I was in my little Honda car in San Francisco—and Viv came out to the car and we were kissing each other good-bye and I was going to miss her so much—and as I was about to drive away, she said, "Remember, darling, remember who you are. You don't have to put out for anybody, because you are perfect just as Paige and you don't have to be a star." This was the greatest advice in the world.

I went to an interview the other day for a soap opera. The role was of a little hooker, and it was a real meaty role. Now that's fun because you can have a real good time with that one. That's not really tits and ass to me, that's . . . if you're a hooker—terrific—you've got some personality. I walked into that interview and I went in in what I usually wear, Ivy League shirt and sort of a normal human thing. The whole room was full of at least thirty girls. Twenty of them were blond, number one, and I'm a brunette, and excuse me, but I'm always going to be up against that. They were wearing these tight little yellow pants, cute little T-shirts and no bra, and just sleaze! Sleaze city. That's hard to compete against.

The manager that I spoke of earlier, the little tiny one, he is known in Hollywood as being a little pimp. It's known that clients of this gentleman—if you want to call him a gentleman—will put out. So his clients work a lot. Now, this is top. He's got stars. And he *makes* stars. He does do it. He is good. He's one of the best because he has energy and he goes and he hustles and gets to those studios and he works with those people, and his clients work all the time. *All the time.*

There is one gal in particular that I know. She literally said, "Listen, I'm going to go to the top, anyway I know how." And let me tell you, she's pretty successful. God knows if she's going to have a nervous breakdown when she's thirty-five. Who knows what's going to happen, because pretty soon you're going to wake up in the morning and you say, "Good morning," and you look in the mirror and it's pretty devastating. It's pretty evident. We look at history and that's the case.

I dream sometimes that I could be like Grace Kelly, that some prince is going to come along and take me away. That's the dream—to split. But that is not very realistic. You've got to get there to be taken away from it. We're all individuals. A person in Iowa is as big a star as someone here.

You've only got your self-respect and your dignity, so do whatever you have to do to hang on to it.

Offensive as it may be to sensitive young actors and actresses, Hollywood's bizarre sexual economics can be a pure godsend for those who possess success and know how to exploit it. Among Hollywood's late-night singles' crowd, few established figures are more renowned than attorney ***Paul Fegen****, who has for years entertained a seemingly unending stream of aspiring young women at his spacious home high above Sunset Boulevard.*

A millionaire lawyer/entrepreneur who has represented entertainment figures such as the late Jimi Hendrix and Connie Stevens, Fegen has never been married and can find no reason to change now. Well into his forties, with a straggly beard and a receding shock of gray-white hair, Fegen cheerfully acknowledges that his powerful Hollywood connection and his luxurious lifestyle provide more of his "sex appeal" than does his physical appearance.

Relaxing in his spacious high-rise office overlooking Beverly Hills, the highly individualistic attorney openly discussed the sexual quid pro quo that has led him into the arms of scores of attractive young ladies half his age.

Single life in L.A. is so good that the temptation to get married is less than *a* temptation to stay single because of *all* the temptations to remain single—all the beautiful girls, all the exciting parties, all the daytime and nighttime happenings. It's conducive to being single with all the excitement and glamour and glitter of the Hollywood life—the parties, the beach, the sun, the weather, just the atmosphere of the people—it's not conducive to raising a family when you're in the single party life. The single party life is such an exciting thing, it's too tempting not to be tied down.

The most beautiful girls all over the country come to Hollywood to live. They think this is the way to get their start. They want to be models and they want to become actresses. So they come to Hollywood and they're in competition with the best-looking girls from other parts of the country. When you put them all together, it's like a beauty contest. A guy like me meets so many girls all the time, that a girl just can't wait at home for a phone call, they have to be aggressive and they have to call up and say, "What are you doing for dinner tonight?" or "What are you doing later tonight?" or some other aggressive remark like "Can I come visit you?" or "Can I come help you at work? Can I come see your new house? Can I drive your new car?" or "I heard you got a new car, can I come to see it? Are you going to be home tonight? Are you going to be at the office tonight? Can I come visit you?" Girls in Hollywood just become aggressive, because of the nature of what's happening here.

Girls tend to gravitate towards the more successful people. There's a lot of good-looking guys in Hollywood; obviously, looks help. But girls are more interested in getting ahead. They want to run around in the right crowd, and they figure if they're going to be with a guy who's successful and wealthy, it's going to rub off on them or they're going to meet the right people. Most of the beau-

tiful girls have met and been with a lot of the good-looking unemployed actors and they want to look for something more secure and more stable. By going out with more successful people, they realize they're running in the right crowd because they could settle down with one of them, they could get married, or they could meet the right people by running around in the right crowd.

It doesn't bother me that, in a sense, they are using my connections, my world. Just as a girl uses my connections, my world, I use her love, charm, beauty, whatever she has to offer. I think it's only fair. I've worked hard to make money, and girls work hard to look beautiful. If they want to enjoy my money, enjoy the good times that I have with them, and I want to enjoy their beauty and their charm, they develop that so it's more or less of a quid pro quo. It's not one-sided.

I would say my single lifestyle has helped me in my professional life. By being single, I'm able to run around and meet more people. Generally, when I date a girl for a long period of time, she wants to spend more time with just me and won't allow me to run around and meet more people. The more people I run around and meet, the more people that get to know me socially and, therefore, want to do business with me. When you meet people socially, if you like them, you want to do business with them because you feel confident dealing with them and you see that they're real. If you meet them socially, you tend to trust them.

Like me, if I meet someone socially that wants to sell me a product, or if I meet someone at a party and they seem nice and they want to work with me, I tend to bend over backwards to hire them because I've already met them and they seem nice. Whereas if someone just walks in and applies for a job from a newspaper ad or someone recommended that I don't know very well, I wouldn't give them as much credit as if I met them socially. I feel a closeness to people I've already met.

As an attorney, I've made many, many social contacts that ended up being business contacts. I've gotten a lot of business through my social endeavors.

There are so many girls around that want to get married. When my mind and head are ready to settle down, I'll do it. If a girl comes around that convinces me, not by her words and not by her actions, but somehow makes me want to settle down with her, I would just settle down—but not out of fear. I would never marry out of security. I don't need security. I have my own security, my natural security. Emotional security I get from my friends. I know enough people and I've got a lot of friends, some real close friends, some not so close. I don't need emotional security. I've got financial security. Emotional security that I may need is the feeling of being with one person, but I don't really need that because I have a lot of people. In a Hollywood life there are so many parties that I flow into a crowd. Generally, when I go to a party, I'm not the first there, but I'm usually the last to leave. I just enjoy the parties and I just fit in.

As a matter of fact, I have friends who are married who say, I don't know how you do it, I wish I could be just like you.

Well, I do have the freedom, the Hollywood life, the fun life, just the freedom, not being tied down. It's wonderful having a family. I mean I love kids; in a way, I wish I had kids, but it does tie you down. It's one of those decisions that I made that I look back and I say it wasn't a wrong decision, because I could have been married, I could have five kids or ten kids. But I wouldn't be the same person I am now. Maybe I would be a very bitter person. You have kids and you've got to constantly reprimand them or constantly train them so you don't have to reprimand them. It's a very draining kind of experience.

Maybe when I'm 100, I may be doing the same thing, but when I'm 100, if I live that long, I may be married. I might be married many years before, I might be married that year, I might be married five years thereafter. I don't know. If I live to be 100. I'm healthy, other than my present cold. I eat well and I don't drink and I don't smoke and I don't take drugs. I eat health foods and I watch my diet and I do a lot of exercising. I jog, juggle, do my handstands.

I am self-centered because I am me. I live as an individual. I am me. I am not ashamed to have my face on my watch. I do it as a joke. I think it's humorous. I love people's reactions when they say, "What time is it?" and then I show them my $10 watch with my picture on it. I could afford a Gucci or a gold watch or a more expensive watch, but that would be showing off. Most people in my position wear expensive jewelry. I have no jewelry other than my $10 watch, which was a gift from someone and has my face on it.

I'm free. I don't go out with one girl all the time. I go to dinners and shows and parties. I go to Westwood Boulevard and hang out with a lot of people, walking around talking, juggling, just having a good time, driving around in my car. I enjoy life. The glamour and the fun. Going to premieres instead of the regular movies.

To summarize, my life is something that is written on one of my tables. One of my secretaries wrote this and this is a little plaque with hearts around it and written within the hearts: "Paul Fegen says he is waiting for the right girl to come along before marriage. In the meantime, he's having a hell of a time with the wrong ones." But I don't really think any of them are wrong; I think it's all right.

Rochelle Tetrault *came to southern California two decades ago, a deflowered Catholic teenager and unwed mother fleeing the constraints of her small town in the state of Washington. Starting work as a secretary in San Diego, the peripatetic, blond-haired Rochelle later became an actress and real estate broker. Cruising around town in her black Rolls Royce with ROCHELLE emblazoned on the license plates, the 38-year-old entrepreneur is now putting together her first full-length feature film production, the culmination of her own personal Hollywood dream.*

Tetrault says she was a "rebellious type" whose trip through convent school was bumpy. It was in public school that she decided "I wasn't going to marry God; that we were just going to fool around." She met a guy, "the James Dean type of guy, went swimming at a lake, drank beer, had sex for the first time—and became pregnant." She told her parents, had the baby, and decided neither to marry the father nor to take care of the baby. "Looking back over my whole life," she says, "I think it was the most difficult decision I ever made, but . . . now of course I can reflect back and say it was the best decision I ever made as well."

She moved to Los Angeles, went to work for attorney Melvin Belli, and learned business. Aside from a brief, and unhappy, marriage to a German actor, Tetrault has remained single. In a $400,000 home she shares with a male friend in the posh Brentwood section of Los Angeles, Tetrault talked at length about the importance of being single for a self-propulsive woman in southern California.

I have had millions of chances to marry various men, but I think my career has been more dominant. I have always been subconsciously aware that my career couldn't be advanced as quickly if I were married. If I were married, it seemed there would be a sudden stop. A halt. Every single opportunity that came along that even seemed vaguely possible, it always represented stopping in my tracks and turning to the man's career. Which was fine—they usually had good careers, but I wasn't *interested* in their careers; I was more interested in mine. And my career was a multitudinous one. It just wasn't . . . medical, legal, real estate, construction, show business. I wrote articles for a Vegas newspaper. You know, I was into writing, poetry. I played music; I liked the music business. I was confused about what I really was going to do for the rest of my life, I didn't feel safe getting married and either putting them through all my changes, which would have made the man weaker, and/or going through their lives 100%,

which would have been required. Therefore, throughout, I had serious relationships, all of which were nice men, wonderful men, but none of whom I wanted to stop dead in my tracks for at that point. In any case, therefore, I continued onward until finally I reached —about seven years ago—I reached a fair pinnacle in my career.

By this time, I had sort of outgrown *anybody*. I was becoming very domineering—not domineering, dominating. I was not the type of woman who would lean on someone.

Most men would rather have you be either a little housewife or have a stable career, i.e., doctor, lawyer, Indian chief, etc. But being an entrepreneurial woman is a very difficult thing, apparently, to ask a man to accept. I get a little pissed at that, frankly. What is it, you know? I'm exciting, I've had an exciting life, I'm going to have an exciting life in the future, and I could never understand why a man couldn't understand my career. I found a few men who I was attracted to, but when anything serious developed, they wanted me to settle down in some way that I can't really define. They definitely didn't like the adventurous nature of my career.

I would get very upset, because I would think that I was unworthy, I would think I wasn't right, I would think that I really fucked up my life, had ruined my chances forever of being married, being in love. In a way, it was a contradiction of the American way. You know, everything I had been taught from my little village was to be independent, to be a driving entrepreneur, to do everything you possibly could.

I'd say I'm a numb head when it comes to men romantically. A man would come along and say, "Rochelle, fly to the moon," I'd fly to the moon and come home from my adventure and they'd say I'd love to marry you, but you know, you flew to the moon. It's a weird dichotomy, in a way.

By this time, I was 32 or 33, and I had two huge houses. I had a wonderful business. I had my Rolls registered, I had good cash flow, I was in real estate, I was making lots of money. I thought, God, I want to settle down. You know, it's like a man does when they say, "Well, when my career gets stable I'll get married." I must have done something similar to that. I said, "Now I'd like to settle down, but who'll have me?" I mean, now all of these guys didn't like my trip. "We love you, Rochelle, but you're just too strong a woman to settle down." I had many friends tell me that, that I was just too strong to settle down. Is that why our divorce rate is 50%: only the weak people settle down in the middle of their lives? I got a little confused. And at that age I wasn't stable enough to figure out what was going on.

And so I met a German actor and he didn't speak enough English to tell me that he didn't like my style, so I ended up marrying this German actor. We had a happy life until he started speaking English and until I started a medical computer company. It was a very large company, employing about thirty people, and I had a lot of pressures: I had around-the-clock people working; I had on-line computers with five major hospitals; 150 doctors—alongside my construction company and my property ownership, etc. What a hell of a load for a girl to be taking. I needed a man who was up to, at least, letting me cry on his shoulder at night. In any case, I couldn't go home and speak English, so I got very frustrated and I think I wanted to destroy my business; I think I wanted to destroy all my financial success.

Everybody feared that this guy would take me to the cleaners and what have you, which he did not. In fact, he was a very nice guy, and looking back, he was all right to be married to. We were *physically* in love, not *mentally*, and he was a nice guy. Our home life was boring, but I needed a boring home life at that time. I just had to have a boring home life to cope with my many business projects. In any case, I went to Hong Kong because I was in the middle of all my business crises and I was going to start another business which was manufacturing clothes—sweaters. During the trip I came to the realization that I didn't care what marriage was supposed to mean to people, it had to mean something more than I had. We separated amicably: no problems, nice guy, we're still friends.

I think, absolutely, that my being single is a good thing. I can't even imagine any other way. I never could imagine having done what I've done, having lived the exciting life I've lived in any way being married. I don't know how I could have done it. Who would have traveled with me to Europe, who would have gone through all these professions, or who would have allowed it all? I never would have had the latitude that I have had. I would never have met all the influential people in my life—the people who said go right instead of left. I wouldn't have been able to meet them, because I would have been married. I would have been maybe cooking dinners and having more babies.

You know, I used to always envy housewives. When I was younger I'd look at them and say, Oh, what an easy life they have, how stupid they are to complain, why don't they just relax and enjoy it? They can raise their children in peace and go to their exercise classes, they don't have to go out and supervise 30 employees and worry about cash flow, and all the crap I had to worry about. Now, I'm totally mobile. I can pick up clothes and furniture and leave. If the economy gets worse, I can always be sure that I'll be OK.

They say the older you get, the choosier you get. That's true. My position now on men is very good. If people could understand, they'd be envious. But I do have a problem.

I have so much respect that I could throw about 50% out of the window. And I think men think of me as much more powerful than the average woman. They get all nervous and they get cold hands and they think, "Gee, you're too strong a woman, Rochelle." I mean, how can you be too strong?

*Being both strong and single has become an essential part of the basic career plan for many of the new generation of women now muscling their way toward Hollywood success. For ambitious actresses like 22-year-old **Jenilee Harrison**, who played the pretty airhead Cindy Snow on ABC's highly popular "Three's Company" series, marriage and family could only undermine the single-minded quest for starlet status.*

A native of Los Angeles' sprawling San Fernando Valley suburbs, the blond-haired, long-legged actress achieved early success as a contestant in beauty pageants, including a stint at seventeen representing the United States at the Miss International contest in Tokyo. Since then, Harrison has worked as a model for nearly fifty different commercial sponsors. Shortly after graduating the University of Southern California, she landed her part on "Three's Company" and has already parlayed that break into appearances on some 28 different network and syndicated programs, including starring in the recent miniseries "Malibu" with James Coburn and George Hamilton and the new feature film "Tank" with James Garner and Shirley Jones.

The deeply private, almost reclusive Harrison insists she has succeeded in Hollywood without making the sexual compromises that have become almost commonplace for aspiring actresses. Over a Tab at Du-par's, a San Fernando Valley hangout for entertainment industry types, the teetotaling actress laid out her plans for being simultaneously single, pure, and successful in Hollywood.

It's a great advantage to be single because our lifestyle is constantly to be on call. It's much easier to have to run off and jet-set it when you are not committed to anybody. I get calls to be in Hollywood or Texas instantly, and luckily, because I am single, I don't have to make plans and arrangements with anybody else. For that reason, I can't even have a dog. I'm not committed to anybody but myself. It makes it easier for me.

I'm not approached by men too often. That has happened my whole life. People see me and here's this pretty, smart, successful girl and she must have guys flogging around her—it's not the case. Ask the beautiful people. What happens many times is people think you're perhaps taken by somebody. They don't want to chance it, or risk it. They assume all these things.

I don't drink, I don't smoke, I don't do anything of *those* things. I went into a bar a couple of months ago and it was very boring for me. I don't live those Hollywood lifestyles.

In some ways, I'm very ignorant. In some ways, I'm very naive, very sheltered. But when you look at me, in some ways for my 22 years, I'm quite worldly. I've been to many countries, I've been on the car-racing circles, I own race horses, I own lots of real estate. But for me, Hollywood is work, and I'm the kind of person who likes to separate my work and my pleasure. It's like a doctor: he goes to work all day long and he doesn't want to go home and fix the neighbor's ankle.

I've never had to deal with the casting couch. I know that people treat me differently, but the people that I'm socially around are people in the business who are usually high-caliber people. I've been sheltered—I saw my first whores on Sunset Boulevard a couple of weeks ago. I just don't know, I don't see the drugs that they talk about and everything. I'm ignorant maybe. I'm sure I do that to myself.

See, this is what I'm saying: nobody would come up to me, a casting director would not come up to me, and even ask me to sleep on a couch. They wouldn't do that. But girls do walk in and ask for it. I see those personalities.

But I am going to get *my* jobs—and I am going to get them—because I try to be a good clean person, I really believe that. You know, people say, "Hey, Jenilee, she's all right. She's got the brains, the looks, and the figure—she's real straightforward." I'm blunt but I'm very businesslike, and there are not too many females out there like that. I have a good business background, and I have a lot to show for it. Somebody's going to sit down and discuss something with me and say, "Hey, this might work." They're not going to come up to me and say, "Hey, sleep on this couch." They just wouldn't do it. There's a lot of bull in Hollywood. Many people think that's what it revolves around, but if you see that and recognize it and work with it, you'll come out ahead. Instead of fighting it.

I don't want to get married for some years. But I do have boyfriends, I usually have very steady boyfriends. And these men are all independent people on their own. They like me for who I am, where I am, and what I'm doing. Obviously, I could not get together happily with somebody from a dampened kind of lifestyle. I mean, I don't want to sound pretentious, but I do have a sort of jet-set, limousine type of lifestyle where I have to pop into bathing suits and appear on the covers of magazines and run around and travel and all that. It would take a hell of a man to understand all that and support all that. But they are out there. But I wouldn't get married to any kind of man right now. I am personally just not ready. I'm only 22, I'm still young and there's so much that I want to do and I'm still very selfish. To get married you have to give up a lot, and you have to think about the other person.

I am selfish, because I want to do what I want to do when I want to do it, and if you're married you can't do that. There's another person who's standing beside you and you have to consider what they want to do. In some respects it saddens me to know that I will never be able to give or have the family life that my mother had and that my family gave to me. But I know that right now I won't settle for staying at home, being a housewife and dealing with kids in the middle of the night because they're sick and feeding them pills and everything else. I'm too selfish about the things I want to do, the places I want to go, the things I want to accomplish. I want to be on the silver screen and stay in this business and be successful in this business. If I gave up part of that now to be a good mother, I wouldn't be happy—it's one thing against another. If you want to have this drive and do all these things, you have to give up other things. Don't get me wrong. I love the institution of marriage. Your family and your loved ones give purpose to all of life, to all of these successes I've been speaking about. Someday I'll be in a wedding gown, but not until I'm good and ready. Then at that time, I'll strive to be like the great mother that raised me.

But until then, here's to being a bachelorette!

WARNER GOES WEST
NEW MORALITY COMICS PRESENTS A TALE of SINGLEHOOD
IN LANTANA, FLA, WARNER BEADY AND HIS GIRLFRIEND BETH WOCKET ARE WATCHING LATE-NIGHT TV...
THOSE ARE SOME GOZANGAS YOU HAVE THERE, ELAINE!
THEY SURE SEEM LIKE THEY HAVE SOME FUN OUT THERE IN HOLLYWOOD!
IF YOU WANT TO TRY IT, GO AHEAD, AND STOP COMPLAINING--- YOU'RE SINGLE-- I DON'T MIND. HAVE FUN!
OH BOY! TODAY'S THE DAY I'M GOIN' TO HOLLYWOOD TO BE A SINGLE! I WONDER IF I'LL GET TO GO TO A PARTY AND GET A CHANCE TO TURN DOWN COCAINE!
NOW GOOD-BYE WARNER — AND BE BAD. BE VERY BAD. I WANT TO HEAR A STOP TO YOUR COMPLAINING ONCE AND FOR ALL!
OK, HONEY, WHAT A PAL!
ON THE PLANE
HEY, AREN'T YOU GUYS SAMMY DAVIS JR. AND BOB HOPE?
HEY BABY, YOU ARE THE GREATEST! I WOULD LOVE TO SHOW YOU HOLLYWOOD SINGLES SWINGING— DIG? YEAH! I LOVE YOU, BABY NUMERO UNO!
HEY, I WANNA TELLYA, THIS KID'S SO INNOCENT, HE MAKES DONDI LOOK LIKE HUGH HEFNER— GO ON SAM, SHOW HIM THE ROPES!
Paramount Pictures
WARREN MAKES IT TO THE LAND OF HIS DREAMS...
OH BOY OH BOY! HOLLLLYWOOD! AH'M GOING TO MEET ME SOME GIRLS, EAT ME SOME COLD SUSHI AND PASTA, TURN DOWN SOME COCAINE, AND CHECK INTO THE BEVERLY WILSHIRE!
AT THE LEGENDARY BEVERLY-WILSHIRE HOTEL...
GIMME A SWELL SUITE— ONE WITH A LOT OF MEMORIES
YEAH— WOW! MY HERO, WARREN BEATTY! I DIDN'T RECOGNIZE YOU!
THAT'S BECAUSE I'M DRESSED FOR MY NEXT GREAT FILM ROLE... AS HOWARD HUGHES!
BUT FIRST I'M GOING WITH MY FRIEND JACK NICHOLSON TO LANTANA— SMALL TOWN AMERICA IS WHERE IT'S REALLY HAPPENING!
WOULD YOU LIKE WARREN BEATTY'S OLD SUITE?
YEAH! DOES IT HAVE HIS OLD ADDRESS BOOK?
WHY, THERE'S MR. BEATTY NOW!
BUT... BUT... DON'T YOU GUYS WANT TO SWING WITH ME-- RIFLE WARREN'S OLD PHONE NUMBERS, TURN DOWN COCAINE?
SORRY SONNY, THAT'S KIDDIE STUFF... ONLY THE GEEKS IN THIS TOWN STAY UP PAST NINE PM ANYMORE... WE'VE GOT EARLY CALLS AT THE STUDIO...
THAT'S RIGHT JACK... WE'RE PIONEERS IN A NEW ERA-- OF LASTING RELATIONSHIPS, EARLY BEDTIMES, HIGH PROFIT— AND WE KNOW
LATER THAT NIGHT IN THE WARREN BEATTY SUITE AT THE BEVERLY WILSHIRE
SO THIS IS THE HOLLYWOOD SINGLES LIFE... GEEZ... I WONDER WHO'S CALLING?
THOSE ARE SOME GOZANGAS YOU'VE GOT THERE, ELAINE!
RING RING!
LANTANA'S ON THE WIRE!
WARNER— THIS IS BETH... I'M SITTING HERE WITH JACK AND WARREN... THEY CAME DOWN TO TELL ME YOU WERE IN DANGER OF FALLING INTO UNHEALTHY DELUSIONS ABOUT YOUR LIFE-STYLE AS A SINGLE!
MAN! DON'T, HONEY! COME HOME... WE THREE NEED A FOURTH FOR MONOPOLY!
AND WARREN SAYS, BRING HIS HOWARD HUGHES SCRIPT (IT'S IN THE NIGHT-TABLE) HE WANTS ME TO PLAY JANE RUSSELL!

8

One of the riskiest parts of being single is that you may begin to see yourself as the media do. The media, after all, pretend to provide a Baedeker to your own emotional terrain. They tell you what you are; they tell you how to understand the world. Naughty, naughty media.

But it's not their fault, really. They've got their work to do. It's your fault, yours, *for not having completed a resistance training program. When you turn on "Singles Magazine" or "60 Minutes" or "Good Morning, Bogaloosa," and they're pushing you around, telling you who singles are and why they whimper and what they wear and when they eat, I don't hear you saying,* "No! That's totally mistaken, Mr. Wise Guy!"

Well, you will, beginning right now.

We want to prepare you to read singles coverage correctly, so that no one, ever, will leave another single stinging with the fury of the misinterpreted. So: read on, and get ready for your resistance conditioning.

Awake!

MONOMEDIA

Covering Singles Issues in America

Special Issue

Nowsweek

June 12, 1984

Singles! Singles! Singles!

Marriage Bites the Dust as Cohabitation Takes the Cake

The New Singles:

Laid-Back 80s Lifestyle Or What?

In Houston, Sally Bodale, 23, rushes home Friday evenings from her $250-a-week secretarial job in one of the city's glittering boomtown oil-company towers, oblivious to the breakneck economic growth that has transformed her 541-square-mile hometown into a roustabout Sunbelt megalopolis—a city some have dubbed "Pizzazz On the Prairie"—and also given it a worrisome set of urban growing pains that resist easy solutions.

Yet on Friday nights, red-headed Sally Bodale does not think about economic expansion or its dislocations. Instead, driven by loneliness, a certain Texas hopefulness and a 1979 Honda Accord, she is intent on finding another kind of Lone Star Action. Indeed, by 8 P.M., she will be one of some 79,000 young, unattached Houstonians jammed into the 430-acre dance floor of Loony's. Loony's, until two months ago a McDonnell-Douglas DC-10 assembly plant, is now one of a plethora of Brobdignagian beer halls that ring the city which, like Topsy, grew by 73% since 1960. Meaningful? Certainly. Sally Bodale: single American.

In tired, frankly uninteresting Schenectady, N. Y. (pop. 76,000), as unlike sprawling Houston as Sparta was unlike Athens—although in a different way—Wilbur Frint prepares for his own kind of Friday night. A library guard at Union College (who, ironically, reads only flour-package recipes) gamely picks the lint from his only suit, probably bought at a harshly lit discount department store. The bittersweetly primping Frint, 45, a widower since 1977, eagerly awaits the second Friday of each month. Then he, along with some 300 unmarried middle-agers, makes his way to a City Hall basement auditorium for a night of free Jon Hall movies, Fresca punch and awkward socializing, a city-subsidized program that some have dubbed "Free Movies and Soda Downtown." Says Frint: "It's great to get to know other folks like myself, have a chat over punch. It's really a pleasure." But beneath that brave, bluff cheer no doubt lies a reservoir of mid-life despair. Wilbur Frint: single American.

Eugene, Ore. (pop. 102,000), is not much larger than Schenectady, but its tempo and its citizens' concerns must be as different from that Northeastern city's as both places are from the brassy, high-rolling, *nouveau*-oil-*riche* upstart on the Gulf Coast of Texas, Houston. And it would be difficult—impossible in just a week or so—to find anyone more superficially distinct from Bodale and Frint than Simone Weinstein.

Weinstein, 32, is a potter and apprentice midwife with a degree in semiotics from the University of Heidelberg. A native of suburban Philadelphia affluence and the mother of an illegitimate daughter by Dead French Philosopher Roland Barthes, Weinstein says ironically that her Friday nights differ little from her Thursday or Saturday nights. "Most nights," she explains, "I come home from birthing classes, make ratatouille for dinner, and read or sketch. Once a week or so I'll go to my friend Michael's, where we make ratatouille, I sketch and he reads." (Her daughter, Vowel-Sound, nine, has her own studio apartment east of Eugene.) Simone Weinstein: single American.

Three seemingly unconnected lives, each separated from the next by at least nine years and approximately 1,700 miles. Three strikingly disparate Americans—but unconnected? Hardly.

They are the New Singles. They together comprise a new wrinkle in the social fabric, or perhaps an old wrinkle in a new place in the social fabric. Their significance is undeniable. According to the 1980 Census, there are now 31 million unmarried U.S. adults—more than twice the population of Australia and 44 times as large as the American Federation of Federal, State, County and Municipal Employees. Some 80% of those U.S. singles are under 35—the young New Singles—while more than 15%—the black New Singles—are black. Single Americans are now more numerous than ever before (*see chart*). The reason? The post–World War II baby boom. The result: a New Singles subculture that includes but is not limited to the well-trodden territory of singles bars, dating services, swinging-singles vacation resorts and U.S. campuses. The prospects for the future? No one knows for sure.

THE SINGLE EXPLOSION

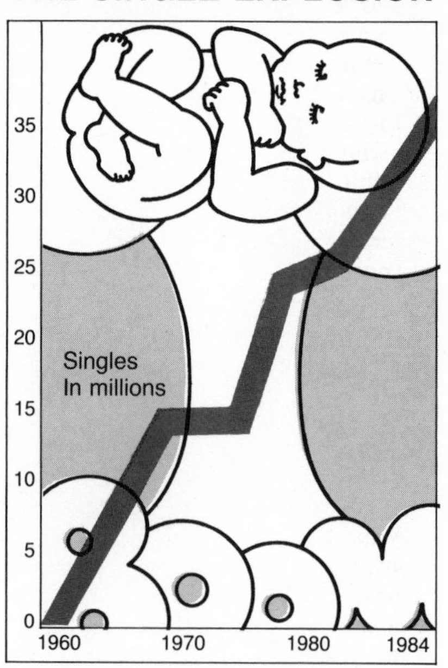

Baby Boom begets Maybe Boom: A generation has not made up its mind, in record numbers, whether or not to marry.

One thing, however, is certain: the New Singles are a powerful force in U.S. society today, affecting the arts, politics (*see box*), business and many other fields.

There have always been single people. England's King Henry VIII, who ruled from 1509 to 1547, was single for more than half of his reign. Jesus, the Christian Savior, was still single at age 33. Yet it is only in the 1980s that so many have chosen to postpone marriage. Thus the New Singles.

Even scholars recognize the importance of the phenomenon. Says Unmarried Sociologist Ballantine Derf: "It is what we call 'salient data.' In other words, there are a lot of single people." Derf, whose *Par-ty! Par-ty!: The Dynamics of Contemporary Monadism* is his discipline's definitive text, has found that New Singles are indeed different from the U.S. population at large. His eight-year study revealed that they talk less frequently while at home, own fewer cars on average, spend less on groceries and profess a greater desire to "engage in sex with persons other than a spouse."

Yet just why are so many Americans opting to remain single longer? Explains Neo-Feminist Psychologist Virginia Schwinner-Rand: "Forces of affective conditioning have loosened. The mate-seeking imperative is more open to idiosyncratic manifestation." In short, there is more freedom. Adds Schwinner-Rand: "Nurturing. Emotive programs. Familial release. Voluntary commitment." Some challenge the implications of Dr. Schwinner-Rand's thesis. But all observers agree that the New Singles are genuinely new and not, as one critic has charged, just an amorphous old notion given artificial new life.

Whatever the intellectuals' explanations, the trend is for the New Singles themselves a stubbornly personal affair. Dianne Willis, 26, a Minneapolis computer saleswoman, has never married. Nor is she actively searching for a husband. She is in many respects typical of the New Singles: a two-mile-a-day runner, she thought Independent Presidential Candidate John Anderson was "neat" and collects decorative salad forks. Willis owns her own one-bedroom lakeside condominium, and is saving to buy a two-bedroom condominium overlooking a larger lake. "I go out with a lot of different guys," she says, "and we have great times windsurfing, watching cable television, drinking imported beers and stuff." Yet she remains reluctant to marry. "None of [my many, many sexual partners] seemed like the right guy, you know? Not the sort of guy I'd want sponge-bathing my body twice a day decades from now, when we're old and I'm riddled with like a paralyzing cancer or something and we're living in an underground ambulatory-care bunker, and the children have drifted out of touch or maybe been killed in a laser war in Southwest Asia."

Her high standards for a prospective mate are by no means a function of gender—or of Minnesota. Says Hospital Vending Machine Lessor Gordon Greenspan of Sarasota, Fla.: "Sometimes it's tough explaining to my parents why I'm waiting so long to marry." Greenspan, 30, says he dates "just enough," and has no plans for matrimony until he is at least 40, or 50, or even older. But his hesitance has none of the macho insensitivity of the "confirmed bachelors" of an earlier era. Explains Greenspan: "My father said he married for sexual intercourse reasons. Our generation doesn't have that need. Sexual intercourse is no big deal to us. It's nothing special to me personally. Sexual intercourse always makes me feel like an awkward boy, or a bad animal. It's so, so *closed in* that it makes my mind burn, sort of." Greenspan, undefensive about his decision to "play it loose for a while," points out that "probably many great scientists and U.N. officials aren't all that crazy about the sexual intercourse part of marriage." (At week's end, spokesmen for the National Academy of Sciences and the United Nations had no comment on Greenspan's claim.)

Like Greenspan, New Singles generally eschew what many have dubbed the "commitment without affection" of old-fashioned marriage, just as they dismiss the "affection without commitment" of previous singles and the "no commitment, no affection" of Japan's state-of-the-art industrial robots (*see following story*). The New Single compromise: a little commitment, a bit of affection and plenty of good-natured après-ski discussions of aerobic conditioning and fine German cameras.

Just who is the New Single? The Bodales, the Willises, some of the Frints—they and 31 million unwitting comrades epitomize this singular style and outlook. Yet in an age when show-business celebrities take on the emblematic luster once reserved for deity or royalty, Actor-Screenwriter Alan Alda, 46, although happily married to one woman for all of his adult life, comes the closest to symbolizing

Singles-Issues Politics

California Governor Jerry Brown, 44, has made two creditable runs for the Presidency, skillfully managed a huge state apparatus during a difficult fiscal period, and frequently enriched the nation's political discourse with his novel ideas and approaches.

Much more importantly, however, Brown has never married.

Bachelor Brown is one of a growing corps of U.S. politicians—growing in notoriety if not, technically, in numbers—proving the possibility of a successful political life *sans* wife.

Brown, especially, flaunts his place in the New Single limelight, dating Rock Singer Linda Ronstadt and forsaking the governor's mansion for his own minimalist bachelor pad. (Indeed, a near-majority of New Single politicians report having dated Rock Singer Ronstadt or "a gal who looks an awfully lot like her.") Yet Brown coyly disclaims any membership in a vanguard. Said the governor ironically: "My private life is not part of the public domain."

Since former widower and New York Governor Hugh Carey's marriage two years ago, he abdicated his reign as the East's leading New Single politico. Heir to the title: Actually Heterosexual New York City Mayor Edward Koch.

While there has been no unmarried President in this century, with Brown, Divorced Senator Edward Kennedy and Ruggedly Handsome Although Still Married Senator Gary Hart all eyeing that office, a New Single commander-in-chief is no impossible dream. Another possible scenario: First Lady Nancy Reagan's untimely death, effectively beginning a New Single Administration before 1985.

The species proliferates abroad as well. Among those who might count themselves as New Singles are Prime Minister Pierre Trudeau of Canada, Cuba's President Fidel Castro (whose ideological father, Communism Inventor Karl Marx, regretted his own marriage), Indian Prime Minister Indira Gandhi and Pope John Paul II.

And the movement comes full circle back to the U.S. It is one of the most prominent New Singles who still basks in acclaim for his portrayal of a U.S. communist: *Reds* Director Warren Beatty.

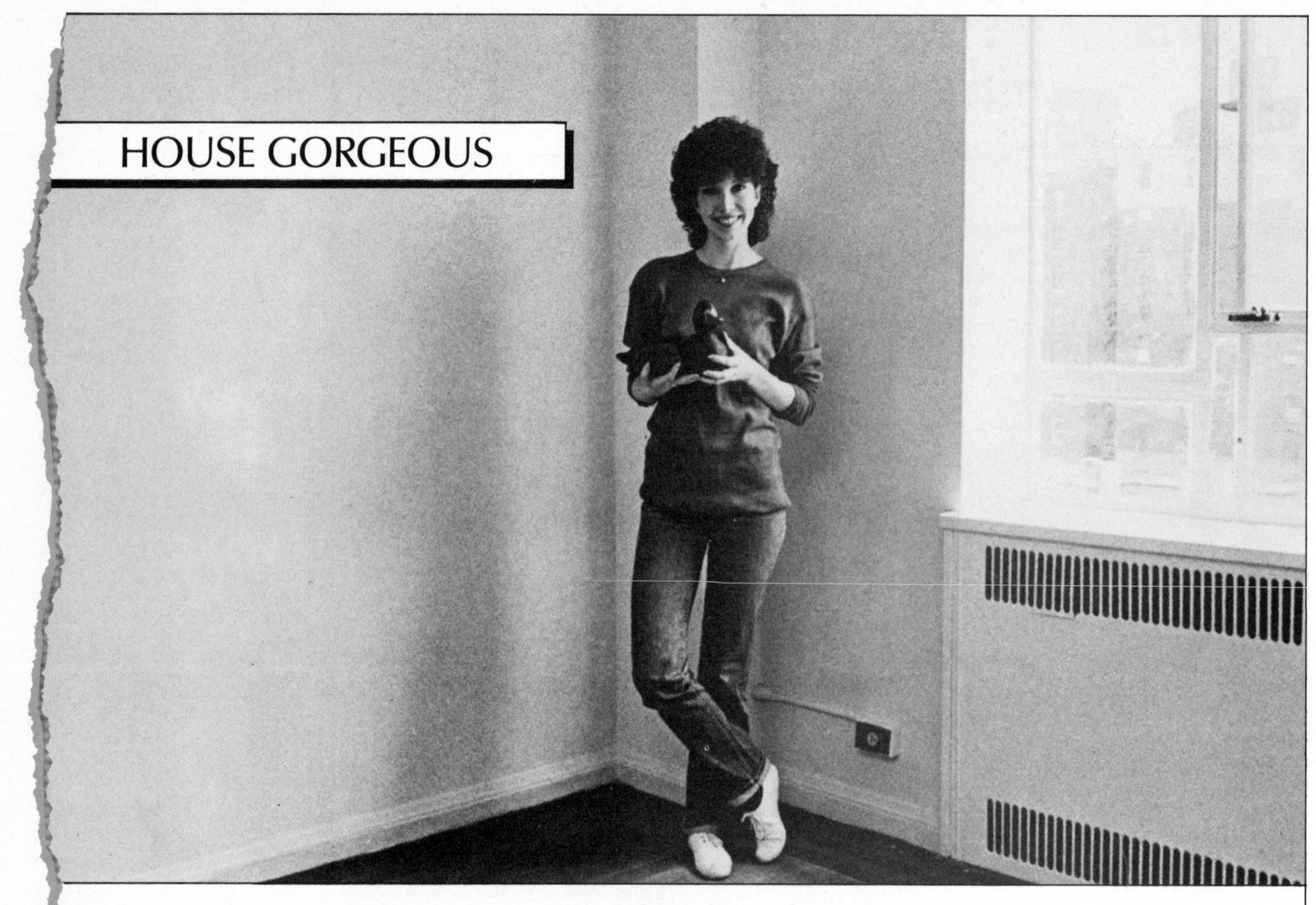

SMALL REALLY IS BEAUTIFUL

A monthly design guide to living alone in a tiny studio apartment, er, flat, and pretending it's elegant.

A wise man once asked if the glass is half-empty or half-full. Sophisticated people between 18 and 34 naturally wonder, "Glass of *what*?" A surprisingly inexpensive Rhine wine to be served at 45° F. in fluted goblets, or one of the bargain California varietals? Yet in fact, the half-empty/half-full enigma is a question of great relevance to residential lifestyle decisions. And there the answer is an unqualified "half-*full*, if a few simple rules are followed."

All it takes to transform your cramped, blank, dry-wall cubicle into a smart little Bauhaus pied à terre is common sense, careful planning, a working knowledge of color and texture, a degree from an accredited architecture school, and no more than half-a-dozen trips to isolated Appalachian hamlets for second-hand furniture buys. Practically overnight, a once-humble apartment can become a showplace, a home where you can show off with pride your collections of folk-art duck decoys and thrift-shop Tiffany lamps.

Before any cosmetic changes can be made, of course, the guts of the apartment will have to be brought up to snuff. Entirely rewiring even a small, one-person apartment can be tricky unless

Continued on page 189

294

BWANAHUE--PROGRAM TRANSCRIPT

TAPED FOR DELAYED BROADCAST 2/14/83

00:00 PHIL: Erika Fedderson is founder of D-E-Sweethearts, a nationwide organization of unmarried young women--each of whom is afflicted with genital and uterine defects caused by their mothers' use of the drug D.E.S. during pregnancy. Ms. Fedderson and her membership want to let the world know that D.E.S. sufferers, in her words, "make good dates and great lovers." This despite the stigma many feel from having surgically built artificial vaginas.

FEDDERSON: "Artificial" could give the wrong impression--

00:30 PHIL: Just give me a chance, I'm short on time here, I'll let you explain in a minute why I'm all wet.

(Audience laughter.)

Next we have Don Blodgett, president of Special People, a firm in Fullerton, California, that has been called by _Newsweek_ "the country's first and only matchmaking service for retarded and brain-damaged Romeos and Juliets." With Mr. Blodgett today is this pair of lovebirds, Wendy Chambers and Mark Jetter, who met through Special People and have been going steady for a year. Finally, Patricia Sissman. Ms. Sissman, with her husband, operates Wheelies, a discotheque in Huntington, West Virginia. The dancers there are mostly young, single--and all paraplegic.

(Audience murmur)

295

Do we have that videotape ready?

(Videotaped scene from Wheelies dance floor, crowded with wheelchairs bumping and gyrating in time to the Olivia Newton-John song "Physical".

02:02 PHIL: We're talking about handicapped romance--some of the special adversities and joys encountered by an estimated one million Americans in seeking companionship, love--and even full sexual functioning.

02:31 (Theme music up.)

04:16 PHIL: Don Blodgett, you started Special People Why?

BLODGETT: Mr. Bwanahue, in 1975 I viewed the motion picture _Charly_, starring Cliff Robertson, on television. That picture gave me my first real insight into the situation of retarded individuals. I got to thinking what I could do as a Christian businessman to alleviate the situation.

PHIL: You were in what business previously?

04:22 BLODGETT: Mr. Bwanahue, I was the owner-operator of three Christian-oriented campgrounds in the Loma Linda vicinity of Southern California.

PHIL: So Special People is a profit-making enterprise for you?

BLODGETT: Yes, sir we are a private, free-enterprise business, yes.

04:34 PHIL: Now how does the service work? Why don't you tell us how Wendy and Mark here were introduced.

296

BLODGETT: Well, sir, Mark's father saw one of our television commercials there that we bought on the local Christian

06:05 cable television. He and Mark drove in to our office--

PHIL: You, what, interview them to find out what kind of young woman Mark is interested in dating?

BLODGETT: Yes, we have a consultation session, and we take some Polaroid pictures of the boy or girl. My niece does the actual matching up. Then we send the boy and girl separate mimeographs we've had our pastor make up, information how dating is a new experience, and with regard to different feelings and all they may feel, regarding

06:23 sexual matters and so on.

PHIL: Wendy and Mark are both twenty-nine. Mark, I know we're putting you on the spot here asking about your love life.

06:42 JETTER: Okay.

PHIL: You want to tell us how you called Wendy for the first time on the telephone?

JETTER: My dad helped.

PHIL: The old man was in there giving you some moral support, huh? (Audience laughter.)

JETTER: What?

PHIL: Wendy, what did you think of this good-looking guy when he came up to your door for the first time?

CHAMBERS: He was real neat and dressed in boots. I laughed!

JETTER: Her house smelled like candy corns, I think.

NEW YAWK

$ingle Strategies / Blare Sable

LOOKING FOR MR. GREATBAR

ALLOW ME ONE TINY PERSONAL observation before getting down to business. I do dearly love New York, but what's this crazy, sexy, incredible, fantastic island coming to when my cleaning woman (Tuesdays, 10 A.M.–4 P.M., $35, no checks) arrives for work in what I could swear was a Versace skirt (Barney's top floor, $425 until 6/10)? And they say the poor get poorer. Tell me another one.

This week only, at the suggestion of my friend Julia Margolin (who only happens to be *the* hottest subsidiary rights director in publishing right now), the column's focus will be slightly narrower. Not only do the establishments listed attract a clientele that meets my usual criteria for recommendation—single (preferably divorced), health club members, six-figure incomes—but the men and women you're likely to meet at this week's selections will also 1) *own* apartments of at least 5 full rooms and 2) regularly charter seaplanes for trips to Amagansett. *Quel* clever parameters, no?

I'd been dying to try *Atlee's* (64th St. and 3rd Ave.) since it opened last winter. I was so right to be so eager: Atlee's is to die for. This little place is only 12 feet square, but with the intimacy comes a thrilling illusion of space—every surface in the place is mirrored, including the floors, walls, ceiling, tabletops and bathroom fixtures. Nobody misses a trick. Atlee's serves only Campari-and-soda at the bar and no food at all, but the conversation—lucrative step deals and telephone gadgetry—is delicious enough.

Go Shoot Yourself: *At Eddie Steichen's watering hole, the Singles Gimmick is, take your own picture, give it to your date.*

Anthony Eden's (72nd St. and Columbus Ave.) is also monochromatic (sort of a gray-peach) except for the witty *trompe l'oeil* mural covering the rear wall: it's an incredibly lifelike view of the South Bronx from the Triboro Bridge, all a gorgeous, smoldering shambles. The crowd: mainly models and deeply tanned furriers. *Very* Milanese. Very eligible.

Back in the late 1970s the only singles who flocked to *H.H. Asquith* (64th St. and 3rd Ave.) were terribly roughhewn young children's book editors and Verazzano Narrows sorts of people. But since Barry Bellin took over and rechristened the place *Neville C's*, the front room has been wall-to-wall Scott-and-Zelda investment banker types who are known to get absolutely outrageous after midnight. (Would you believe an arm-wrestling match with some funny little Russian cab driver somebody invited in? I'm serious.)

Gladstone & Balfour (72nd St. and Columbus Ave.) is absolutely packed most nights with talent agents and a spritz of cosmetics executives. G & B doesn't *open* until 4 A.M. (I love this insane town, I love it). There is no menu, but if you have to ask they don't know you. The only meal served: Brie-burgers and Dr. Pepper ($9.50, cash only). New Wave does not have to mean cheap. Or inelegant—some regulars have started bringing their own custom-made sushi with them, ice-packed in leather valises (Mark Cross, $580). Wild! A very special place that will make you feel like an artist in Paris (Air France, $759 round-trip APEX) in the 1920s.

Even if *Disraeli* (64th St. and Third Ave.) is not my sort of *boite*, well-fixed-women-hungry young men of my acquaintance say that

Photograph by Jim Marchese

COZMOPOLITAN

Solitary Refinement:

By Randy Cleavage

PHOTOGRAPH BY JIM MARCHESE

Sexy Games Solo Girls Play While Waiting For the Phone to Ring

Sitting at home alone with a closet full of slatternly mail-order lingerie does *not* have to be a night of self-loathing hell!

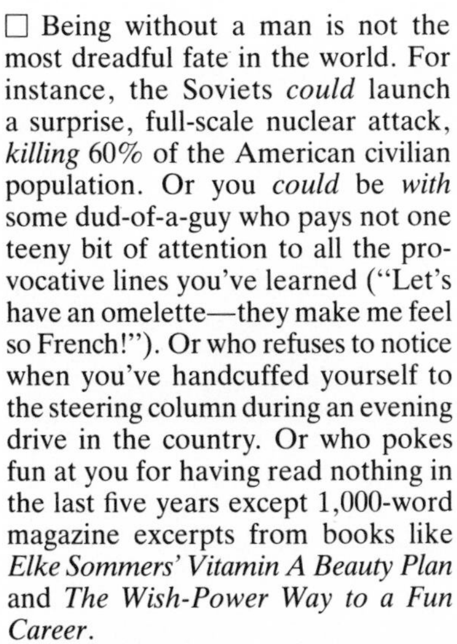

☐ Being without a man is not the most dreadful fate in the world. For instance, the Soviets *could* launch a surprise, full-scale nuclear attack, *killing* 60% of the American civilian population. Or you *could* be *with* some dud-of-a-guy who pays not one teeny bit of attention to all the provocative lines you've learned ("Let's have an omelette—they make me feel so French!"). Or who refuses to notice when you've handcuffed yourself to the steering column during an evening drive in the country. Or who pokes fun at you for having read nothing in the last five years except 1,000-word magazine excerpts from books like *Elke Sommers' Vitamin A Beauty Plan* and *The Wish-Power Way to a Fun Career*.

Yet as hard as she tries to please herself *and* her men, *every* girl is once in a while "between lovers." And that's just when you'll feel like staying in bed and crying for a week, dreaming up ways to meet Phil Donahue, and binging on caramelcorn. Wrong! There are ways of surviving until the next Mr. Right comes along that are lots less fattening—and more *fun*.

Psychologists say that *feelings*, after all, are really just *healthy emotions* that come and go, and that *single women* especially should not feel threatened by feelings of abandonment or a profound sense of *rootlessness*. The experts tell us that all of a woman's feelings together make up her *personality*. Each of us has her own unique *personality*, and the no-beau blues is one way the personality plays *psychological tricks* on us. The solution is to play some tricks right back!

Ten Tricky Turn-Ons for Home-bound Single Girls

1. Playing a word game may sound like a confusing bore, like something the frizzy-haired man-haters in your junior college dorm did on Saturday nights. 'Tain't necessarily so! Borrow a friend's Scrabble board for the night and improvise a one-girl tournament. *Don't* worry about scoring points or dictionary spellings. Instead, just tease yourself by laying down the little letters to form words that make for giggles and private shivers. Words such as "squeeze," "suede," "peach" and "thong" are peppy—and surprisingly *potent*.

2. Toss some big fluffy pillows on the floor, curl up in your soft nest and pretend you're a cat—or a *kitten*. (Maybe you're the royal pet of some ancient Egyptian pharoah. Or the California kitty of Tom 'Magnum P.I.' Selleck!)

3. It's 1943 during World War II. Write a letter to your make-believe serviceman boyfriend who's on a battleship somewhere in the South Pacific. (You don't know *exactly* where he is because *that's* Top Secret.) Tell your sailor-boy you're worried sick, and describe your imaginary hair-do to him—one of those nostalgic styles like on the Late Movie!

4. Slip into an oversized man's dress shirt (and nothing else!), and make yourself a late-night snack of toast and English marmalade (plain old low-cal jelly will do). Then find a thick book and read it *out loud*. If that doesn't make you feel almost cuter and cozier than you can *bear*, light a scented

[*continued on 203*]

PLAYBUY

For Greg Wallace, ending an affair is no bowl of cherries, but the bittersweet fruit of experience is simply there on the menu at the contemporary male's movable feast

fiction

By Dan Rack

10:47. ALWAYS GOOD to know the correct time.

Out of bed, Greg-boy. Ignore the hangover. What was it? A quarter-bottle? A third of a bottle in one sitting? What it was was fine, 30-year-old Scotch, the best. I'll survive. And then some.

10:49. Thank God my video-cassette recorder has the digital chronometer built in. She didn't figure on the VCR; typical. Barbara took every last clock with her when she left. Eight days ago, cleaned out of clocks completely. Okay, they were all hers. But it was just like Barbara, thinking she could inflict one last, dramatic uppercut, the lioness's final swipe, by taking time itself with her through the door, down to the elevator, around the rock garden in the lobby, past the doorman, into the parking garage and out of my life for good. Am I reeling? Think again, honey. Our six months were special, I'll give you that, but *recherche du temps perdu* is not this man's style.

Other exes just drifted away, things dissolved; there had always been a vague . . . understanding, an instinctual *ciao*. But with Barbara, it was different. She wanted to talk it out, she said. If verbalizing is your trip, I told her. . . .

"You know, you don't *live* life in any meaningful sense," she said on that last night. Then she was screaming, suddenly. Sexily. "You buy things. You act a life. I'm through being some kind of . . . *component* in Greg Wallace's little dream world."

I let the "component" crack pass. If there's one thing I need to make no apologies for, it's my stereo system. But I don't live life? Right. Diving the Grand Caymans every spring for two weeks is not living life. Trading a Corvette for a Saab turbo in the early 70's is not living life. Free-basing coke in a Beverly Hills Hotel suite with two Emmy-award-winning lighting directors is not living life. Sure thing. Right.

Maybe life in the fast lane was more than the lady could handle, I don't know. Maybe she was always too busy fretting about gas-mileage and speed limits. But I'd made it clear to her at the beginning: I'm a strictly high-performance driver down life's *autobahn*. The house odds may be the house odds, but a real player keeps tossing the dice. Again. And again.

"I loved her and I loved no one else and we had a lovely magic time while we were alone." Hemingway; I always reread Papa after a break-up. Funny thing, Barbara liked that about me, liked the book club membership, liked all the magazine subscriptions. Most of all, she once whispered, she liked my gentleness, that and my resemblance when I smile to Marlo Thomas's boyfriend on *That Girl*. She said she liked that I was a man who knew how to cry.

Not that she ever saw me cry. And I'm not crying now. I could if I wanted, could bawl like nobody's business if I were in the mood, but I'm not. In fact, I feel like singing. *Life is a cabaret, old chum, life is a cabaret*. . . . Funny thing, it really is.

11:02. Out of the sack, *now*. Sunday morning coming down, and no more Barbara, Barb, BB. Alone again. Does not compute: make that *single* again, free, free, free at last.

No cuticle cream on the dresser. Her fancy-pants Japanese architecture magazines, gone. Good. No Judy Collins albums stacked—*stacked*—on the Bang & Olafson. Great. No diaphragm sitting like some big poisonous mushroom on the bathroom sink. Even better.

Switching to the diaphragm. That was just like Barbara, too. Maybe it hadn't been a snub, bitchy provocation, deliberate hassle. Maybe. But any way you cut it, it still comes down to the same refrain: living life in the fast lane, safety belts are not standard equipment. She never understood that, couldn't understand. Or perhaps wouldn't. *Wouldn't? Wouldn't.* The truth isn't always pretty.

Take shaving. This may be the best fucking shave I've had in the last six months. The razor: deadly instrument, daily duty. War. Honor. No-nonsense hygiene. Men shave; women

(continued on page 196)

REMOTE
Gross

When we began this project, we knew that you know better than we do how happy you are where you live. Nevertheless, we traveled and interviewed and surveyed, and came up with a report on 12 American cities and how each provided for singles. We worked day and night, night and day speaking to bartenders, pushing maitre d's against the wall, putting residents under hot light bulbs and making them talk.

So here they are: urban landscapes for the night voyagers who are singles. If you're holed up inside and scared to go to these joints, scared of ogling and Goodbarism and meat marketing, the one generality we can offer is that the best places in any city are usually the ones where you can talk to the personnel. If the waiters answer you and the waitresses know how to laugh, you may be home. It's in their eyes.

We don't claim that our small and idiosyncratic précis is definitive, only that we listened to voices and tried to find whether capitalism was doing its work for singles in New York, Boston, Washington, Minneapolis, Miami, Houston, Dallas, Chicago, San Francisco, Los Angeles, New Orleans, and Philadelphia. We think it is and we think it's not. We groped throughout the nation, and we came up with hot nights and free hors d'oeuvres, saddles hanging from the rafters and slow fans moving warm fronts of cigarette smoke against cold fronts of air conditioning. You know what a singles bar looks like late at night as well as we do, and you've taken beer on the lap and the elbow jabs of angry drunks. But when you're single, when you're alone, and in the middle of a night where you've got to meet somebody or go home to the cold glow of the television and the silence of a dark bedroom, you brave these things. It's a battleground; we fight to win.

That's what we found, anyhow, in the Single Cities of America.

SINGLE CITIES

Boston

Boston is a city full of intellectual pretensions. It's also full of singles: hundreds of thousands of them to be exact. You're supposed to be in Boston to cultivate your mind, not your heart, so it's considered uncool to be "on the make." The word "singles" isn't really part of the Bostonian's vocabulary, and some denizens deny that there is a singles scene at all. "Of course there is," counters a single woman who has spent all of her 28 years in Boston and Cambridge. "It just wears wirerims."

Actually, in the downtown, business section of Boston you find the same typical singles bars you'd find in any other city. There are franchise outfits called Fathers One, Fathers Two, up to six at last count. These are local franchises of such national chains as the Rusty Scupper. These bars pack in clerical workers by offering gimmicks such as Ladies Night or Vodka Night, when all Vodka drinks cost 50¢. There are fern and basket bars, one of the nicer being St. Botolph's Street behind the Prudential Center. *Hampshire House* (84 Beacon St.) appeals to the pretensions of "proper" Bostonians. It's a four-story Georgian townhouse at the foot of Beacon Hill that houses a disco, a basement pub, and a dining room that attracts a tweedy but friendly crowd.

In collegiate Cambridge and its funkier neighbor, Somerville, singles hang out in places where they can pretend to be doing something other than looking for a pick-up. Soulful-looking eggheads sit for hours on end at the small square tables at Cafe Pamplona and Cafe Algiers in Harvard Square, sipping exotic coffees and reading "important" books. But they're all sitting there hoping, secretly, that someone will talk to them, so don't be afraid to draw anyone's nose out of a book at any of the Cambridge cafes.

Any laundromat in Cambridge or Boston is a great place to meet singles. *The Kirkland Street Laundry* near Savenor's (92 Kirkland St.) market is livelier than any nightclub. A lot of singles actually hang out in laundromats hoping to strike up friendships as their permapress clothes become permawrinkle from too lengthy a spin in the dryer. Ask to borrow some fabric softener and see what develops from there.

Bread and Circus (115 Prospect St.), a fresh produce market near Inman Square, is jammed with singles squeezing the overripe honey dews. Sexuality oozes from the aisles. *Steve's Ice Cream* (191 Elm St.) in Somerville always has a huge line, so it's impossible not to strike up a conversation with the other people waiting. Ditto for the even longer line outside the *No-name* (15½ Fish Pier) restaurant down by the docks in Boston that dishes up some of the best seafood at moderate prices in New England. *1,007 Plays* (1007 Massachusetts Ave.), a video emporium has also become a singles haunt. It's definitely hip to play Pac-Man.

Boston

Since Singles in the Boston area put L.L. Bean on the map, there are a lot of outdoorsy types. The banks of the Charles River are filled with cyclists and joggers. A lot of singles sun themselves on the banks of the Charles immediately after the winter thaw. Outdoor concerts at the *Esplanade* during the summer attract flocks of singles, especially on the Fourth of July, for fireworks and the Boston Pops.

A passion for sports is a prerequisite for happy living in Boston. Many beautiful friendships have flowered in the bleachers of *Fenway Park* (24 Yawley Way) (of course, there have been even more fist fights). It's hip to be into the Celtics. Health clubs are a big deal in Boston. Two particularly popular clubs, both with good facilities and open membership policies, are the *Back Bay Racquet Club* (162 Columbus Ave.) and the *Boston Athletic Club* (653 Summer St.). The latter attracts the likes of Boston Mayor Kevin White, and jocks Bobby Orr and Mike Torrez, of Red Sox renown.

Because public transportation shuts down at midnight, it's pretty crucial to own a car in Boston. People don't take taxis in this city. Pre-1970 vintage Volvos are considered super-hip, preferably with the back seat loaded with old paperbacks. Cars are also necessary for day trips when the Boston-Cambridge lifestyle begins to drive you crazy. A day trip to the Amherst-Northampton area of western Massachusetts is a must for any single. The countryside is beautiful, and there are a lot of great places to go. In the summer, tanned nymphets go skinny-dipping at *Chesterfield Gorge* near Amherst. In the winter, the ski rental huts around *Cummingtom* are stacked with cross-country enthusiasts, most of them single and looking to meet people. The ferries to Martha's Vineyard and to Provincetown (which has the liveliest summer gay community in the country) are also terrific places to meet other singles. For longer travels, the new low-fare planes run between Boston and New York by People's Express are crammed with singles, most of whom need someone to share the taxi from Newark, where the planes land, to Manhattan and back again. On any college holiday, Amtrak hops between New York and Boston.

Closer to home, there are quite a few good clubs and bars in Cambridge and Boston that attract singles in droves. The "in" bars in Cambridge seem to be *Ryles* (212 Hampshire St.), a two-story brick establishment, and the *Harvest* (44 Brattle St.), a top-flight restaurant in the Design Research Building whose lively bar attracts graduate students from Harvard and young architects from the surrounding area. Most of these people pretend they've eaten at the Harvest, when more than likely they've been chomping mediocre tacos at *Chi-chis* (1001 Massachusetts Ave.), another Cambridge singles haunt. The more collegiate set can be found posing at the *Casablanca* (40 Brattle St.), waiting for Ingrid Bergman to walk in the door. *The Inman Square Men's Bar*, despite its name, is filled with loads of singles of both genders and offers good rock and roll acts almost every night. *The Oxford Ale House* (36 Church St.), one of Cambridge's oldest singles' haunts, seems to have come out of a decline in the mid seventies and also offers live music and plenty of Watney's ale. For some grittier rock-and-roll, try the *Rathskeller* (528 Commonwealth Ave.) in Boston, which packs 'em in to hear and dance to new wave bands (many are local and excellent) every weekend. *The Plough and Stars* (Massachusetts Ave.) is for serious drinkers in Cambridge: the light beer and stout on draught remain the best in the city. Although it's been overtaken by students, a lot of the native Boston Irish still come to the Plough, so never mention the Oxford Ale House here.

In Boston, the restored *Faneuil Hall-Quincy Market* has become the most popular singles cruising scene in the city. There are a number of bistros and bars, the most popular of which are currently *Cricket's* and a trio called *Seaside, City-side* and *Dockside*. All the bistros in Quincy Market are slick, expensive, and more than a bit on the pretentious side. But then again, this is Boston.

If you're not a student, it's important to have an after-work bar in Boston. The *Copley-Plaza Hotel* (Copley Sq.) has restored its bar to original splendor and it now resembles, once again, a British outpost in India. There are large antique fans fluttering on the ceiling, and the drinks are large and stiff. The martinis come in individualized shakers. There used to be a highly objectionable singles bar called the Merry-Go Round in these quarters, filled with secretaries trying to snare a rich husband. The gimmick? You guessed it: the whole bar turned in circles. If you feel like rotating, there is the *Hyatt* (575 Memorial Dr.) in Cambridge. We are very glad that the Copley decided to abandon this ill-conceived piece of razzle-dazzle and restored its bar to its well-deserved elegance.

Keep in mind that Boston is not a late city. There are discos and jazz clubs, but activity winds down pretty early, around one A.M. The blue laws are strict, so no place stays open past two. If you're a late-night bloomer, you won't be very happy in this city. Natives of Boston and Cambridge do not thrive on going out, as their counterparts in New York do. They prefer to congregate in one another's apartments, cooking informal meals, drinking beer, and listening to records.

One long-time native of Boston sums up what the atmosphere is like for singles. "Boston and Cambridge are laid back—sort of like the West Coast, only without the sunshine."

Keep in mind that Boston is not a late city... activity winds down pretty early, around one A.M. The blue laws are strict, so no place stays open past two. If you're a late-night bloomer, you won't be very happy in this city. Natives of Boston and Cambridge do not thrive on going out, as their counterparts in New York do. They prefer to congregate in one another's apartments, cooking informal meals, drinking beer, and listening to records.

One long-time native of Boston sums up the atmosphere for singles. "Boston and Cambridge are laid back—sort of like the West Coast, only without the sunshine."

Chicago

The Midwest. Talk to a New Yorker and you'll discover that the Midwest begins on the other side of the Hudson. It ends, apparently, just to the East of Los Angeles. All he really knows for sure is that it's out there, somewhere. It's where the polls are taken, and where the TV shows get their ratings. But is it something more than that? Is the Midwest more than just some great cultural sinkhole, a huge receptacle for the disposal of countless disposable situation comedies, Jojaba commercials, and cartoon-illustrated official handbooks? The answer is a definite yes, and to think otherwise is an act of naive and dangerous provincialism.

The urban heart of the Midwest is Chicago, a great city of American cities, a city of neighborhoods, and a university town. There are staggering quantities of happy and fulfilled people here, living on tree-lined streets and going out at night to dine on some of the finer ethnic food around, including lots of Mexican. This is important to know, if you're single and living in any large city, as food is undoubtedly one thing with which—in the absence of certain others—you'll want to develop as intimate a relationship as possible. Aside from that, there is the fabled community of Chicago musicians, an undercurrent in the infra-structure that residents tend to take an excessively boring amount of pride in. There is a ton of theater out here, too, and a very big lake, which doesn't cost any money at all to hang out around. Some of the places which do cost money are listed below.

On Broadway (5246 N. Broadway). This small concert club is a good place to catch just about anything live. Take your pick from rock 'n' roll, new jazz, old jazz, traditional blues, domestic and imported reggae, you name it. Most of the acts are local, and the sound system is good. Better yet, the bar tab won't absolutely bust you, so it's a good place to take a date. If you're alone, this may or may not be a good place to strike up a conversation, depending on who is playing, and whether or not you can even hear. If you have to go home alone, at least you heard some riffs. Okay?

The Earl of Old Town (1615 N. Wells). This is one of the older, more well known clubs, going back a good twenty years. Folk is what they play here, and they play it better than anybody else in the Grain-belt. Some of the best have come through the Earl, among them Steve Goodman and John Prine. The place is small and unimposing, in an old brick building, with a small stage at one end, and a select audience of true faithfuls, all sucking rye. In a time when folk is out of favor, when most clubs are having to expand their repertoire, there is still a core of regulars here large enough, in the words of one club spokesman, "to keep the bar open." It's a good thing. There's something special about bars which do what they do and do it well, and stick with it over the years, like the Earl of Old Town has. More should.

Orphans (2462 N. Lincoln). This is one of a huge scattering of bars in the Lincoln Avenue area, to the north of downtown. This particular house is older than most of the others, offering simple "glass and brass" comfort, rather than the more

Chicago

highly decorated and thematic kind so popular in the eighties. Come here to watch Joe Daley and his band play BeeBop, for not a whole lot of money. But money shouldn't be a problem here, anyway. In the words of one club manager, "when the times get bad, the music gets better." That's as it should be, particularly when you're talking the blues. So spend now because you may not have it tomorrow. Even if you will have it tomorrow, spend it now. After all, what else is it for?

Park West (322 W. Armitage). This is a big concert house, not a barroom as such. But it is a place to hang out and drink, and the acoustic shell design means the sound of whatever you're listening to should be clear even when you're not. This is the place to come for the national acts, of absolutely all kinds. Dave Edmunds, Patrice Rushen, John Mayall, Teardrop Explodes, A Flock of Seagulls, Frankie Valle—something for everyone. You can even catch live boxing here several times each year. Something for the whole family. The seating is at tables, all on tiered risers backing off from the stage and dance floor, so it isn't impossible to achieve a level of intimacy. Park West is a great place to impress a date, particularly if you don't wish to talk to him/her. It's great. You can have your kir royale and slam dance to The Jam at the same time. This is the modern world.

Misfits (6459 N. Sheridan). This is one for those who don't want any foolishness mixed in with their rock and roll. Nowadays, as the rock and roll ethos as a lifestyle makes more and more sense, it's good to have at least a few places around to cater to it. Sandwiched between parochial Loyola college, and a smaller institution called Mundelein, this is still not a student bar, partly because the drinking age in Chicago is a whopping twenty-one, and partly because the Loyola kids prefer to stay indoors where it's safe. So, while there are some kids here, they don't dominate. There are blue collar guys, a handful of professional types—whoever really feels the need to catch *James White and the Blacks,* on some Tuesday night. *Fear* and *The Ruts* have stomped through here, too, though the bar is trying to get away from the nihilist scene. It just doesn't pay in the long run, according to the management. The crowd is cheap and they mess the place up. Who needs it? That's not a very punk way of looking at it, but....

"The original singles' bar of all times." The place is old—it goes back to 1961, older than the baby-boom generation, whose pocketbooks Butch and his pals so gleefully empty each night. The bar used to be a lot of things, but Butch finally figured out how to make it work, which was to get the women in *alone*, so the men would follow.

Incidentally, Misfits is reputed to have some of the most awesome women in town, and the hippest. But it seems to be on a look-but-don't-touch-or-I'll-have-my-skinny-boyfriend-apply-his-pointy-black-boots-to-your-kidneys, creep basis. Besides, says one observer, "they're probably all crazy, anyway." All the better.

Harry's (18 W. Quincy).This is one of the most popular after-work bars in Chicago. Not to be confused with Harry's Cafe, on Rush Street. This is a Loop bar catering mostly to the crowd from the Federal Building next door, who come to drink their lunches and look goggle-eyed at something besides legal documents for a while. The range is from immigration to IRS, clerks to Secret Service, great guys all. There is also the Arthur Andersen contingent, there with their secretaries, no doubt, trying to knock back a few or just find their office mates or kill time before the train. Everyone needs an after-work bar. Where else will the typing pool find executive escorts to Rush Street? By the way, it's not a good idea to just assume that that woman at the bar is looking to climb. At Harry's if you make the wrong guess you'll be emasculated so fast you won't even know what happened to you. Chicago is gradually being taken over by good-looking females who work for Playboy Enterprises.

Rush and Division Streets. The Rush Street area is where the singles' scene lives in Chicago, at least the visible part. It's where you tell your friends you don't go on a Saturday night, even though you always seem to wind up there anyway, at some point, somehow... if only this headache would go away... and what the hell is her name...? Check out Rush Street. There must be fifty bars up here, on the Near North Side, all glitzed up on the inside, all full of three-piece suits. Here are a couple of the landmarks:

Butch McGuires (2020 W. Division). This is the bar known in Chicago as "the original singles' bar of all times." That is as it may be, and the place is old—it goes back to 1961, which makes it considerably older than the coming of age of the baby-boom generation, whose pocketbooks Butch and his pals so gleefully empty each and every night. The bar used to be a lot of things, including maybe a strip joint, but Butch finally figured out how to make it work, which was to simply figure out ways to get the women in *alone*, so the men would follow. They used to have Flight Attendant night, of all things, based, one imagines, on the fact that the majority of flight attendants are attractive young women. Thank you, Hugh Hefner. Now, however, the place is just another antiques and mahogany "Irish pub," with all sorts of "Irish pub" stuff hanging off the walls and the beams. There are some plants, too. Just what young, upwardly mobile professionals need in order to meet and ensnare sleeping partners. This is the model for the cliché.

The Snuggery (15 West Division). Right across the way from Butch's is the place with the name that's hard to beat. The Snuggery. Roll that around in your mouth for a minute. The Snuggery. There are four in the Greater Chicago area, but this is the main branch. It's a giant, two-level cube space fitted out with all kinds of Victorian-looking junk and "objets," stained and cut glass, lots of plants. You know the scene. There is even an atrium with a greenhouse effect at the top of this dancehall monster. In the words of one bar spokesman, "We create an ambience which is conducive to young Americans." Whatever that means. But you can bet on one thing. This is a singles' bar extraordinaire, a muscle-flexing shopping center that claims to be the number-one spot in town. They've got the best sound sys-

Chicago

tem, the best D.J., the best music. Who knows, maybe they have the best food, too. And the best view? Maybe the best art on the walls? Who knows, in this the best of all Snuggery Worlds, why not just say that this low-rent mishmash bar is simply the best place in Chicago? One thing's for sure, as the management says, "Everybody finds some kind of comfort here." Yeah, and a lot of people find herpes.

Sick of bars? Listen, don't bother with this Rush Street mess. At least don't go there on purpose. Find yourself a local and get to know the bartender. That's what Chicago was made for. If you take the time to get to know the people in your neighborhood, you won't feel so alone here, even if you are so alone. And if you're a student, you should really have no fears. This is a university town, if there ever was one. Circle Campus of the University of Chicago is the hub, down in scenic Hyde Park. The students don't do much, but that's okay. They're supposed to be smart. To the west is DePaul, and there is Loyola, and Northwestern, not actually in Chicago. It's town is Evanston and Evanston is dry, so those kids trek over to the big city periodically. Unfortunately, the blue laws make a night on the town tough for kids, so most students probably just hang out in their frats and dorms drinking beer from hand-held aluminum cannisters, which they later discard. So, next time you're out prowling Butch's, don't be disappointed if you don't wind up with a nice young co-ed majoring in philosophy. You can always look for student sex on campus, but if you're not actually a student, that can be a pretty alienating experience. You're a townie, which is a bad thing to be.

As far as residential considerations go, the Gold Coast is the hopping place for all you swingles with law jobs. Buy a condo and have sex in it. It's the way to relieve boredom. Otherwise, make do with one of the older and more attractive neighborhoods. Chicago is a great city. Just get off your ass and explore a little. Here, do this. Get a piece of paper, eight by eleven. Write down some plans. Then, implement them. When you've implemented them, reap the rewards. Life in the Midwest isn't so bad. Pass the word.

Dallas

Now that Dallas has been firmly inscribed on our national consciousness as the home of just so many manipulative centerfolds and corporate villains, like J.R. and his crowd, it might do to elaborate a bit on some of the differences between media myth and reality.

First, Dallas has a sense of tradition, of history, that some of the newer Texas cities lack. A lot of the money here is controlled by the older families. That makes it harder to break into the financial arena, though rewarding when you do. But there is also a share of Houston-style boom-town madness going on here. Particularly for the single man or woman, it can be a very confusing scene.

Often, success in Dallas boils down to pure appearances. What seems simple and right at first glance turns out to be a sophisticated veneer of symbolism. For instance, it is a well-known fact that there is nothing known to modern man that can come between the native Dallasite and his Luchese ostrich-skin boots. They are his symbols of a kind of antiquated "Texas nationalist pride." In the words of one resident, if Dallas had its way it would "issue green cards to all the northerners and secede." But even though Dallasites see themselves as the final word in all things Texas, they still have this wistful gaze to the East. They

Dallas

do wear Brooks Brothers suits over their ostrich skins.

What does all this have to do with the single Dallasite? For a start, it means that living happily in this city depends on the rapid assimilation of some purely western trademarks, along with the cultivation of slick Eastern sensibilities. Appearances come first. Money and sexual companionship, cars and apartments, follow accordingly. Here are some places where you may want to work on getting your accent down pat:

Greenville Bar and Grill (2821 Greenville). This place calls itself the oldest bar in Dallas, and it probably is. It's an unimposing beer and burger sort of place that specializes in not getting in your way while you're trying to relax. On Thursday and Saturday nights there is some authentic Dixieland jazz from Hal Baker and the Gloom Chasers.

Since the Bar and Grill is one of the only hangouts in Dallas over five years old, it does tend to get pretty crowded. But that's okay, because the spirit in here is right. The only real problem with the place is that it is too close to S.M.U.

Longhorn Ballroom (216 Corinth). Just south of Downtown, in industrial Dallas, this is truly the "house that Bob built." As far as the locals are concerned, this is the original kicker palace, the watering-hole dream of the late Bob Wills. There is a lot of big-name country music here, as well as a fair amount of people who can actually two-step. The Longhorn is a large bar literally crammed with western murals and decor, even phony cactus that pretends to hold the ceiling up. And even though it seats 2,000, the management claims that you won't get lost in the shuffle here. Says one spokesman, "Our main concern is the public. We kiss these people's ass." Well, there's some southern hospitality.

Stricktly Tabu (4111 Lomo Alto). The Tabu is something of a class act from the past. Named for its former exclusive membership policies, it is Dallas' main jazz house, the home of the better local fusion talent. Structurally it is a cube space divided up into tiers and levels, a miniature monument to someone's version of 1950s deco-moving-into-the-future architecture. As one patron notes, entering the club is like "walking into a Warner Bros. set." Still, the place is comfortable and dimly lit. The drag at Stricktly Tabu is the realization that fusion jazz, no matter how good it is, is little more than complicated sound for nervous people.

Stoneleigh P (2926 Maple). The P may well be one of the most popular small bars in all of Dallas. Located in the trendy Oaklawn District, between downtown and S.M.U., it will on any given evening be full of artistes, professionals, college kids, and, as one patron has it, "the sort of people who watch public TV." In the P (named for the old pharmacy that once stood here, pictures of which now fill the mild earth-tone walls), there is a general assumption you are here because you're an interesting and vital person.

Cafe Dallas (At the corner of Greenville and Lovers' Lane). The address of this spot is almost too good to be true. It's located in the midst of a dense collection of "swingles" apartment complexes. If you can't find conversation, companionship, or sex here you will have no choice but to play video Defender for the rest of your life.

Billy Bob's has no mechanical bulls. It has real ones . . . only thing that hasn't been tacked on is an auto dealership.

Eight-O (2800 Routh). When Eight-O first opened a few years back, it fast became known as the place to see and be seen by the best of Dallas' professional bohemians. Now, Eight-O, in all its high-tech splendor, is a stainless steel and plastic plaza where people in berets can come and commiserate over their kirs. Just for the record, when one member of the management was asked how he felt about the singles' scene at Eight-O, he replied simply, "We're not middle-class enough to talk about that." Good for you.

Nostromo (4515 Travis). Owned by the makers of Eight-O, this place was apparently designed to outdo its predecessor in absolutely every detail. This is now the *only* place to go in Dallas. It doesn't matter who you are. If you deserve to live, and you want to prove it, there is only one thing to do. Put on a jacket, stroll in the front door, sidle up to the bar, and order up a white wine spritzer. You are now validated as a successful human being.

Billy Bob's Texas. This monster beer palace is actually in Fort Worth, but that's beside the point. Billy Bob's may be one of the most frightening things that has happened on this continent in about a million years. There is just no way to fully understand what is happening in your mind as you enter this most awesome spectacle of Wild West decadence. So don't try. Just don't. Billy Bob's exists. It is fact. There is only one thing that can possibly save you from dangerous confusion, and that is the rapid consumption of massive quantities of alcohol at any one of Bob's forty-three—count 'em—forty-three bar stations.

This is truly the largest bar in the world. Here's why: Billy Bob's Texas has over 100,000 square feet of available floor space, all sticky from spilt beer; three separate restaurants (one of which is an oyster bar), a jewelry store, clothing shops, shoeshine girls all over the place, a hair salon, as well as—ready for this?—a live indoor rodeo! Billy Bob's doesn't have mechanical bulls. It has real ones. About the only thing that hasn't been tacked on is an auto dealership. In your face, Gilley's!

Now, there are some places besides bars where people go and do stuff. Dallas may not be the lively arts center of the Sun Belt, but it does have a fair amount of theater and music. The Dallas Theatre Center, in Oaklawn, is the main resident house. This is a two-stage, commercial company that does its popular main season upstairs and more experimental new work in the smaller downstairs area. Good, entertaining fare. There is also a smaller company called Stages, which does a lot of new scripts. S.M.U. offers a good bit of student theater in their Bob Hope performing arts complex, where you can see some of the more reliably trained actors in the south. If you're into ballet, probably the best thing to do is drive to Houston and see theirs, though Dallas does have its company, and there is also an opera company, which is more of an opera club. They perform in November. In May, though, the Met hits the provinces for one single week. Buy tickets early.

Most of the music in town is confined to the clubs.

Houston

Houston, Texas. If you're young and single and looking to buy into the American dream, this is the place to start. It's a truly awesome town, a space-age monument to some vast, archaic, Wild West mythology of expansion and wealth, a staggering network of glass-enclosed office plazas and freeways, peopled with Horatio Alger characters all hunkered down over the tops of rosewood desks and clutching the wheels of expensive automobiles. Next time you drive down I-10 or the Gulf Freeway, have a look around. See the guys in their Mercedes. Take in some of the platinum blondes, fresh off the set of Dallas. *Who are these people? What are they doing here? Chances are, if you were to ask them, you'd find that each is on some private journey toward Houston's one collective destiny: the accumulation and subsequent disposal of massive sums of money, at the fastest rate, and in the most opulent manner, ever witnessed by anyone in the history of the planet.*

Sound fun? It is, especially if you're single and ambitious and feel you've nothing to lose but your savings.

Downtown: Nothing much happens here, except business, during the day. At night it all pretty much closes down. There are, however, the *Alley Theatre*, where you can catch last year's Broadway hits, and *Jones Hall*, a beautiful performance space that houses the Houston Grand Opera, and the Ballet. The Ballet, incidentally, is one of the finest in the world. Opening nights at Jones Hall are awe-inspiring occasions.

For after theater eats, follow the crowd to *Nick's Fish House* (1001 Fannin, in the First City Tower). Nick's is definitely a man's place. Its decor gives brute masculinity new meaning, with enough solid oak and walnut to fuel all the wood stoves in Vermont, all hewn into these massive "power center" booths, and all covered in enough thick black leather to make new jackets for all the Hell's Angels who ever lived. The best thing about Nick's are the phone jacks at each table. Ostensibly they're provided for conference calls over salmon steak lunches, but they're best used to ring up that sweetie at the next table, whose escort has just gone off to dispute his American Express limit. When you talk at Nick's you're talking big. Big men. Big decisions. Big tabs. Wear a jacket.

As you move out of downtown, toward the south and southwest, there are plenty more restaurants of the macho-meets-steak variety. There is also an enormous assortment of clubs and discos and country/western bars. Here are some more notable spots:

Todd's (5050 Richmond Ave.). Todd's is the definitive pick-up bar of Houston, Texas. It is an unashamed meat market. They like to come to Todd's. Fair enough.

Houston

If you get tired of Todd's you can try the local branch of *T.G.I. Friday*, next door. There's also a place called *Cooter's*, and another named simply *Cowboy*. All in all there must be a dozen big singles' hangouts in the Windsor Plaza area off Richmond, the "magic circle," as it is known by frequenters.

Élan (1885 St. James). Owned by the people who own Todd's, Élan bills itself as Houston's high-fashion disco. It's a members-only house that features a lot of plush chairs filled with debutantes and ex–University of Texas wild men who stand around in groups and talk about their corporate futures. Structurally, the place is a kind of windowless cube that has been chopped up into various private and semiprivate nooks, each with some theme or other, like the "library," which is a balcony area decorated with shelves of books, none of which seem to get much of a workout. Says one employee: "At Élan, when people meet each other they talk about their jobs, about how much money they are making, and about the titles they hold. Titles are big."

Cody's (3400 Montrose). Cody's is a pretty good jazz club that features a fairly consistent local lineup, but which has its real attraction in its positively beautiful view of the Houston skyline from the patio on top of its office plaza home. Located in the old Montrose district of Houston, Cody's tends to draw a slightly more hip crowd than will be found in the newer suburbs to the west. There are also a fair number of displaced New Yorkers.

120 Portland St. (120 Portland St.). Though not a singles' joint as such, 120 Portland deserves mention as one of the finer small restaurants in Houston, if not the entire Southwest. It makes its home in an old house, and its interior is simple and clean and unobtrusive. Chef Theodore Schmitz's menu changes every two weeks, which is a nice thing to find in a city of chains. This is a good place for single women to have a drink and not be bothered, possibly because 120 Portland St. is owned by a woman. Her name is Nanette.

Birraporetti's (1997 West Gray). Here we have a hugely successful Irish bar, set down in a mall, that serves pizza, and is filled with more antique beer signs, plows on the wall, and even deco fittings, than you can begin to take in at a glance. There are a lot of good-looking young preppies here, which is probably where the success of the bar lies. Birra's tends to be over-priced, but it is always overcrowded.

Gilley's (Pasadena, Texas). A few years back, Mickey Gilley decided to build himself a bar. His creation is a monster testament to all that was huge and good in the Old West. Located in industrial Pasadena, this bar comes in at somewhere near 150,000 square feet, with a reported capacity of 15,000 beer drinkers. This is the original mechanical-bull bar, the place where John Travolta rode out a movement that overnight became the industry most of us now associate with Houston above all others: the Urban Cowboy. Besides the bull, there is also a recording studio and a radio station used to broadcast Gilley's live shows to over 400 other radio stations nationwide.

Mickey Gilley decided to build himself a bar. His creation is a monster testament to all that was huge and good in the Old West. Located in industrial Pasadena, this bar comes in at somewhere near 150,000 square feet, with a reported capacity of 15,000 beer drinkers. This is the bar where John Travolta rode.

There are literally thousands of folks who come here to drink staggering quantities of Lone Star beer. Thanks to the bar's location, it supports a healthy number of kickers (mean guys in pointy-toe boots, known as shit-kickers), but there remain the dudes from town and the European tourists, who come to gawk, and of course a healthy number of single cowgirls. All in all, this can be an extremely rowdy bar. Asked about fights at Gilley's, part owner Sherwood Cryer replies: "Aw, hell, some of them guys (kickers) 'll start playing some grab-ass with each other 'till one gets mad and knocks someone up 'side the head and we just throw 'em out of there." Well said, Sherwood. Not to worry. So come on over and check out the neon beer signs and the hardwoods all over the place and the beer on the floor. It may not have much to do with the Old West, but it does all make a perverse kind of sense in the eighties.

La Carafe (813 Congress, on Old Market Square). This small actors' roost near the Alley requires at least one visit by everyone in town. It occupies the oldest standing building in the urban center, and is so unchanged from the last century that the dust piled over the scads of junk and "objets" is worthy of note as a special form of soft-sculpture. This is not a singles place in any sense of the word, but if you drop by La Carafe you won't be lonely. It is one of the friendliest bars in Houston.

Of course, there are those for whom the bar scene, no matter how lively and inviting, is still not an answer to the frustrating problem of being single in Houston. For those who don't like to go out at night, or who just don't want to sit at a bar stool alone, here are a few alternatives:

Memorial Park. This is Houston's main drag for the health-conscious. Some of the best public jogging in the Southwest can be had here, along with some of the best public joggers. The sheer quantity of tanned, firm, young flesh is frightening to behold. A lot of single lawyers run here on their lunch breaks.

Metropolitan Museum of Art. All things considered, this is a very fine museum, and there is often some excellent walking art here as well. Museums have always been famous spots for pick-ups. Houston's is no different.

Rice University. Rice students are unbelievable. Don't go looking for girls or guys here. They're all much too busy sitting around in their rooms alone. The student bar is generally empty. There is some speculation about whether or not Rice actually has any students. Few campuses have so little influence on the surrounding community.

Finally, if you're single and gay, have no fear. Houston has one of the largest and, by all accounts, healthiest gay scenes in the country. Its focus is Montrose. Stay in Montrose and all is well. If you're straight, Montrose is still the trendy, hep place to be. It's full of quiet little fern and basket places and wine bars and galleries, kind of a Georgetown South. It's worth a trip.

Los Angeles

Single people come to L.A. and stay in L.A. because somewhere, as far away as New York and Kansas City and as close as the San Fernando Valley, they heard that Hollywood was a golden land of opportunities. In the olden days, the young flocked to become stars. In our own particular recession, real estate and made-for-TV movies are the draws. You'll find guys in open collars sporting gold chains talking about mortgage financing and MOWs—that's movie of the week to you greenhorns.

You can flock to the Valley or Marina Del Rey if you want to see the real laid-back people really lay back. But they're all waiting for the right mate to come along to sponge off of. You'll find a lot of that in L.A. The real nightlife for the fairly upwardly mobile L.A. single is in West Los Angeles, Hollywood, and a few downtown watering holes that are slightly off the beaten track.

L.A. is an early town. You'll come out of a late movie and find there aren't a hell of a lot of places to drop into even for a quick beer or a cup of coffee. Most people have mellowed off to bed. (If you can't say "take a meeting" without a snicker, don't try. The natives will understand you fine if you just say you've got a meeting to go to.)

The Studio 54 phenomena could never happen in L.A. It's a stay-at-home town. Los Angelites have cars and love to visit each other in them. Souls are sold for Rolls Royces. The tourists are the only ones who stop and stare. The Rolls and the more discrete Mercedes, Porsches, and BMWs can easily be parked in front of someone's home for a dinner or brunch where you'll meet new mates and business contacts.

Life in L.A. is always colored by the fact that it is the capital of the entertainment world.

The more painfully fashionable evening spots in Los Angeles cater to the on-the-way-up, primarily single inhabitants of the entertainment industry. At these places, people-to-know meet other people-to-know so they can learn what gossip to spread in the morning at the studio. Not everyone can be a studio executive, but that news has yet to reach the other 50 percent of those frequenting L.A.'s poshest niteries. They're aspiring to the movie-television-music fantasy career world. While transacting business or plugging away for that big break, all these people eye each other carefully. One never knows. One could find that special star or starlet. Or even life-long happiness with a fellow exec at a neighboring studio. It never hurts to have all the bases covered.

Perhaps the more bearable of the latest trendy spots is *Kathy Gallagher* (8722 West Third Street). It's one of the least pretentious of the pretentious waterholes. Kathy Gallagher, an emigré from New York City, has set up a gimmickless bar, something that's rare in these parts. The place consists of a long bar and bar table area. A restaurant off to the side serves adequate Continental food. All this is not to say that Kathy Gallagher doesn't cater to the run-of-the-mill L.A. killer trendy. The difference is that the young William Morris agents and ever-present studio executives can be seen at relative ease here. Also, the L.A. caste system seems not to

Los Angeles

be enforced here. Young working class types (attractive, of course) can be sighted sidling up to those at the top.

The *China Club* (8338 West 3rd St.) is the nerve center of the "Melrose scene" which consists of several niteries lining Melrose Avenue, a little south of dying Hollywood. It is an incredibly noisy combination Chinese restaurant/New Wave bar. New Wave music is played very, very loud. The single animal prowling near the very large bar is a very experienced, sophisticated version of the professional single. The usual entertainment types and lawyers prevail. These folks are universally savvy; they think they're at the top of the world. "Single" is the last word they'd use to describe themselves, even though technically most of them are. That about sums up the clientele. "I call it new punk," says a screenwriter. "It's sort of beyond punk. It's rich punk. It's people who are dressing punk and paying $400 for a jacket. You know, upper-echelon lawyers who are slumming." When checking out this chichi bar, take note that it is designed down to its teeth. Almost literally. "It's designed to the way the food is on the plate," says an impressed casting agent. "It's incredibly fashionable."

Madam Wong's (949 Sun Mun Way) is a distant cousin of the China Club, although it's somewhat more tame. In Chinatown, during the early evening hours, Madam Wong's is an honest to God Chinese restaurant complete with lanterns dangling from the ceilings. As the evening grows later, the food is whisked away and the place becomes a club featuring New Wave bands. This is a music place, not so much a bar-type scene, frequented by music business types, eighteen-year-olds, and anyone else interested in the latest sounds.

Joe Allen's (8706 West 3rd St.) is traditionally known as a show biz bar. It has a lively but casual bar scene. People come to drink, not necessarily pick each other up, although of course that does happen. You can leave that $400 jacket at home and relax. Also, points out our screenwriter friend, you can actually get a hamburger "for less than $12,000."

Spago (8795 West Sunset Blvd.) is a pizza place. But as Michelle, one of its managers, says, "It doesn't compare with any other pizza you've ever tasted." It seems that Spago's rather expensive and rather small pies are baked in two of the only four wood-burning pizza ovens in the United States of America. Oak wood only, thank you.

More importantly, Spago is ultra in. If you don't belong at Spago, well, you just don't belong anywhere. If you hated that attitude in sixth grade, you still might hate it at Spago. It was founded in 1981 by Wolfgang Puck, former co-owner and chef of Ma Maison, a restaurant so outrageously trendy that its phone number isn't listed. The younger, mostly single film and studio set has gravitated with Wolfgang to Spago. Says Michelle: "Wolfgang has a following that goes back years." Remember that name.

Make reservations two weeks in advance. (That's two.) Then be prepared to stand in line for an hour or so. This, if anything, adds to Spago's spectacular popularity. "Just treat people badly, just be rude, and people just line up outside," says one film type who had just made reservations.

Is it worth it? Well, you'll probably wait longer than it takes to get into Spago before you find a neighborhood pizzeria that serves duck sausage pizza or pizza topped with leeks, double-blanched garlic, artichokes, Santa Barbara shrimp, and, yes, smoked salmon.

For dancing, there's *The Circus Disco* (6648 Lexington Ave.). which can be found in Hollywood. To some of you Hollywood may still mean movie stars and celebrity footprints on the sidewalks. Although nowadays you can still see the old, art deco Hollywood through neon signs, it has largely been replaced by sleaze and roughneck nightlife. Still, singles venture in to frequent The Circus and a few other night spots. The Circus, aptly named, was built in the tradition of New York's barn-like discos. Singles and others come to dance and watch each other dance from an overhead walkway connecting two rooms. In one, disco music is blasted. In the other, New Wave is pumped. In the disco room, dress is any variation on casual. New Wave/Punk clothes predominate in room two, where one woman was slightly dressed simply in a lingerie teddy and spiked shoes. A young lawyer questioned about the place recalls the time he somehow lost his shirt. He still doesn't recall how. The crowd, he says, consists of "a lot of young people, a lot of teeny boppers, a lot of gays, and then your everyday people." Business deals are not struck here. People at The Circus are serious about dancing and The Circus serves the purpose.

In Los Angeles there is almost a hierarchy of where the bands play. At the top of the heap is the *Roxy* (9009 Sunset Blvd.). This places is used as showcases by the record companies and so is frequented by those who consider themselves to be hipper than thou. In other words, at this place, the studio executives rub elbows and coke spoons with the record company executives who rub elbows with the television executives who elbow out everybody else having a good time.

The Roxy is hard to get into. Large chunks of tickets are often snapped up by the record companies ahead of time. But the fact that it's hard to get in only

Make reservations two weeks in advance. Then be prepared to stand in line for an hour or so. This, if anything, adds to Spago's spectacular popularity. "Just treat people badly, just be rude, and people just line up outside."

Is it worth it? Well, you'll probably wait longer than it takes to get into Spago before you find a neighborhood pizzeria that serves duck sausage pizza or pizza topped with leeks, double-blanched garlic, artichokes, Santa Barbara shrimp, and, yes, smoked salmon. . . .

At the Circus, one woman was slightly dressed simply in a lingerie teddy and spiked shoes. A young lawyer questioned about the place recalls the time he somehow lost his shirt. He still doesn't recall how.

infatuates the Los Angelites. It makes them want it more. If by some distant chance this doesn't appeal to you, you might try *Rissmiller's Country Club* (18415 Sherman Way) in nearby Reseda. It's bigger, a little nicer, and easier to get into. And the musical menu is up to Roxy standards.

Musso & Franks (6667 Hollywood Blvd.) is a Hollywood restaurant that deserves mention for its excellent, red-meaty menu and for its atmosphere, which is perfect for a cozy dinner. Unfortunately, because of Hollywood's state of decline, this old scriptwriter's hangout is beginning to suffer a little in the popularity department, although you can still find a line at the door. If you're willing to ignore the slutty activity outside, enter this dark cavern and sink into a soft leather banquette and a juicy thick steak.

Another restaurant currently in vogue is *The Original Pantry Cafe* (877 South Figueroa), which can be found with some difficulty in the heart of downtown Los Angeles. "It's really sleazy," says one gourmet, show biz–type who went back. "The atmosphere is a bizarre diner." The food, which is excellent, consists primarily of steaks, cole slaw, and pickles. But what attracts denizens of the fast lane is that the restaurant is staffed by ex-convicts. A sign indicates how long each waiter has been working at The Original Pantry, i.e., been out of the joint. Needless to say, people line up to get in.

The after-hours club phenomena is fairly new to the early-to-bedders of L.A. But they've learned to love it. The bastion of these clubs is *At Sunset* (8907 West Sunset Blvd.), which is a little straighter than the rest and attracts an older youngish crowd of entertainment and business people on the way to the top. At Sunset becomes an after-hours bar only on Friday and Saturday nights (2:00–5:00 A.M.). Sometimes there is a D.J., other times there are live bands, as the owner's whim dictates. Beer and wine are served. You can dance or just hang out, even in the kitchen if you really want to. (The place used to be a restaurant; now munchies are served.) During the week, anything goes at At Sunset. There are acting workshops, video tapings, and canvases painted. You can browse while you sip at night. Just wander in and see what's happening and "bring your ideas," advises one who has. Private parties are often held on week nights, but sometimes spontaneous partying erupts. Drop in and see.

Club Lingerie (6507 West Sunset Blvd.), situated in Hollywood on the Strip (the sleaziest section), starts out as a regular club with a complete bar. But as the witching hour nears it becomes an after-hours club that doesn't close until around 4:00. Live bands play and dancing occurs. The crowd is largely professional, but on the punkish side of those who frequent At Sunset. Singles come to Lingerie with sex on the mind, but this is not a meat market. One can emerge unscathed *or* no longer alone.

Singles come to *Club Lingerie*, but this is not a meat market. One can emerge unscathed. Of course L.A. abounds with the usual on-the-make singles bars, places where the music reaches unprecedented decibels and people are judged simply by how they look or how much beer they can consume. One such bar is the *Fox Inn– Rathskeller* (2626 Wilshire Blvd.) in Santa Monica. Featured is a pianist playing dirty songs while chugging beer. "He stands on his head and chugs pitchers," says one fan. "It's pretty rowdy, it's pretty fun." (If you like that sort of thing.) At Fox Inn, people are in a mood to get crazy and all that goes along with it, including seemingly unconnected hands grabbing human parts you consider private. Don't expect witty repartee.

Fun and approachable New Wave can be found in Hollywood at the *O.N. Klub* (3037 West Sunset Blvd.)

As *People, Time,* and *Newsweek* have already informed you, Venice, California, is for roller skating. Youngish people, and some rapidly marching toward middle age, can be seen skating up and down a strip of asphalt near the ocean. They are usually scantily dressed in bizarre clothing, ears glued to Sony Walkmen or suitcase-style radios. Not too far from the beach is *Rose Cafe and Market* (220 Rose Ave.), a coffee house–restaurant frequented by the slightly less spaced out Venetians and by the crowds who come to watch them space out. These, often as not, are young professionals escaping corporate/movie studio L.A., just a few miles away. The Rose has a salad takeout table area where you can easily chat with the natives, and a little California objet de junk gift shop. A restaurant section has pretty white cloth-covered tables, some of which are outside. The desserts are great. So are the espresso and dessert wines. "It's just a neat place to go and sit, and a lot of interesting people hang out there," says a devotee.

Of course L.A. abounds with the usual on-the-make singles bars, places where the music reaches unprecedented decibels and people are judged simply by how they look or how much beer they can consume. One such bar is the *Fox Inn–Rathskeller* (2626 Wilshire Blvd.) in Santa Monica. Featured is a pianist playing dirty songs while chugging beer. "He stands on his head and chugs pitchers," says one fan. "It's pretty rowdy, it's pretty fun." (If you like that sort of thing.) At Fox Inn, people are in a mood to get crazy and all that goes along with it, including seemingly unconnected hands grabbing human parts usually considered to be private. Don't expect witty repartee.

Along the same lines, but with a country twist, is *The Palomino* (6709 Lankershim Blvd.) in North Hollywood. The music is country and the raison d'être is drinking. These people are in a good mood. Your object should be to leave saying you've never been so drunk in your life.

The *Cowboy* (1721 South Manchester Avenue) is an imitation cowboy bar in Anaheim. Those aspiring to upper crustdom with a penchant for gettin' down to some real rowdy fun, drop by to ride a mechanical bull, which is in action a few times a week.

The Oar House (2941 Main Street) is bigger than the Saloon, but the basic premise remains the same. It's racy and a bit more college oriented.

Los Angeles

The one pickup-type bar that few seem to take too much exception to is *Merlin McFly* (2702 Main Street) in Santa Monica. Merlin's attracts a true mix of single life; some are beer-drinking rowdies and others are more subdued suit-laden execs having a good time. The place attracts college kids and their elders. It's a pickup place but more relaxed. If you venture in alone, most likely you'll survive. If you go, make sure to check out the bathroom. "You go to comb your hair and Merlin (the magician) appears in the mirror behind you," says a visitor. "Very freaky." Indeed.

One thing a newcomer will immediately notice about Los Angeles is that nobody, but nobody, walks the streets. One just doesn't saunter down the street taking in the scene. Foot traffic has nothing to do with L.A. life. There are a few interesting exceptions. One is *Little Tokyo*, an area of L.A. near dowtown, which seems self-explanatory. There you can peruse Japanese shops and sushi bars. A less popular spot to wander is *Koreatown*, which runs parallel to the mid-Wilshire area. *Westwood*, the area near UCLA, is packed on Friday nights with people showing off and walking around. College types and older guys sporting gold chains are the inhabitants of these streets.

An easier place to meet people is your corner health club. They are sprouting all over L.A. Your goal should be to find a group you want to know better and get yourself invited to a ski weekend where they'll become your best friends. In L.A. you must learn to play racquet ball. It's tennis one generation removed. One safe bet is the *Sports Connection*, which has four branches, each with their own distinct flavor. Try the Santa Monica branch. If you're stuck with extra cash, you might try the *Century West Club*. You'll find monied folk and Beverly Hills matrons in a more luxurious atmosphere.

San Vicente Boulevard in Santa Monica is *the* place to jog. Runners meet, mate and deal-make huffing and puffing along this condo-lined lane and its central mall. Another jogging spot is the grassy stretch on Santa Monica Boulevard on the border of Beverly Hills and Los Angeles.

Miami

The first thing you'll need to learn if you're single in Miami is not to take the tourist-class madness too seriously. What you need to do is have a good fling with the city, play Miami as a huge and ultimately inconsequential game, like Pinball. Flip off Bayshore Drive and light up a number on Key Biscayne. Speed over the Rickenbacker Causeway and up the mainline into downtown, and then pop through the Cricket Club for a Perrier.

If you're a single man down here, you'll always need to carry a bankroll. Own a fast car. Wear silk. Keep an unlisted phone and two apartments. Make sure there is always gas in your Cigarette speedboat. If asked, say you are in Import/Export. Forget your past.

If you are a woman, meet a man in Import/Export who owns a fast car. When the passenger door opens at the red light on Bayshore, just get in. Don't ask any questions if he disappears for extended periods of time without warning. Just don't do anything but shop at Mayfair when he gives you money, or stay at home and watch color TV, or lie out back naked in the sun.

You might gather that Miami is a fast lane of recreational chemicals and professional tanning. You might gather right!

Is it worth it? You're damn right it is. That's why you're here, for a little excitement. It isn't everyone's idea of a good game, but, baby, it's the way Miami works, so strut into the center of this exquisite dime arcade and flash a little bit. Here's where:

Monty Trainer's (2560 S. Bayshore Drive). Monty's used to be a great place to go sit outside and have raw conch salad and a few drafts. It wasn't that crowded, because it was strictly a Coconut Grove hangout, in the days before the Grove became the chic and fashionable condo community it is today. Now Monty's Conch is crowded, and there are even a lot of high-school kids with fake IDs keeping low profiles around the lounge. All in all, though the place is not what it used to be, it is nonetheless a good bar for the under-twenty-five crowd. It has calypso music and party lanterns—and it still has good conch salad. What more could you want?

The Village Inn (3131 Commodore Plaza, in Coconut Grove). This is a good place to catch the chic on their nightly rounds. The bar itself is like a lot of other big bars in Miami, all decorated up in the Caribbean-rum-runners-and-smugglers-on-the-wharf-with-gold-doubloons theme. The exceptionable feature of the Village Inn is that it is located on what most consider to be Miami's most beautiful street, and the people are not in contrast. As they drift from point to point in this miniature sea of boutiques and bars (Bananas, Tarus, etc.) they are observing each other and themselves in glass window-fronts, admiring the sheer beauty they each bring to this idyllic landscape, this mellow and sophisticated island of sun and sex. Go into the Village Inn and be one of them. Have a planter's punch. Love the sounds of Jimmy Buffet.

Bubba's (1624 East Sunrise Blvd, in Ft. Lauderdale). Bubba's is the only house in the Miami/Fort Lauderdale area metroplex in which to catch national jazz acts. Woody Hermann plays here, and

The Yorkshire (6521 Bird Road) is the latest in hot spots. It is a giant complex in which there are three separate areas: a restaurant, where you eat; a disco, where you get down; and a piano lounge, where you come down. Make no mistake, this is environmental marketing at its very best.

Mel Tormé, as well as the likes of Eddie Davis and Joe Pass. This is the real thing, and it's worth the drive if you live down south. The cover is usually reasonable, and you don't have to put up with a lot of decorative hype. This is simply a tastefully designed music and supper club, dimly lit, with walls in deep earth tones, and good acoustics. There are two shows as a rule, at 9:00 and 11:00. Check it out.

Faces-in-the-Grove (Mayfair in the Grove). A few years back someone decided that Miami didn't have enough expensive stores in which to buy Pierre Balmain shirts and Polo ties and designer bicycle shirts. So now there's Mayfair, an elaborate and stunningly rich mall. On the third floor is a disco known as Faces, a membership-only club. What you see when you arrive is a red and blue and purple L-shaped room full of backgammon tables, two glitzy wood and copper bars, and, on a tiered upper level, a row of white tablecloths and professional waiters. At ten o'clock the music cranks on, through a marvelous little technological toy of a sound and light system, and by 2:00 A.M. there is some serious madness going on.

The Yorkshire (6521 Bird Road). The Yorkshire is the latest in hot spots. It is a giant complex in which there are three separate areas: a restaurant, where you eat; a disco, where you get down; and a piano lounge, where you come down. Make no mistake, this is environmental marketing at its very best. There's a set for every play you want to try.

Incidentally, the minimum age for membership here is twenty-three, so expect some of the older crowd at the Yorkshire. While you're there, check out the handsome imported brass revolving doors. They really are quite nice.

The Candy Store (1 North Atlantic Blvd., Ft. Lauderdale). Chances are you've heard of this one before. This is the bar known the world over (or so the management claims) as "the wet T-shirt capital of the world." It 's always full of barely post-adolescent males who stand elbow to elbow, holding paper cups full of draft beer, all ogling a tiny stage upon which five or so nubile young girls allow themselves to be doused with ice water in order to maybe win the fifty-dollar cash prize. The Candy Store has a name just laden with meaning, and right now there's something for women, too. Seems they've come up with a wet nightshirt competition for male entrants. Never a dull moment at the Candy Store. This is definitely a place where you can "party down" and "kick out the jams" all night long.

The Sand Bar (301 Ocean Drive, Key Biscayne). The Sand Bar is a little bar/restaurant attached to a small Key Biscayne Hotel called the Silver Sands. It is a lovely place, chiefly because it is so small and unimposing. You can order a rum tonic or a planter's punch and take your shoes off and simply stroll up and down the beach. Just a few hundred yards from the Hotel Sonesta, the Sand Bar lacks all the Miami Beach–style pomp and glitter of that newer, bigger concrete pyramid. Occasionally, in the afternoons, there will be a bunch of University of Miami kids out here quaffing brews and soaking rays, but the beach is big enough to get away from anything resembling a crowd. You can also escape the abundance of monster portable radios which clutter Crandall Park with so much evil top-forty sound. This can be a great place to take a date whom you want to impress with your romantic sensibilities.

Miami Beach (Miami Beach). Native Miamians never go to Miami Beach. It just isn't done. Everyone out there is old and all the Deco hotels are falling apart. It's a rip-off.

The Vita-Course (South Bayshore Drive). This is the social meeting place for all the health nuts who can't seem to psych out the impossible bar situation. It is a public jogging trail that winds through Kennedy Park, just off Bayshore Drive, in Coconut Grove. Every afternoon, hundreds and hundreds of South Florida's best physiques come out here to walk around, stand around, stretch out, and maybe even trot a few yards, depending on what quarter the moon is in. After a tough workout, stop off at Monty's for a pitcher of something. You deserve one.

Minneapolis

Once upon a time there was a little town in the woods that no one knew much about, except everyone had heard it was a nice place, and friendly and peace-loving. All the people who lived in this faraway time were rumored to be among the happiest and healthiest in the land.

It just so happens that this town was way up north, almost to the border of another land, and so in winter it was really cold, and snow covered the ground much of the time. But in summer everyone came out of their hibernation and swam and went boating in the hundreds of nearby lakes.

It was also true that in this particular town many of the inhabitants were both intelligent and good-looking at the same time, which is a remarkable thing. How this came about is uncertain, though it has been said of the original settlers that they were descended from a proud and noble Nordic stock, were well adapted to the rigorous winters, and not at all afraid of hard work. Travelers have told of tall blond women with high cheekbones and men who could chop down the trees to make way for buildings. Together they made families, and as they did the right thing, their prosperity grew, and so too did the name of their town spread far and wide among the idealistic young people from other towns, who sought out new frontiers in which to make their home. And soon the town in the woods was a big city.

Minneapolis.

But it's still the town in the woods. If you're single and alienated, what you probably need is a good dose of Minneapolis. As one resident has noted, being single here is "like being single in the country, except there are buildings." In a world increasingly resembling a huge Houston, that can be a refreshing option, particularly if you're settled with yourself and what you're doing and don't feel you need to compete for some sort of spotlight. Because in Minneapolis, they couldn't care less about the big time. Or could they? Is it possible that this is really just a sickeningly nice burg full of boring people who make a special form of pretension out of drollery and lack of ambition? Is it possible that this is a city that keeps to itself only out of some massive, collective inferiority complex? There's only one way to find out: go and meet some of the folks in one of these places.

If you're single and alienated, you need a good dose of Minneapolis. Being single here is "like being single in the country, except there are buildings." In a world increasingly resembling a huge Houston, that can be refreshing, particularly if you're settled with yourself.

The New French Cafe Bar (128 North Fourth St.) This is the obligatory waiting room restaurant bar for the New French Cafe, downtown Minneapolis' premier house of nouvelle cuisine. The operation was started a few years back by two women who, according to the management, thought that "Minneapolis should have a restaurant that served good food." That's nice. An honorable sentiment, if a bit passé. But the Cafe and Bar are doing quite well, drawing in large crowds of the local artist community who come to sip white wine on the rocks and chat each other up. Apparently, the place has a certain broad appeal. As one fan says, "I like it because on each table there is a candle, and it's dimly lit, and so it's romantic." Sounds like those Minneapolis trendsetters have done it again. As to the food, the management had this to say: "Nouvelle may be going out of style now, but we're still going strong."

Sweeney's (960 North Dale, in St. Paul). Located in traditional old Irish Catholic St. Paul, to the east of Minneapolis, this is one bar that is what it is and knows it. "We're a fern bar," says one of the owners, and that is exactly what Sweeney's is, right down to the hardwood floors, dark, antique-looking bar, and deck chairs strewn all over the place. This bar is only a few years old, but the name goes back to 1906, to a Sweeney's general store, which occupied the same space. So of course there is plenty of general-store-type decorative material lying about: old tins and signs and flour canisters and burlapy stuff. If you don't like drinking with that kind of dreck around, you can go into the next room and try their brand-new Deco champagne bar. Either way you cut it, you're still talking ferns. Enough said.

Classic Motor Company (4700 Excelsior Blvd., Bloomington). This is it. If you want to get picked up, this is the place to do it. All you have to do is brush up on your vocabulary and put on your best polyesters and drive out to this unholy shopping mart and stand around for a while. And while you're there you can check out this bar's one truly amazing feature: the car. That's all there is here, really. You see, the gimmick at this place is to take an old car, a Bugatti or a Stutz or something along those lines, and set it on one of those showroom platforms, right in the middle of the bar. That's it. Oh, there are some other levels, some staircases, a certain amount of pointless and silly architectural variance designed to give strangers private nooks for necking. But at the center of it all, there is just this car.

"Do you like it?"

"What?"

"The car. It's a Bugatti Royale."

"Oh."

"It's a classic, you know. Very fine machine. Expensive. 1935, probably."

"Uh-huh."

"Yep, sure is something. Don't make them like that . . ."

"No . . ."

"Say, need a refill?"

". . . Um, uh-huh . . . okay."

"Say, my name's Brad. Prefer a Stutz, actually."

Sergeant Preston's of the North (221 Ceder Ave., South). Sergeant Preston's, named for the Canadian radio and TV personality, is by far Minneapolis' definitive concept bar. The theme is something along the line of "Canadiana," with pictures of the Sergeant and Canadian Mountie murals and flags and odds and ends and memorabilia everywhere. There's a dog sled over one of the bars, and a giant birchbark canoe over another.

What most people don't seem to think about, in terms of a bar like this, is that under all the veneer of objects and thematically relevant decorative elements lies nothing more than an anonymous and shallow superstructure. This stuff didn't accumulate over the years. Somebody went out and got it all from god knows whose garage, and then distributed it around this big room to make it look like it had accumulated. But it really didn't. What that means is that beyond the creation of some new and temporary visual sense of place, some imitation of spatial reality, there is in fact no reality at all, just an effect. It is an elaborate marketing conceit posing as someone's idea of Canada, or something about Canada, but the idea itself is corrupt. It is a vague sort of Disney attraction that really has nothing to do with drinking beer, and everything to do with being with other people in the vaguest and least defined (historically speaking) turf possible, which is exactly why everyone flocks here. It is easy to be inside this big room full of red and wooden stuff. Chalk one up for the management. You may be getting drunk and laid, but they're making money.

The Loon Cafe (500 First Ave, North). Owned by the manufacturers of Sergeant Preston's, this is now the hot downtown bar in Minneapolis for those who want to see and be seen. More austere and less cluttered than its partner house, this is a kind of glassed-in street level wine bar that may or may not be a pickup bar, depending on who you talk to. Suffice it to say that good-looking and affluent young singles do in fact get picked up here, if they want to. For others it is probably enough to just be trendy, and leave it at that. The Loon isn't for everybody, but you might check it out. The only real criticism of the place came from a patron who said simply, "The wine is bad." But then who cares about the wine?

Night Train (289 Como, in St. Paul). If you feel cheated by bars that go out of their way to look like something they're not, if you feel smothered by the heaps and heaps of junk and symbols, if you want to just rip them away and expose the plywood underneath, maybe you should stay away from the Night Train. Or, maybe not. This is the ultra-environmental barroom. It goes the route. For this theme house, the owners have actually used real Pullman cars, two of them, with a bar section in between, and a stage where mostly local jazz talent holds down every single night. You can bet there's more brass and mahogany railroad refuse tacked up in Night Train than you'd ever want to inventory, and all of it real. In fact, the award for conspicuous authenticity definitely goes out to Night Train, right down to the real gas lamps and the Pullman seating. What it all has to do with jazz is unclear, and whether the novelty will continue to hold interest is anybody's guess, but for now this bar is pulling in a healthy crowd from both sides of the river. The Twin Cities have traditionally been good towns for music, and Night Train is a good place to catch some of it, if you can take it. There's no cover, but there is a two-drink minimum, which seems to upset some patrons. Sorry, folks, but after all, that's the way it is everywhere else too.

Stub and Herb's (227 Oak St., S.E.). Stub and Herb's is the main college bar for the University of Minnesota, downtown campus, and that's saying a lot. This school enrolls about 50,000 students, so it's fair to assume that Stub and Herb's is crowded a lot of the time.

Minneapolis

This is *the* bar, dating back to the twenties, with all the requisite banners and pennants and signed photos of past athletic teams, all actually acquired in logical temporal order. Since the bar is located across the street from the stadium, Football Saturday is a mob scene of ungodly proportions. When the Gophers win, Stub and Herb's sells a shitload of beer. Or, when they lose. So, if you're a student, or if you're not, go there soon and have a pitcher. On Tuesday nights they're only two bucks. Stub and Herb's is a dying breed: a real college bar with real history.

Walker Art Center and The Guthrie Theatre. This is a museum/theater complex that is quite large, and an excellent place to spend as much time as possible. There is a restaurant at the top of the museum, called Gallery 8, which actually serves some good food, and where can be found attractive art students reading brochures. The Walker is definitely a good place to see fine art, both on and off the wall. The Guthrie, on the other hand, while it may not be your idea of a prime social event, does happen to be one of the finest and most widely respected theaters in the land. Besides, there is a bar backstage which is ostensibly reserved for the actors, but the inside scoop is that audience members can actually buy memberships. So now you can go backstage after the show and knock a few back with the company.

In general, Minneapolis is not a big bar town. Nor is neighboring St. Paul. The blue laws on both sides of the river are tough, so tough, in fact, that a bar cannot even open without first obtaining an already existing license. That means the number of establishments serving spirits remains pretty constant, even though the city is growing. Particularly in winter, when it's just too damn cold to go out, a lot of the population stays in and drinks at home.

But who needs to drink, when you get down to it? Minneapolis is a great town. It's pretty and the lakes are nice and the crime rate is low. Relax. Enjoy life a little. You don't need an expensive car here. A VW bus is much more practical, and you can use it for camping trips in the summer. So sit back and stoke up the fire in your fireplace. Just relax. This is Minneapolis.

New Orleans

The city of New Orleans occupies a unique space in the American landscape, and no one is more pleased about that than its residents. New Orleans is a special and sometimes confusing town, in that it is at once a sophisticated and historically rich "European" city—more so than any other in the country—and at the same time the urban heart of the deep, deep South. But the two aren't that far apart, really. Both represent highly traditional, stratified societies that grew out of broad racial and cultural mixes. Both hold onto their sense of history as though it were a purely personal matter, which it is. And both are ultra-sensitive about change of any sort, particularly change from the outside. The result is a New Orleans inner city that is physically gorgeous, and very much alive, though not in a 1980s sense.

So here are all these people in this hot southern town, most of them derived from exquisite combinations of African and Indian and French and Spanish and English heritages, all moving at their own speed and in their own way, to this singular swaying, steamy, sexy, white silk suit rhythm. Heat is the most potent destroyer of inhibitions, short of rum (that both are in ample supply is annually proved at Mardi Gras), which means that, regardless of who you are and where you fit in—or even if you don't fit in—this town is always wide open for romance.

At its best, New Orleans is one of the greatest places in the country to be single. The rule is this: find the tone, the

But the folks down here don't care much about that. What they do care about, in the words of one resident, are three things: "Food, drink, and jazz." The locals are quite content to let New Orleans simply keep on being New Orleans, in its own fat and happy way, for as long as is possible.

beat, the rhythm, and learn to move to it. There are those who take life in New Orleans to the point of something like a love affair. If you take your time, and learn your way around, you'll find that this is definitely a city that will respond to you. New Orleans is just too old and real and mixed up not to. It is city-as-art, and that is the highest cultural calling card a town can offer. What follows are a few of the places to prowl out the heart of New Orleans, while you prowl out the heart of a mate.

The Fauberg (626 Frenchman). This two-year-old jazz house located just outside the French Quarter has been described by the management as a "discreet singles' bar." What that means is unclear. Either it's a good place to look for a secret affair, or it's full of people who just don't want to admit that they're actually here to get picked up. Probably both. Either way, you can always pretend you're there for the music. This austere, arty hangout is constructed on several levels, with an assortment of different rooms, so it's good roaming territory. The walls are full of local art, which is for sale, naturally, and the stage features an assortment of local musicians, like the Hot Strings, and James Booker, "The Piano Prince of New Orleans." The place looks as though everyone who is anyone is here at some point during the evening, and at times the crowd gets pretty racy. To quote the management, "There are certain nights when fifty percent do cocaine." Well, that's in the jazz tradition if anything is.

Tipitina's (501 Napolean). This is one of the better uptown bars for music. Near the river, and near Tulane, Tip's specifically features an aficionado crowd sitting around in berets, unshaven, and smoking as many Gitanes as it takes to fully appreciate the blues. This is not a pickup bar, but then once you get here, you probably won't want to get picked up anyway. It's more fun to stay. Just settle back and suck gin and hear horns.

The Maple Leaf (8316 Oak St.). This is another uptown music bar, all-kinds-of-music bar. The best thing about the Maple Leaf is that it defies categorization. There's some jazz happening, and there are people drinking Dixie Beer. There are also some fascinating old tin walls to look at, and a patio to sit in. It's great. Oh, there used to be a laundromat here too. Seems the owner decided he was tired of taking his dirty clothes out and paying all that money, and having to stand around in the Coin-Op, which is always a dismal prospect, so he just installed his own machines right there against one of the far walls. You could go in and swill and hear tunes and leave with clean clothes, which must have been an incredible high. But the laundry is now a deli. Sign of the times.

If you're into poetry reading, you can catch Everett Maddox and friends here on Sundays. In a way, poetry still makes sense in New Orleans. The Maple Leaf even publishes a little journal of it, *The Maple Leaf Rag*, which you can read at the bar. About the only thing you can't do here is play Pac-Man.

Tyler's Beer Garden (5234 Magazine). Just eight little blocks away from Tip's, this place is worthy of mention only in that it is very popular with those who fancy themselves as "hip" and "in the know." It's another new bar in an old building, which is a pretty common phenomenon in New Orleans (better than new bars in strip shopping centers, at any rate). Anyway, this is a split-level, ranch-style house that features more progressive jazz, this time with red checked tablecloths, and walls full of arty jazz festival posters and portraits of musicians. The great thing about Tyler's Garden is that there is no garden. Just a bunch of ferns by the window.

The Hired Hand Saloon (1100 S. Clearview). You just know you made a mistake, the minute you walk in. This is just one more version of the same boring, repetitive theme we've had so many times before: the Urban Cowboy Disco, High Tech style. Blech!

4141 (4141 St. Charles). When asked what sort of crowd featured this posh, plush, and velour society factory, the inside reply was simply, "the cream of the crop." This blue suede and mirrored deb stable over St. Charles is a marketplace for those who desire to see and be seen. There's a disc jockey and a dress code, of course.

Napolean House (500 Charters). This one is right in the middle of the French Quarter, which gives it some validity as a cool bar. It's nice. It has all the usuals, except that they play canned classical tapes instead of Dixieland. The bar got its name from the story that the building was originally designed as a home for Napoleon in Exile. It didn't work out that way, but the architecture that remains is quite stunning. All things considered, this is an easy and quiet place to be. It's a good after-work bar.

Bourbon Street (in the French Quarter). Bourbon Street these days is little more than a strip of peepshow houses and T-shirt shops. It's fun to stroll down and people-watch, but don't plan on an extended stay.

New Orleans really is one of the most beautiful towns in the country. All you need to do is exercise a little choice and discretion in your social decision-making. You'll find that you are learning things most American city dwellers never get to learn, because you're living in a city unlike any other. And, the best thing about New Orleans is that it is a year-round proposition. Granted, Mardi Gras is one of the awesome festivals of bacchanalia available anywhere. The city plans for it for the whole year. Everyone, gays and heterosexuals and kids and senior citizens, participates. The streets are unbelievable. Everyone is drunk. But when it is over, the spirit of it stays on. It's always there, in the music and the food, and the people who really know New Orleans. Seek out good places. Find a favorite. You'll be quite happy you did.

New York

New York is a city that loves brains, guts, heart, sex, and hard cash, in no particular order. To love New York is to love life in the fast lane, with a bumper-to-bumper traffic jam every five blocks. To be single in New York is to practice a sort of social Darwinism gone haywire.

The sheer variety of things to do in New York can be instantly overwhelming. New York is "cheesebugga, cheesebugga," and it's haute cuisine. It is a glittering cocktail party on Park Avenue and a block party in the East Village. New York is a vast anonymous ballroom packed with a thousand people you've never seen before and will never see again, and it is the neighborhood dive where the bartender knows your cat's name.

Every day, three million people commute into Manhattan. They come to drink coffee, publish novels, sell sequined bikini underwear, and restructure the debt of Black Africa. They ignore one another as they stand rattling belly to groin on the subway. Then they fight over taxis, line up for the afternoon paper, and complain about the high cost of living. And they go out.

For some New Yorkers, daybreak comes at a time that the rest of us call dusk. For them, night is signaled by the dawn, and the chauffeur's yawn, as others feed the pigeons breakfast at six A.M. Unfortunately for office-centric earth dwellers, the incredible high life of Manhattan—silver Lincoln limos, sky's-the-limit expense accounts, international dough all over—sets such a lofty (and costly) tone that one is tempted to forget it all and stay home.

But going out—to lunch, after work, or just before dawn—is what living in New York City is all about. People in the Big Apple don't ask each other how they've been lately, they ask where they've been or what they've done lately. If you make some intelligent choices about where to go, and are willing to venture off the overly well beaten track of singles bars on the upper east side of Manhattan, you will find that New York is the star maker, heart breaker, and international capital that it's been cracked up to be.

If you make intelligent choices and are willing to venture, you will find that New York is the star maker, heart breaker, and international capital that it's been cracked up to be.

Not that all the singles bars on Third and Second Avenues should be avoided. On a weekday night, *Jim McMullen's* (1341 Third Ave.) can be a lot of fun if you enjoy people-watching. The place gets jammed with models and advertising execs by nine each night. *Camelback and Central* (1403 Second Ave.) has a long, attractive bar, and the cool design of the place, sort of like a dimly lit submarine, is conducive to good conversation. Young, rich professionals, basically the same crowd you'll find at the slightly pricier McMullen's bar, hang out at Camelback every night. If you want to gawk at sports stars and other celebs, *Oren & Aretsky's* (1497 Third Ave.) can be an amusing pit stop. Reggie Jackson used to hang out there during his glory days with the Yankees. *Willie's* (1426 Third Ave.), a little lower down, also attracts a sports crowd; a lot of hockey fans come to watch the Rangers on the bar's color television. This bar has great burgers, a good jukebox, and a comfy red-checked tablecloth decor and pub atmosphere. *Martell's* (1469 Third Ave.), also on Third Avenue, has an outdoor cafe where young professionals, mostly lawyers who live on the Upper East Side, drink during the week and on weekends (when they're not in the Hamptons). The cottage fries at Martell's are justifiably famous.

Two archetypal Third Avenue bars/restaurants, *Hoexter's Market* (1442 Third Ave.) and *J. G. Melon's* (1291 Third Ave.), are often four-deep at the bar with hungry hopefuls, who are only too glad to wait interminably for tables.

But overshadowing these pleasant oases on Third and Second Avenues, there are the meat-rack bars, some of which actually have names as blatant as *Singles* (951 First Ave.), *Auctions* (1403 Third Ave.), and *Adam and Eve* (141 E. 45th St.) (every city seems to have one of these). These places are crowded and expensive. The people who flock to them, mostly on weekends, are likely to be members of the bridge and tunnel set, suburbanites acting out a misconceived fantasy of what being single in Manhattan is all about. Slightly less offensive is *Maxwell's Plum* (64th and First Ave.), probably still the most famous singles' haunt in the city. The food here is actually quite good (but very pricey), and it's a pleasant place to have Sunday brunch. But the crowd at night is strictly bridge and tunnel, and on weeknights the place really thins out as the regulars race to catch the 12:02 to Fort Lee.

If you don't mind venturing off the beaten track into Manhattan's less glitzy neighborhoods, the allure of most of these Upper East Side establishments fades quickly. Manhattan's lower depths, the downtown area above Wall Street, including the East and West villages, are where you'll find many of the best bars, restaurants, and clubs.

More than anything else in New York, music seems to bring out singles in the largest numbers. There are a number of really good clubs on the East Side below

14th Street, where the live acts don't go on until after midnight. But the doors open at nine or ten, and people drift in to drink at the bar, talk, and listen to taped music. This is the best time to come if you're hoping to meet people or snag a dancing partner. The following clubs are highly recommended:

CBGBs (315 Bowery): This raunchy hole may have spawned the New Wave movement. When 1976's punk rockers were still sticking safety pins in their cheeks, they came here. Things have calmed down a bit since then, and you'll find all types at CBGBs' long bar, from preppies to punk poseurs. The tables at the back of this gritty club are reserved for those who want to see the live bands, and the music can be intolerably loud. On Sundays, CBGBs offers brunch concerts that get underway at three or four P.M. The scene is a little more serene on Sundays, and the cover price is cheaper. The bloody mary's, sadly, are terrible, so stick with beer.

The Ritz (11th St. between Third and Fourth Avenues): This big, musty ballroom, which reeks of grander times gone by, is a fun place to dance, watch rock and roll video above the big dance floor, and people watch from the tables on the balcony. On weekends, the limos stack up outside, the cover price is steep, and the scene is a little frenzied. On weeknights you can sometimes get in the doors for just a few bucks, and you'll find a crowd consisting of burnt-out airheads, celebrities (yes, Mick comes here a lot), and even boring businessmen.

Danceteria (30 W. 21st St.): This multilevel pleasure palace for the ultra chic has taken over some of the cachet once reserved for uptown clubs like Studio 54, which never has been able to recapture the glamour it lost when its owners went to jail two years ago. Unless you're properly dressy (which means anything from punk miniskirts to tails), it's tough to get past the bouncer at the door. On weekends, the wait can be long, but is worth it. On three different levels, you can either dance, hear live acts, eat (the restaurant is really quite decent), or watch video. Danceteria brims over with energy, and if you enjoy hobnobbing with celebrities (Mick comes here a lot) and watching the upscale cruising scene, this disco is a good place to splurge. Be prepared to blow your wad.

Danceteria has a lot of imitators uptown, but these discos are even pricier and more attuned to the limousine crowd. Unless you want to drop $20 for cover and $4 a drink, it's probably best to avoid Xenon, the Red Parrot, and Studio 54.

If you find yourself in the predawn hours with the urge to prowl, there are several likely after-hours clubs in the extreme eastern section of Manhattan known as "Alphabet City." (The avenue names are "A," "B," "C.") Be cautioned that this is a dangerous part of town and that public transportation is sporadic in the wee hours. If you go, take a cab. Many of these clubs have no visible markings and are indistinguishable from the tenements that surround them. If gaunt, anemic-looking types who never sleep appeal to you, feast your eyes and ears at the *Pyramid Club* on Avenue A, which looks like an English pub gone punk, For something active, try the *Bowling Club* (110 University Pl.), forty-four lanes on University Place that draw a hip, young crowd after midnight on Mondays thru Wednesdays. Even if you hate bowling, this is a great place to drink beer and meet people.

If you still have the urge to roam after these places shut (post 5 A.M.), or to wind down with some nourishing food, a number of Ukrainian coffee shops near Alphabet City draw an interesting breakfast crowd of singles. Most of them are just finishing their evenings out, trying to get the buzz out of their heads with some eggs, kielbasa, and some strong coffee. However, some of the local writers and artists who live in the East Village actually do eat a proper breakfast at these establishments before starting work. Before you settle down at the *Kiev* (7th St. and Second Ave.), the *Odessa* (117 Ave. A), or *B&H Dairy* (127 Second Ave.), pick up the morning paper,

New York

cigarettes, maybe an egg cream, at *Gem Spa* (St. Mark's Pl. and Second Ave.) on Second Avenue. If you've struck out on the club scene, you're more likely to meet someone appealing at the Gem.

Since many singles are put off by the throbbing trendiness of the rock club scene, there are alternatives. Two country-western clubs, the *Lone Star* (61 Fifth Ave.) and *City Limits* (125 Seventh Ave. S.), offer nightly country, bluegrass, and progressive acts, dance floors where you can two-step the night away in a congenial, less raunchy atmosphere. Both of these clubs went a little too far with the Texas-chic phenomenon (there's nothing more obnoxious than a New York sophisticate trying to pass for redneck), but those days, thankfully, seem to have passed. A lot of Rich Texans in New York on business actually do hang out at the Lone Star. *The Eagle Tavern* (355 W. 14th St.) is more relaxed and less pricey, with a bent toward bluegrass. This 1911 vintage workingman's bar on West 14th Street is a good place to come alone, listen to music, and meet people. The atmosphere is friendly, more like a neighborhood bar than a club, and the regulars usually sing along with the groups. *Tyson's* (755 Ninth Ave.), a little west of the theater district, also offers the feel of a neighborhood bar and live music, country and show tunes, the favorite of aspiring and would-be actors who hang out there.

To live happily as a single in New York, it's extremely important to find a neighborhood bar near your apartment that will serve as an after-work decompression chamber, an after-dinner social club, or a place to get a quick cash infusion. (Your friendly neighborhood bartender is far more pleasant than the Citicard computer when you need to cash a late-night check.) There is no shortage of such establishments. In the West Village, the *Corner Bistro* (331 W. 4th St.) is quiet (except when the terrific jazz jukebox is loaded up) and friendly, always filled with regulars. In the East Village, the *Grassroots Tavern* (20 St. Mark's Pl.) is as good a place as any to be a neighborhood barfly. On the Upper East Side, *The Bailiwick* (1244 Madison Ave.) is a relaxing spot, with terrific bartenders. Just ignore the ugly zebra-stripe interior. For a slightly more dazzling neighborhood bar on the Upper West Side, try *Cafe Central* (320 Amsterdam Ave.). It gets crowded, but for some reason some of the most beautiful women in New York flock to this bistro-bar. This place started out as a quiet neighborhood bar, but those were the days before the likes of Paul Simon and actor Michael Murphy moved into the neighborhood. (Maybe that's why there are so many beautiful women here.) For good looks, *Cafe Un Deux Trois* (123 W. 44th St.) in midtown is also recommended; the French food here is also passable. Cafe Un Deux Trois attracts basically the same crowd as Cafe Central, and even has the same crayons on all the tables for the artistic among its clientele.

To live happily as a single in New York, it's important to find a neighborhood bar: an after-work decompression chamber, an after-dinner social club, or a place to get a quick cash infusion. (Your friendly neighborhood bartender is far more pleasant than the Citibank machine when you need to cash a late-night check.) It's also important to have an after-work bar. Some of the best bars in New York empty out after eight, but throb with activity around five or six.

For jazz lovers, *Bradley's* (70 University Pl.) has a cozy atmosphere, consistently good jazz, and best yet, usually no cover charge.

Besides the neighborhood bar, it's also important (if you drink) to have a regular after-work bar. Some of the best bars in New York empty out after eight, but throb with activity around five or six. *P.J. Clarke's* (915 Third Ave.) is probably the most famous after-work bar. It's in an old tavern-style red building, and you can order one of the best burgers in town there. Be prepared for a three-person-deep crowd at the bar. *Peartrees* (1 Mitchell Pl.), near the U.N., is also hopping with young professionals cooling down after work. A lot of writers hang out here and at *The Cowboy* (60 E. 49th St.), around the corner from the *Newsweek* building. Some of the bars in the big hotels—*The Algonquin* (59 W. 44th St.) (still a favorite meeting ground for would-be Dorothy Parkers and James Thurbers), the Art Deco bar at the *Sherry Netherland* (781 Fifth Ave.), and the Oak Room at the *Plaza* (Fifth Ave. and 59th St.) (sometimes a bit too sedate)—are also filled with upscale, young professional types who come after work or gather during business trips to New York. Be prepared to pay upwards of $4 a drink at any of these.

In New York, it's perfectly possible to meet people almost anywhere. While marketing, for example. Check out the young singles examining the out-of-season asparagus at *Fairway* (Broadway and 74th St.), a great fresh produce market on the Upper West Side. On any given Saturday at *Zabar's* (Broadway and 80th St.) there are more singles buying lox for their Sunday brunches than you can count. If you hang around the smoked fish counter long enough, maybe you'll snag a brunch invitation. Singles also flock at night to the gourmet ice-cream stands that dot Broadway and the Village—Häagen-Dazs, Frusen Glädjé, Bassett's, or Sedutto's.

On the weekends, the city's museums are notorious singles' haunts. Although everyone pretends it's the paintings that interest them, it's really the pickup scene. Saturdays at either the *Metropolitan Museum* or the *Museum of Modern Art* are particularly busy. In summer, in the MOMA sculpture garden there are at least ten singles to every statue.

Lastly, the parks are probably the best place to meet other singles. Joggers are everywhere in Central Park and Riverside Park. Washington Square Park is a good place to stroll and pick up drugs. All parks are good places to meet gay singles, as well.

In general, the gay scene and the straight scene in New York are well integrated. Gays hang out at almost all the places we have mentioned, without branding any of them as a "gay" bar or "gay" club. At most of the downtown bars and clubs mentioned, the racial mix is also pretty good. One of the best things about New York is that any lifestyle is tolerated, and because of the crowds everywhere, people blend into the environment more easily.

Philadelphia

Philly has never been known as the fast sister of the Eastern seaboard. It isn't the middle Atlantic city that young entrepeneurs and aspiring artists flock to in order to make their reputations, and though Frank Sinatra may have the odd late night meal at Pat's Steaks, he does not sing a song about Philadelphia, PA.

Which is not to say that nothing ever happens here. Rather, Philadelphia, for all its sprawl, for all its tough-guy labor and ethnic associations, is an alarmingly relaxed city. Sandwiched between Washington and New York, it is as though all the drive and ambition of those two cities sort of oozes along some imaginary periphery, never really invading all the solid old traditions urban progress so unwittingly destroys in more transient and less secure environments. Philly may not be a lot of things, but *secure* it is. As one resident puts it, "Philadelphia is livable."

But be warned. Much of Philly's landscape gives urban decay new meaning, with some of the roughest ghettos and meanest slums you could ever want to think about. And the hordes of policemen, all armed to the teeth and doing things like leading German shepherds through subway cars, seem more of a reminder of the city's crime rate than a deterrent. The living can be cheap, though, and often highly attractive, and there is one benefit of living here that far outshines any of the drawbacks a hundred renegade Philadelphia expatriates could list up: the food.

Just in the last ten years there has been a movement in the restaurant business here, a kind of renaissance, that has resulted in growing numbers of restaurants and even what some call a "Philadelphia cuisine." Now, much of the social life of the city revolves around its restaurants and bars. There aren't a whole lot of discos, and the singles' bar, as such, is more the exception than the rule. There are some, but for the most part, an evening out in Philadelphia is an evening out dining. Here are some places to start, and some more to miss:

Downey's (526 South Front Street).

Downey's is one of the cornerstones of Philadelphia's South Street waterfront area. It's not that old, only seven years, but still it looks old. The interior is all from Ireland—an assortment of antiques from a Dublin bank, and some more stuff out of a Cork pub, gives Downey's a kind of beery Irish feeling that is mostly authentic. Lately, this part of Philadelphia has become something of a tourist area. People stroll along the riverfront, and sit outside at Downey's outdoor cafe, one of the more recent additions to a constantly growing restaurant. Wednesday and Friday nights are the big ones for singles, according to the management. If you're willing to pay the prices (Downey's draft beer will set you back) and you feel that you can suspend disbelief on entering this warehouse of Irish antiques, Downey's may be a very good place indeed to meet some young lawyer or dentist for some extended foreplay.

The Happy Rooster (118 S. Sixteenth). This one deserves mention because it is specifically *not* a singles' bar, or at least so the owners claim. Asked why this is so, they will tell you that here, the bartenders will actually refuse to send a screwdriver down the bar to that young lovely you just made eye contact with, but to whom you have little if nothing to say. In fact, at the Happy Rooster, the bartender may even refuse to *make*

Philadelphia

a screwdriver. This is the best-stocked bar in Philadelphia, with hundreds of spirits and liquors, and an enviable collection of cognacs. If you want to try a glass of Martell Extra, but you can't see dropping a week's pay for the bottle, come here. In the meantime, there is a decent restaurant and a fair amount of architectural nicety going on.

Ripley's (608–610 South Street). Ripley's is on South Street, but it's not a restaurant. It is a concert and dance club. People like James Chance play here, and the Motels, and the Missing Persons, Lary Coryell, etc. They also feature something called Rock against Reagonomics, on odd week nights, when you can get in free. Of course, if you plan on doing a lot of drinking once there, they'll make up the difference on you. Get faced ahead of time, then go.

The Bijou Cafe (1409 Lombard). Another place that is not a restaurant is the Bijou. What it is is a smaller live-music house, not far from Ripley's. They also feature national acts, as well as some locals, but in a slightly more intimate setting. The seating is at tables, and there's an upstairs area from which you can peer down at the stage. Incidentally, the people who own the Bijou also own some of the bigger spaces in town, like the Spectrum—Philly's sports arena—and some of the outdoor pavilions in Fairmount Park. Which explains why they get some of the acts they do. It may help to know that the club closes down in the summer. Apparently there is too much competition from the park pavilions and the Jersey shore to make it worth staying open.

La Terrasse (3432 Sansom Street). La Terrasse is a woody little place where U. Penn students spend large sums of money on gin and tonics. Most everyone stands at the bar, the better to break in those new topsiders. The regular clientele at this place tend to be some of the more obvious preppies around.

Frog (1524 Locust). A few years back Steven Poses, then a student at the University of Pennsylvania, took a look around and decided that there just weren't a whole lot of places in town where *he* wanted to eat. Just how he became one of Philly's leading restaurateurs in such a short time is a story that would probably defy most of what all those marketing analyst types over at the Wharton School base their jobs on. As he puts it, "I just wanted to make a restaurant that *I'd* like to eat in." He did, and he called it Frog, and it is still one of the better known and favored of Philly's host of young dining rooms. Since then he has branched out, and now owns several other popular Center City restaurants, including the *Commissary*, on Sansom Street.

Very simply put, Frog is one of the finer serious restaurants in Philadelphia. Its decor is simple, the food is a combination of French, Chinese, and American cuisines, and the prices are moderate to high. It's a good place to impress, though Frog is good for other things besides impressing. Mostly it's good for dining.

The Commissary (1710 Sansom). The Commissary was something of a risk when it first opened, because all it really is is a glorified cafeteria, line and all. But it, like Frog, hit. The folks in Philly like cafeterias, one supposes, or at least they like this one. It is generally packed. It also manages to sport, in a mainly business oriented section of town, the City Center, a real singles' scene. The reason seems to have something to do with convenience. Also some sort of twisted reasoning that suggests that since it is a cafeteria, the Commissary will be the *obvious* place to eat alone, and is therefore a *good* place to eat alone, and therefore *the* place to eat alone and not be bothered. Add it all up and you have a place where people are able to meet each other specifically because the restaurant is known as a place where you don't have to worry about all that. Make sense? It does, and to prove it one need only look at the record of the bar next door, which used to be the Piano Bar at the Commissary, but is now just the Bar at the Commissary. Success follows Mr. Poses like a retriever puppy. Incidentally, there is also a more formal dining room upstairs, which costs a little more. And elsewhere in the building is a market, the Market at the Commissary, which is a cute little place full of cute little bags of ground exotic coffees, and cute little slices of famous Commissary Carrot Cake—everything you need to make life meaningful.

Sixteenth Street Bar and Grille (264 S. Sixteenth). Last but not least in Mr. Poses' lineup of winners is this little Art Decoish number on Sixteenth Street. It's a lot of things that Frog is not, like inexpensive, for one. You can get an 85¢ draft here, and the usual burgers and all the rest. The Bar and Grille sports a copper and marble bar, behind which work bartenders who are, in the words of the management, "pretty friendly." This refers to their willingness to talk, to tell jokes, to dispense counsel, in short, to offer all the services bartenders have traditionally offered their customers, but which in recent years have been harder and harder to come by. In the days of computerized drink machines, the better sound system, membership only, jungles of banana trees and Australian ferns, chrome and glass, and tight jeans, there are those out there who are at least making a pretense toward establishing some sense of the traditional reasons why bars existed. The real old bar is hard to find. If you can't find one, the Sixteenth Street Bar and Grille can fill the gap.

Élan (at the Warwick Hotel). Élan is a chain. If you want to know about this fairly awful members club, see under Houston.

Philly is a good bar town, not a great bar town, but it is getting better. Some of the better neighborhood bars are located down in South Philly, but your best bet is simply to wander and search those out for yourself. If you're lazy, you can always just stick to the South Street area. Some of the recommended clubs along here are City Lights, Dobbs, and Downey's.

If you're not into bars, don't worry. There's other stuff to do here. Fairmount Park is about as big as Rhode Island, and it's located in all of about sixteen different neighborhoods. This is a great place in the summer, with a lot of concerts happening in the outdoor pavilions, and a lot of running going on everywhere. It's everything a park should be—everything about fifty parks should be. There are also some good museums. One resident has noted that the Pennsylvania Art Institute is the best place in town to meet people. Nice. Every city needs its civic-minded museums. And of course there's Penn, and Temple, and the Schuylkill and Delaware riverfronts, and a lot of buildings in the City Center, and elsewhere. But if you're in Philly, be content with feeling like you're in a small town, because that is what it invariably boils down to. It's a big village. Sometimes a messy village. Usually a politically tense village. But a village.

San Francisco

Above all else San Francisco is a real looker. Marin County's green hills in the distance, the world's most famous bridge straddling its most beautiful bay, and the morning mist rank San Francisco just behind Paris on the universe's most romantic cities list.

But not everything is right in San Francisco. While the city has earned its reputation as a magnet for social pioneers, the home of est, hippies and whole earthies, its denizens are now retrenching, if not retreating to the comfortable environs of the old-fashioned singles bars. In these fern-laden havens upscale professional singles ponder a subject of pure insanity: Are all the men in the Bay Area gay, and if not, will there be enough straight men to go around? It's an issue that's been debated for so long and so many times that at this point it's boring enough to be left to the sociologists. The whole issue is a cloud over single San Francisco, enough to transform its balmy weather into stormy weather.

But the news is not all bad. There is a pleasant residue of casual spaciness left over from the hippies in the sixties and even the beats in the fifties. When you've had enough of the singles scene in the Union Street bars, head over to North Beach. In between the Carol Doda big-breasts signs and the sex shops, you'll find cozy cafes and bars that are eons more tolerable. Then there's Berkeley, filled with present-day students and those who never left, which helps mellow out the tense social scene downtown. If you don't work for Bank of America and you're avoiding the suit and tie set, it is possible to find your own kind of laid-back scene, northern California style, and enjoy the mist and other mushy stuff that makes San Francisco everybody's favorite city. And if you're upwardly mobile and gay, you'll find that San Francisco has one of the most pleasant climates anywhere. Half the city's night spots were built with you in mind.

At the certain kind of bar that runs rampant in San Francisco, it almost helps to wear a suit or the casual equivalent just so everyone knows you're the financial district lawyer–type you inevitably are if you're frequenting these places. The best known of these bars is probably *Henry Africa's* (2260 Van Ness Ave.). This woody bar is always full of greenery and affluent young professionals in their twenties and thirties. The place also attracts San Francisco's ver-

San Francisco

sion of Beautiful People, described by one media-type as the "quasi-jet set, or people who know rock stars and talk about New York and Los Angeles a lot." Next in line is the *Balboa Cafe* (3319 Fillmore Street), which is perhaps even more of a pickup scene than Henry Africa's. Nondescript music accompanies wall-to-wall professionals and secretaries eyeing each other out and assessing various nonfinancial assets. Designer shoes and "fuck me" shoes are in vogue here. The training ground for Balboa's and Henry Africa's is the *Dartmouth Social Club* (3200 Fillmore Street), which attracts management training types in their early twenties. Run for cover if you're allergic to preppies. *Perry's* (1944 Union Street) was one of San Francisco's first classic singles bars. It's frequented by the well-to-do of Union Street who like to see their names appear in Herb Caen's social commentary column in the *San Francisco Chronicle*. Good jobs, good looks, and good money abound. Another jet-set spot is *MacArthur Park* (607 Fort St.). Only those who wear 100 percent silk may enter here. If you're looking to meet someone, stop in at the *Royal Exchange* (301 Sacramento), a primarily after-work joint frequented by those who after 8:00 depart to try their luck at Balboa's Cafe. Secretaries, lawyers and stockbrokers pack a modern, woody room with at least two rectangle bars and wall-to-wall people.

For those who are a little too tired of the above hectic scenes there is *Lord Jim's* (1500 Broadway), which attracts an early thirties crowd touched with a little mellow. Chrysanthemums and other flowering plants thrive here as do professional divorcees.

If you're not so concerned about whether or not you're going to have sex tonight, try *Tommy's Joynt* (corner of Garry and Van Ness), a classic San Francisco bar that serves cheap food of varying quality. The menu includes buffalo stew. A mixed and fun-but-not-rowdy crowd thrives here, more bohemian and down-to-earth than anything you'd ever find at Henry Africa's. Chic is not popular here. *Vesuvio's* (225 Columbus Ave.) is a good, unpressured bar in seamy North Beach, left over from the days when it attracted the true bohemians. The feeling's still there. People sit, play chess and backgammon, and drink. The City Lights Bookstore (261 Columbus Ave.) is next door. Poets and writers and readers wander into this stained glass haven for really anyone who wants to come and have a good time at a comfy, but fashionably unfashionable bar. Businessmen co-exist with hippies. This is a good place to buy yourself a drink. Nearby, in a hard-to-find back alley, is *Specs* (12 Adler St.), which attracts the same clientele as Vesuvio's with more of an emphasis on old-fashioned salty San Francisco types and beer-drinking regulars. At Specs, you get more fashionably off-beat young people and no heavy professionals. A good place to avoid the beautiful people. *Achille's Heel* (1601 Haight St.) caters to singles who never managed to leave the late sixties behind. These folks, caught in a time warp, ask each other if they were in SDS while picking each other up to the tune of piped-in sixties records.

***Vesuvio's* is a good, unpressured bar in seamy North Beach, left over from the days when it attracted the true bohemians. The feeling's still there. People sit, play chess and backgammon, and drink. The City Lights Bookstore is next door. Poets and writers and readers wander into this stained glass haven for really anyone who wants to come. Businessmen co-exist with hippies.**

Affectionately referred to by some as the Fab Mab, *The Mabuhay Gardens* (443 Broadway) is a bopping New Wave place with a good, very large bar. Tables face a large stage featuring fine New Wave groups. The Fab Mab attracts a mix of people, including, says one visitor, classy professionals who "still go a little crazy at night." It's fun, attractive and tolerably pick upish. For more high quality New Wave, try the *I-Beam* (1748 Haight St.), especially on Wednesday nights. Sometimes the I-Beam is a gay bar but on Wednesdays it's pure music. This New Wave caters to the slightly bohemian punkers, especially art school types dressed in black with skinny ties and ankle boots.

For country music, try *Last Day Saloon* (406 Clement St.). Live country bands serenade cavorting singles in cowboy boots and designer jeans. *Earthquake McGoon's* (Pier 39) plays all styles of jazz and has a lively bar scene. It's big and rowdy and gets written up in Herb Caen's column in the *San Francisco Chronicle*, which is the equivalent, in this town, to being blessed by the Pope. You can "dance your ass off," says a visitor, to Earthquake McGoon's old-fashioned jazz band. On the waterfront, this place is often packed but it's well worth wading through the crowd for. *The Boarding House* (901 Columbus Ave) is a small club that offers the best folk, rock, and jazz to be found in the Bay Area. Featured are low ceilings, lots of tables and not much room for dancing. Its coziness stems from the fact that it looks something like a bomb shelter. *The Great American Music Hall* (859 O'Farrel St.) is much larger and books rock and jazz but no punk or New Wave. The music is great, but there is no room for dancing. *The Old Waldorf* (444 Battery St.) is in a big old theater with tables for drinking and a big area in front of the stage for dancing up a storm. Rock and New Wave predominates.

Life is more relaxed and down-to-earth in Berkeley, where you can find bars and hangouts with a little more "atmosphere." The fern bar mold seems to have been broken before it crossed the bay. One such place is *Shattuck Avenue Spatls* (1974 Shattuck Ave.), a bar and restaurant lined with overstuffed chairs with lion claw legs and deer heads staring down from the walls. Professionals and former students and others hang out, get comfortable and sometimes a bit sloshed here. *The Starry Plough Pub* (3101 Shattuck Ave.) plays an odd combination of rock and Irish music, left over from the days when this was solely an Irish bar. This is a haven for Berkeley radicals. This is a jeans—and we don't mean designer jeans—place. There is some dancing, and some radical style picking up. *Brennan's* (720 University Ave.) has "no atmosphere at all but everybody goes there," according to one Berkeley resident. This old-time Berkeley bar and eating place attracts professionals, cops, hippies, old Italians, and blacks. In the center of this brightly lit room, there's a huge rectangular bar. Huge tables line the rest of the room. If you want to drink, sit near the bar. If you want to eat tons of excellent and cheap food, sit nearer the walls. "It's the perfect place to meet the ultimate mixture of everyone you'd ever want to meet in Berkeley," says the Berkeley resident. For more of a college crowd try *McNally's Irish Pub* (5352 College Ave., Oakland), an Irish bar semi-taken over by frat types, although in the afternoon the Irish still reign. This place sucks in college graduates, nurses, and community people. Bumper pool is popular here. There are tables and a bar, and you need not exit alone.

For music in Berkeley try the *Keystone Berkeley* (2119 University Ave.). Good bands play rock or jazz, and there's a big dance floor surrounded by tables. Here, people are serious about music and each other. For a more raunchy time the *Townhouse* (5862 Doyle St.) in Emeryville, a tiny town wedged in between Berkeley and Oakland. By day, the political establishment of the town hangs out here, including the city's powerful police force. By night, country music bands play up a storm under the dark, beamed ceilings of this ramshackle bar. Freestyle, let-loose dancing happens on an adequate dance floor, and everybody in sight has a real good ole time.

Night life in Berkeley and San Francisco tends to end at about 2:00 A.M., when bars, by law, must close. There is no such thing as an after-hours club here. Many people travel into the city from suburbs and exit early for Marin County and other far-off American dream lands. Another notable omission to San Francisco's night life is the large barnlike discos that populate New York and other cities.

The gay community is lucky to have an exception. *Trocadero* (690 Fourth St.), a predominantly gay, extremely intense disco, rocks from midnight until noon. Drugs, including acid, poppers, MDA and crystals, are popular here. At about 3:00 or 4:00 A.M., the straights wander in, including coked-out Iranians and jet-set types who have left Henry Africa's. After the action winds down at Trocadero, dancers roll over to the *End up* (401 6th St.), a gay bar with music that services the clean-up crowd from Trocadero. Castro Street and the industrial area south of Market Street are where to find the gay bars. *The Stud* (1535 Folsom St.) serves a mix of hippie and other gays. Disco and New Wave are played, and there is a dance floor. The *Alta Plaza* (2301 Fillmore St.) draws an affluent gay crowd. Mellow rock is piped into this bar. *The Trinity Place* (25 Trinity St.) serves the affluent gay community in the financial district. This is a haven for gay business executives.

San Francisco is home to numerous coffee houses. They are more low-key than bars and it's perhaps easier to approach someone and chat if you like the book or magazine they're reading. One neighborhood to explore is Noe Valley, the place the hippies moved to when they decided to settle down. "Everybody's more real," says one San Francisco single. "They're not for show, they're more into the intellect. They're kindred spirit types as far as everybody's trying to find a common ground." *The Meat Market* (4123 24th St.) is the exact opposite of what the name says. You can sip coffee and read the paper at a table that won't match the one sitting next to you. You can play a game of chess and the waiters and waitresses won't bat a lash. The *Acme Cafe* (3917 24th St.) is a bit more restaurant-like but still relaxing. It's a good place to hang out on a Sunday morning. The jukebox is chock full of Bruce Springsteen and friends. The *Noe Valley Bar and Grill* (3945 24th St.) is a bit classier. It's a full-scale restaurant and bar.

On impact, North Beach looks like a haven for massage parlors and strip joints. Note the famous sign advertising the breasts of one Carol Doda on Broadway. Actually, North Beach is a great neighborhood to wander around in. Once you get off the main drag (Broadway), the old bohemian beat flavor comes through. After you're finished drinking at Vesuvio's or Specs, check out the *City Lights Bookstore* (261 Columbus Ave). Pick out a shelf you like at this old beat hangout. If you stay put long enough you might very well find a mate. At the *Savoy-Tivoli* (1438 Grand Ave), in an Italian section of North Beach's Grant Street, you can sit in an open-air section drinking coffee and eating desserts, or retreat to a cavernous room in the back where New Wave is blared. The *Caffe Trieste* (609 Vallejo St.) features its owner singing opera. This place attracts "intellectuals" and writers. Big espresso and cappuccino machines adorn this cafe. Outside of North Beach, a slightly more touristy cafe, known for its Irish coffee, is *Buena Vista Cafe* (2765 Hyde St.). This bar and restaurant is just slightly above the bay. The Union Street version of a coffee house is the *Coffee Cantata* (2030 Union St.), which has an open-air front area and serves good desserts and drinks. Beware, however, of the upper crust crowd you may be going to a coffee house especially to avoid.

If none of this works for you, try the *Modern Art Museum* on Wednesday nights. It's free. Corduroys and tweeds are fashionable here. Most gallery hoppers are holding scripts from Woody Allen's *Play It Again, Sam*.

Night life in Berkeley and San Francisco tends to end at about 2:00 A.M., when bars, by law, must close. There is no such thing as an after-hours club here. Another notable omission to San Francisco's night life is the large barnlike discos that populate New York and other cities.

The gay community is lucky to have an exception. *Trocadero*, a predominantly gay, extremely intense disco, rocks from midnight until noon. Drugs, including acid, poppers, MDA and crystals, are popular here. At about 3:00 or 4:00 A.M., the straights wander in, including coked-out Iranians and jet-set types who have left Henry Africa's. After the action winds down at Trocadero, dancers roll over to the *End up*, a gay bar with music that services the clean-up crowd from Trocadero.

Washington, D.C.

There are two Washingtons: the inner city of lifetime residents, which is 70 percent black, and the younger, transient population of robots in blue suits and hornrims and ingenues in espadrilles who flock to Capitol Hill after every election. These young wheelerdealers set the tone of single life in our nation's capital. Politics snakes through all of their relationships just as the Potomac slithers through the city.

This is not a town of sensitive individualists. Many of the 559,000 folks employed directly by the Fed, as it is affectionately known, are largely indistinguishable from one another, even by gender, unless by degree of raw ambition. For single men, this homogeneity means wearing a tie at all hours of the day or night, including Saturday (unless one is jogging or playing raquetball). Still, Washington can be a very hospitable environment, where, to paraphrase the Jan and Dean song, there are just about two girls for every boy.

Young ladies from Ohio and West Virginia come to town for a taste of the Eastern establishment. *The Washingtonian* (the Bible for young, white, professional Washington) aptly described the typical ingenue as being "cute, clever, slightly sophisticated, and Eternally 21—a sweet-faced young thing with a brain like an Apple II. . . . She can spot a Cartier tank-watch at 100 yards." These coquettes learn quickly to spot (and blandly reject) the too-fast come-on, the standard opening, and other trappings of single-speak. A fly on the wall at any of the basic boy-meets-girl fern and basket bars would hear most singles chatting about their jobs and their bosses, or trading inter-agency gossip.

Even if they don't arrive that way, most Washingtonians quickly become political junkies. Therefore, one most fertile ground for the single hunt is at any of the many receptions held each day by delegations, lobbying groups, candidates, public interest concerns, and the like. A generally neat appearance and arrival in groups will get you in the door at these free-for-alls, although the diplomatic circuit is a good deal tougher to crash. The hors d'oeuvres alone at these bashes provide more than an ample dinner (Congressional staffers have been known to subsist on mini egg-rolls and chicken drumettes for years). Once you meet the significant other of your dreams, it's a quick ride (by cab or the ever-ready Fairmont) to the entertainment zones along Connecticut, Massachusetts, or Pennsylvania avenues, to Georgetown, with its Broadway—Wisconsin Avenue—and adjoining side streets, the best territory among them being F, K, M, and O streets.

Along these well-worn sociopolitical meeting paths, there are even young, singles versions of some of the famous gathering places for older pols, such as *Mel Krupin*'s (1120 Connecticut Ave., N.W.), *Joe & Mo's* (1211 Connecticut Ave., N.W.), and *The Palm* (1225 19th St, N.W.). Downtown, one of the best places for young staffers to trade office gossip and table-hop is *The Class Reunion*. While this bar enjoyed its greatest following during the Carter Administration (a giant mural of young James Earl Carter as a young navy lieutenant adorns one of the bar's walls), it's still a prime hangout for youthful pols and journalists. Associates from many of the big downtown law firms congregate here for lunch. Like most Washington bars, the crowds are most intense right after 5 P.M. (almost everyone in Washington who doesn't have to carpool it home to the 'burbs goes drinking after work) and the place begins thinning out by 10 P.M.

John Kennedy once remarked that Washington is a town with southern efficiency and northern charm, and much of that redounds to the detriment of the capital's singledom. It's not exactly life in the fast lane, and during the week the city virtually shuts down after midnight. Beer drinking, jukebox oldie tunes, and relaxed conversation at bars is the prevailing lifestyle for singles.

Around Capitol Hill, *Bullfeathers* (410 1st St., S.E.) and *Pendleton's* (501 2nd St., N.E.) are reliable standards for Senate staffers and young prepettes. Downtown, their equivalents are *Rumors* (1900 M. St., N.W.) and *Sign of the Whale* (1825 M. St., N.W.). In Georgetown, *Clyde's* (3236 M. St., N.W.), a wood-paneled page from the bar book as written in California, attracts an even preppier crowd. It has spawned a number of paler imitations, including the *Third Edition* (1281 Wisconsin Ave., N.W.), *Nathan's* (3150 M. St., N.W.), and *Mr. Smith's* (3104 M. St., N.W.). *F. Scott's* (1232 36th St., N.W.) is where you go to guzzle beer and Lindy to oldies.

Washington is also home to thousands of college students, and campus coeds from Georgetown, George Washington University, and American University hang-out at *Numbers* (1330 19th St., N.W.), a popular dance and drink establishment that sits above Dupont Circle, and the *21st Amendment* (2131 Pennsylvania Ave., N.W.), which boasts a D.J. Tuesday through Thursday and live music on the weekends. Inspired by its college-age population, the city has long been a home of much good rock and roll. *The Bayou* (3135 K St., N.W.) has filled in the vacuum left by the closing of the Cellar Door, long the area's best rock venue. It features local and national acts. *Desperado's* (3350 M. St., N.W.) in Georgetown gets down with R 'n' B and country rock. For the more adventurous, the *PsycheDelly* (4846 Cordell Ave.) in Bethesda features some of the better New Wave activity, including regular appearances of Washington fixture Root Boy Slim and the Sex Change Band, progenitors of the "boogie-til-you-puke" school. *The 9:30 Club* (930 F St, N.W.) is the district's hard-core punk venue. Check your brains at the door. *Winston's* (3295 M St., N.W.) plays oldies but goodies. Western clubs have hit it big in Washington with the advent of former cowboy Reagan, and *Annie Oakley's* (Wisconsin Ave. and M St., N.W.) and *Bronco Billy's* (1821 L St., N.W.) are both popular with young westerners (west of Pittsburgh, pardner).

While a drab preppiness, which never seems to change from decade to decade, overhangs single life in Washington, the city has proven extremely susceptible to a number of recent crazes. Video games have caught on with a vengeance, and Pacman meets Pacwoman at *The Far Inn* (3433 Connecticut Ave., N.W.), where there's a back-to-back club and game-room in a giant basement setting. Physical fitness is an obsession for many singles, and almost everyone belongs to a health spa. *The Saga Health Club* (1000 Potomac St., N.W.) is one of the chicest, and a good place to meet other body-conscious singles. Jogging on the C&O Canal or Tidal Basin and biking along Rock Creek Park are de rigeur activities on the weekends.

Single people from other big cities, such as New York, Boston, and Los Angeles, most frequently complain that unless you're on the A list for the diplomatic parties, Washington lacks sophistication. There are, however, a few places where the atmosphere is less provincial. A New Yorkish style prevails at *Café de Artistas* (3065 M St., N.W.), with a wide range of music in a quieter, but still active, setting. Many of the hotel piano bars are also hospitable to singles, including those at the *Fairfax Hotel* (2100 Massachusetts Ave, N.W.), the *Four Seasons Hotel* (2800 Pennsylvania Ave, N.W.), and the *Embassy Row Hotel* (2015 Massachusetts Ave, N.W.).

Since most singles come to Washington to spend a few years in Congress, some agency, or even a newspaper to make a name for themselves, it is more than likely that if you are one of these folks for whom Washington is only a temporary assignment, much of your social life will revolve around your job. Many singles love this aspect of Washington because, unlike life in New York or other big cities, it obviates the need to go out every night to meet other singles. If you're a GS-10 working at the Commerce Department, it's more than likely that there are at least thirty other people on your floor who are also single, under thirty, and college educated. Others complain that too many young people in Washington derive their sense of identity from who they work for, their GS level, or other trivial government/political trappings. If you don't like politics, it's unlikely that you'll like Washington, whether you're twenty-two, thirty, or fifty. If you do, and you don't mind the fact that everyone under thirty looks just a bit too much alike, you'll probably be very happy here.

The *PsycheDelly* in Bethesda features New Wave activity, including Washington fixture Root Boy Slim and the Sex Change Band, progenitors of the "boogie-till-you-puke" school.

Singles Books: A Selected Bibliography

Lifestyle

Single Minded, Gail Sheehy. Why young professionals on the rise have allowed their social lives to take a back seat to their careers.
Hey! You Single?, Cordelia Lear. Foolproof guide to finding Mr. Right.
Dateless and Desperate. Highlights from the popular National Public Radio program.
Everything But the Kitchen Single, Julia Child. Cooking with leftovers.
Hi! I'm Single!, Eric Weber. Tips for getting the most out of business conventions.
One Plus Zero Equals Zero, Isaac Asimov. The mathematics of loneliness.
Miss Smith? Party of One?, Ann Landers. Etiquette guide to dining alone.
Singles Say the Darnedest Things!, Studs Terkel. Taped soliloquies.
Hey! You Still Single?, Cordelia Lear. Guide to seeking True Love, for women in their 30s.
On Our Own, Singles Anonymous. Singles in search of a cure.
We Are Not Alone, Eric von Daniken. Extraterrestrial beings offer new hope for singles.
Nice to Meet You, Andy Rooney. 101 ways to say hello to strangers.
How to Be Single, Penelope Ashe. How-to.
Living and Loving Alone, Rabbi Moishe Lindenthal. Controversial prescription for self-satisfaction.
Singles Who Need Singles. Stark black-and-white photos of Singles bars.
We're All Singles beneath Our Skin, Alistair Cooke. Based on the popular PBS series examining how cultures throughout the world cope with the singles problem.
Going It Alone, Steve Birnbaum. Sidestepping double-room occupancy fares, and other useful travel tips.
Pick Up This Book, Abbie Hoffman. Advice on getting your way with women and other authority figures.
Single Belles! Single Belles! Single All the Way! Sister Maria Conti. How nuns cope.
Hey! What'sa Matter? You Still Single?!, Cordelia Lear. Alternatives to marriage for women over 40.
How to Enjoy Singlehood, National Singles Association. How-to pamphlet.
Why America Hates Singles, John Le Boutellier. Why singles pay more taxes yet don't get their own designated bus seats and parking spaces.

Humor

It's a Single's World! Cartoons and essays from *Single's World* magazine.
Hark! The Harried Singles Age! Erma Bombeck. Reflections on her children's social lives.
Modern Civilization, Fran Liebowitz. Tart observations about all kinds of stuff.
You're a Single Kinda Guy, Charlie Brown! Charles M. Schulz. The Peanuts gang taunts its leader about his perpetual alienation.
Kids Letters to Singles, Bill Adler. Culled from actual correspondence.
The I-Hate-to-Date Datebook. Diary with daily suggestions for things to do by yourself.
101 Uses for Dead Singles, Simon Bond. Illustrated.

You Know You're Single When . . ., Bruce Feirstein. How to separate the real men from the married men.
Singles Are Only Skin Deep, Chris Cerf and Henry Beard. Parody of popular PBS series.
Singles Guide to Life, Bruce Jay Friedman. Previously published as *Lonely Guy's Guide to Life.*

Fiction

Single, Tommy Thompson. Husbands of wealthy Houston socialites are found mysteriously missing or murdered.
Catcher in the Rye, J. D. Salinger. Ribald misadventures of a single man in 1950s New York.
Single Life, Ken Follett. British secret agent uncovers diabolic Nazi plot to exterminate singles.
Soup for One, Jonathan Kaufer. Novelization of minor cult film.
The Fan Man, William Kotzwinkle. Hapless misadventures of a single man in 1960s New York.
The Singles Syndrome, Michael Crichton. An entire Midwestern town wakes up one morning and finds its marriages have been mysteriously annulled by alien beings.
Looking For Mr. Goodbar, Judith Rossner. Ribald, hapless misadventures of a single woman in 1970s New York.

Unauthorized Biographies

Screwloose and Fancy-Free. On the lonely campaign trail with Jerry Brown.
K. The life and times of Franz Kafka, a single writer.
A Man Is a Man Is a Man. But a good woman is a smoke: the private life of Gertrude Stein.
Still Single after All These Years. Heaven can wait, and so apparently can eternal bachelor Warren Beatty.
Star Crossings. Up-and-coming actress Juliet Capulet divulges names and conversations of real celebrity bachelors she's run into, and some she'd like to run into.

Authorized Autobiography

Singled Out. Watergate-era dirty trickster Donald Segretti breaks silence to reveal that President Nixon wanted him to take the rap for the entire White House, reasoning that he had no family to support.

Games and Pastimes

Solitaire Strategy. 101 time-consuming card games for singles.
The Simple Solution to Singles. Unraveling the maddening puzzle that only eight-year-olds seem to be able to master.
How to Win at Singles. Directions for scoring high on new Atari video game. "Woman" in singles bar fires "barbs" at invading "men."
Single or Swim. In support of the buddy system.

The *Single States* authors: Personals, and Other Information

Peter W. Kaplan: editor of the book, Kaplan is 5'11½", a former editor at *Esquire* and *New Times*. He has written regularly for *Esquire*, and for *Playboy*, *Life*, and the *Washington Post*. From South Orange, N.J., he lives in New York City. As of this writing, he is not married.

Randy Cohen: author of "Monophobia," is a New York writer. His work has appeared in *New York* magazine, *New West* magazine, *The New York Times* and the *Washington Post*. A book of his correspondence, entitled *Modest Proposals*, was published in 1981. As of this writing, he is not married.

Charlie Haas: author of "How to Drink Alone," lives in San Francisco, California, where he writes screenplays and magazine pieces. His work has appeared in *Esquire*, *New West*, and *New Times*. He co-wrote the movie, *Tex*, among others. As of this writing he is married; when he wrote his essay for this book, he wasn't.

Marilyn Johnson: author of "How to Feed Yourself (F)," is an editor at *Redbook* magazine, and wrote *Esquire*'s "Ladies Entrance" column in 1980. She has written for *Seventeen* and several poetry magazines. She is a native of Ohio, Tennessee, and California. As of this writing, she is not married.

R.D. Rosen: author of "The Speed Chef Method . . . for Single Guys," is a writer who lives in Cambridge, Massachusetts. He has written for the Boston *Phoenix*, the *New Republic*, and *Esquire*. He is also the author of *Psychobabble*, and is at work on a novel. As of this writing, he is not married.

Franie Ruch: author of "How to Dress Yourself," is a writer and fashion expert from Princeton, New Jersey. She has worked for *Esquire* and *Spring* magazines and she reads many Condé Nast publications. As of this writing, she is not married.

Barbara Simmons: author of "How to Set Up House," is a New York interior designer who lives and works in Manhattan. As of this writing, she is not married, although she has designed the homes of many married people.

Jerry Lazar: author of "Technodating," is a Los Angeles writer and editor of the Republic Airlines flight magazine. He has written for *California*, *New Times*, *Esquire*, and many other magazines of a respectable kind. A strapping fellow, as of this writing, he is not married.

Mark P. O'Donnell: author of "First Lines," "Last Lines: the Collected Letters to Dear John," and "Living Alone and Liking It," is a New York writer from Cleveland, Ohio. He has written for many magazines, including *Esquire*, *New Times* and *Film Comment*, wrote for "Saturday Night Live," and is the co-author of *Tools of Power*. His play "Fables for Friends," was produced in New York in 1983, and, as of this writing, he is not married.

Sally F. Carpenter: author of "For Women Only," lives in Shaker Heights, Ohio. She is working on her first book. As of this writing, she has three children.

Frank Goldman: author of "Promiscuity and You," is from Guatemala and Boston, Massachusetts. He lives in New York, and his fiction has appeared in *Esquire*. He is currently working on a screenplay for IPC Films, and it's his second. When he wrote his chapter, he wasn't married. As of 1982, he abdicated his singlehood.

Dean Valentine: author of "How to Cohabitate," was born in Rumania, but lives in White Plains, New York. Formerly an editor of *Next* magazine, he is currently working for the Time, Inc. magazine development group. As of this writing, he is not married, but he does cohabitate.

Maud Lavin: interviewer of Eileen Walsh, lives in Philadelphia and New York, where she is pursuing her doctorate in Advanced Art Studies at the City University of New York. Her articles have appeared in *Art Forum*. As of this writing, she is married.

Dr. George Thomas and Dr. Lee Shreiner: authors of "Single Diseases: Tissues and Answers," are both physicians at Harvard Medical School and authors of *Ten Diseases You Were Better Off Not Knowing About*. As of this writing, neither is married.

Mr. "X": author of "I Have Herpes Simplex," is a writer who has lived and worked and shaken hands with hundreds of people in many of the great cities of America including Minneapolis, Philadelphia, New York, Los Angeles, and Boston. As of this writing, he is not married.

Joel Kotkin: author and interviewer of "Hollywood Singlehood," lives and works in Los Angeles, where he has written for *California*, *Esquire*, the *Village Voice*, the *Soho News*, the *Washington Post*, and many others. He is, with Paul Grabowicz, the author of *California, Inc.*, a nonfiction book on the rise of the state, and alone, is writing a novel. As of this writing, he is married.

Kurt Andersen: author of "Monomedia," is a staff writer for *Time*. Born near Wahoo, Nebraska, he lives in New York. He is the author of *The Real Thing*. As of this writing, he is married.

Jill Abramson, Don Antrim, Henry L. Griggs III, and Ellen Joan Pollock: authors of Singlopolis, are writers of diverse background. Ms. Abramson is an editor of the *American Lawyer*, so is Ms. Pollock. Mr. Antrim has written for the theater, mostly in Texas. Mr. Griggs is a political consultant. Mr. Antrim went to Brown University and Ms. Pollock went to Brandeis. Ms. Abramson and Mr. Griggs are both married, to each other. As of this writing, Mr. Antrim and Ms. Pollock are not married.

Acknowledgments

Acknowledgments are a dangerous business when as many people are involved in a book as were in this one: twenty three writers have people to thank.

Let me, however, mention a few people without whom this book would never have even come up for air a second time:

Our editor, Peter Gethers, was steadfast, imaginative, and supportive to the extent to which this is very much his book.

Susan Wallach, now of Villard Books, was patient and firm, which were necessary, and kind and funny as well.

This book would not have existed without my friend and agent Amanda Urban, who brought me to it and followed through with an incisive sensitivity that is all hers.

Don Antrim, Byron Dobell, Rob Fleder, Paul Friedland, Suzanne Gluck, David Hollander, David Michaelis, Richard Reeves, Philip Seibel, Richard Weigand gave generous and warm counsel.

Paul Slansky read the manuscript with an attention he otherwise only gives to biographies of natives of Yorba Linda, California. It's nice to have critical friends.

Philip Weiss, Cal Fentress and James Kaplan gave more than they would allow me to say. My parents and my brothers gave me their inestimable support.

Most of all, I'd like to thank Audrey Walker, with whom I was single but never alone.

—PWK